Manhattan Conspiracy

Manhattan Conspiracy

Blood On The Apple

Ken Hudnall

Authors Choice Press
San Jose New York Lincoln Shanghai

Manhattan Conspiracy
Blood On The Apple

Authors Choice Press
an imprint of iUniverse, Inc.

For information address:
iUniverse, Inc.
5220 S. 16th St., Suite 200
Lincoln, NE 68512
www.iuniverse.com

ISBN: 0-595-20399-X

Printed in the United States of America

To Sharon, who never fails to be supportive.

INTRODUCTION

In 1992, I lived in Trump Tower in New York City. Being an avid reader, I explored the many book stores which abound through the city. I collected several hundred books in my one bedroom apartment, which I devoured every evening. One of the books was called the Control of Candy Jones by Donald Bain.

Candy Jones, born Jessica Wilcox, was a very well known model during World War II, and later ran her own very successful modeling agency. She was a very patriotic young lady and when she was approached by an F.B.I. agent who requested her to allow her place of business to be used as a 'mail drop' for the Bureau and 'another government agency' (presumably, the CIA); she gladly accepted the proposition. The clandestine world is a relatively small place and eventually, Candy came into contact with a 'Dr. Gilbert Jensen,' who worked, in turn, with a 'Dr. Marshall Burger.' (Both names are pseudonyms.) Unknown to her, these doctors had been employed by the CIA to work with a program called MK-ULTRA. This was the U.S. Government's mind control program.

Using a job interview as a cover, Jensen hypnotized Candy and found her to be a particularly responsive subject. She was felt to be the perfect subject for Jensen's research and he proceeded to use her as other scientists would use a rhesus monkey. She became a test subject for the CIA's mind control program. She was so perfect a subject that she was programmed with another identify that could be activated on command. Her job—insofar as it is known—was to provide a clandestine courier service during her travels in Europe using the cover of the modeling agency.

Dr. Estabrooks, a CIA researcher had outlined a plan years earlier to create what he called a perfect secret agent. This plan was the impetus for the design that became the prototype for the current research:

Induce hypnosis via a disguised technique;

Give the messenger information to memorize;

Hypnotically 'erase' the message from conscious memory; and

Install a post-hypnotic suggestion that the message (now buried within the sub-conscious) will be brought forth only upon a specific cue.

If the hypnotist can create such a courier, ultra-security can be guaranteed; even torture won't cause the messenger to tell what he knows—because he doesn't know that he knows it. According to the highly respected Dr. Milton Kline, 'Evidence really does exist that has not been published' proving that Estabrooks' perfect secret agent could be successfully evoked. Candy was one such success story.

I began to think that it this program could produce the perfect courier, then why not the perfect assassin. The killer personality lies dormant until needed. Thus it is almost impossible to find the assassin unless he is caught in the act.

From this germ of an idea came the series which begins in Manhattan Conspiracy. I hope you enjoy it.

Ken Hudnall
New York City
1993

PART ONE

THE DREAMS

CHAPTER ONE

The gathering in little San Antonio, New Mexico would have been news any place in the world. The main business in this small New Mexican town is a very famous restaurant known as The Owl Café. The Owl Café had gotten its start serving food and offering scant entertainment to the personnel working on the Manhattan Project in the 1940's. Now it was a fixture, know far and wide.

Normally, it had a very steady clientele of diners from the local area, as well as numerous travelers on Interstate 25 who knew of the small out of the way establishment. Folks in San Antonio were friendly and tended to mind their own business and the Owl Café served the best chiliburgers between Albuquerque and Las Cruces.

On this day, in addition to the large contingent of the normal people who took their meals in the Owl Café, the Café was host to two different groups of travelers. The first to arrive consisted of one Partain Turner, the CEO of the Brennan Corporation, a major defense contractor, tall, slim and patrician, as well as several of his senior staff and security people. Serge Mortonsen, six foot eight and almost four hundred pounds, bodyguard for Partain Turner entered first, to arrange for a private corner for his boss. The former KGB agent had a way of getting whatever Mr. Tuner wanted. He went from worshipping the State to worshipping Partain Turner. The owner, sizing up the situation, quickly set his obviously important guests in the far corner of the room behind the bar. He didn't have to tell the regulars to give Turner privacy; the glowering presence of the huge bodyguard took care of that.

An hour later, Patrick Monahan, the five hundred pound CEO of Paterson Scientific Services entered with his own security people. Slowly he walked down the length of the long wooden bar, his beady eyes missing nothing as he noted the hundreds of dollar bills tacked to the walls and ceiling of the Owl Cafe. He was puzzled at the unique custom demonstrated by the current and former patrons of the café. Partain had once told him that it was considered a coup for one to have the chance to place a dollar bill in a vacant spot on one of the walls of the restaurant. As of yet, Monahan could see no purpose or excitement to giving a way a perfectly good dollar.

He paused at the end of the bar, uncertain of which way to go. Finally, a low call directed his attention to the group gathered in the far corner of the room behind the bar, happily enjoying their green chiliburgers. In a few moments, he had lowered his not inconsiderable bulk into a waiting chair across of the dapper Tuner.

"Partain," he growled, carefully dusting off the table in front of him with a lily-white handkerchief before he rested his massive forearms on the checkered tablecloth, "interesting place you picked for this meeting. Why not some place that at least had some topless entertainment?"

"Patrick, you have no class," said Turner, his mouth full of a juicy green chiliburger. "In its own way, this place is every bit as much of a gourmet restaurant as anything in New York City. Not everyone can make a perfect green chili hamburger"

Turner paused to wipe his mouth with a white paper napkin and swallow his mouth full of chiliburger.

"In fact, here," he said, pushing another burger sitting on the table by his elbow toward his companion, "take this one. I'll order another. You will taste a sensation unlike anything you have ever imagined."

Monahan looked over at the second burger that had set in front of Turner with visible disdain. He reached forward with one well-manicured hand and gently lifted the top of the burger to look at the mass of green chili strips piled atop the patty, then shivered.

"No thank you, Partain. I wouldn't want to deprive you of such a, uh, delicacy. I didn't work all of these years to climb to top of the heap to eat a hamburger."

Partain shrugged and pulled the second burger back towards him.

"Suit yourself, Patrick, but you have no idea what you are missing."

Partain Turner took a big bite of the second burger and chewed it slowly. He obviously found it very much to his liking. Monahan waited impatiently for the other man to finish, but finally could contain himself no longer.

"See here, Partain, I came over three thousand miles to meet you here in the middle of no where as you asked, but I want to assure you that I have other things to do besides sit here and watch you feed your face." complained the big man.

With a sigh of disappointment, Partain Turner pushed the remains of his second burger away and carefully wiped his wide mouth. Very deliberately he folded his soiled napkin and laid it carefully beside his paper plate. Slowly, he shook his head, his dark eyes sadly studying his companion.

"Patrick, my man, as I said, you have no soul. I bring you to a little known haven of civilization in the midst of a bare dry desert and you turn your nose up at one of the real reasons to live. But very well, I'll humor you. So tell me, why did you demand this meeting?"

Monahan looked carefully around the room, but he need not have worried. Massive Serge Mortonsen had planted himself between the two businessmen and the main area where the bar was located. Turner's other associates had unobtrusively moved to other tables, leaving the two men alone. They were assured of privacy. He had a momentary sense of unease when the failed to see his three security personnel.

"Well it's like this, Turner" he began, he deep voice kept as low as possible, "Some of the others are concerned as to whether it's really possible to pull this off. After all, if we fail, it could be called treason. I was asked to act as a spokesman for the group. Some of the group want some type of concrete assurances of success, or at least of no prosecution if this thing fails."

Partain Turner nodded slowly, taking time to take a small sip of his soda from a paper cup before he responded.

"Patrick, please do not misunderstand me, I understand your concern. However, remember, we can't fail since some of the highest placed people in the country are going to be helping us when the time comes. Even more importantly, the intelligence, military and internal security units that will normally be major obstacles to a venture such as ours, will be otherwise engaged at zero hour."

Monahan sighed and waved one pudgy hand.

"I've heard all of this before. In fact, that's part of what bothers me, uh, I mean us, Partain. We are all businessmen in this venture. We all got where we are by assessing the odds and going with what we feel are good gambles. It seems fantastic that the military will turn a blind eye to a coup being conducted in its very midst. Another thing, how can we be assured that this mysterious person you say is running this venture can really do what he says he can do. We've seen nothing to support that this person even exists.

After all, Partain, I didn't get where I am at buying a pig in a poke. I would like to seem some proof."

Partain Turner was a very patient man. He had built a financial empire and an international conspiracy that was on the verge of toppling the United States Government using that patience. Patrick Monahan represented many millions of dollars to the cause and had to be handled very carefully.

"Patrick, the reason that you haven't yet met the head of our movement is very simple. This person is so highly placed that there is no way that he can dare reveal himself personally. If there were even the slightest rumor or hint of impropriety associated with him, the project would be over. That's why he works through people like me."

"How highly placed?"

Turner smiled and fixed his eyes on his companion.

"I assure you that he is at the very highest level."

Monahan rubbed his triple chins and pondered the situation. He had to flush out this mystery man for several reasons. Most importantly, he was sure that if he could meet the leader, he could convince him that he was a better front man than Turner and, secondly, he needed to be able to assess the ability of this mystery man to do his part.

"Turner, even so, no matter how high the level, I still don't understand how one person, no matter how highly placed can so effect the system as to enable us to simply take over."

Turner made a supreme effort to keep his anger and frustration from his voice. Motioning Monahan to come closer, Tuner lowered his voice even further and leaned across the table.

"Patrick, we have people working for us who are not even aware that they are working for us."

Monahan scowled at Turner and shook his head.

"Turner, I have to hand it to you. You can really make a sales pitch. But I have to admit that I find some of what you are selling a bit hard to believe."

Turner leaned back in his chair and shrugged his silk clad shoulders.

"So what will make you believe?" he asked softly.

Monahan thought for a moment, making it appear he was undecided. But he knew when he had won. He allowed himself a slight smile.

"I'm sorry Turner. You are asking me, and others, to risk everything they have worked a lifetime to achieve. I need a meeting with the head man."

Turner nodded his head and stood, studying his companion as he slowly buttoning his suit jacket.

"Very well, Patrick. I'll be in touch."

Tossing some bills on the table, Turner strode grandly from the room, waving his good bys to the owner as he passed the register. The silent Serge Mortonsen pacing behind the magnate like a huge shadow. An old desert rat, clumping along in his down at the heel boots, followed them both. In the back room, Monahan still sat calmly at the table, seeming to stare at the bills laid lying beside the partially eaten burger. He had just pulled off what could e the biggest coup in his career. He had forced a meeting with the headman.

Monahan sat motionless, as visions of his soon to be elevation to the heights of power filled his thoughts. He was pulled from his reverie as another individual dropped into the vacant chair across from him.

"Well, Patrick, what did he say?" queried the new comer; his weather beaten features expressionless.

Monahan jumped as if he had been goosed.

"Uh, Frederick, what are you doing here?" quavered the big man. He hadn't expected to meet this man here in the backside of nowhere.

Frederick Mason, President of Mason Pharmaceuticals was not a well-known media figure, but he was a mainstay of New York City high society. Dressed as he was, like a cowboy in well-worn jeans and a dirty white Stetson, not even a member of his own board of directors would have recognized him.

"Came to see what's what, boy." Mason responded, waving at one of the waitress' for service. "And a damn good thing I did."

He paused to give his order to the waitress and waited until she had left before turning back to Monahan.

"Boy, that Partain Turner is a real snake oil salesman. He's done well, but he's just like his daddy. I knew his daddy forty years ago and he was ever bit as big a crook as the boy. Now what's he got us into?"

Monahan rubbed his hand across his face before answering.

"Well, it's like this Frederick, I have my doubts about what is going on here. I wanted Turner to give me some more reassurances that just thing wasn't going to blow up in our faces. He couldn't do it so I demanded to speak to the man in charge."

Frederick Mason smiled slowly and rubbed his hands together in anticipation as a large steaming green chiliburger was placed in front of him.

He smiled up at the young lady that had brought his meal.

"Thank you, darlin'. Looks great."

As the young woman walked off, Mason took a big bite of the steaming burger before wiping his mouth with a napkin.

"Patrick, I don't want to tell you how to run your business, but sometimes you just have to roll the dice and take your chance. A lot of time and money has gone into getting this thing in place. It's a little late for doubts. Besides, though Turner pretends to be harmless, he'll cut our throat in a New York minute."

Monahan watched in fascination as Mason took another huge bite out of the burger, pieces of green chili hanging out of the side of his mouth. Neither man paid any attention to the quiet middle-aged man in the dark jacket that took a seat across the room, near the entryway to the rest rooms.

Finally, Monahan broke the silence. "Frederick, unlike you and the others, I wasn't born with a silver spoon in my mouth. I started on the docks and fought my way to the top. I'm not afraid of Turner or his trained Russian monster."

"Well, it's your funeral. But Patrick, I would urge you to just wait and watch what happens." he continued as he swallowed the mouthful of burger, "your doubts at this stage of the game could place us all in jeopardy. If anyone outside our group knew what we were doing, we would all be in serious trouble."

Monahan shook his head stubbornly.

"Frederick, I don't want to cause any waves. After all, we are agreed that our movement is the best and last hope for the country. I have personally contributed over three million dollars to the cause. But I need some reassurances that it is not all wasted. I, for one, do not want to spend the rest of my life in prison or worse if this thing fails."

Frederick Mason finished his burger and carefully wiped his lips, folding his napkin carefully and placing it beside his plate, almost mirroring the earlier movements of Partain Turner. He got slowly to his feet and looked down at Monahan.

"Patrick, old friend, I urge you to just let things take their course. Don't be making demands right now. Things are at a critical juncture and distractions such as these are really not needed."

Monahan hauled his bulk to his feet and faced his old friend.

"Frederick, I have demanded a meeting with the top man. I'm a businessman and I want to deal as a businessman. If the top person can't talk with me, then perhaps I need to reconsider giving this plan the support of Paterson Scientific Services. I have no desire to spend years in a jail cell for treason. Because in case you haven't noticed our little venture is treason of the highest order."

Frederick Mason nodded his understanding and glanced around the room. The man in the dark jacket sat sipping a soda from a paper cup. He turned his attention back to Monahan and shrugged slowly.

"Well, a man's each gotta do what a man's gotta do as Duke Wayne once said. Good night, Patrick."

With that, Frederick Mason walked across the room and disappeared around the bar, leaving Patrick J. Monahan, multi-millionaire standing alone. Annoyed Monahan looked around for his own security people, but saw none of them. This was simply unsatisfactory, He'd see about the lack of attention shown by those worthless people when he returned to New York.

Outside in the darkened parking area, Partain Turner glanced at his watch by the light of the single illumination in the parking lot. He looked over at Mortonsen.

"You are sure that Monahan's security people have been neutralized?"

"Yes sir. Their bodies have already been loaded in the limo," rumbled the big man.

Inside the Owl Café, Monahan decided to freshen up prior to starting the long trip back to Albuquerque and the airport. He hated feeling dirty and just being around that stinking green chili had made his skin crawl. He walked down the short corridor and entered the tiny men's room. Carefully he washed his hands and patted his face with water. He finally began to feel clean.

Turning off the water, he straightened his suit coat and turned toward the door. Leaning against the inside of the closed door was the quiet middle-aged man in the dark jacket that had been sitting near the entrance to the back room.

"Excuse me, young man," said Monahan, trying to squeeze around the man who blocked his way.

"Not so fast, big fella." replied the other, not moving from his spot. "I have a message for you."

Monahan looked the smaller man up and down with disdain.

"Yes? What's the message?" He asked insolently.

"Just this, fatso. You shouldn't ask questions of your betters."

"Bah." snapped Monahan, brushing past the smaller man. "I don't know who you or your employers think they are, but this decided me. Tell your "betters" that I quit."

"No," came the quiet answer, "you're fired."

"What?" Monahan asked in confusion, turning to look at the young man "I'm what?"

Silently, the young man pulled a silenced automatic from his pocket and fired two well-placed shots. Both punctured Monahan's already overtaxed heart. The big man collapsed back against the wall. Holstering his weapon, the assassin half carried and half supported the big man in stumbling back into the toilet cubicle, depositing him on the commode. Pulling the door shut, the assassin smoothed his hair back in the mirror, washed his hands and stepped from the rest room, closing the door behind him.

Pausing to make sure that no one had noticed anything unusual, the assassin strolled calmly back to his table and finished his meal before walking calmly out of the café. At the cash register he paid his check, pausing only to pick up a book of matches. The book of matches was small, black and had the Owl Café logo imprinted on the back. Outside the café, he paused in a lighted area to light a cigarette. Across the parking area, two men entered an idling limo and drove slowly away. The assassin walked to another car and got into the back seat. That car headed up the road and entered the interstate.

CHAPTER TWO

THE PRESENT

Carter Davis Hughes was a moderately wealthy man, had a fantastic job, a beautiful, wealthy wife, two swell kids and a large apartment overlooking New York's Central Park. He should have been on top of the world, but on this day, he was a very disturbed man. On this particular night, he was actually afraid to sleep, for fear that he would dream. Not that normal dreaming is something to be afraid of, but his dreams were not just normal dreams.

Already dressed for bed, wearing a dressing robe, Carter Hughes paced the floor, his razor sharp mind dealing with the many ideas that flooded his senses. The dreams were so real that he had trouble separating them from being awake. Pausing, he picked up a cigarette from a pack on the table and lit it. Tilting his head back, he drew the smoke into his lungs and blew it toward the ceiling. Logically, he knew, he was just simply having nightmares. The problem was, he dreamed of places and people that he felt that he should know, but in his waking state he knew that he had never seen the people or been to the locations.

Then there was the discussion with a friend of his, Dr. Stanley Parmentier. Dr. Parmentier, a very expensive clinical psychiatrist who had gone to school with Carter had told him that the dreams probably were an attempt by the subconscious mind to work out some type of psychological problem. It was the job of a clinical psychiatrist to figure out what the psychological problem was and help the subconscious solve it. One other factor Dr. Parmentier had mentioned was that dreams normally used familiar places as the backdrop for the "mental movies". The most disturbing thing about Carter's dreams was that he had absolutely no memory of every having been in the locations he saw in his dreams.

Moving toward the open balcony door, Hughes stepped out into the warm afternoon breeze. Leaning against the railing, Hughes studied the people crowding the streets below. He watched the sun slowly setting, dreading the arrival of dark. He turned at the sound of a key in the lock. The door swung open to admit two small children and a stunningly beautiful young woman of about thirty, followed by an older matronly woman.

"Daddy!" screamed the children as they dashed across the room.

With a laugh, Hughes swept both children into his arms and planted a kiss on the check of each.

"And how are my two balls of fire today?" he laughed.

"Full of energy!" exclaimed the young woman, coming over to plant a big kiss on is check and pulled the younger child into her arms. "We've been in every toy store in Manhattan, this afternoon."

Turning to the older woman, Martha Hughes handed her the younger child, named Janice after her grandmother.

"Matilda, take the children in for their baths."

"Yes ma'am." Responded the taciturn woman.

Matilda Masters took the other child, David, from Hughes' arms and set him beside his sister.

"Come along, you two," she said sternly, "Time for your bath."

"But Daddy," wailed the boy, pulling loose from Matilda, "We haven't had any time with you"

Martha intercepted the little guided missile and steered him toward the bathroom, along with his sister, the stout Matilda rolling along in their wake like a clipper ship under full sail.

"David, your Daddy's not well and needs his rest. You'll have plenty of time with him this weekend and remember, on Friday, he's taking the two of you to see Santa Clause."

"Goody," exclaimed Janice, clapping her hands, trying to turn back to her father.

With the experience of a good mother, Martha intercepted her daughter and tugged her into the bathroom. Once the two were behind the door of the bathroom, with the water running and Matilda in full charge, Martha came back into the living room. She found Carter sitting in a stuffed chair; a glass of scotch in one hand, his head laid back, eyes closed. She perched on the arm of his chair, pulled him forward and began to slowly rub her husband's neck.

"Is it the dreams, again?" she asked softly.

Without opening his eyes, Hughes nodded slowly.

"Yeah, it is. I'm afraid to sleep. Each time I close my eyes, I'm some place else. It's driving me crazy."

"Carter, perhaps—-" she began, falling silent, but continually rubbing his neck.

When she didn't continue, Carter Hughes twisted his head, taking her hand in his.

"Perhaps, what?" he asked.

"It's nothing, just —-perhaps you should have professional help."

Slowly, he shook his head.

"No, dear. You know that I don't believe in all that claptrap. No, it's just something I have to work out for myself."

With a deed sigh, Martha Hughes stood up and took the glass from his hand.

"This stuff isn't helping, my sweet. I'll fix you something that will make you feel better. Then I want you in bed early."

Against his better judgment, Hughes obediently got to his feet and walked into the bedroom, tossing his robe on a nearby chair. His wife walked into the kitchen and returned with a glass half full of some clear liquid. As she crossed the living room, she began to flip off some of the lights. She paused in the bedroom door and by the light of the single lamp on the bedside table, she watched Hughes dawdle, actually afraid to get into bed. Finally, he ran out of things to do, then, under the amused eyes of his wife, he crawled under the cover and settled back against the pillow. His wife waited until he was in the bed before she leaned over and tucked him in, handing him the glass.

"You drink this and I'll check on the kids and be right back, my dear," she murmured as she reached up to switch off the bedside table lamp. "It'll be fine, my dear. Just rest and I'll be back in a few minutes."

She walked from the room as Hughes slowly drained the glass, switching the light off in the living room as she entered the room. There was no sound from the street and little light in the master bedroom end of the apartment to disturb the darkness.

"Rest," he muttered to himself as he stretched slowly, sitting the empty glass on t he bedside table. "I wish I could rest."

In spite of himself, Carter Hughes began to doze. From the doorway, out of sight of her husband, Martha Hughes stood silently, a slight smile on her beautiful face as her husband began to breath deeply. Once she was sure that he was asleep, she glided over to the phone and punched out a number.

"It's me," she whispered when the receiver was picked up on the other end," he's asleep. But he is somewhat agitated tonight."

She listened to the conversation.

"He's been more agitated than usual since he got back from the trip."

She listened intently as the individual on the other end gave some muted instructions to her.

"Yes sir. I understand."

Gently, she sat the receiver back onto the phone and looked across the darkened room toward the master bedroom. Crossing the room, she pulled the door closed on left her husband alone with his dreams to wrestle with his own personal demons. Moving over to a bookcase, she removed two books and flipped a small switch. A tiny red light came on, illuminating a dial, which showed a draw of power. A small low energy generator imbedded in the mattress beneath Hughes began to emit an energy field.

CHAPTER THREE

Almost as soon as his eyes closed, Carter Davis Hughes was catapulted to another time and another place. Instead of lying in his own bed, he found himself sitting in a large room, with numerous other individuals, all wearing Army uniforms. He glanced down and, somehow, wasn't surprised to find that he was also wearing an Army uniform. He believed the uniform was referred to as dress greens. From the black stripe on the side of his pant leg, Carter deduced that he was, himself, an officer. At the front of the room, stood an individual wearing the silver leaf of a Lieutenant Colonel.

"Gentlemen, the summer in the Panama Canal Zone is typical of tropical areas, it rains every day. Old hands in the tropics swear that you can set your watch by the rains. There is a steady downpour at ten o'clock in the morning, but by 1:30 in the afternoon, anyone soaked in the torrential morning shower will be as perfectly dry as if there had never been any rain. At almost exactly two o'clock in the afternoon, a second torrential storm will hit and completely soak everyone who was just dried out by the tropical sun. It can truthfully be said that the Panamanian Rain God has a sense of humor."

He paused for a minute, paying idly with the swagger stick he carried under his right arm.

"No one is really sure what the American population of the Canal Zone might be at any one time, but it is probably in excess of fifty thousand, most of whom are civilians employed by various American interests. The Smithsonian Institute has a research facility that studies jungle wild life, the Central Intelligence Agency has several listening posts that keep an eye on everyone within a thousand miles, and of course there is our own organization, the United States Military.

Before I brief you on the current situation, it is only right that I first give you some history of the Canal Zone. During the 1800's, Panama was owned by the country of Columbia and treated pretty much like a backwater colony. The famous Commodore Vanderbilt and some of the other 19th century American robber barons treated most of Central and South America as their own private fiefdoms. There had been much discussion about building a Canal across Central America long before Vanderbilt died, but nothing other than negotiations were undertaken. There was no question that there was a need for a canal to speed up travel from the Atlantic to the Pacific, but the problem was determining where the canal would be built.

Actually, there was a better place for the proposed Canal much further south of where it was finally built. There was an area in Southern Columbia that would require very little work in order to connect several existing rivers in order to make a water passage from the Atlantic to the Pacific. Unfortunately, the backers of the original canal project could not get the required concessions. One result of the heated exchanges between the Columbians and the Canal builders was the choice of Panama as the location for the canal as a punishment of the arrogant rulers of Colombia.

The U.S. Marines established the first United States Military facilities in the province of Panama. Even before the first spade of dirt was turned in the building of the long-awaited Canal, there were numerous backstabbing, underhanded deals made by the various interests who saw the citizens of the various countries below the Rio Grande as pawns in a huge game. Shrewdly, the powers that backed building the Canal proceeded to create unrest among the Panamanians. When the

Panamanians finally rose in open rebellion against their greedy over-lords the Columbian military was ordered to begin a move into Panama with instructions to squash the revolutionaries like a bug. However, U.S. Marines were landed at the south end of the area coveted by the leaders of the revolution to insure that the Columbian occupation forces in Panama would receive no reinforcements from their main forces in Columbia. Knowing that they couldn't take on the United States military and hope to win, the Colombians wisely agreed to allow Panama to become independent. In return, the Panamanian government agreed, at the urging of its' new friends from the north, to give permission to build the Canal.

The first group to try and push a canal across the Isthmus of Panama was backed by a French consortium. As most everyone knows, the jungle, the Indians and disease stymied the French. This does not even take into account; the rumors of sabotage allegedly carried out by other groups that had failed to get the contract to build the canal. Dozens of skilled workers in the pay of the French left their bones in the marshes and swamps of the jungles of Panama. Faced with potentially tremendous financial losses, the French Consortium sold their rights to an American Group.

This new group, after having had the opportunity to study the mistakes of the French determined that the best route for the Canal was already owned by the railroad that cut across the isthmus. Naturally, the owners of the railroad company were not about to share their monopoly with outsiders. Suddenly, the railroad company began to have some of the same problems that had plagued the French Consortium. Negotiations resulted in the group who owned the railroad joining with the power brokers who wanted to build the canal.

Panamanians were naturally overjoyed to be free and thought it was wonderful that the rich North Americans were concerned enough to make large loans to rebuild the infrastructure of the newly liberated country. It was a few years before the natives noticed that only a few of the more prominent families were actually getting any benefits from the gifts of Panama's new friends from the North. Even so, the average Panamanian was relatively content, because those who supported the regime were rewarded with well paying, for Panama, jobs on one of the military bases.

The United States Government very quickly decided that, having been responsible for the independence of the new Republic of Panama, the new country needed advice, guidance and most of all, financial assistance. Militarily, according to the United States Government one of the most important things that had to be done was to protect this new possession of the United States. With typical military wisdom, protection of the new canal actually began long before the Canal was built.

The United States Government sent not only the Army, but also the Navy, the Marines and later the Air Force. The Army sent the 193rd Infantry Brigade, made up of three infantry battalions, a medium boat company, a signal company and other assorted support units. The Navy sent several units supplemented by the Marines and the Air Force built several major air bases around the country.

Naturally, to house all this personnel, the Army built three bases: Fort Clayton on the Pacific side of the Isthmus; Fort Howard on the south side of the Isthmus; and Fort Davis on the Atlantic Side. The Air Force later built its own facilities and the Navy also built several bases.

As the years progressed, the U.S. Military tightened its grip on the Canal Zone. Fort Clayton became the home of the 4th Battalion (Mechanized) 20th Infantry Regiment, a medical company, a signal company, a military police company and a military intelligence company. Fort Howard, which grew up around the Air Force Base consisted of Howard Air Force Base, and the 3rd Battalion, 7th Infantry Regiment. There was also Fort Amador, near Fort Clayton, but this post became primarily an administrative base, home of the Headquarters elements of the 193rd Infantry Brigade. Fort Davis was the guardian of the Atlantic side of the Isthmus.

At Fort Davis were the 4th Battalion, 10th Infantry Regiment, a Headquarters Company, and a medium boat company. The Navy had a base called Farfan, which supported Naval presence in the Southern Hemisphere. Finally, there was Fort Gulick, also on the Atlantic side, home of the School of the Americas and the Special Forces Detachment.

Since the Panama Canal Zone was, and is, considered vital to national security, the Department of Defense made it a point to keep all units at full strength. Due to the location, personnel were able to get very low-cost trips to the South American Vacation spots. Panamanian women dreamed of marrying a G.I. Which is something that is tightly controlled.

I might also make note of the fact that due to the peculiar laws in this 'protected' country, Panama was one of the few places in the Western Hemisphere where a man could be legally married to two women at the same time. Due to a quirk in the treaty that gave the United States eternal ownership, Panama didn't recognize marriages between its citizens and United States Citizens conducted in the Zone, and the United States didn't recognize marriages between its' citizens and Panamanians conducted in the country of Panama without US permission.

Panama has long been considered a plum tropical assignment. Since most of the country was covered with jungle as thick as any place in the world, when the Vietnam War started, the United States Army established the Jungle Warfare School at Fort Davis. Units from all over the world were brought to Fort Davis for training. The Special Forces Detachment at Fort Gulick was used by the Pentagon as a ready reaction force for troubled spots all over South America. In fact, though the military tried to keep it a secret, it was a sniper team from this Unit that actually killed the famed Cuban revolutionary leader, Che Guevera. "

At this point, Carter Hughes mentally tuned out the briefing officer and glanced around the room at the others seated near him. All appeared to be young infantry officers, judging by their branch designations pinned on the lapels of their uniform coats. None of them could be over their mid-twenties.

Glancing down, Carter saw several papers scattered on the table in front of him. Picking up the top most, Carter saw that it was a letter. Listening to the briefer with only half an ear, he scanned the letter.

"On the whole most Americans find themselves adopting the lifestyle of the natives, quitting work at noon for siesta and returning at three o'clock. The workday usually ended at six or seven in the evening. Although the same amount of work got done as in northern climes, the pace is much slower. But, beginning about the late 1950s, after the great red scare, the pace of the military activities began to slow. By 1975, Panama had become a pre-retirement posting; there were second and third assistant positions filled with people who killed time on the golf course day after day as they counted down the days until retirement.

All of this came to a screeching halt in mid 1975. That year, Brigadier General William R. Goodrich took command of the 193rd, (shortly before he became Major General William R. Goodrich) and brought the Canal Zone into the twentieth century. According to legend, he slipped into the Zone a day before he was due to arrive. At noon on a Wednesday he went to Brigade Headquarters to conduct an inspection, and found a corporal in charge of the Brigade. The rumor is that he was so angry that he became totally incoherent. When he asked the Corporal why there were no people at Brigade Headquarters, the Corporal directed the angry general to the golf course and promptly made himself scarce. By dark, Goodrich had relieved over forty staff officers and twenty assistant and second assistant Sergeants Major of their duties. The next day, the 193rd Infantry Brigade rejoined the United States Army.

Major General Goodrich may have changed the appearance of the 193rd Brigade and the Panama Canal Zone, but he did not and could not change the true nature of some of the things that went on in the

Zone. There were many things that took place within the area under his command over which the military had no control.

I know your interest in U.F.O.s, so you'll be fascinated with what can be find down here. According to the story making the rounds, not even General Goodrich had a clearance high enough to allow him to set foot in the guarded compound that sits on the southern plateau above the slow-moving water of Lake Gatune. When anyone asked the General about the large red building that dominated the sky-line above the jungle, he gave basically the same answer that Air Force General Curtis LeMay gave Barry Goldwater when Goldwater asked to go inside the hangar that supposedly contained captured Unidentified Flying Objects, known as Hanger 18. The answer was not just, no; but an emphatic, hell, no. In fact, the mere existence of the building was considered top secret. It has its own security force that report only to some big shot at the Pentagon.

There is something else that you need to know my friend. When you get here, you need to walk softly, for there are secrets in this command that not even the General is aware exist. I've also managed to discover that there is a secret society existing among his command. An organization that calls itself the Brotherhood has members in almost every unit of the 193rd. Through these many inroads, I believe that the Brotherhood is able to influence every decision normally made by unit Commanders. The leader of the Canal Zone Brotherhood probably has more control over what took place in the 193rd, as does General Goodrich.

I've done my homework good buddy, I've found out that the Brotherhood is not a newly created organization nor was its operation just limited to the 193rd Infantry Brigade. As far as anyone knows, the Brotherhood came into existence during the American Revolution, formed by the Officers that served under General Washington's personal command; firm believers that Washington's views on government were the only proper ones for an American, they were men who worked behind the scenes to make sure that their programs controlled American foreign policy.

According to what I can find out, not only are there members of the Brotherhood in every branch of government, but also there are chapters in every Battalion in the entire Army. There were even three General Officers who are supposed to be senior members. No area of the military had been overlooked, for even the Reserve forces is supposed to have its Brotherhood representatives. I met an old retired officer down here who knows the whole story and boy is it a whopper.

It seems that no enterprise is too large or too small for the Brotherhood to take a hand: through its' Southeast Asian connections, the Brotherhood assisted C.I.A. renegades in arranging distribution routes for the drug trade. As a result of this relationship, there was a 'you wash my back and I'll wash yours' rapport between the Intelligence community, Organized Crime and the Brotherhood.

Knowing your interest in conspiracies, I think you'll have a great time here, that is if you can keep your hands off that gorgeous wife of your long enough. Well, I've written enough, got to go to work. Tell Julie I said hi. Sincerely, Emil.

Carter slowly closed the letter and noticed beneath it, an envelope addressed to Lieutenant Bill Jennings. He remembered that a few other times, he had heard some of the dream folks refer to him as Jennings. It made no since. He knew his name was Carter Hughes, but here it seemed right to respond to the Jennings name. This had to be some kind of delusion. Maybe he was losing his mind. But there was one way he could prove it to himself.

On a hunch, he leaned forward and placed his hand firmly on the shoulder of the man in front of him. The man turned, a quizzical expression on his broad face. Hughes shook his head and the man turned back to the briefing officer. Hughes was far more shaken than he showed, for the shoulder upon which he had placed his hand was firm.

Somehow, it seemed, he was physically present in this place and at the time.

Suddenly, Hughes felt nauseous; a loud clanging filled the air. Slowly, he fell forward and things got dark. Slowly, he realized the sound he heard was the ringing of a telephone, so loud it drowned out the drone of the speaker. He felt a hand on his should and heard a soft voice calling his name. With a start he jumped and opened his eyes find himself safely in his own bed and saw the beautiful face of Martha hovering over him, lit by the soft glow her bedside lamp. Her filmy negligee covering very little of her curvaceous body.

"Carter, it's for you."

The sudden transition from the briefing room to the bedroom had him somewhat disoriented, so he took the phone from her without really understanding what she was saying. Slowly, he placed the phone to his ear.

"Uh, yeah. I mean, hello."

"Is this Mr. Carter Hughes?" asked a low muffled voice.

"Uh, yes, it is."

"Mr. Hughes, I have some information that I think you would like to have."

Hughes sat up in the bed, pressing the phone to his ear.

"Yes?"

"Mr. Hughes, have you ever heard the name William Jennings?" queried the caller.

For a moment, Hughes found himself back in the briefing room. He reached down and tilted up the nametag pinned to his uniform jacket. It read Jennings. He closed his eyes tightly and tried to calm himself. He opened his eyes and found himself back in his bedroom.

"Why, uh, yes. I believe I have heard the name." He stammered. "Who are you?"

"That's not important, I'll be in your office tomorrow at precisely ten o'clock. Is that satisfactory?"

"Why, yes." Hughes paused and collected his scattered senses. "It most certainly will be satisfactory." He finished in a firm voice.

Without another word, the phone was hung up on the other end. Hughes dropped the phone in his hand back on the cradle. So intent was he with his own thoughts that he didn't hear the slight click of a third receiver being replaced. He also failed to notice the intent stare from his wife.

"Who was that dear?" she inquired softly.

"Who, oh," he thought swiftly, " why that was a client wanting to meet me to morrow. It might be a good sale."

Outwardly accepting the very flimsy explanation, Martha flipped off her bedside lamp, pulled him back under the cover and moved over to rest her head against his broad chest.

"That's nice, dear. Now forget all of that business stuff and all of your bad dreams and think of me." She purred as she gently began to rub his chest, her soft hand moving ever lower.

Snuggling close to her smaller frame, he buried his face in her sweet smelling hair. The last coherent thought Hughes had was that he wife definitely knew how to get someone's attention. What he didn't see was Matilda sitting in the living room, her hand still resting on the receiver.

CHAPTER FOUR

Carter Hughes snapped awake hours later. He knew that they had gone to bed very early. He glanced over at his wife's figure curled up in a ball, the faint light from the open living room door showing one full breast, the nipple soft. He smiled to himself as not to many hours ago, he had been licking that same nipple and it had been standing tall. Her strong even breathing assured him that she was fully asleep. Carter listened intently, but heard no sound from beyond the open bedroom door. He couldn't remember if the door had been open or closed when they had gone to sleep.

Slowly, so as not to disturb his wife, Hughes slid from the bed and slowly crossed the room to peer cautiously into the darkened living room. He heard not a sound, but he knew with every fiber of his being that he had been awakened by something moving in the room. Slowly, silently, he paced the room, checking each darkened corner. He found no sign that anyone had been in the room since they had gone to bed. Finally, he returned to the warmth and safety of his bed, to snuggle up behind his wife. Slowly, he drifted into slumber, once again. Once again, he became his dream identity, in that other time and that other place.

THE DAY BEFORE THANKSGIVING, 1975-PANAMA CANAL ZONE

Carter Hughes once again found himself inside the head of the young army officer. Though this time, he was a solely a spectator, just along for the ride. Though he did experience each and every emotion felt by the young officer, he was totally unable to influence any of his actions. In one other way, this time was slightly different, however, as this time was the first time he had seen the officer's wife, Julie.

Julie was tall, slim and absolutely gorgeous. Her figure was simply outstanding, a true traffic stopper. On this day, her eyes were sparkling and she was obviously excited. Actually, both were excited by their first visit to a foreign country. Once the plane came to a complete stop, the young couple stepped out of the plane and paused at the top of the ramp. In spite of the fact that they had been told that it was a tropical assignment, neither of them were prepared for the literal wall of intense heat that face them when they began to descend the ramp. By the time they reached the bottom of the mobile stairs that had been pushed against the side of the plane, Bill Jennings' khaki uniform blouse was quickly turning dark from sweat. His wife's blouse usually so crisp and white was showing severe sweat stains. It's going to be a long three-year-tour, he thought to himself.

Halfway across the thirty-yard gap between the plane and the hangar, it began to rain, not a soft, light civilized rain, but a raw primitive rain that fell in driving sheets. In the space of four steps, they were both soaked to the skin. The rain was so intense for the first few seconds that they became disoriented and were unable to see the terminal. It was the arrival of one of the terminal attendants that allowed them to finally reach that shelter.

The Howard Air Force Base International Terminal was primitive by U.S. standards, but then it was never intended for paying customers. The building had been thrown together to give newly arrived personnel the impression that they were still near civilization. It was basically one huge room, divided into one area for new arrivals and one for the departing passenger area. As Bill and Julie staggered in with their arms loaded with carry-on luggage, they saw there were forty or fifty people pressed against the glass door of the building staring, hungrily, in the direction of where the plane had been sitting on the tarmac. Even though the driving rain hid the plane from sight, many still strained their eyes for any sign that it was still there.

To the departing passengers, that plane represented freedom, their magic carpet to the land of the big PX. At the far end of the barn-like room was an area that appeared to be set up as a snack bar. A few tables and chairs were placed near the snack bar so that the items of food served could be eaten in relative comfort. The overall feeling was one of anticipation from the new arrivals and relief from those leaving. All in all it was rather pitiful.

A military police corporal directed Bill and his wife over to the customs inspector. Sweating profusely in the slowly moving customs line, Bill began to understand that being an officer was not going to be a piece of cake after all. Slowly, they shuffled their way to the head of the line, as, one by one; the belongings of those ahead of them were pawed through by two laughing military police, supervised by a member of the Customs staff. After the almost hour-long wait for the customs inspection, their actual customs check lasted less than ten minutes.

Quickly, Jennings and his young wife gathered their bags and bundles and pulled them over to the small snack bar located at the edge of the reception area, where they were to have been met by Lieutenant Emil Larson, a college friend of Jennings' and best man at their wedding. Emil had also been assigned to Panama a month before Jennings received his own orders. An hour passed before Julie Jennings began to get worried.

"Bill, don't you think you ought to call someone?' She looked up at him from her soda. He grinned, when she was tired, no one had to look at her to know that she had been born in Mississippi.

"Emil has been late ever since I met him. He wasn't on time for class more than once or twice during his entire college career." He reached in his pocket for change for the phone. "But if it'll make you happy I'll call for him."

Sipping on her straw, she smiled one of her special smiles. He was a sucker for her slow sensual promising smile, so he happily made what he considered to be an unnecessary call, glancing toward the door, sure that Emil would barreling in late as he always did for his college classes. Checking his pocket notebook to make sure he had the phone number correct, he dialed the local number. After two rings the phone was answered.

"Company A, 4th of the 10th, Corporal Addison speaking, may I help you sir?"

Bill nodded at the phone and then caught himself. "Er, yes, this is Lieutenant Jennings. I'm newly in the Zone and assigned to your unit. I'm looking for my sponsor, Lieutenant Larson. Is he there per chance?" he asked as he glanced back at Julie.

"Lieutenant Larson?" stammered the voice on the other end of the phone, "Uh, sir, let me refer you to the First Sergeant."

In less than a minute he heard a brisk efficient sounding voice. "First Sergeant Hendricks, may I help you?"

"Yes, this is Lieutenant Jennings, my wife and I have just arrived at Howard Air Force Base. I'm assigned to your unit. Lieutenant Larson from your company of the 4th of the 10th is my sponsor and was to meet us here. We've been waiting here about an hour, I was calling to make sure that he had left to meet us."

"You're at Howard now?" asked the First Sergeant.

"Yes, I am." Jennings replied, "We'd like to get to our quarters fairly soon, we're both soaked and tired."

"What, oh, I see you got caught in our usual two o'clock rain." Chuckled the voice on the other end of the phone, "Get use to it, sir. It rains every day at the same time. Just wait there and someone will be there shortly."

With that, First Sergeant Hendricks broke the connection. Carter Hughes was a good enough judge of men to know that something was wrong, but Bill Jennings simply stood and looked at the receiver, totally baffled at his reception. Where was Emil? Surely, he wouldn't just abandon him. They had been best friends until graduation. It made no sense.

"Problem, Lieutenant?" asked a quiet voice behind him.

Bill turned around quickly to see a grizzled old Sergeant Major with a chest full of ribbons on his khaki uniform blouse and creases in his uniform pants that were so sharp that he could have shaved with them. From the top of his neatly trimmed gray hair to the tip of his beautifully spit shined low-quarters, he was the perfect poster soldier. Bill noticed that the nametag on the right pocket of his uniform read Morton.

"Well, our transportation seems to be late, Sergeant Major," said Lieutenant Jennings, concern causing him to glance over at his wife. He relaxed when he noticed Julie having an animated conversation with another young woman of about her own age. She caught him glancing at her and waved gaily, Bill waived back.

Sergeant Major Morton spun on one heel and began to march across the terminal floor. Jennings had to almost trot to keep up with the older man, even though Jennings was taller and had a longer stride.

"These things happen, Lieutenant," said the Sergeant Major, paying no other attention to the Lieutenant, "don't let it give you the wrong impression about the efficiency of the good old 193rd. Come to my office and we'll make some telephone calls."

Lieutenant Jennings hesitated for a moment, looked over and gave Julie a weak grin before he obediently trotted along behind the ramrod straight Sergeant Major. Julie gave him a thumbs-up, but never missed a beat of her conversation with her new friend. At the far end of the terminal, Sergeant Major Morton pushed open the door to his office and stood aside to let Bill enter ahead of him.

"Just have a seat, Lieutenant and we'll get this matter straightened out shortly." He sat down behind his metallic green desk. Pictures of the Brigade chain of command filled the wall behind and above his head. The senior NCO reached out toward the Lieutenant.

"Let me have a copy of your orders, Lieutenant."

The question caught Jennings by surprise. "My what?"

The Sergeant Major looked at the Lieutenant sadly, as if he had just been told that his dog had died, then he focused his gaze on the light fixture on the peeling ceiling.

"Begging the Lieutenant's pardon, but generally, Lieutenant, in this man's army, when a lot of taxpayer money is spent to send some wet-behind-the-ears child to a post to be trained by adult NCOs, the child is given a piece of paper that tells him where he is going and when he is supposed to get their.

Now, Lieutenant, you have to understand that since the Army has its own name for everything, the Army calls these children Second Lieutenants. These pieces of paper I mentioned, which are called travel orders, are given to the Second Lieutenants because, if left to there own devices, the Lieutenants would immediately get lost. Begging the Lieutenant's pardon."

Getting the hint and realizing that he really did appear foolish, Bill jumped to his feet and began to back toward the door.

"Just a minute Sergeant Major, I'll get my briefcase and be right back. Won't take a minute, be right back," he babbled almost incoherently, trying to hold onto some shred of dignity.

"If you're not back in ten minutes, I'll organize a search party. It's easy for certain people to get lost in this big terminal," observed the Sergeant Major as he continued to study the light fixture above his head in great detail. The last thing Bill heard as the door swung shut was the Sergeant Major laugh softly and say, "Second Lieutenants!"

Pausing, to give his face a chance to return to its normal color, Bill looked around for Julie. He had left his briefcase containing, among other things, the precious orders sitting by their table. In the hustle and bustle of people gathering to be escorted to the waiting plane, it was no longer possible to see his wife.

Very much aware that the Sergeant Major was waiting for him, Bill quickly made his way through the mob of soldiers and their dependents eagerly waiting to board the plane and looked around for his wife. Finally, he found her among a small group of chattering women. From the appearance of things, they were all bemoaning their fate of being sent to the wilds of Central America. When Julie saw him coming, her face brightened and she half-rose from her chair.

"Is he here yet?" she asked eagerly.

He shook his head as he leaned over and grabbed up his briefcase. "Not yet, babe. Sergeant Major Morton is calling about it, but he needs a copy of my orders."

He paused as he caught sight of the very revealing low cut blouse that one of the young women was almost wearing, then turned red as, out of the corner of his eye, he caught sight of Julie grinning at him.

"Uh, be back in a moment." he stammered as he literally trotted back to the Sergeant Major's office.

"See you made it without a guide," observed the Sergeant Major, who was still studying the light fixture, as he held out one hand.

Silently, Bill handed over a copy of his orders to the senior NCO. Mumbling to himself, Sergeant Major Morton ran his finger down the page, laid it precisely in the middle of the desktop and reached for his phone. Eyes still riveted on the copy of orders on his desk, Morton dialed a number, six digits instead of seven, since the Canal Zone exchange was so small seven digits had never been needed. He held the phone to his ear in silence until he received an answer.

"Brigade Personnel, Sergeant Muldavo speaking."

"Yeah, Muldavo, Sergeant Major Morton, give me Sergeant Major Clancy," snapped Morton as he began to reconsider the light fixture.

"One minute, Sergeant Major, he's on the phone with Brigade."

For what seemed like an eternity the Sergeant Major and the new Lieutenant sat silently in the small office. For lack of anything else to do, Bill began to memorize the names and faces of the Brigade chain of command from the row of pictures on the wall behind the Sergeant. He wanted to get up and pace, or go check on Julie, or just wander around the terminal, but he didn't want to get the Sergeant Major started on any more of his observations regarding the need of a Second Lieutenant for a keeper. The room had become so quiet that when Morton spoke again, Jennings jumped a foot out of his chair.

"Clancy, Morton over at Howard."

Sergeant Major Clancy had such a booming voice that even Jennings could hear what he said.

"Jim, my man, how's it hanging? Understand that you have a small problem."

" Yeah, I got another Lieutenant who seems to be a little disoriented. His orders say that he's assigned to Company A, 4th Battalion, 10th Infantry. Unfortunately, his sponsor never arrived to pick him up."

"Seems to be another screw up by old Hardtack Hendricks. Don't know how he managed to get to be a First Sergeant. Who's this lost lamb's sponsor supposed to be?"

"Yeah, typical Hendricks snafu. Hold on." Morton rested the receiver on his right shoulder and suddenly riveted the uncomfortable Lieutenant with a piercing glance.

"Who's your sponsor, Lieutenant?" he snapped, as he pulled a black Government Issue ballpoint pen from a penholder set approximately six inches from the front edge of the desk and began to make notes.

"Er, Larson, Lieutenant Emil Larson."

"He with Company A?" demanded Sergeant Major Morton.

"Yes, he's with the Second Platoon. Assigned there two months ago."

Morton put the receiver back to his ear. "His sponsor is a second luey named Larson, Emil Larson. Assigned to Second Platoon, Company A. What?"

Jennings could tell that something was wrong from Morton's tone of voice, but he was totally unprepared for what came next. Morton simply sat and listened quietly, making no comment but writing copious notes. Periodically, he shot sharp glances at the increasingly uneasy Lieutenant. Finally, he hung up the phone and for the first time he dropped his ramrod straight posture.

"Well Lieutenant, I hope the rest of your tour does not go like your arrival. You represent a king size problem to us." he said as he went back to studying the light fixture.

Lieutenant Jennings had immediate visions of being cashiered out of the service for some totally obscure reason, but for the life of him, he couldn't figure out what he might have done. He was certain that Second Lieutenants were given more than one chance before they were thrown out of the service. He had no idea what he could say to Julie if they threw him out.

"What do you mean, Sergeant Major?" he managed to stammer as he tried to figure out what to do with his hands.

"Well, first as to your assignment. You won't be going to Company A of 4th Battalion, 10th Infantry. You are being re-assigned, probably to the 4th battalion (Mechanized) Twentieth Infantry. I know that they have some platoon leader slots open right now. You'll like it, it's a good unit."

Now the Lieutenant knew that he had offended someone, his new unit didn't want him. Try as he might, he could think of no reason why he was being re-assigned. For a moment, he was torn between wanting to know why he was being re-assigned and just wanting to get away from the ferocious Sergeant Major. His curiosity won over his fear.

"Sergeant Major, why am I being assigned?"

"Nothing to worry about, Lieutenant, these type of personnel changes happen all the time." The Sergeant Major actually seemed to be fidgeting in his chair. He kept glancing at the phone as if he were impatient to get rid of the Lieutenant.

"Well, is it possible to ask that I remain in my original assignment?" Jennings leaned forward in his chair, trying to read the notes the Sergeant Major had taken. He always had trouble reading upside down.

"Fraid not, Lieutenant. After all that trouble over there, most of the newly arrived Lieutenants from the last flight were sent to the 4th of the 10th. They now have a full roster, so there is no room for you. Personnel is now cutting orders assigning you to a new position, so don't worry about it." The Sergeant Major glanced at his army issued watch for the fifth time since he had hung up the phone.

"What kind of trouble?" asked Bill as he leaned back in his chair. He'd decided to hope for the best and was merely making conversation.

"Oh, the usual, racial unrest and things like that. Yesterday a Lieutenant was killed in a training accident. Things like that can cause a lot of trouble in a unit." He went back to studying the interesting light fixture above Bill's head.

Bill froze as he studied Morton's face. To his surprise, the dominating Sergeant Major refused to meet his eyes. He sensed that Morton was trying to hold something back.

"Sergeant Major Morton, who was the Lieutenant who died?" he asked in a firm voice, as he sat straight in his own chair.

"Well, Lieutenant, I hope he wasn't a close friend of yours but yesterday, according to what I was just told, Lieutenant Emil Larson was killed."

At the news, Hughes could feel the pain and anguish felt by Jennings. The world began to spin.

CHAPTER FIVE

Jennings swayed in his chair and turned white as a sheet as the realization of what he had just heard really struck home. What the Sergeant Major was saying to him was that he would never see his best friend again. Second Lieutenant Emil Larson was dead, the victim of a silly training accident, killed while in the field playing war. It was impossible, for his best friend, his friend since the third grade, to be dead. Not Emil Larson, 6' 4", 250 pounds, with the laughing blue eyes. Of all the people who might be dead, why did it have to be Emil?

Even though he was just along for the ride, so to speak, Hughes was amazed at how real the pain felt to him.

"Lieutenant Jennings? Sir, are you all right?" asked the Sergeant Major loudly, finally glancing away from the light fixture, a look of concern on his face.

It was really difficult for Jennings to focus his attention on the Sergeant Major. He couldn't grasp the idea that he would never again hear Emil's famous battle cry of 'Who's got the beer?'. It was a major struggle not to break down in front of the man, but, finally, he pulled himself together when he felt the Sergeant Major's hand on his shoulder.

"Son? You O.K.?" he asked in a softer concerned tone of voice as he bent over the pasty-faced, swaying lieutenant.

"Uh, yeah, I guess. I mean, how did it happen?"

Assured that the young man was not going to come face to face with the office floor, the Sergeant Major dropped back into his chair and dialed the phone. It appeared that this lieutenant knew the dead man very well; that could cause some complications. "I don't know, son. All I know is that the scuttlebutt was that a Lieutenant with the 4th of the 10th was killed yesterday. Then Clancy confirmed that your friend, Lieutenant Larson, was the dead man. Until then, I only knew that someone had died, not how." he responded as he leaned back in his chair, the phone to his ear.

"Yeah, Muldavo, this is Sergeant Major Morton, get me Clancy," he snapped as he pinned the phone to his ear with his shoulder, while he fished in his pocket for a crumpled pack of Marlboro. He hesitated, and then offered the pack to Jennings before putting a cigarette to his own lips. As he reached for a match, Sergeant Major Clancy came on the phone.

"Yeah, Morton, what's ya need?" he asked in his broad Brooklyn accent.

"Got the assignment for Lieutenant Jennings yet?" he rasped as he lit his cigarette, still holding the phone to his ear with his shoulder.

"Yeah, just came through from Brigade Headquarters. He's to report to Captain Pritchart, S-1 at 4/20. They are arranging for his family quarters now and a driver is in route. Have him, his family and his kit at the front entrance of the terminal in about ten minutes."

Morton nodded, as he blew a stream of smoke out of his nose.

"Thanks Clance, see you at the NCO club later. Got some news."

"What is it?"

"Tell you tonight."

Morton dropped the phone back into the cradle and finished making his notes. Finally he looked up at Bill.

"Lieutenant, you doing all right?" he asked in concern as he gently tapped his cigarette on edge of the glass ashtray, knocking off the ash.

Lieutenant Jennings stood and straightened his uniform blouse. Morton knew in that moment that this kid was made of good stuff, if anyone could break what was going on, his money would be on this young man. Be interesting to watch what happens, he thought to himself.

"I'm fine, Sergeant Major. Emil was a very close friend. The news caught me by surprise. Do you know if anyone has notified his family?" he asked as he reached for his briefcase.

The Sergeant Major shook his head. "No idea, Lieutenant, as I said, I just knew that he was dead. If you want to follow up on it then you might call his Company Commander."

He paused as he picked up his sheet of notes.

"As for you, you and your wife, I assume that young lady you were grinning at is your wife, need to be at the entrance to the terminal in about ten minutes. You will be picked up by a driver from 4/20, he'll take you to Battalion Headquarters over at Fort Clayton."

Falling silent, the Sergeant Major leaned back and began to study his light fixture some more like there was a lot he wanted to say, but it really wasn't his place. With a grunt, he almost sprang from his chair and held out his hand.

"Best of luck to you Lieutenant. If I can be of any help, call me."

Solemnly, Jennings shook the NCO's hard hand. "See you later, I guess. Thanks for your help."

Jennings' mind was spinning, he felt lightheaded as he turned from the Sergeant Major's desk. Without another word to the NCO, he opened the door and walked back into the confusion of the Terminal.

With the illogic of a dream, Hughes found himself still in the room with the NCO after Jennings walked slowly out of the office. For a long time after the Lieutenant left the office, Sergeant Major Morton starred at the ceiling, considering the various course of action open to him. Finally, Morton pulled the phone close to him and carefully dialed another number. Holding the receiver to his ear with his shoulder, Morton fumbled with his crumpled pack of Marlboros.

"Brigade Sergeant Major's Office, Private Benjamin speaking." said a rather sexy female voice.

"Benjamin, Sergeant Major Morton at Howard, get me Sergeant Major Ashe. This is important," he said emphatically.

When Morton bluntly asked for the Brigade Sergeant Major and didn't try to make a pass at her, Private Sarah Benjamin knew that something was long, so she lost no time in finding the Brigade Sergeant Major. Sergeant Major John Ashe also wasted no time in charging into his office and shutting the door.

"Morton, you old dog, what's the problem? You didn't come on to sweet little Benjamin and she feels rejected." Boomed the big black Sergeant Major over the phone.

"John, we are going to have some problems, so you need to be ready." said Morton bluntly as he stuck his last cigarette in his mouth.

"What the fuck are you talking about?" demanded the Brigade Sergeant Major in perplexity as he reached into a humidor on his desk for a Havana cigar. Lighting up, he blew a stream of aromatic smoke toward the ceiling.

"You know that Lieutenant Larson that died yesterday over at Fort Davis on the range?" he asked as he lit his own smoke.

Ashe grumbled to himself as his cigar went out and struggled to relight it. "Yeah, so what. He's dead and that's the end of that."

Morton snorted into the phone. "You couldn't be further from the truth. I don't think that this thing is over. It's not over by a long shot," he said, nervously puffing away on his diminishing cigarette.

"What the hell are you talking about old man? That nosy Lieutenant is dead, how much more final can that get?" demanded the angry Sergeant Major. At almost seven feet tall and well over three hundred pounds, the big black Sergeant Major was one person no one wanted to anger. To make it worse, he had a hair trigger temper.

Morton waved away the cloud of smoke that formed around his head and leaned back to continue his study of the light fixture.

"A new lieutenant arrived today." began Morton as he allowed himself to sink lower in his leather covered chair.

"So what." interrupted Ashe angrily, "What does that have to do with the fucking price of tea in fucking China? We have new lieutenants arriving everyday. Most of them haven't got the sense to pour piss out of a boot. Sounds to me like you losing it, old man."

"Well, you stupid son of a bitch, this particular new lieutenant was a good friend of Lieutenant Larson. In other words, there is someone here who I believe will want to look into what happened!" snapped Morton as he swung his chair around and stretched out his legs.

"How do you know they were friends?" asked a suddenly calm Ashe.

"Because Larson was to be this new guy's sponsor and, when I told him that Larson was dead, he turned white as a sheet and almost passed out." responded Morton.

"Hmmmmm. This could potentially cause serious problems. I'm going to have to tell the old man. What's this kid look like?"

"Oh, he's about six feet, two inches tall, sandy hair, well groomed. His weight is about one hundred and seventy five pounds, seems to be fairly well muscled. I got the impression that he could be a mean one in a fight. He's fucked up right now, but when he gets his act together, he could well be hell on wheels.

He's married to a real fine looking filly. I got a look at his wife; she's about five foot, four inches tall, very well developed. Long blonde hair, looks almost white in the sun. Be a pity to make a young widow out of her, now wouldn't it?" mused Morton in a bland voice as he grinned into the phone at Ashe's obvious discomfort.

"You're enjoying this aren't you, you bastard?" rumbled Ashe.

"You bet I am. You big shots have really fucked this Larson matter up. If this new kid finds out what really happened to his friend, there could well be some heads rolling in this outfit."

"God damn! God damn!" yelled Ashe as he slammed down the phone.

Morton held onto his phone, listening to the dial tone and laughing loudly.

With a snap, Hughes found himself once again floating above Lieutenant Jennings. He watched as Jennings made his way through the crowded terminal. He would have rather have gone off by himself to grieve over his friend's death, but he didn't want to let Julie know what had happened. When he found her again, Julie looked up at him with such a bright smile that he knew he was right not to break the news about Emil's death now.

"Get things straightened out?" she asked brightly as she moved over on her chair to make room for him to sit.

"Sure, thing, babe. Typical Army efficiency, someone will be here to pick us up in about ten minutes."

Julie tossed her soda can into the nearby trash and began to help her husband gather up their carry on baggage. Arms loaded, they struggled through the still crowded terminal to the large front doors. Their timing was almost perfect, for as they dropped their bundles and bags on the side walk, an Army carry all screeched to a stop at the curb, and a tall lanky private first class in camouflaged fatigues jumped out. Bill noticed that the bumper markings were for the 4th Battalion, Twentieth Infantry.

"You Lieutenant Jennings?" the private drawled, around a toothpick clenched in the side of his mouth. He then threw Bill a sloppy salute.

"Yes, I am. If you'll open the rear, we'll get this stuff loaded and then we need to get a couple of bags at the baggage claim area." said Jennings as he grabbed up one of his bags.

"Shucks, Lieutenant, you and the little lady just get in the front. I'll handle this here stuff," said the Private, taking the bag from Bill's hand.

"Have you all at Battalion Headquarters in two shakes of a lamb's tail." boomed the lanky Private as he jerked open the driver's door and jumped inside. "Just gotta swing by the baggage claim area and pick up your other things."

With a roar and a jerk, the carry all moved smoothly around the circular drive and turned into another parking lot on the side of the terminal. Bill noticed that a small crowd was gathered near a conveyor belt that ran along the south wall of the building. Periodically, one of the people clustered around the belt would lean forward, grab a suitcase and pull it off the belt. Whistling to himself, the driver stomped on the brakes, swinging the carry all into a marked parking spot. Leaving the motor running, the driver jumped from the driver's seat and then turned and put his head back into the car.

"You all got your claim checks?" he inquired slowly, holding out his hand.

Julie fumbled in her purse for a while and then held out several buff colored baggage claim checks. "Here they are. You need Bill to help you?" she asked with a worried look on her pretty face. "Those bags are heavy."

"No thank you ma'am. I can handle it. You all just sit tight and I'll be back shortly," he mumbled around his toothpick as he turned and ambled over to the baggage claim area. They sat and watched in complete fascination as the lanky, slow talking, Private sorted through the small mountain of unclaimed bags until he found the matching set of Samsonite luggage that had been their wedding gift from Julie's father.

"My God, it's like watching a movie in slow motion," said Julie as she began to giggle. Bill looked at her fondly and began to laugh, harder and harder as he watched the young soldier grab all four bags and start the long trip back to the carry all. It helped him to laugh. He'd decided that he would tell Julie about Emil later.

Finally, all their bags were loaded and the Private was back behind the wheel. Once again, with a jerk, he dropped it into gear and pulled out of the parking lot. Bill leaned back against the seat and tried to compose himself. He tried to appear cheerful, but all he could think about was Emil. What could have happened to his friend?

"What's your name, Private?" Julie asked as she craned her slim neck to try and take in all of the colorful scenery they passed.

"Private Jonah Ralph, Ma'am." he said politely.

Bill was amused to see Ralph try to watch Julie in his rearview mirror. From Julie's expression, Bill saw that she was flattered at the attention.

"How long have you been in the Canal Zone? Oh, what's that?" she asked pointing at a multi-colored bus, people hanging out of the windows. Bill glanced at it and was surprised to see a crate of chickens tied to the top of the bus.

Private Ralph glanced over at the bus, which was pulled over on the shoulder of the road as a large crowd tried to pack themselves on board and grinned. "Well, ma'am, I been in the Zone about a year. As for that thing, it's called a Chiva Chiva bus. Basically it's a Panamanian idea of how to run a bus line. You do see some sights on a Chiva Chiva bus."

"Private Ralph, how far is it to Fort Davis?" she asked as she turned in her seat, her attention focused on a road side-stand that had numerous signs advertising the sale of original works of art.

The private glanced over at the young woman. "Fort Davis, Ma'am?"

"Oh, I didn't tell you, babe," interjected Jennings, "they changed my assignment. Instead of sending me to 4/10 at Fort Davis, I was reassigned to 4/20 here at Fort Clayton. I'm sorry I didn't tell you, I was just pre-occupied."

Out of the corner of his eye, Bill caught Julie's look of surprise. He could kick himself. With her quick mind and extremely accurate intuition she had already guessed that there was something unusual about this reassignment. The look that she was giving him made it clear that while she wouldn't make an issue out of his oversight in front of the Private, he would definitely have some questions to answer after they were alone.

He was relieved when she turned her attention back to the scenery and started her chatter with the Private again.

"How are the quarters at Fort Clayton?" she asked as she leaned forward to rest her arms on the back of the front seat.

"Well, ma'am, you have to understand that I live in the barracks so I'm not really familiar with most of the quarters. The NCO quarters are nice, but I don't know anything about the officers' quarters. I do know that most of the bigger officer places are at Fort Amador," he answered absently as he negotiated the turn onto the approach to the Thatcher Ferry Bridge.

Fort Amador was a name that Bill hadn't heard before, or if he had, he wasn't really sure where it was.

"What's at Fort Amador?"

Spinning the wheel and stomping on the brakes to avoid a collision with a stalled ancient car that appeared to be held together by bailing wire and primer, Private Ralph continued his conversation without missing a beat.

"Fort Amador is where the Brigade Headquarters is located. Tain't much else there except the Headquarters, maybe a couple of research stations and one or two small support units."

Private Ralph paused for a moment as he pulled over to the shoulder of the road at the edge of the entrance to the bridge.

"Got something to show you that you may like." He opened the door and jumped to the ground.

"Why not?" Julie slid out the door, gallantly held open for her by Private Ralph.

Bill followed his wife and the Private as they walked along the shoulder of the road toward the Bridge. To their right was a wall of greenery. To their left was an almost solid wall of cars crossing the bridge toward Panama City, Panama. Try as he might, Bill could not figure out a reason for this little impromptu stroll in the heat. He wanted to get to his new assignment and find out about Emil. Increasing his pace, Bill hurried to catch up with his wife.

Julie and her escort were at the edge of the Bridge when Jennings immediately forgot his objections. Laid out before them was a view that should have been on post cards around the world. Before them was the broad bay that led into the Panama Canal, full of sailing craft of various sizes and types. The panoramic view allowed them to see the Capital City of Panama, the closest lock of the Canal and a bit of the river. It was a beautiful country. Unfortunately it was also a poor one.

As Bill remembered from his pre-assignment briefing, Panama's current political strongman was General Omar Torrios, commander of the Panamanian armed forces. Torrios ruled the little country with a firm hand, all the while skimming off all of the available foreign aide money from the United States to his secret bank accounts in Switzerland. The average Panamanian worker, who didn't work in the zone, earned about ten thousand dollars a year. As far as the average native was concerned, an American was a millionaire. Law enforcement in the country was arbitrary and discriminatory; the Policia for the slightest infractions arrested people. The dream of every Panamanian was to get a job in the Canal Zone working for the Post Exchange. Those who did, lived a life of luxury undreamed of by their less fortunate neighbors.

As he remembered the story, until early 1975, an American Officer could hire a full time live-in Panamanian maid for the equivalent of thirty dollars a week. In fact, he had been told that almost all of the older officer's quarters came complete with attached maid's quarters. The cost of living was about equal to what it had been in the United States in the 1950s. It had been a paradise, until the American Civil Liberties Union decided to put an end to it. Their attorneys' descended on the sleepy Canal Zone town of Balboa and proceeded to file suit after suit, asking the Courts to apply America's minimum wage laws to the citizens of Panama. Finally, in settlement, it was decided and decreed by the Military and Pan Canal Corporation powers-that-be that henceforth, American standard minimum wages would be paid to Panamanian workers who worked in the Zone. No one ever discovered who had called the ACLU.

Bill started slightly when Julie grabbed his arm.

"Isn't it just beautiful? Isn't it like a paradise on earth?" she asked as she breathed deeply, taking in the softly scented sea air. Then as a cloud of monoxide floated over them from a passing Chiva Chiva bus she began to cough loudly.

"Well, even Eden had a serpent." She laughed, trying to stop her coughing fit.

"O.K. poet, let's get out of here before I suffocate or our friend goes to sleep." Bill took her arm and began to steer her back toward the carry all. Their slow-talking, slow- moving escort had already returned to the comfort of the air-conditioned carry all.

Forgetting that public displays of affection were frowned on by the Military, she slid her arm around her husband's waist and hugged him close. "I know we'll be happy here," she said as she stretched up on her tiptoes to kiss his check.

Bill glanced back at the city gleaming in the afternoon sun and felt a shiver run down his spin. He remembered an expression of his grand-mother's. He now knew what it meant to get the feeling that someone had just stepped on his grave. He didn't want Julie to know how he felt, but he really wished he had been sent to Germany or Korea instead of Panama.

CHAPTER SIX

Hughes started and opened his eyes. The world of Lieutenant Jennings vanished like smoke. Hughes glanced over and saw that Martha was sleeping soundly, her hair spread out around her like a halo. Rubbing his face, Hughes laid his head back on the pillow and closed his eyes. Immediately, he found himself back watching the life story of Bill Jennings.

Bill was so lost in his thoughts that he really didn't remember much of the trip from the Thatcher Ferry Bridge to Fort Clayton, other than that Julie continued her cheerful chatter with the Private as they crossed the Bridge and entered 4th of July Avenue, and the whizzing cars threatened to kill them at every intersection. Panamanian drivers all appeared to have learned how to drive in an area where there were no obstacles that required them to learn how to steer their vehicles. To compound the problem, the drivers seemed to know of no speed other than full speed ahead. Death was just a swerve away at all times.

They worked their way through the backed-up traffic jam to the main intersection between Panama City and the entrance to the Canal Zone. On one side of the street were smartly uniformed members of the Panamanian police force; on the other side were United States Army Military Police. The two forces had enough weapons to start a small war.

"I like their uniforms much better than ours."

Julie tapped Bill on the shoulder to get his attention. When he still didn't respond, she leaned over the seat and pressed her lips to his cheek.

"Earth to Bill. Are you still with me?"

"Sorry, babe. I've got a few things on my mind. What were you saying?" Bill looked out at the traffic.

"Those guys in uniform over there." she said pointing out at the Panamanian police patrolling to their right. "Their uniforms are much fancier than your drab old uniforms."

Bill looked them over with great interest. He did tend to like their high-pitched dark uniform caps, but their dark green uniforms and knee-high riding boots were a bit too showy for his taste. At that moment, the Panamanians had a changing of the guard. Bill was amused to watch the new guards actually goose step to their posts.

"Interesting, but their uniforms look a bit too much like Nazi uniforms to me," he observed turning to keep them in sight.

"Spoil sport. You're so proud of your own uniform that you can't see anything else."

"Well, I worked damn hard to get it, so I have no desire to trade it in on another this soon."

He glanced back at the Panamanian police one last time but a marring of the building facade behind them drew his attention. As they passed another building, he saw the same apparent damage. Looking back along the Panamanian side of 4th of July Avenue, he noticed what seemed to be a row of pitted areas on the front of the buildings. The marks really looked like a giant woodpecker had made them.

"Private Ralph, what's that peculiar defect on the front of that building?"

Ralph threw a bored glance at the building and then returned his attention to the road. "Reckon they's bullet holes, Lieutenant," he remarked as he slowed in front of the main entrance to the Zone. "Probably came from one of our 50 caliber machine guns."

Braking to a stop, Private Ralph rolled down the window and leaned out to talk to the M.P. who approached the car.

"Where you been, Private?" demanded the M.P. as he made a note on his clipboard.

Ralph hooked a thumb over his shoulder toward the Lieutenant.

"Picking up a new officer fer the Battalion." The M.P. craned his neck to get a good look at Julie, who leaned back against the seat and crossed her legs. When she noticed the M.P. gawking at her, she rewarded him with a bright stunning smile.

The M.P. waved Ralph to drive on through the main gate. Once they were moving again, Bill repeated his question.

"Those marks on the buildings across the way, you were telling me what caused them." he reminded the Private.

Private Ralph glanced at the Lieutenant out of the corner of his eye as he kept his main attention on the traffic.

"Well, sir, there's better than me that can tell you about them, but from what I've heard, it happened about ten years or so ago. The Panamanian Army kind of attacked the Zone and the Army had to stop them. One of the other guys told me that those marks you were asking about are where our .50 caliber machine guns knocked the chunks out of the brick. For some reason, the Panamanians never fixed the place."

"I hadn't heard about any trouble down here. Is it safe?" Julie worried, leaning forward over the back of the front seat.

Private Ralph laughed shortly. "Shucks, ma'am that was ten years ago, we're all friends now, more or less."

"What caused the trouble?" Bill sat a little straighter in his seat.

"I don't rightly know, Lieutenant. According to the story that I have heard, the Natives got upset about something and tried to storm the Zone. The ole 4/20 met them at 4th of July Avenue, that's that main street that divides the Zone from Panama City, and there was a regular brawl at first, before everybody decided to get under cover and start shooting at each other from safer locations. From the stories, it was like the Hatfields and the McCoys for a while, until the General ordered our side to quit firing."

"Why'd he do that?" asked Julie.

Private Ralph shook his head slowly. "Don't rightly know, ma'am. Remember, that was ten years ago. Anyway, our folks just kept their heads down. The Panamanians put some snipers on those buildings you was looking at. According to the story, the snipers really were more of an aggravation than a real danger, until one of our boys stood up at the wrong time. The sniper got him right in the head."

"Oh, how horrible!" exclaimed Julie, with her hand over her mouth. "What happened?"

Bill could see a small grin playing at the edges of Ralph's mouth and knew that he was enjoying Julie's reactions.

"Well, ma'am, according to the story, there was a Department of the Army observer with the troops, he was a Bird Colonel. He ordered our troops to fire and of course, they refused cause of the General's orders. Well, this here Bird Colonel just climbed up on one of the armored personnel carriers, jerked back the lever on one of the big .50 calibers and let her rip. He not only hit the sniper, but he made a mess out of about a dozen others who tried to return fire. According to the stories I've heard, it was his bullets what knocked those chips out of the buildings.

Well, that type of shooting kind of ended the stalemate, the Panamanian military just vanished. Next thing you knew, the streets were empty. You couldn't find a Panamanian anywhere near the zone. It seemed to shock them that we would fire back. Well, since there was no more enemy to shoot at, why, naturally our folks just packed up and went back to the post."

Julie thought over the story in silence and then leaned forward again. "I guess that Colonel was a hero."

Again, Private Ralph gave his horse like laugh. "Well, not exactly, ma'am. Seems like he got congratulated for killing the sniper and then arrested for disobeying the General's orders. Well, we're here, folks."

Jumping out, Private Ralph quickly opened the rear door for Julie to step down from the vehicle. Bill opened his own door and, grabbing his briefcase, walked around the front of the vehicle to meet his wife. For a long second he stood and looked at the front door of the Battalion Headquarters. In an arc over the door large raised red letters spelled out 4th Battalion (M) 20th Infantry. His new home for the next three years.

The majority of the buildings in the Canal Zone were built in a peculiar style known as tropical architecture. In areas such as Panama where the humidity can easily reach 100% and tropical storms can cause major flooding, it was discovered that normal building styles used in North America and even in Mexico were simply not suitable. This led the U.S. Military to experiment with new building techniques that took into account all of the major considerations of life in the tropics. One of the main considerations in building in the tropics is air circulation. So most barracks were designed with internal walls that did not go all the way to the ceiling. Non-load bearing walls are built only seven feet high, from this height to the ceiling, screen wire is nailed, thus allowing complete air circulation and giving some security. Additionally, the rooms are built around the outer wall of the building, with wide airy halls running completely around the inside of the square. In the center of the floor, were the showers and latrine facilities. The buildings were also built on high ground and were uniformly three or more stories tall.

Another important consideration was the flooding that could be caused by tropical storms. This led to the designing of buildings on large pylons. Taking advantage of this design technique, the first floor was usually used for storage, and actually considered the basement. The first floor is one flight of stairs up. At the top of the stairs, Private Ralph turned left and led them through a set of double metal doors. Immediately before them was the office of the Battalion Sergeant Major, Sergeant Major Jorge Villanueva. The door was shut, but Bill could hear loud voices coming through the flimsy wooden door.

Further down the hall on the left was the Battalion orderly room, where the Battalion Commander's clerks worked. Off this room, were the offices of the Battalion Commander, Lieutenant Colonel Lyman Green and the Battalion Executive Officer, Major John Durgle. Across the hall from the orderly room, on the right, was the office of the Battalion Adjutant, the officer in charge of personnel and assignments for the Battalion. It was into this office that Private Ralph led Bill and Julie.

"Here they are, Captain," said Private Ralph as he stopped in the doorway to the Adjutant's Office.

"Well, damn it, Ralph bring them on in here instead of letting them stand in the hall!" came a rather high-pitched voice from in the room. With more speed than they had come to expect from Ralph, he jumped out of the way and shooed them into the office. The Adjutant, a slim Engineer Captain, wearing a set of camouflaged fatigues that were so starched that they could have stood by themselves, came around his desk to offer his hand to Bill.

"Good to see you, Lieutenant. Have a seat."

Before Bill could say anything, the Captain dropped his hand and turned to capture Julie's. "And I am so glad to see you came with him, always good to have another woman here to join our little family."

Leaving Bill to find his own way, the Captain, still holding Julie's hand firmly in his own, led them over to a sitting area furnished with a couch and two overstuffed chairs. Bill noticed that the furniture was grouped around a beaten-up brown coffee table, with one cracked leg that contained a few dog-eared magazines. The office was large, probably twice the size of Bill's college dorm room, but painted an atrocious puke green, typical army colors. Near the couch was a partially closed door that seemed to open into another office.

"I'm Captain Bert Pritchart, Battalion Adjutant." he introduced himself as they all settled themselves on the battered furniture. "And you are

Lieutenant William Thomas Jennings and you are his wife, Julie. Correct?"

Bill nodded as he crossed his legs. "Yes, sir. I'm sorry that I don't have any orders, but they were changed at Howard Air Force. I was originally scheduled to go to Fort Davis, but then I was told to come here."

Pritchart nodded his head as he turned to the door to his right. "Malone. Sergeant Malone, where are you?"

No one answered, but a tall, gray haired Sergeant First Class, smoking a pipe that appeared older than dirt, wearing red bedroom shoes, came wandering into the room. Surrounding his partially baldhead was a wreath of pipe smoke.

"Yes, sir?"

"Malone, call Brigade and asked them about Lieutenant Jennings' orders. Tell them that, pending receipt of the orders, we are going to assign him as Assistant Adjutant. Once orders arrive, then we'll permanently assign him to a rifle platoon." Pritchart tried to look at Julie's magnificent legs and appear to be paying attention to Malone.

"Yes, sir." answered Malone as he took his pipe out of his mouth and examined it closely. Apparently satisfied with the condition of his pipe, Malone ambled around and shuffled out of the room. He had never once raised his eyes to look at the Captain. Julie, meanwhile, was getting a big kick out of the whole situation. She always did love to be the center of attention and attention was what she was getting from Pritchart.

With something close to amusement, Bill sat quietly and watched the Captain watch his wife. He was curious as to how long it would take for the Captain to realize that they both knew what he was doing, but he quickly found out that the Captain didn't care if they knew he was ogling Julie or not. It was actually Bill who broke the silence.

"Uh, Captain, did I understand you to say that I would be assistant Adjutant until my orders arrived?" he asked as he shifted uncomfortably in the battered chair. Pritchart was now opening ogling Julie's tanned, well-muscled legs, which her mini-skirt showed off to perfection.

"Uh, yeah, Lieutenant, we'll have something for you to do since it'll probably be the first of the week before you are officially assigned to this outfit. This will give you a chance to get the lay of the land, so to speak, before taking over your platoon." said Pritchart as he leaned back and stretched, his arms in the air.

Bill was ready to make a comment that would probably get him in trouble, when a big bulky Lieutenant Colonel came walking into the office.

"Bert, where the hell are you?" he bellowed, a sheaf of papers clutched in one massive hand.

Bert Pritchart sprang to his feet and almost fell over his chair in his eagerness. "Right here, Colonel." He waved for Bill and Julie to join him. "Meeting the new arrivals."

Lieutenant Colonel Lyman Green was the Battalion Commander of the 4th battalion (M) 20th Infantry. He was certainly one of the biggest men that Bill had ever seen, not that he was especially tall, but his sheer mass was simply overwhelming. Next to the Colonel, Captain Pritchart, who was about 5' 10" and weighed around one hundred and-seventy-pounds looked like a dwarf. Pritchart handled the introductions.

"Colonel Green, this is Lieutenant William Thomas Jennings and his lovely wife, Julie."

The Battalion Commander engulfed Bill's hand in his own and liter-ally crushed it in the power of his handshake. With Julie, however, he was almost courtly in his manner as he almost bowed over her hand.

"Pleased to meet both of you. Are you signed in yet?" he asked mildly, raising one eyebrow as he glanced at the Adjutant.

"Not yet, Colonel. He was scheduled for the 4th of the 10th, but was diverted to us at the last minute. It will probably be Monday or Tuesday, before we have hard copy orders assigning him here."

Green put his fists on his hips and looked Julie over with great appre-ciation. "Well your good fortune, Lieutenant. Fort Davis is considered a backwater in the Zone. Here at Fort Clayton, you'll get not only a good military education, but even more importantly, you'll be associating with General Goodrich almost weekly. A very good way to make connections that will be useful in the future."

The Colonel paused for a second and then glanced at his Adjutant.

"Bert, have you arranged quarters for them yet?" he asked as he tossed the crumpled papers in his hand onto the Adjutant's desk.

"I called Collier over at Housing and he said that subject to Colonel Holden's approval, that they would be assigned to the quarters that Captain Martin had occupied. Near your quarters, if you will remember." responded the Adjutant as he leaned over the desk to examine the papers thrown down by the Colonel.

Green nodded and turned toward the door. "I'll call Holden and make sure that he approves. Call Collier and tell him to have someone meet them there in about thirty minutes."

The Colonel stood in silence for several moments before pointing at the crumpled mass of papers on the desk.

"In the meantime, Bert, you look at those statistics. I am not satisfied with any of them; Goodrich just finished reaming me out over those damn reports. I want them modified to meet his requirements," ordered the Colonel in a hard voice as he stomped out of the office.

Pritchart looked at the papers and then at the door. He sighed, shook his head and dropped the papers on his desk. He looked up at Bill and grinned. "Some days it's a zoo around here. You've got to keep your sense of humor."

He picked up his phone and dialed quickly. "Captain Collier, please." He searched his desk drawer for a pencil.

"Collier."

"Bert Pritchart here, Steve. Colonel Green told me to call you and ask you to have someone meet Lieutenant Jennings and his wife at the old Martin quarters in about thirty minutes."

"Well, Bert, that may be a problem, Colonel Holden wanted to give those quarters to Major Jeffrey Amos, a new officer assigned to the

Communications Company. In a contest between a Lieutenant and a Major, I'm afraid that the Major will win."

"So what quarters can you give to the Jennings'?" asked Pritchart frowning up at Julie.

"Fraid there are none available, Bert. They'll probably have to live on the economy in Panama City. At the rate officers are rotating, we'll probably have a vacancy in a year or so." said Collier in a bored voice.

"Call you back, Steve, Colonel just came in." said Pritchart to end the call.

Dropping the phone back into its' cradle, Pritchart looked over at Bill and shrugged his narrow shoulders.

"Watch the fun. No one tells Lyman Green that one of his officers has to take second place to a support weenie. Sit tight and I'll be right back."

He jumped up and hurried out of the office.

Julie turned and looked at Bill with laughed. "What a bunch of kooks. I think this place is going to be a million laughs before we get out of here."

Bill shrugged and shook his head sadly. "That may well be, but it looks like we are going to be living among the little brown natives. After all, in this army rank has its privileges. As a second Lieutenant, I have no rank and thus, no privileges." he said as he reached over and squeezed her knee. "Well, maybe a few privileges."

"Letch! Wait till I get you home, where ever home might be." she promised in a teasing tone, leaning forward to give him a good view of her super structure.

Suddenly, they both jumped.

"Holden wants to give those quarters to who?" roared a voice from outside the office, "Where's the damn phone?"

Julie began to giggle as she realized that the bellowing was the Colonel yelling at Pritchart about their housing problem. To their surprise, they heard Pritchart's higher pitched voice yelling back at the Colonel with as much gusto as the Colonel. The gist of the conversation seemed to be that as far as Colonel Green was concerned, if Colonel Green wanted the Jennings in a particular set of quarters, then that was where they were going to live. That's all there was to it. Pritchart was pointing out that the Post Commander, Colonel Holden, seemed to want to have a say in the matter.

"I didn't know the little guy had it in him." observed Julie clapping her hand over her mouth, as her giggles got worse.

"Hush, they'll hear you," said Bill in a low voice as he made a face at her, trying his best not to smile in response.

Obviously, Green had gotten Colonel Holden on the phone. Bill made a note to himself to always remember that the walls were not soundproof. Though he knew that he shouldn't be listening to his superiors, it was difficult not to, since the Colonel's voice was of sufficient volume to rattle the windows. His main regret was that he could only hear one side of the conversation.

"Jim, Lyman Green. What's this shit about not letting my new lieutenant have those quarters near mine?" bellowed the big Colonel.

"I don't give a rat's ass what rank this new guy is, Jim, he's a Commo weenie. I want good infantry types living around me. After all, I've got to raise a family in that neighborhood. It simply won't do to have a support type that close to my children."

"If I have to call General Goodrich, I'll do it. I don't want that guy living near me. I was saving those quarters for my new lieutenant."

"What? Goodrich told you to assign the quarters to this Commo guy. Well, I'll call you back." There was a thud that shook the pictures on the wall, as Green slammed down his phone.

"Why that lily-livered jackass. I'll take this up with Goodrich," he bellowed to the world in general. Obviously, Green called the General because, in a second, they heard him talking to him.

"General, Lyman Green. I've got a bone to pick with you," he said politely.

"He's toned down quite a bit," observed Julie in a whisper to Bill.

"Shush, they'll know we're listening." cautioned Bill as he slumped in his chair. First day in his new assignment and he'd caused a fight between his commander and the Brigade Commander. They'd probably ship him back to the states on the next plane.

"I have been saving those quarters near mine, here at Clayton for my new Lieutenant and now Holden tells me that you've told him to give those quarters to this Commo Major. Sir, I don't want that guy in my neighborhood, he's not Infantry."

"I feel strongly enough that I may bring a complaint to the Brotherhood. Yes sir, I know a complaint like that made to the Brotherhood could cause you a great deal of trouble, but I am serious about this housing thing. After all, it doesn't matter where this Commo guy lives, but I like to have my officers close to the Battalion area in case of an alert. Besides, remember that giving me these quarters is the least that you can do for me since I'm going to pull your chestnuts out of the fire for you on this training accident thing."

"What's the Brotherhood?" Julie whispered to her husband.

"No idea, now hush." Bill responded, trying to hear more.

"Right, I understand. Can you call Holden now so that I can let these poor kids get some rest? They've been exposed to Pritchart for the last couple of hours and that would tire anyone. Thank you, Sir"

There was another thud as Green slammed his phone back down into its cradle and a low murmuring of voices as the Colonel gave instructions to Pritchart in a more reasonable tone of voice. In a few seconds, they heard Pritchart's voice more clearly as he opened the door to the Colonel's office.

"Yes, sir. I'll take care of it," he said as he escaped from the Colonel into the hall.

The Pritchart that came back into his office was not quite the dapper calm individual who had entered the Colonel's office. He dropped in his chair behind the desk, opened a bottom drawer and pulled out a small bottle of bourbon. Unscrewing the cap, he took a long pull straight from the bottle before sitting back in his chair with a deep sigh.

"You know," he observed as he held the bottle up to the light to measure the level of alcohol remaining, "Some days are worse than others."

With another deep sigh, he screwed the cap back on the bottle and returned it to the drawer. Pulling himself up straighter in his chair, he smiled at the couple in front of his desk and glanced at his watch. They all sat in silence for a long time, with Pritchart appearing to be timing something. Finally, Pritchart spoke.

"Now, five, four, three, two, one and there." he smiled in satisfaction as his phone rang. He let it ring for several rings before he picked it up.

"Fourth Battalion, Twentieth Infantry, Captain Pritchart speaking, May I help you? Oh, hello Steve, what can I do for you?" he inquired politely as he smiled at Bill.

"O.K. you bastard, send that Lieutenant out to the quarters at Clayton. I'll have someone meet them there in about twenty minutes." said Captain Steve Collier of the Housing Division.

"Always a pleasure to do business with you." said Pritchart as he hung up the phone.

The Adjutant allowed himself a chuckle.

"Well, it was a tough fight, ma, but we won. You are being assigned quarters in about twenty minutes. I'll have Private Ralph run you over in the carry all and pick you up tomorrow. Now as for more permanent transportation, did you ship a car?" he asked as he swiveled his chair around and reached in a box sitting behind him on the credenza to pull out a list.

"Yes, sir. We did. According to what they told me when I shipped it in New Orleans, the car is supposed to be at Fort Davis on December 1." replied Bill as he checked the date in his pocket notebook. "According to the Transportation Office at Fort Banning, our household goods should be here about the same time."

"Good, enough." replied Pritchart as he made some notes on his desk pad, "When your car arrives, we'll send Ralph to carry you over to pick up your car.

Now to other matters, we need to get you a sponsor here in the Battalion. Let's see, how about Lieutenant Phillips, he's the executive officer of A Company. That should be satisfactory, his wife is a best friend with my wife. You'll like her, Julie, her name is Carol, as a matter of fact, and she is about your age. I'll call her about seeing you tonight." Pritchart said as he continued to make notes on his pad.

Finally, he finished and looked up at them.

"I'm going to have Ralph take you over to the quarters that have been picked out for you. Check out the place and decide what furniture you'll need to be comfortable. When you know what you want, we'll requisition it from Housing's furniture division and get you set up. Anything you need, just ask." he said with a smile, and then he paused, tapping the desk with his pen.

"About tonight, I guess, I'll make you reservations at the Post Guest House. It's too late in the day to get furniture from Housing so you won't even have a bed until after Thanksgiving. You see, with tomorrow being Thanksgiving Day, there aren't a dozen people working right now. So the easiest thing to do it put you up at the Guest House, it's nice, you'll like it," he said as he turned to Malone's door.

"Malone, hey Malone." he yelled as he scribbled on a small piece of paper.

Julie turned in her chair to see Malone peer around the door as if he was afraid to enter the room.

"Yeah." he mumbled.

"Get Ralph in here." he yelled as he searched through his desk drawer.

Malone's head disappeared back into his office and then they heard some mumbling from the office. In a few minutes Private Ralph came stumbling into Pritchart's office, still buttoning his uniform blouse as he came. Hat in hand, he came to a semblance of attention in front of Pritchart's desk.

"Sir, you sent for me?" he asked as he kept trying to straighten his uniform.

Pritchart nodded without looking up as he pulled several booklets from his desk drawer.

"Yes, Ralph, I want you to take the Lieutenant and his wife over to quarters number 2040-A here at Clayton. Somebody from Post Housing will be there to let them look at the quarters, then take them over to the Post Guest House. They will be staying there tonight. I'll call and make the reservations while you are en route." said Pritchart as he placed the small pile of booklets on top of his desk.

"Now, Julie, these informational booklets are for you. They tell all about the Post services, such as PX and grocery shopping. Some time after you get settled, someone from the Officer's Wives Club Welcome Committee will come to visit you. They'll help you get settled. Now you better get over to your new quarters before something else happens." he said with one last lingering glance at Julie.

Bill got to his feet and held out his hand to Captain Pritchart. "Thank you for the help, sir. I don't know what we'd have done without your assistance."

To everyone's amazement, Julie went around the desk and kissed the Captain on the cheek. "We really do thank you," she said with a twinkle in her eye as she turned and gave him a front row view, as her rather full mini-skirt swirled out and revealed more of her stunning legs.

Following Ralph, the happy couple left the Headquarters building and got back into the Carry All that was still parked out front. The morose Private started the vehicle and drove them over to the address he had been given by the Captain. Waiting for them was a military sedan parked by the curb. As they pulled up a tall slim black woman got out of the sedan and waited by the car for Bill and his wife to join her. Ralph waited outside.

"Lieutenant Jennings?" said the black woman in a low, monotone voice.

"Yes, I'm Lieutenant Jennings and this is my wife Julie." he replied as she held out her hand.

"I am Sherry Kovina from Post Housing. Captain Collier asked me to show you these quarters and see if they were satisfactory," she said in her peculiar monotone as she led the way toward the front door of the quarters.

Bill stood near the door as Ms. Kovina took Julie on a tour of the house. Besides the living room, there were three bedrooms, two baths, a small eating area and the kitchen. Out the kitchen door was a walkway and then a small room that had, in earlier years, been maid's quarters. As a first home, Bill thought it would be quite satisfactory. As the women came back to rejoin him, he could tell that Julie liked it as her eyes were dancing and she looked like she was almost walking on air.

"It's perfect, Bill." she breathed as she took his arm.

"Good, then we'll take it." he said to his wife as he looked over her head at Ms. Kovina.

"What do I sign to make it official?" he asked raising his eyebrows at the housing representative.

Without a word, Ms. Kovina held out her clipboard to Bill. On it was a form that, when translated into common English stated that he was assuming responsibility for the Quarters located at 2040-A, Fort Clayton. With a flourish, he signed and waited while she tore off a copy of the form for Bill. With a timid smile, the Housing Representative handed Julie a ring of keys and then quietly slipped out the door, leaving the couple in their new empty home.

"Our first home together." sighed Julie as she hugged her husband close to her.

"We can make it into a very nice home." agreed Bill and he bent down and kissed her tenderly. Suddenly, there was the sound of a horn honking and they both started. Glancing out the window, Bill grinned at his wife. "Looks like Ralph is impatient to get off duty. Well, let's lock it up and get over to the Guest House."

Quickly, they checked to make sure that all of the doors and windows were tightly locked before they locked the front door behind them. Forgetting himself for a moment, Bill held his wife's hand as they walked down the sidewalk to the waiting Carry All.

"Sorry to take so long, Private." Bill said as he helped Julie back into the vehicle. "Now, I guess we need to get over to the Guest House."

"Yes, sir." answered Ralph as he started the vehicle and pulled away from the curb.

Bill glanced back at their new quarters in time to see what appeared to be a very sad face pressed against the window in the living room. A face that seemed to be starring at him with sad eyes. The same room that he had assured himself was empty. He raised his hand to tell Ralph to stop, but then the angle of the light changed and the face disappeared. Was it an omen, he wondered?

CHAPTER SEVEN

Bill Jennings opened his eyes to a beige painted ceiling, for a moment he had no idea where he might be, then he remembered his new assignment and the fact that this was the Guest Quarters at Fort Clayton. Stretching, he turned over in the bed and smiled tenderly as he saw just the top of a tousled head sticking out from under the covers. That was one thing he always found amusing about Julie, the way she burrowed underneath the covers until she disappeared.

Reaching over, Bill slowly pulled the cover down until he could see her face, almost completely covered by long blonde hair. Leaning over, he gave her a small kiss on the cheek, then jerked his face back as she swatted at him. Occasionally, waking her up this way lead to other things much more intimate. He could only hope.

Slowly, he pulled the bed covers down lower, exposing more and more of her lovely little body. Julie was a surprisingly broadminded young lady; in fact, she had some habits that could occasionally surprise even her husband. She always slept in the nude, even when they went for visits to her family. Bill laughed silently to himself when he remembered the first time that they slept together in a motel near their college. He had been terribly embarrassed when she stripped, he had never even considered sleeping in the raw before he met Julie, but after she had introduced him to the idea, he now liked it as much as she did.

They had been married a little over six months and he still marveled that such a stunningly beautiful woman would want to marry him. Many nights he would lie awake and just watch her sleep. He had memorized every curve of her body, every mole, every small dimple. Her breasts were medium-sized, 36-C, but full, almost perfectly formed. He had been with many women of all ages during his college years, but he had never seen a woman whose body was so perfect that the mere sight of it unclothed could give him trouble breathing, until he met Julie.

As he pulled the covers lower and lower, revealing more and more of her shapely body, he saw his favorite feature, her legs. They were perfectly formed. Some nights he would just lie awake and run his hands over her legs, especially concentrating on the heart-shaped birthmark at the top of her thigh. God, he loved her. Silently, Hughes agreed that Jennings had a beautiful wife.

Gently, he began to tickle her nose, causing her to slap at his hand. He kept at it until he saw her eyelids begin to flutter. Sighing deeply, she twisted over in the bed to lie close against him.

"You bastard, you woke me up." she complained in a sleep-thickened voice.

He leaned over and kissed her deeply, tasting her morning breath, but not caring.

"Remember we have to be ready at ten o'clock for Ralph to pick us up." he said as he broke the long kiss.

She pouted prettily as she snuggled deeper into her pillow.

"But Bill, I'm so sleepy. Can't we just skip the lunch and get something around here?"

"No can do, babe. Got to dress up and meet the General today, honey. Always good to meet the boss."

Leaving her to wake up in her own good time, Bill jumped into the shower and quickly lathered. It had felt good the night before, to wash off all of the grime from their travels of the previous day. He had also believed that showering in the evening would mean he didn't have to

shower first thing in the morning. However, after his first night in
Panama he had learned a very valuable lesson, that in the humidity of
the tropics, even asleep, the human body could work up a good sweat.

As he shaved, again, Bill reflected that it was very appropriate that
this was Thanksgiving Day as he had a great deal to be thankful for. Julie
as his wife, a good paying job as an Army Officer and a nice home to
look forward to.

Then he remembered the news he had received about Emil's death.
Big strapping, laughing Emil, they had been as close as brothers for
years. In fact, it had been Emil that had introduced Bill and Julie. If
nothing else, he wanted to find out how Emil had died, it was the least
he could do. He wondered if Emil's parents had been notified of his
death.

The Battalion Thanksgiving Dinner was a very fancy occasion. Every
officer and senior NCO in the battalion, as well as many of the brigade
Staff were in attendance. For some reason, General Goodrich had a special place in his heart for the 4/20; he spent much more time with this
battalion than with the others under his command. Officers that started
out in the 4/20 always went much further, faster under Goodrich's command than officers from any other unit. As soon as they had arrived at
battalion headquarters, Colonel Green had made it a point to introduce
Bill and Julie to the General and his wife. Julie was a major hit with both
of them.

The meal was a stunning success, as far as Bill was concerned. Green
had doted over him and Julie as if they had been his own two children.
He had made a major effort to insure that Bill was formally introduced
to every other officer who attended the dinner. It was very gratifying to
have such a reception at his first assignment. It wasn't until after the
meal that Bill found out why he was receiving such a royal treatment.

At the conclusion of the meal, all of the officers and their wives had
left the Headquarters company building where the mess hall was

located and walked the hundred yards to the Battalion Headquarters where a small celebration was scheduled for the battalion Day room. The General and a selected group of officers adjourned to the Colonel's office for drinks and good cigars. Usually, this was a time of mutual congratulations for a job well done, but this time there were more serious matters to discuss.

"Are you sure that he can handle it?" the General asked around the big Havana cigar clenched in his teeth.

Colonel Green shrugged and poured himself a drink from the secret bottle he kept in his desk.

"I think he can, but if he fucks it up then we point to his inexperience and let him take the brunt of the heat. Either way, it clears us."

"I think we should have taken care of that nosy reporter from the Armed Forces Network. She has really been digging into what happened. She's been back to Fort Davis on three occasions asking more questions." offered Colonel Grace, Brigade Executive Officer.

Green tossed back his drink and rubbed his hand across his mouth.

"Glad it was Colonel Mellon's fuckup and not mine. I don't understand why he let the kid get that close to the truth before he stopped him." said Green as he poured himself another drink.

Goodrich looked troubled as he leaned on the edge of Green's desk.

"It's really not important, but I wish I had been consulted before you people took such drastic steps." he complained as he grabbed the glass out of Green's hand and tossed it back. "After all, I am in command of this Brigade."

Green's head snapped around and he glared at the General. "What do you mean, you people?" he demanded as he gazed intently at his commander.

Goodrich starred at his subordinate in confusion. "Why I had assumed that what happened was because the Brotherhood had decided to sanction the young man. No one has told me any different." he paused and swiveled his chair around so that he could look out at the parade ground.

"You seem surprised, Lyman. Are you meaning to tell me that the Brotherhood did not order the hit?" he demanded over his shoulder.

Green got heavily to his feet, swayed slightly and walked around to face the General.

"If the Brotherhood had anything to do with the hit, I didn't know anything about It.," declared Green as he rubbed his chin. "But this is all the more reason to use someone who is not only young, but gung ho army as well as someone who has just arrived in the Zone as the Investigation Officer on the death of that young officer. No one can accuse him of taking sides and better yet, he can find out what that damn reporter knows about the death."

Goodrich nodded slowly as he reached behind him for the bottle on Green's desk.

"Do it. In fact, get that young Lieutenant in here and let's talk to him now," ordered the General.

Bill and Julie were talking to Captain Pritchart and his wife Lola when the Colonel summoned Bill. Actually, Bill was glad to get away from the Captain and his lady, though he had to admit that Lola Pritchart had a build that was even more spectacular than Julie's. However, she looked like a slut where Julie was always a lady. Hughes had to agree that Lola Pritchart looked like a streetwalker. Her dress was so constructed that it forced her large, full breasts to stand out in front of her chest like a cowcatcher on the front of an old time locomotive.

"Lieutenant Jennings, Colonel Green wants to see you in his office." said Sergeant Moody, the Colonel's chief clerk, coming up behind Bill.

"Well, babe, duty calls." he said to his wife.

"If you will excuse me," he said to the Pritcharts' as he turned to follow Moody.

Moody walked him across the large day room where the officers and their wives had gathered out into the hall. Leading the way, the Sergeant opened the door leading into the command section and stood to the side. "The Colonel is waiting for you in his office. I'll be around if I am needed."

Silently, Bill walked down the hall, turning to the right into the orderly room. The door to Colonel Green's office was closed, but he could hear the voices of the Colonel and the General. He wasn't sure whether to knock or not, but his decision was made for him when the door opened and the Brigade Executive Officer, Colonel Grace glanced out.

"Oh, Jennings, glad you're here." he turned from the door and looked at the General, "Lieutenant Jennings is here, sir."

"Well, bring him in.," snapped the General as he poured himself another drink.

As expected of a young lieutenant coming before a superior officer, Lieutenant Jennings came to attention before the desk and executed a textbook-perfect salute. General Goodrich returned his salute and waved him toward a chair.

"Glad you could join us, Lieutenant. The Zone can be good duty and the lifestyle is unbelievable," mumbled the General, who was slightly worse for wear from his visits to the Colonel's bottle of bourbon. Green glanced over at Grace and smiled, Grace shook his head and leaned back in his chair.

"Lieutenant, I have a favor to ask of you." began the General as he reached for the bottle again. "You don't have to accept the assignment. In fact, it's not an assignment, but rather a request. I know it's a lot to ask, but it would be of service to the Brigade. I never forget those who help the Brigade."

"Yes sir." prompted Bill as he leaned forward in his chair.

"Why don't I fill him in, General?" Colonel Green watched the General try to pour a drink and miss the glass completely.

"Good, idea Colonel, I seem to be having a slight problem." The General concentrated his full attention on trying to pour the whiskey from the bottle into the glass. Bill was a little uncomfortable having to sit and watch the General getting plastered, actually, he really didn't want to the be in the room. Green obviously picked up on his feelings and smiled at him in encouragement.

"Two days ago, a Lieutenant Larson assigned to 4/10 at Fort Davis was killed in a training accident. Even though it was just one of those unfortunate things, the press is trying to blow the matter up into a big scandal. The Department of Defense has ordered that an officer of this command, but from a Battalion other than the 4th of the 10th, be assigned to conduct a full-scale investigation into the death and determine the cause.

Quite simply, the General would like you to conduct the required full-scale investigation into all phases of the training accident. See if anyone was at fault, if so what they did that endangered the Lieutenant. Was the Lieutenant, himself, negligent if so, how? You are to be given full support of all 193rd Brigade personnel, if you want something to assist the investigation, then it's yours."

For a moment, Bill had no idea what to say. Of all the assignments they could have offered him, Bill never expected to be asked to investigate Emil's death. For a moment Bill almost told them that Emil had been his closest friend, but for some reason he didn't. It was just a feeling, but something told him to keep his mouth shut. Green mistook his indecision for a desire not to undertake the investigation and took steps to sweeten the offer.

"Lieutenant, you will have the full backing of the General himself, you will even be able to give orders to me if you require something from this Battalion to assist in your investigation. It's very unusual for someone as junior as you are to be given such power. It just goes to show how much confidence the General has in your ability. This could result in an outstanding Officer Efficiency Report such as few junior officers have received. Reports like this lead to early promotions, it could make you one of the chosen few on the fast track to Field Grade." he offered as he looked intently at the young lieutenant.

Feeling an unexplained tension growing in the room, Bill finally nodded his head firmly. Instinctively, he knew that there was something that they were not telling him, something that seemed to mean a great deal to them. At least, he could now officially look into Emil's death, which he had planned to do anyway.

"I'll be happy to accept the mission, Sir," he said darting a quick look at the General who was struggling to pour another drink in his glass.

"Excellent." boomed Colonel Green as he walked over to clap the Lieutenant on the back. "Tomorrow's Friday, but it is an official holiday for the command. So be prepared to start your work first thing Monday. I'll expect you here first thing to pick up your orders and review the files. You'll probably be over at Fort Davis for several days.

Now get that pretty wife of yours and get the hell out of here. I am sure that you're still tired from that long trip from the states."

Bill stood and grinned at the Colonel. "Thank you sir, we are both tired. Getting up this morning was not easy."

"Especially with a wife that looks like yours." quipped Colonel Grace as the other officers laughed uproariously. Bill turned a deep red as he joined in the laughter.

"Leave the kid alone, Karl." Green laughed at Bill's discomfort, as he waved him toward the door.

"Go home and I'll see you Monday," ordered the Colonel as he looked over at the General. Goodrich waved one hand toward the Lieutenant and then swiveled his chair back toward the window. Bill executed another perfect salute and escaped into the hall.

Determined to follow Colonel Green's orders to the letter, he took Julie aside and told her that they were leaving. She objected since she was having fun.

"Sorry, babe, the Colonel just ordered me to get you and go home." he told her as he held out her light jacket.

"But why?" she pouted as she allowed him to help her slip into the jacket.

"Because as of Monday I am going to be traveling to the Atlantic side on an assignment. I may be gone several days and I want to get us settled before I have to leave." he responded as he led her out of the Day Room and down the stairs toward the ground floor.

"Already? I thought you'd be here for at least a few days. Why you?" she demanded, rubbing her face against his uniform blouse.

They left the building and walked over to the Carry All idling at the curb. Private Ralph sat morosely at the wheel waiting to drive them. Bill helped Julie into the back seat of the vehicle and then jumped into the front.

"Home, James." he said with a sigh.

Private Ralph looked over at the Lieutenant with a puzzled look on his face.

"Sir, my name is Jonah, not James," he said slowly as he turned to glance at the woman in the back.

Julie giggled as Bill slowly shook his head.

"Uh, sorry. Just take us to the Guest House." he said to the staring Private.

Obediently, Ralph pulled away from the curb and drove them back to the Guest House. Silently, Bill helped Julie out of the vehicle when they arrived and, hand in hand, they started for the door.

"Be back Monday morning, Lieutenant." yelled Ralph through the open window. Bill's only response was a wave of his hand.

Once in the privacy of their room, Bill dropped down into a chair and kicked his shoes off. Julie tossed her jacket onto the bed, jumped in his lap, put her head on his shoulder and her arms around his neck. To Bill's surprise, she seemed to be crying.

"Hey. What's this?" he asked as he cuddled her close.

"I'm going to miss you," she sobbed into his shoulder.

He pushed her face away from his shoulder and looked into her red, swollen eyes. Gently, he wiped her tears away and put a finger under her chin.

"Hey, babe, there's nothing to cry about. I'll only be gone a few days." he said as he pulled her close again.

"Why do you have to go?" she demanded, as her arms tightened around his neck.

This was the moment he had been dreading all along. He had debated about whether to tell her about Emil, but now that he had been assigned to investigate his death, Bill felt that he had no choice. Slowly, he pulled her arms from around his neck and made her sit up straight in his lap.

"Babe, something has happened that I know is going to upset you. Now, you have to stay calm." he said as he tried to decide how to break the news to her.

Her big blue eyes searched his face. He could tell that she was bracing herself for the worst. "What is it?" she asked in a trembling voice. Instinctively, she seemed to know that it was something that would affect them.

"It's Emil."

"Wha-what's happen to Emil?" she demanded, grabbing him by the shoulders.

"Emil's dead." he said flatly, "He was killed in a training accident two days ago."

For a moment Julie just stared at him speechless. "How? How could this happen? I liked him so much. He was a good friend." Bill held her for several hours as she cried herself to sleep.

Sergeant Major Villanueva sat at his desk, phone clutched tightly in his hand and waited patiently while the bartender went and found Brigade Sergeant Major Ashe. He had known that at this hour, the massive top sergeant of the brigade would be at Julio's Bar just across the street from the main entrance to the Canal Zone. Normally, he wouldn't have dared interrupt Ashe's drinking, but this information was so hot that it could destroy them all.

"Who's this?" Demanded the Brigade Sergeant Major.

"Villanueva. I've got some news for you." He toyed with the dud grenade he had long used as a paperweight.

"What the fuck you botherin' me here for? There's nothing that couldn't wait until Monday," roared the angry Sergeant Major.

"By Monday, your big black ass may be in a sling," snapped Villaneuva.

"What the fuck you mean, Spic?"

"I mean that Green has manipulated the General into appointing a 4/20 Lieutenant to investigate the death of that Lieutenant over at Fort Davis."

As he suspected, the news brought the Brigade Sergeant Major up short.

"Which Lieutenant?" he asked quietly.

"The new one, Jennings."

"Oh, shit!" exclaimed Ashe.

"What's the matter?" demanded Villanueva sitting higher in his chair as he sensed that this was not good news to the man on the other end of the phone.

"That Lieutenant was originally scheduled to go to the 4th of the 10th. The dead Lieutenant was scheduled to be his sponsor. According to Morton out at Howard, Jennings told him that he and the dead Lieutenant were best friends for years."

"Oh, shit is right!" exclaimed Villanueva. "This could blow the lid off the whole can of worms. Investigating the death of a dead man you don't know is one thing, but investigating the death of a friend is something else. He's liable to uncover more than is good for him or us. Should I tell the old man to assign someone else?"

"Hell, no." answered Ashe, "Listen, call all the group. Tell them we're meeting at the Tarpon Club tomorrow afternoon at 4:00 p.m. Tell them to come ready to make some decisions."

"What decisions?" asked Villanueva, but Ashe had already hung up the phone.

Muttering to himself, Villanueva dropped the receiver back onto the cradle and swiveled his chair around to look out at the Battalion Street.

"Maybe I should consider retiring, soon. I would definitely live longer." he murmured to himself.

CHAPTER EIGHT

Hughes had the feeling of impending doom, and tried to end the dream, but try as he might; he was unable to wake up. Next, he found himself inside Jennings' head. It was a Monday morning, but not just any Monday morning. On this Monday morning, sitting in the dark in front of a partially opened window watching the sun come up, was a very troubled Bill Jennings. Slowly, he stood, stretching and yawning, before rubbing his face and padding into the bathroom. Finally, under the hot stinging shower, he began to wake up and start to feel more optimistic about his new assignment.

Julie was still peacefully sleeping as he stumbled around in the darkened bedroom trying to find all the pieces to his uniform. He had to remember, in the future, to lay out his complete outfit before going to bed. Finally, fairly sure that he was properly dressed, briefcase in hand, he eased himself out of the apartment door and locked it behind him. As quietly as possible he walked down the long red-carpeted hallway to the reception area. The only person he saw in the building was the desk clerk who merely looked at him and yawned.

Still feeling a little groggy, Bill stepped out onto the front porch of the Guest Quarters. He liked the feel of the building; he had noticed that it was an old one, built in 1934 proclaimed a plaque on the wall beside the front door. Reveling in the peace and tranquility of the place, he breathed deeply of the crisp tropical air. Promptly at six o'clock in the morning, Private Ralph screeched to a stop in front of the Guest House and waved at the young Lieutenant. Bill jogged down the long walk way and climbed in the passenger seat. Without so much as a greeting, Ralph pulled away from the curve and headed back for Battalion headquarters. Bill was just as glad that Ralph didn't want to talk; he was feeling more and more uneasy about this assignment.

As the Carry All pulled into the Battalion Area, Ralph had to come to a complete stop as a long formation of soldiers in white t-shirts, gym shirts and jungle boots went jogging through the main intersection. Bill realized that it was the full Battalion when he saw that leading the formation was Colonel Green and the rest of his Battalion Staff. The noise made by the several hundred runners was deafening.

By the look of the many blue banners (guide ons in military parlance since the formation was expected to guide on the flags) fluttering in the early morning breeze, every company assigned to the Battalion was represented in the formation. From the number of people Bill could see, he could well believe that every man in the Battalion, over seven hundred well conditioned soldiers, was following the Colonel down the street, lustily singing jody calls. Fascinated, Bill sat in the car and watched as line after line of soldiers came through the intersection. It was a sight that could make your blood run hot in your veins. He was proud to be a part of such a well-trained battalion. For the hundredth time, he wondered what rifle company he would be assigned to after this first assignment was completed.

"Does the Battalion do this mass run every morning?" asked Bill as he kept his eyes glued to the troops.

"No sir. Just some Mondays and every Friday morning. The Battalion Commander will tie one on the night before and then work it out with a good long run the next morning. Problem is, he don't like to go alone." drawled Ralph, not looking at the officer.

"How far do they go?"

"Well sir, it depends on how much the Colonel tied on the night before, or to be frank, if he got any. If he's just a little soused, then he only does four or five miles. If he's plastered, then after about three miles he has troubled standing up and gets a terrible urge to piss. When that happens he drops out when the formation passes his house and the XO brings the unit back to post. Those days we only go about three and a half miles," responded Ralph as the last of the troops pasted through the intersection and he put the vehicle back in gear.

With a flourish, Ralph wheeled the vehicle into his parking spot in front of battalion headquarters. Bill jumped out and walked importantly into the building, his first official day in his first Battalion assignment.

Two at a time, Bill climbed the stairs up to the Command floor, and pulling off his garrison cap, he entered the hall to the Colonel's Office. As soon as he came through the door into the Battalion Commander's outer office, a short, 5' 7", powerfully built, Hispanic wearing camouflaged fatigues came from the Colonel's office.

"Lieutenant Jennings?" the Hispanic asked as he noticed the young officer.

Bill noticed that the man wore the chevrons of a Command Sergeant Major on his collar and his stitched nametag said Villanueva. "Yes, and you are?"

"Battalion Sergeant Major Jorge Villanueva. Good to meet you, sir." he said as he offered his hand. Bill took it, feeling the raw power emanating from the man.

The Sergeant Major turned back to the Colonel's office and walked over to pick up a file lying on the corner of the desk. He returned to stand before Jennings.

"Colonel left a file for you to read. Said he'd be back to meet with you after breakfast." he said holding out the slim file toward the Lieutenant.

"I would suggest, if you don't mind, that you read it over breakfast." continued the Sergeant Major as led Jennings back down the hall, stopping before a office which had the Sergeant Major's name on it. He stepped inside only long enough to pick up his fatigue cap. "As a matter of fact, I'll join you."

Following the stocky Sergeant Major, Bill walked across the gap between Battalion Headquarters and the building housing the Headquarters Company, Captain Otis Schultz, commanding. Entering the side entrance, the two mounted the stairs to the first level where the main mess hall for the battalion was located. At this hour of the morning, with the Battalion run still under way, there were few soldiers other than the mess hall staff present, so the Senior NCO in charge came over to meet the new Lieutenant.

"Well, heard we had a new Lieutenant," said the NCO as he held out his hand.

Bill shook his hand and introduced himself. The Mess Sergeant was Staff Sergeant Horace Mansfield. Ignoring SSG. Mansfield, Sergeant Major Villanueva picked up a tray and moved over to the food service line.

"Any of this slop you call food, ready yet?" he grumbled to the white dressed noncommissioned officer standing at the head of the serving line.

"Sure thing, Sergeant Major. Got some good S.O.S. for you, and bacon or sausage, or toast." laughed the black buck sergeant waving a large spoon toward the chow line.

"Come with me, Lt. and we'll get you fixed up. The first meal for an officer is always on the house." said the Staff Sergeant as he led the Lieutenant over to the meal line. In less than five minutes, Sergeant Major Villanueva and Lieutenant Jennings with his precious file were seated at the officers' table enjoying a surprisingly good breakfast.

Slowly, as he ate, Bill read through the report. It was rather scanty; apparently, Emil had been running a .50 caliber range for his Battalion. As Senior Range Officer, Emil and his driver had driven around the training area as they checked to make sure that no one had wandered onto the range.

Due to the limited amount of land area inside the Canal Zone, the area laid out as ranges was fenced off so that no one would wander into them by mistake. This was a little difficult since some of the back roads led across the ranges. These roads were blocked with gates that were to be closed during live fire exercises. One major duty of the Range Officer was physically closing and locking those bright yellow gates. There had been a great deal of ground fog that day when Emil and his driver had driven off to check the gates and visibility had been bad. Due to the lack of available training sites inside the Zone, this particular firing area was facing one of the main roads to the other training areas. To insure that no one drove into the area by mistake, there were three gates, instead of the usual two, that had to be closed to block off the training area.

No one knew what had happened, but while Lieutenant Larson was gone, a voice came on the radio frequency used by Range Control and gave the command to begin the training session. The senior officer present at the training site, another Second Lieutenant had radioed back that the Range Officer was still downrange. The voice on the radio had responded that the Range Officer was at Range Control meeting with the Colonel. The order was again given to fire.

At the command of the Lieutenant, twenty-eight .50 caliber machine guns had opened up on the numerous man shaped silhouette targets spotted on the various hills around the range. In addition to the silhouette targets there were also several old stationary vehicles spotted about the range. Unfortunately, one of the stationary targets fired at by the gunners turned out to be Emil and his jeep. The big .50 caliber rounds had literally destroyed both the jeep and its occupant. Both Jennings and the presence that was Hughes Carter were a little surprised to see that Lieutenant Larson was the only casualty. Where was the driver?

That was all of the report. Lieutenant Jennings looked up at the Sergeant Major with a frown.

"You know anything about this accident, Sergeant Major?" asked Bill softly.

Before the Sergeant Major answered the question, he took a long drink of his coffee and pursed his lips.

"Lieutenant, you have to remember, shit happens, especially in an area like the Canal Zone. I wasn't there when this screw up happened, but I will say this. I have no idea how it could have happened by accident. I didn't know Lieutenant Larson, but he had been there long enough to know not to skyline himself on a live fire range. Besides, according to what I heard, he had no need to be up on that hill where he was killed. He should have been on a road almost a mile away."

Lieutenant Jennings nodded slowly. A vague idea was beginning to form in his mind and it was not a pretty picture.

"The file doesn't make mention of it, but did anyone find out who gave the radio order to begin the exercise?"

The Battalion Sergeant Major shook his head.

"Not that I know of. Lieutenant, the only thing I can do to help is to recommend that you keep your own council. I'd like to do more, but, unfortunately, that is all I can do." he said as he finished his coffee and stood.

Bill nodded and then as if he finally heard Hughes screaming at him, asked a question that Hughes had immediately formed.

"It makes no mention of his driver being killed. What's the story on that?"

The Sergeant Major studied his coffee cup intently for a minute.

"Afraid I can't help you, sir. If the Lieutenant will excuse me, I have a mountain of paperwork."

His mouth hanging open in surprise, Bill watched the Sergeant Major carry his tray over to the window to the wash area and hand it to one of the Panamanian civilians that staffed the kitchen. It was obvious that the Sergeant Major knew more than he was letting on. But he also knew enough about the prerogatives of a Command Sergeant Major to realize that no power on earth could make him talk if he didn't want to do so.

Bill dawdled over his breakfast as long as he could, reading the report over and over. Unfortunately, he couldn't get anything more out of it than he did the first time he read it. He couldn't put his finger on what bothered him about what he had read, other than no mention of the driver, but he knew Emil. He knew that, in spite of his reputation as a party animal, Emil was a careful, cautious individual when it came to his own or someone else' safety. From his comments, the Sergeant Major apparently also felt that there was something peculiar about the accident.

Finally, he sighed and closed the folder, time to get this investigation underway. He glanced at his watch and saw that it was almost eight o'clock, the number of uniformed soldiers that were piling into the mess hall also told him that the Battalion run was over and that the Colonel would soon be looking for him.

Finally, he stood, put the folder in his briefcase and picked up his tray. As he approached the window to the kitchen, the Mess Sergeant met him.

"Let me help you, Sir. I'm sure that you have more important things to do than mess with your tray." said SSG Mansfield as he took the tray from Bill's grasp.

"Why, thank you, Sergeant." he said, as he turned toward the door. "As a matter of fact, I have an appointment with the Colonel."

"Too bad." sympathized Mansfield, "Well, on the bright side, better you than me."

Grinning, Bill left the mess hall and the building. As he headed back for Battalion Headquarters, he saw Colonel Green, in a crisply starched camouflaged uniform, getting out of his car. Not seeing Bill, Green returned the salute of some soldiers walking up the Battalion Street toward the mess hall and then entered Battalion Headquarters.

Bill followed more slowly, trying to get a firm grip on the questions he wanted to ask.

Entering the doors of the Headquarters building, Bill walked slowly up the stairs and down the hall to enter the command area. The Sergeant Major's door was shut, so Bill continued down the hall to the Adjutant's Office. Glancing in, he didn't see any sign of Pritchart. Having no alternative, Bill finally entered the orderly room and looked around. Sergeant Moody was sitting at his desk across the room, while two PFC's on a couch to his left flipped through a couple of newspapers.

"Colonel in?" asked Bill as he hesitated just inside the door.

"Just a minute, sir and I'll see." replied Moody as he walked over to the Colonel's closed door and knocked. At a call, he entered and shut the door behind him. Bill stood awkwardly in the door to the orderly room, not quite knowing what to do next. The two PFC's simply ignored him.

Bill didn't have any idea how much time had passed, but in a few minutes, Moody came out of the Colonel's office and motioned to Bill.

"Colonel will see you now, Lieutenant," he said formally as he held the door open.

Self-consciously, Bill straightened his uniform and marched into the Colonel's office. Seated beside the Colonel's desk was Major John Dancer, the Battalion Executive Officer. Pulling himself to attention in front of the Colonel, Bill once again, executed a textbook salute, which the Colonel solemnly returned.

"Have a seat, Lieutenant," said the Colonel waving an arm at a chair in front of his desk. "Hope you are ready for your mission. Have you read the file I left for you?"

Bill balanced his briefcase on his lap and pulled out the file he had been given, Sergeant Major Villanueva's warning to keep what he knew to himself very much in his mind.

"Yes sir," he said heavily, "I have read it thoroughly and frankly sir, I must submit that the report just doesn't make sense."

"Oh?" said Green as he short a quick glance at Dancer. "And what about it doesn't make sense?"

"Well, I find it difficult to believe that Lieutenant Larson would go and park on an exposed hill across a valley from an active .50 caliber range. I don't understand why he would do such a thing, since, according to this file, this was the third time he had run this particular range." He dropped the unopened folder in his lap.

He noticed that Green relaxed after hearing what Bill had to say. This confirmed his suspicion that there was more information known about the death of Emil than he was being told. What he couldn't figure out was why everyone was making a mystery out of what appeared to be a simple training accident. As bad as a death was, especially that of a close friend, Bill was old enough to know that training accidents did happen.

"Well, hell, Lieutenant, that's what you're being paid to find out. Why did Lieutenant Larson stop on that particular hill? I don't have any earthy idea. He had no business being there. You're absolutely right, he should have known better than to pick that particular hill." He glanced at his watch.

"There will be a helicopter here to pick you up in about twenty minutes and it will bring you back this afternoon. Now get this, Lieutenant. Each day, and I do mean each day, I want you to prepare a written report of your findings for that day and leave it with Sergeant Moody. In other words, you keep me fully informed of everything that you do.

Oh, and see Pritchart, he has your authorization papers from the General to empower you to carry out a thorough investigation." Colonel Green said as he stood, signaling that the meeting was over. Major Dancer immediately shot to his feet.

"Yes, sir." said Bill as he saluted, again, gathered his briefcase and the precious file, executed an about face and left the Colonel's Office.

Crossing the hall, he stuck his head in the Adjutant's office and saw that Pritchart was at his desk sorting through a stack of stapled documents. From the look on his face, he was not a happy camper.

"Excuse me, Captain Pritchart," he said as he stepped into the office.

Pritchart looked up with a frown that broke into a grin when he saw who had interrupted him.

"Yes, Bill, come in. How was your first weekend in Paradise?" He leaned back in his chair, indicating that Bill should take a seat in one of the chairs in front of his desk.

"Not, bad. We went into Balboa and bought a few things from the San Blas Indians around the square. Julie loved their handicrafts."

Pritchart folded his arms across his chest. "Well, those things are sometimes over- priced. First chance we get, Lola and I will take the two of you up to some of the Panamanian Villages in the hills. You won't believe the things you can buy for just a few dollars."

They sat quietly for a moment, Bill not knowing what else to say and really not wanting to get started into his investigation. Not wanting to find out that Emil had, perhaps, been killed by his own stupidity. Or worse.

"Well, what can I do for you, today?" asked Pritchart as he leaned forward and picked up a 4/20 mug filled with steaming coffee.

"The Colonel told me to check with you for a letter of authorization from General Goodrich. There's a chopper coming in about fifteen minutes to take me over to Fort Davis."

Like a shot, Pritchart came up out of his chair.

"Don't move, Malone must have it. I know that a Brigade courier came a while ago and dropped off a package." Pritchart said as the little Captain darted across the lobby and into Malone's office.

Bill heard the sound of angry voices and in a few minutes Pritchart came striding back into his own office, a letter clutched in his hand.

"Here you are, Bill. Malone wanted to process it, even though it's addressed to you and marked for your eyes-only. Some days I wonder about him." said Pritchart as he passed over the envelope.

As the Adjutant watched curiously, Bill tore open the envelope and glanced at the letter. It was address to Whom It May Concern and ordered the reader to give full cooperation to the bearer on direct orders of the Brigade Commander. It was a great deal of power to give to a new Lieutenant. Slowly, Bill returned the letter to the envelope and dropped it into his briefcase.

"Well," said Bill as he stood. "I guess it's time to go. See you this afternoon, sir."

Deep in thought as he left the Adjutant's office, Bill strolled down the hall toward the exit. He had a very bad feeling about this entire project, even though he had written proof of the General's full backing. He was so engrossed in his thoughts that he actually jumped when Sergeant Major Villanueva stuck his head out of his office and called to him.

"Lieutenant Jennings, can I see you a minute?" he asked as he opened his door wider.

Bill walked into the small office and looked around with interest. The Sergeant Major had an office with windows on two sides. Directly behind his desk was a window that looked out at the buildings that housed the Rifle Companies, to Bill's left, the windows looked out over the Battalion street and the small parking lot across the road from Battalion Headquarters. Bill actually preferred this office to the Colonel's; of course the Colonel's office was probably three times larger.

"Yes, Sergeant Major, what can I do for you?" asked Bill as he looked around the office.

"Lieutenant, I shouldn't do this, but I'm going to tell you something you need to know. Now I'll deny it if you tell anyone. Do you understand?" he finished as he played with what looked like a hand grenade.

"Sure, I understand." answered the puzzled Lieutenant.

"O.K. When you get to Fort Davis, look up a Staff Sergeant Mort Crawford. He's assigned to A Company, 4th Battalion, Tenth infantry or he was. Crawford was the first man to get to the Lieutenant and he told a story to Sergeant Major Smith, that didn't quite jive with the report that the Battalion Commander made to the General. Crawford was Larson's senior Platoon NCO and, if he will, he can probably help you," said Villanueva as he began to toss the hand grenade from one hand to the other.

Bill pulled out a pen and made several notes on the inside of the folder he was carrying. "Anything else?" he asked, looking expectantly at the Sergeant Major.

Villanueva shook his head emphatically. "Nope, you're own your own, Lieutenant. I would just suggest that you play your cards close to your vest. I found out that you were a close friend of Larson's, from the States. I would suggest that the Lieutenant definitely not mention any previous relationship with Lieutenant Larson."

Starting, Bill looked at the Sergeant Major intently. "Why not?"

"Well, Lieutenant, all I can say is that accidents do happen," returned the Sergeant Major as he put down the grenade paperweight and pulled a file out of his in-box.

Bill took the hint that the meeting was over and, without a word, turned and left the office. He now had even more to think about. It seemed to him some of the people sending him on the assignment, for some reason, appeared to be nervous regarding what he might find out at Fort Davis. The Sergeant Major was indirectly warning him to watch his ass and at the same time giving him leads to possible information sources. It was a very confusing situation. Emil had been his closest friend; he was more determined than ever to get to the bottom of what happened to Emil. Besides his concern over what happened to his friend, he also had the promised reward of an outstanding Officer Efficiency Report.

Lost in thought, Bill wandered over to the marked-off helicopter landing zone that was about a half a mile down the street from Battalion Headquarters. He was so engrossed in thought that he didn't notice the small, dark green Volvo parked under a nearby palm tree. Nor did he notice that there were two men seated in the car who seemed very interested in him. Hughes, on the other hand floating along behind

Jennings, paid very close attention to the vehicle and the soldiers seemingly aimlessly wandering in the area.

On the other hand, the two men parked in the dark green Volvo didn't notice the trio of soldiers that were strolling along the side of the street toward them. It began to be clear to Hughes that Sergeant Major Villanueva was going to make sure that nothing happened to the Battalion's newest Lieutenant, at least while he was still on Fort Clayton. Since Bill's attention was directed toward the helicopter that came in low over the fence toward the landing zone, he never noticed the soldiers jerking the two men out of that dark green Volvo and starting to work them over.

Suddenly, Hughes was hovering in a corner of the Sergeant Major's office. Sergeant Major Villanueva was waiting patiently in his office for news that the occupants of the suspicious car had been brought into the basement of the Battalion Headquarters. A knock on his door was the signal that the snatch had worked to perfection. Reaching into his desk for a .45 automatic, he wrapped it in a newspaper, carefully placed it under his right arm and walked down to the basement area. He had long since learned, that in this man's Army, if you wanted something done right, do it yourself.

Once in the basement with the door securely fastened, he pulled out the pistol, letting the newspaper fall to the ground. Waiting for him were Master Sergeant Ernesto Lopez of Company A and two of the biggest, meanest privates in the Battalion. They were standing guard over two very rumpled individuals of obvious Hispanic extraction. Villanueva paused just inside the door to study the captives closely; they glared back defiantly. Their attitudes changed, however, when he pulled back the slide on the pistol, chambering a round, and held it loosely in his hand, pointed at the ground.

"Now, gentlemen, I want to know who you are, who sent you and why you were following Lieutenant Jennings. And I want to know now!" roared the stocky Sergeant Major as he pointed the automatic toward the face of the smaller of the two prisoners.

For a moment, Hughes almost clawed his way back to consciousness. He was momentarily aware of Martha and an older gentleman studying him intently by the subdued light of the bedside lamp.

"He's fighting it." Said Martha, leaning over to run her hand gently over his forehead.

"I don't understand." Mumbled her companion. "The conditioning should have kept him under completely."

He paused for a moment, then leaned forward and raised one of Hughes' eyelids.

"You gave him the sedative?"

Martha nodded emphatically.

"Certainly. And started the subliminal tapes just like you instructed."

For a long time her companion simply studied Hughes unconscious figure. Finally, he shook his head and stepped back from the bed.

"Well I suppose it is one of those unexplained mental quirks that go with brain conditioning. Nothing to worry about, I'm sure."

He looked at Martha as if for the first time, eyeing her as she stood there in her filmy negligee. Slowly he raised one hand and pushed on of the thin straps off one of her creamy smooth shoulders.

"Since we have a long time to wait, suppose we enjoy ourselves?"

Hughes struggled to move, but was still held tightly by the effects of whatever she had given him. To his horror he watched her smile and raise her hands to completely remove the nightgown. Naked she stood before the stranger before dropping to her knees and reaching for his belt. Raging inside, Hughes felt himself falling into darkness as he heard his loving wife begin to noisily please the stranger. Neither Hughes nor the nocturnal lovers noticed the bedroom door open wide enough for a single eye to observe the occupants of the bedroom. Grimly Matilda watched silently before easing the door shut.

Flying on a military chopper is like no other type of flying there is. Hughes had never served in the military, but, suddenly back with Jennings, he recognized that the helicopter that had come for Lieutenant Jennings was one of the type known as a Huey. This aircraft had been the workhorse in the Vietnam War, with the capability of carrying eight passengers beside the three-man crew. Another characteristic of flying in this type of helicopter was that the side doors were usually left locked open when the helicopter flies. With the wind whipping along the side of the helicopter tearing at the passengers, it was probably the closest sensation possible to flying like Superman.

As Bill also quickly discovered, flying with a 193rd pilot at the controls had other major differences from normal flying. A combat trained pilot flew in a manner known as nape of the earth. This meant that he kept the helicopter flying only a few feet higher than the contour of the land over which he flies. In a country with as many changes in contour as Panama, this meant that the helicopter was constantly changing altitude. To the young Lieutenant, it felt like he was on a roller coaster.

Being unused to flying in general, the constant roller coaster type motion began to make Bill regret his big breakfast. As soon as he could get used to one altitude, they would make a major increase or decrease depending on the land below them. Seldom had he been as relieved as when the air craft broke out over a last clump of large jungle trees and he could see the 4th Battalion, 10th Infantry Battalion area laid out below them like a model city. The multi-storied whitewashed buildings with their red slate tile roofs were laid out in an orderly pattern around a large grassy parade field. As Bill felt the aircraft begin to drop toward the grassy area, he decided that he had a chance to get on the ground before he lost his breakfast. As the helicopter settled down to a gentle landing, he slipped out of the craft to the ground, bent low and ran out from under the whirling blades.

Waiting for Bill were several camouflaged clad officers. He recognized the 4/10 Battalion Commander, Lieutenant Colonel Mellon, by the silver oak leaf on his uniform collar. With the Colonel were two Infantry Captains and a Second Lieutenant. Straightening, Bill gave the Lieutenant Colonel a salute and nodded to the other officers.

"Colonel Mellon, I'm Lieutenant Jennings from 4/20. General Goodrich sent me to investigate the training accident that took place last week. This is my authorization." Bill opened his briefcase, pulled out the General's letter, and handed it to the Colonel.

Colonel Mellon was a tall man, in his stocking feet, he stood close to 6' 8" inches, but he didn't weigh much over two hundred pounds. Coupling his appearance with a constant facial expression indicating that he had smelled something bad, had given the troops a great deal of enjoyment thinking up new semi-obscene nicknames for their commanding officer.

Mellon completely ignored Bill's salute, but instead opened the envelope with his long slim fingers and stood for a long time looking at the General's letter of authorization. From his stance and general demeanor, Bill knew that the Colonel wanted very much to have him thrown off the Post, but didn't quit dare. Secretly, Jennings was glad he hadn't been sent to Fort Davis, a sentiment to which the ever-present Hughes fully agreed. Finally, Lieutenant Colonel Mellon grunted, thrust the letter at the Captain standing beside him and, without a word, spun on his heel, and stalked off across the Post back toward his Battalion Headquarters.

Bill stood with his mouth hanging open. In his wildest imagination, he hadn't expected this type of reception. Why would Colonel Mellon adopt this attitude toward an investigation ordered by his own Commanding Officer regarding the death of one of his officers? Did the Battalion Commander know something he wanted hidden? Since arriving, Bill had been faced with nothing but questions. Puzzled, he looked at the Captain holding the General's letter.

"Well, sir. When do I start?" he asked politely.

The Captain looked at the Colonel's retreating back, dropped his eyes to the letter and then looked at Bill.

"Well, er, I suppose whenever you like." he said pausing for a moment before handing back the General's letter. "You have to forgive the Colonel for his attitude. He feels that this investigation is an insult to the unit and the fact that its being conducted by a Second Lieutenant from another Battalion, makes it a major insult to him personally. He can't refuse to allow the investigation to take place, but he seems to feel that he doesn't have to actively cooperate."

As Bill put the General's letter away, the Captain held out his hand.

"Forgive my manners, I'm Captain Randy Mosley, Battalion Adjutant. This is Captain Frederick Finch, Company Commander of A Company. The Lieutenant is Johnny Ragsdale, XO of A Company," said the Adjutant, indicating each officer.

Bill smiled and offered his hand to each in turn. "Glad to meet you, sirs. I guess, I need to get started with my investigation. As I understand, Lieutenant Larson was in A Company." He referred to the notes jotted down in his pocket notebook.

"That's right, Lieutenant." said Captain Finch, "He was in charge of second platoon. If you go with Lieutenant Ragsdale, he'll take you over to the company."

The Captain turned to his Executive Officer.

"Johnny, Lieutenant Jennings is to be given full cooperation. Anyone who does not cooperate will answer to me," said the Captain, glaring at his subordinate.

"Yes, sir. I'll see that everyone cooperates." answered the Lieutenant as he motioned Bill to come with him. "Let's go, Lieutenant."

The two Captains stood, eyes narrowed, watching the two lieutenants walk off across the grassy field.

"Anything he can find, Fred?" asked the Adjutant.

"The place is clean, Randy. We've gone over everything with a fine toothcomb. Anyone who might possibly know anything about what happened is on emergency leave. Sergeant Crawford should be in Florida by this time. I personally made sure that he left on a C-47 out of Howard yesterday afternoon."

The look on Finch's face was pensive.

"But, Randy, what's the General going to say about us shipping those folks out of here so quickly? He's bound to know why we did it. You saw that letter, he ordered full cooperation." asked Finch nervously as he looked around to see the Colonel just now entering the Battalion Headquarters.

Mosley looked over at his companion and snorted in derision.

"Fred, my first loyalty is to Colonel Mellon. We are part of the 4th battalion, 10th Infantry. If the Commander of the 4th of the 10th wants the facts regarding the training accident hushed up, then, by God, that's what we are both going to do? You'd better remember who writes your efficiency report." He gripped Finch's shoulder.

"Besides, Goodrich no more wants this thing to break open than you or I. If the truth got around, it'd have his fancy brass ass in a sling in a heartbeat. He may bitch and moan and make wild accusations about all of the emergency leaves that were approved, but I made damn sure that every set of leave orders is accompanied by very valid supporting documents. So don't sweat it."

"I also know the penalty for murder, Randy! If this Jennings guy finds out everything that really happened, then we could all be on the carpet." snapped Finch as he shook off Mosley's hand and walked toward his Company area, head down.

Intently, Mosley watched the Commander of A Company march off across the field. He had the strong impression that Finch might break and spill what he knew if pressured. That could be most unfortunate for everyone. Well, field exercises were dangerous operations. It was a miracle that more troops didn't die in these jungle-covered hills. If necessary, another unfortunate accident could be arranged. With one last look toward the A Company area, he swung around on his heels and quickly walked toward the Battalion Headquarters.

CHAPTER NINE

Lieutenant Ragsdale led Bill into the building that housed A Company to an area in the back of which opened several small rooms.

"Each Platoon Leader has a private office in this area where they keep their more sensitive equipment, records and so forth. Lieutenant Larson's was the second door on the right," he said as he led Bill into a room slightly bigger than a closet containing two desks and four large double door wall lockers.

The two NCOs sitting behind the desks stood as they saw that their visitors were officers.

"Sergeant Muldoon, this is Lieutenant Bill Jennings from 4/20. He is the General's personal appointee to investigate the death of Lieutenant Larson. You are to give him full cooperation under the direct orders of both Captain Finch and General Goodrich. Any questions?" he asked as he stood with his hands on his hips, glaring at both of the NCOs.

"None, sir." snapped Sergeant Muldoon, answering for both of them.

Lieutenant Ragsdale glared at the two of them for long moment before nodding in satisfaction and turning to Bill.

"My office is over in the command section, Bill. If you need anything come see me." he said as he offered his hand to Bill.

With another glare at the two NCOs, Ragsdale slammed the door behind him. Bill looked from the door to the two NCOs standing at rigid attention. Hughes was surprised to find that he found the

Battalion area, the Company area and the office strangely familiar, but wrote it off to the illogic of a dream. He watched as Jennings sat his briefcase down on the floor and dropped into one of the straight-backed metal chairs in the corner.

"Well, guys, I need to talk to you. Have a seat, don't stand on ceremony," he said as he threw his garrison cap onto the desk.

After a look at each other, the two NCOs gingerly resumed their seats and slowly relaxed. With a grin at their nervousness, Bill put his briefcase on the desk and pulled out a legal pad, which he placed carefully in front of him. He also took out the letter from General Goodrich and passed it over to Sergeant Muldoon.

"As you can see, Sergeant, this inquiry has been approved at the highest level in the Brigade. So don't be afraid to tell me anything that you may know." said Bill as he pulled a pen out of his blouse pocket.

Sergeant Muldoon passed the letter over to his companion and waited until the NCO handed the letter back to Bill before he spoke.

"Well, Lieutenant, we would be glad to help you, if we could, but we don't have anything to say." offered Sergeant Muldoon.

Bill placed his elbows on the desktop and leaned forward.

"Weren't you at the .50 caliber range when the accident happened?" he asked as his eyes searched their faces.

"No sir, neither of us was there." Muldoon concentrated on picking an invisible piece of lint off of the jacket of his fatigues.

Bill was experienced enough to know a stonewall when he ran into one. Leaning back, he threw down his pen and considered the two men in front of him. Muldoon appeared to be in his mid thirties. From his accent, he was probably from the northeastern part of the United States. His silent companion was a little older, black and extremely uncomfortable.

"Let's make sure that I have your name correct. You are Sergeant Muldoon, and your name is?" he asked glancing over at the hereto silent black NCO.

"Casey, Sir. Staff Sergeant Amos Casey." he mumbled, refusing to meet Bill's gaze.

"Well, Sergeant Muldoon, Sergeant Casey, I am going to have your assistance on this investigation. If you do not cooperate with me as of now, I will call General Goodrich and let you explain to him why you are not giving me the required cooperation," declared Bill calmly as he raised his legs to rest his feet on the edge of the desk in front of him. He then tilted his chair on its back two legs and dared them to meet his eyes. Bill was prepared to sit there as long as he needed to in order to get their unreserved cooperation.

Finally, Sergeant Muldoon broke the silence.

"Lieutenant, you don't know what you're asking. We can sure enough, get our tails in a wringer big time over this." he complained with a guilty glance at the door.

Neither Hughes nor Jennings knew what to make of this.

"I don't understand you people," snapped Jennings, "you just heard your Company XO order you to cooperate and this letter from General Goodrich orders the same thing. So what's the problem?"

Casey still just sat silently, staring at the cigarette-burned desktop. He rubbed his face for a moment with one big hand and sighed.

"What happened ain't right, but in this Battalion, many times what is said is definitely not what was meant."

Deciding it was time to play hardball, Bill dropped the front legs of his chair back onto the floor and stood.

"Fine. I'll see you guys later." he said, as he packed his legal pad into his briefcase.

"Where are you going, Lieutenant?" Muldoon watched the Lieutenant with puzzled eyes.

"I'm going back to Fort Clayton to tell the General that I can't obey his orders because you gentlemen won't cooperate." he said, snapping his briefcase closed as he turned for the door.

"Uh, wait Lieutenant. O.K. We'll talk. But you can't ever tell anyone what we tell you or even that we told you anything. You may think that Ragsdale meant those orders and he may have, but word has already gone out to say nothing." Muldoon glanced again at the closed office door.

Making it a point to keep his face blank, Bill dropped back into his chair and put his briefcase back onto the desk.

"Who gave those orders to not cooperate?"

Muldoon shrugged and went back to gazing at the floor.

"Can't rightly say, Lieutenant. We got the word is all that is important."

"All right, Sergeant. I want to know what's going on here and I want to know now."

With a sharp jerk, Hughes found himself once again hovering like a bat near the right shoulder of the 4/20 Sergeant Major.

Sergeant Major Villanueva was getting more worried about the state of the Brigade to the point that he really didn't know what to do anymore. He still had those two men locked in the basement of the Battalion Headquarters, though they were now a little the worse for wear. They hadn't wanted to tell him anything, but after encouragement from some of the Battalion's bigger 'persuaders' the two had sung like birds. He had hated, however, to hear what they had to say.

His .45 still held loosely in his hand, the Sergeant Major walked slowly back up the stairs to his office. This was a fine kettle of fish, he thought, it would appear that the fat was getting ready to drop into the fire. Closing his office door quietly behind him, he wearily dropped into his chair, tossed the .45 onto his desk and grabbed the phone. Almost savagely, he dialed the number and clamped the phone to his ear with such force his knuckles went white.

"Sergeant Major Ashe, please." he said politely when the clerk answered at Brigade Headquarters.

"Ashe." snapped a deep voice in his ear almost at once.

"Ashe, this is Villanueva," he said wearily as he pulled open his upper right hand desk drawer and pulled out a brochure on retirement property in Florida. He had decided that it really looked better the longer he considered it.

"Yeah?"

"Early this morning, one of my guys reported a suspicious car in the Battalion area. I had some of the troops search and we caught two guys staking out our Chopper Pad. They seemed to be especially interested in Lieutenant Jennings and where he was going. We searched the car and found a high powered rifle in the trunk."

Villanueva paused for a moment, gathering his thoughts.

"And?" prompted Ashe.

"I had some of the guys 'persuade' them to tell us what they wanted with the Lieutenant. You ain't going to like it." finished Villanueva as he mentally calculated what it would cost to make a down payment on a retirement lot in sunny Florida.

"So what ain't I gonna like?" prompted the Brigade Sergeant Major.

"They were members of the Panamanian DENY."

"The DENY!" exclaimed Ashe. "What'd the Panamanian version of the CIA want with a U.S. Army Officer?"

"According to what they said, their assignment was to make Jennings disappear. They had planned to shoot down the chopper as it came back this afternoon," answered Villanueva. He watched out of the window as the two disheveled members of the Panamanian DENY, the local version of the CIA were hustled, head first, into the back of a military Carry All. One was definitely in a lot of pain.

"Shit!" exclaimed the Brigade Sergeant Major, "that tears it. I'd better let the old man know that there may be an attempt on that Lieutenant over at Davis."

"I've got an even better question for you, Ashe." said Villanueva as the Carry All

disappeared down the road.

"Eh, what's that?" asked Ashe.

"The official orders for the Lieutenant's assignment only came in here today. I would assume that they were not typed over there until this morning." began Villanueva as he began to toy with his hand grenade paperweight again.

"Yeah, so. I oversaw the cutting of the orders at about 6:30 this morning. The General's letter of authorization was typed at about the same time." he answered, a thoughtful note in his voice.

"Well, since we caught these guys at about 8:00 or so this morning, how did they know where he was going and when he was coming back? It's unusual to send a chopper for a Second Lieutenant, so how did they know he would go by helicopter?" asked the Battalion Sergeant Major.

For a few minutes Ashe was totally silent. Villanueva could almost hear the wheels turning through the phone lines. He didn't have to spell it out for Ashe; it was obvious that there was an information leak at Brigade Headquarters. Somehow, someone on the General's own staff had leaked the information about the investigation to the Panamanians. Why would the investigation of the death of an American Army Officer be of such concern to the Panamanian military that they would send one of their CIA trained assassination teams into the Zone to kill another American Army Officer and risk an international incident? It just didn't add up.

"What have you done with those two guys from the DENY?" asked Ashe.

"What two guys?" asked Villanueva as he began to toss his grenade into the air.

"Good enough. Keep a lid on it, or it could take us all down." growled Ashe as he slammed down the phone.

Feeling like a yo-yo, Hughes found himself snatched back to hover above Jennings again.

"It's like this Lieutenant, if we talk, we can't do it here in the Company area. Someone might hear us," said Muldoon in a low voice, as he shot another glance at the office door. "These walls have ears."

Bill nodded quickly, he didn't know what to make of their attitude, but he could at least tolerate it.

"Then where would you suggest we talk?" asked Bill as he again leaned back in his chair.

Muldoon couldn't think of a place, but Casey showed that he had a sharp mind behind those brooding eyes.

"Why not out on the range? If you are going to investigate, you have to go out there anyway, don't you?" he asked, still studying the scarred desktop.

"But won't whoever you're afraid of believe you are talking to me?"

Casey allowed himself a slight smile.

"What can we do if the Lieutenant orders us to go out there with him?"

Jennings had to smile in spite of himself.

"But, I still have a lot of people to talk too here. In fact, my instructions were to talk to everyone involved and then report back to the General," protested Bill.

Sergeant Muldoon took a deep breath before leaning forward across his desk.

"Well, Lieutenant, actually the only way you're going to learn anything is out on the range. There ain't nobody in Garrison at the moment that can tell you a thing about what happened out there."

Bill looked down at his notes for a moment and then at Muldoon.

"How about Sergeant Crawford, I understand that he was there when it happened."

Sergeant Muldoon nodded and grimaced.

"He was there. But he ain't here now."

"What do you mean?" demanded the Lieutenant.

"I mean that Crawford left the Zone yesterday for the states. According to what I heard, his mother died. So he left on emergency leave."

Bill considered this unfortunate piece of information as he quickly jotted a few notes in his folder.

"Well, I guess I can call him at his home in the States. Did he leave a phone number?"

Muldoon glanced back at the door and this time his voice was lower when he spoke.

"You don't understand Lieutenant. Crawford is an orphan, both his parents died years ago. They sent him away so that he couldn't talk to you. God knows where he really is."

Bill looked at the Sergeant in disbelief. "Now, just a minute Sergeant. Are you saying that the Officers of this Battalion are involved in trying to conduct a cover-up?"

Muldoon shook his head emphatically.

"No, sir. I ain't saying nothing like that, Lieutenant. What I am saying is that Crawford went home to the States to go to a funeral for someone that has been dead for years. Maybe it's just Army inefficiency."

Bill licked his dry lips and scanned his notes.

"How about Private Curtis Dalton, Lieutenant Larson's jeep driver?"

Casey shifted nervously in his chair.

"Well, sir, that's another little matter that is hard to understand."

Jennings shifted and scowled.

"Now what do you mean by that? Surely you know who drove the Lieutenant."

"Well, normally, Curtis Dalton was the Lieutenant's RTO and driver. But —-"

"But what?" demanded Jennings.

"Well, it appears that Dalton didn't drive the Lieutenant that day."

"Well, if Dalton didn't drive him that day, who did?" demanded Jennings.

Muldoon stood and waved his arms for emphasis.

"Lieutenant, we just don't know. Crawford told me that he saw Larson drive off and he saw someone in fatigues driving, but it weren't Dalton."

"Was Dalton out on the range that day?" questioned Jennings.

Muldoon nodded slowly and walked over to open the door and glance out in the hall.

"He was. But he didn't drive the Lieutenant."

"What has Dalton said about who drove?"

Sergeant Casey shook his head and interjected his comments in the conversation.

"Nothing at all. Far as I know ain't no body asked him nothing."

Jennings got to his feet and put his briefcase on the desk. He raised the lid and dropped his legal pad inside, closed it and snapped the clasps.

"Well, let's go talk to this Dalton."

Casey leaned his elbows on the desk and fixed his eyes on the Lieutenant.

"Dalton went on pass Saturday and didn't come back."

"AWOL?" asked Bill, in surprise.

"No idea, Lieutenant." answered Muldoon. "We just know that he didn't come back from pass."

"So you see, Lieutenant, if you want to find out anything useful, you need to go out to the range. Besides, the Lieutenant's jeep is still sitting out there," said Casey, nervously clicking his ballpoint pen.

For some reason, Bill was reluctant to go to the range, but finally, he agreed that they would drive out to where Emil had been killed and talk along the way. It took but a moment for Bill to arrange with Lieutenant Ragsdale to use the Company Commander's jeep, so within ten minutes he was sitting in the back of an open jeep driven by Muldoon, with Casey in the passenger seat.

As Lieutenant Jennings and the NCOs drove past the Battalion Headquarters, two sets of angry eyes followed their passage. Hughes once again found himself drifting above people he didn't know, listening to conversations that puzzled him.

"What if he finds out?" asked Lieutenant Colonel Mellon as he watched the jeep drive out of sight.

His well-dressed companion shrugged, wiping his sweaty face with a monogrammed handkerchief. "Then we stage another training accident." he answered as he signaled from the window to a man in civilian clothes that had a car parked nearby.

The men in the window watched as the civilian car sped after the jeep. The man in the expensive civilian clothes was the first to move.

"Colonel, I suggest that we leave matters such as these to the experts. I am more concerned about the breach of security caused by your Lieutenant Larson. We may not be so lucky next time."

Mellon turned from the window and shrugged his skinny shoulders. "As far as we can find out, he didn't tell anyone he was planning on sneaking into the Kito Research Facility. Hell, I don't even know what goes on in that place."

His companion took one last glance out of the window in the direction the jeep had disappeared, before accompanying the Colonel back to his office.

"Well, my dear Colonel. What goes on at the Kito Facility is of no concern of yours. You have more pressing concerns to attend to if you want to save your career."

Mellon allowed his visitor to precede him into the office and shut the door behind them.

"I was a fool to let your people talk me into closing my eyes to those shipments you people ran out of the Golden Triangle. You haven't given me a moments peace since Saigon." Mellon sighed as he dropped into his chair.

His companion sat primly in another chair, crossing one Gucci clad foot over the other.

"My dear Colonel Mellon, you took the money and enjoyed our support in the various promotions you have received in the last ten years. So the least you can do is be civil about the whole affair."

Mellon frowned as his eyes were drawn to his visitor's large gold signet ring.

"But I never counted on murder. God, Martell, what you people did to Larson was just simply murder. When I told you what Larson was up to, I thought you'd just arrange a transfer, not murder."

At those words, Hughes went cold. Things went dark and when he opened his eyes again, he was looking at the ceiling of his bedroom. He felt exhausted, like he had run a race. Slowly, he swung his legs over the side of the bed and struggled to his feet. By the bedside clock, he saw that it was only two a.m. Remembering his dream within a dream of his wife with another man; he glanced over to see Martha lying peacefully beside him. Giving in to his suspicions, he slowly pulled the cover back to see that Martha's nightgown was bunched up under her armpits; she was naked below that. With trembling hand he slowly felt between her legs, he felt dampness. Unable to resist, he pushed a finger into her velvety interior and pulled it back.

Holding his hand out from his side, one step at a time, he crossed to the bathroom and dropped onto the commode. Reaching up he turned on the night-light. To his shock, he saw that his finger was covered with a thick milky mucous; it was sperm. Another man's sperm was in his wife. He hadn't been dreaming. Without thinking, he wiped his hand on the towel hanging on the rack. Suddenly he felt something close to relief. He hadn't been dreaming. Silently, he returned to the bed, hoping to be able to sleep without dreaming. He needed to consider his next step. His wife had betrayed him.

However, once his eyes closed, like a runaway train, Hughes found himself falling.

Like returning home, Hughes found his trip to the range with Lieutenant Jennings very familiar. The part that was still Carter Hughes knew that he had actually been there before.

Bill was fast finding out about the rapid changes in the weather in the Canal Zone. When he had left the Clayton Guest House that morning he had actually been a little cool, now at mid-morning he was sweating profusely in his starched khaki uniform. He made a note to himself to take time out the next day and get his basic issue of camouflaged fatigues from the Battalion S-4 shop. He noticed that neither Muldoon nor Casey appeared to be overly hot, in their fatigues.

When they hit the first major bump in the road, Bill also made a note to himself to get a check up, since he was sure he had just lost a kidney when his body left the seat and then slammed back against the thin seat pad. The metal seat had no give to it at all. It was only his death grip on the edge of the windscreen that kept him from being flung out of the vehicle all together. Military jeeps did not come equipped with seat belts.

Hearing him grunt, Casey glanced back at Bill with a knowing look and for the first time met his eyes.

"Hang on, Lieutenant. This is the paved road. Soon we'll turn off on to a dirt road and it'll get a little bumpy."

Bill groaned as the jeep made a two-wheeled curve and bounced off the ground as it entered a rutted overgrown unpaved road. Weaving through the twisting and turning road they descended into a stretch that had been used for so long that its' surface had dropped almost eight feet below the level of the surrounding terrain. Muldoon reached a long straight stretch and floored the little jeep. It seemed to leap ahead, stirring up a thick cloud of dust that was kept confined to the sunken road by the high embankments on either side. Finally, the level of the road began to rise as they started up a low hill. At the top, they came to a screeching halt; a closed metal gate blocked the road.

As Casey got out of the jeep to open the gate, Muldoon turned back to Bill.

"There are three gates like this one that are used to close off the area when a live fire exercise is underway. Lieutenant Larson was out checking to make sure that they were all shut when he was killed."

"What's it mean when they are closed?" asked Jennings.

"Exercise underway. Keep out."

"Then why are we going in?" he asked.

Getting the point, Muldoon laughed out loud, his black face shining in the bright sunlight.

"Don't you worry none, Lieutenant. This gate's closed cause the General ordered the range sealed until the investigation. Ain't nobody out there."

Casey opened the gate and held it back while Muldoon drove the jeep through and then braked. As soon as the black NCO had jumped back into the jeep after closing the gate behind them, Muldoon slammed into first gear and drove slowly along the rutted dirt road. Bill looked around in great interest as they slowly drove up the hill toward the staging area of the firing range.

At the Range Officer's hut, Muldoon braked to a stop. Muldoon was right, as far as they could see; there was no one in the area. Muldoon cut off the jeep and stepped to the ground, turning to watch with amused eyes as the Lieutenant painfully extracted himself from the cramped rear section of the vehicle. The Sergeant's grin widened as he saw how completely dust covered the Lieutenant's nice khaki uniform was, as a result of their trip. Sergeant Casey's laugh turned into a coughing fit as Bill shook his head sorrowfully and surveyed his ruined uniform.

"Well, the things I do for the military." He mumbled.

He began to brush the thick layer of dust off his blouse. Accomplishing little, and finally, giving up the effort as a lost cause, Bill began to clean his sunglasses with his relatively clean handkerchief as he squinted around the barren windswept hill. In every direction, were hills covered with low brush that led up to complete walls of jungle foliage. Periodically scattered around the high ground downrange from the firing line were clumps of man sized silhouette targets and wrecked vehicles that were used also used as targets on this particular range.

"O.K., we're here. Now let's talk." began Bill as he replaced his sunglasses and walked into the scant shade offered by the Range Officer's hut.

Muldoon and Casey followed him into the warm, musty smelling, little hut, each taking their seats on one of the many metal folding chairs left for range observers. As usual, Muldoon took the initiative.

"First off, Lieutenant, we were telling you the truth, back at the Post. We don't know anything about the death of the Lieutenant. Neither of us were here that day." he said, pulling a package of chewing tobacco out of his pocket. Solemnly he opened it, took out a handful and put it in his mouth before offering it around to Casey and lastly, to Bill. Casey took out a handful, but Bill declined.

"Then why did you bring me out here to talk, unless you just wanted to try and kill me by suffocation?" demanded Bill as he stood and began to pace around the tiny hut, glancing out of the open windows in every direction.

Muldoon grinned suddenly, but when he realized that Bill was not exactly happy, he wiped the grin off of his face.

"No, Lieutenant. That will be for your own platoon to do. We did bring you out here to talk, but we want to talk about some of the weird things that have happened since the accident.

You see, for us to have not been at the range that day was highly unusual. We are, or were, Lieutenant Larson's two senior NCOs. Rightly, Casey and I would have been the ones to go to check the gates. Not the Lieutenant." responded the Sergeant as he leaned over and spit out of the window facing the entrance to the Range.

Bill turned to make a comment that froze in his throat as Muldoon raised his hand in caution.

"There's somebody coming up the road, Lieutenant," said Muldoon in a low voice.

Bill glanced over in the direction Muldoon indicated and saw a small cloud of dust hanging in the air.

"So, this is still an active training range, isn't it?"

"Certainly, but there is no training scheduled until Thursday and the general ordered this range area sealed. That's why we came out here. No one has any reason to be here except us," replied the Sergeant as he walked out to the jeep and peered down the road.

Bill was utterly dumbfounded by the actions of the two NCOs. They acted like their lives were in danger just from talking to him. Like most other things about this assignment, their actions made no sense. He swung around toward Casey.

"Stop this cloak-and-dagger bullshit and tell me what the fuck is going on!" he demanded.

Sergeant Casey was a man of few words, but when he did say something, it was straight and to the point.

"Lieutenant, this cloak-and-dagger bullshit, as you call it, may just save all our lives. There's things happening in this outfit that shouldn't be happening in our Army, but they are. Muldoon and I are taking a hell of a chance by talking with you, so you let us decide how and when we're going to talk." said the Black NCO as he walked out to join Muldoon.

Not knowing what else to do, Bill followed them. Muldoon was still intently studying the cloud of dust. He glanced around as Bill joined them.

"Let's go on up to the hill where the Lieutenant was shot." said the Sergeant as he climbed back in to the jeep.

With a shake of his head, Bill sprang into the back and Casey got into the passenger seat. Muldoon started the jeep and they drove across the grassy plain toward the hill to the left of the firing line. A normal car would have quickly bogged down on the uneven terrain, but under Muldoon's expert guidance, the jeep went right up the side of the hill, though there were a few times when Bill had to hang on and pray that the jeep didn't flip over. Finally, they reached the crest of the hill and Muldoon pulled up by one of the wrecks that he had seen from the Range Control shack. As Bill jumped to the ground, he noticed that a burned-out armored personnel carrier was sitting some one hundred feet further up the hill; close to him was a jeep that had so many bullet holes in it that it looked like a sieve.

"Well, Lieutenant, here we are." Muldoon walked over to the ruined jeep.

Bill looked at him, puzzled. "Where is here?"

Muldoon slammed his hand down on the hood of the destroyed jeep.

"The scene of the accident, if you want to call it that. This piece of junk was Lieutenant Larson's jeep," he said sadly.

Without a word, Bill walked over to the jeep and began to examine it almost inch by inch. He winced as he ran his hands over the huge holes in the metal frame; it looked like someone had taken a giant can opener to it. Hughes could feel the waves of anguish emanating from Jennings.

"What caused these big holes?" he asked curiously as he measured one of the three-inch-wide holes with his hand.

".50 caliber rounds from the firing line down there." said Casey as he leaned against their jeep, watching the Lieutenant's investigation.

Bill's jaw dropped as he considered the amount of power it would take to do this kind of damage to a heavy framed jeep. The firing line was almost a mile away, downhill, and the rounds had literally disintegrated parts of the vehicle.

Bill walked around to the passenger seat and studied the shredded seat cushion. He could see some light reddish stains on the seat that he didn't need to be told were bloodstains, Emil's blood. He leaned forward, eyes closed, and pressed his hand against the back of the seat, and his friend had died here.

To his surprise he felt a lump inside the pad. He stepped back from the jeep and looked at the shredded cushion from the side. From this angle he noticed that it was about three inches thick, much thicker than a normal military jeep seat cushion. He glanced over at the jeep that had brought him out and confirmed his suspicion that the seat pad in that one was not as thick as in Larson's jeep.

A sudden thought occurred to him.

"Where was the driver when all this firing was going on?"

"Good question, Lieutenant." growled Casey, studying the ground around the jeep. "Whoever drove Larson simply disappeared. We asked Dalton questions, or tried to, but Dalton refused to answer. All he would say was that he had not been the driver. Crawford brought the matter to the Old Man, and the next thing we known, Crawford is heading for his mother's funeral on emergency leave."

Resting one foot on the running board on the passenger side if the destroyed jeep. Bill paused to consider everything he had seen and heard. It was sounding less and less like a simple training accident. Idly, his eyes went back to the shredded seat pad on the passenger seat.

"Muldoon, why is this seat cushion so much thicker than the one in the jeep we have?" he asked as he fingered the shredded material.

Muldoon walked around the jeep to join him.

"Lieutenant Larson hurt his back about a week before he died. He complained that the bouncing of the jeep made the pain worse and asked to have this extra thick one put in the jeep in place of the regular, thinner one. It's no big deal, Lieutenant, lots of you officers use them," he said turning his eyes back toward the dust cloud approaching the range shack.

Pulling out his pocketknife, Lieutenant Jennings leaned over the seat and began to dig the point into the material that filled the cushion. Slowly and carefully, he cut away ragged strips of the pad until he had dug a hole about two inches deep. To his delight, he found exactly what he expected to find, a misshapen lump of metal. He used the point of the knife to pull the lump out into the palm of his hand.

He had been aware that Muldoon and Casey had walked over to lean over his shoulder, watching quietly as he worked.   He closed his fist over what he had found and turned to face the NCOs.

"Sergeant Muldoon, was the pad installed on this jeep for Lieutenant Larson new?"

Muldoon nodded.

"Yeah, it was. In fact, Casey here picked it up from supply and had Dalton install it."

Jennings glanced at Casey who nodded earnestly.

"That's a fact, Lieutenant. I took it out of the box myself. There were absolutely no holes in it when I gave it to Dalton."

"What'd you find, Lieutenant?" asked Muldoon.

Wordlessly, Jennings held out his hand and opened his fingers.

"What is that thing, Lieutenant?" asked Muldoon as he studied the lump of metal in Jennings's hand.

"A bullet, Sergeant Muldoon, looks like a .45 caliber." said Bill as the sun glinted off the cooper-coated lump.

"Now, gentlemen, I have a question for you." he spoke in a low tone of voice, his eyes riveted on the small lump of metal in his hand. "You have both stated that this range is used only as a .50 caliber range and by the General's order, no one has been on this range since the accident. Sergeant Casey, you have stated that this pad was new when you installed it in this jeep."

He paused to let his listeners consider what he had said.

"If all of those statements are true, then why is there a .45 caliber bullet embedded in Lieutenant Larson's seat just about where his heart would be if he was sitting in this jeep?"

The Lieutenant turned around and looked at the two NCO's with a hard stare. It was obvious from their expression that they were puzzled. However, Hughes understood exactly what Jennings was driving at with his questions.

"I don't understand what you are talking about?" said Muldoon. "I don't know what you're driving at, but I know that there is something strange about the bullet. Only officers carried .45s that day."

"Simply this. If Emil Larson was killed by a .50 caliber round, then why was this .45 caliber round embedded in the seat cushion at about the level of his heart? Are you ready to talk to me now?" he asked, very much aware that their eyes were riveted on the bullet in his hand.

CHAPTER TEN

In another of those dizzying jumps, Hughes found himself hovering over the Sergeant Major.

Sergeant Major Villanueva was worried; he was pacing the floor in his office doing his best to put all of the pieces of the puzzle together in his head. What could the DENY have to do with the death of an American Army Lieutenant? From his personal knowledge, the DENY was the Panamanian version of the CIA reporting only to Colonel Manuel Noreiga, who in turn reported to General Omar Torrios, the real power in Panama.

He remembered all of the rumors that he had heard making the rounds about some of the black projects allegedly being conducted in the Zone. He also remembered that one of Lieutenant Larson's men had been shot by Security while looking for relics near the Research Station. Larson had naturally been upset that one of his guys had been shot and had vowed to get to the bottom of that incident. He didn't believe that the shooting had been an accident. There was only one person he could think of who might give him a clue as to what might be going on. He went back to his desk and quickly dialed a number. After a large number of rings, the phone was answered.

"Yes." answered a very cultured sounding voice.

"This is Sergeant Major Jorge Villanueva of 4/20 at Fort Clayton. I need to talk to Mallory," he said, the hand grenade paperweight gripped tightly in his right hand.

"One moment, Sergeant Major. I will see if Mallory is in."

In less than sixty seconds he heard the unforgettable voice of Mallory on the phone.

"Yes, Jorge. What can I do for you?" asked the sultry female voice.

"Mallory, I need help. It's important," he said as his grip on the grenade became tighter.

"What do you need to know, Jorge, and how do you propose to pay me?" she asked with a low laugh. "I give away nothing, as you well know."

"Mallory, this is more important than anything else I have ever asked you for, it can get me and many others killed if you don't help me." he pleaded, sweat pouring down his shiny face, his eyes squeezed tightly closed.

"Well, in that case Jorge, tell me what you want and we'll consider the question of price later."

Silently praying to himself, Villanueva asked his question.

"Mallory, what do you know about Project Resurrection?"

For a moment Mallory was silent, she made no answer, but he could still hear her heavy breathing on the line.

"Jesus Christ, Jorge, do you know what you are asking me?" she spat at him, her voice as shrill as a fishwife's.

"Mallory, please hear me out. I wouldn't ask you if it wasn't terribly important. I've got one dead Lieutenant and another who's being stalked by a DENY hit team. I've got to get to the bottom of this before anything else happens." he pleaded as he slammed the grenade against his desktop.

"Jorge, we go back many years. You've done me some good turns and never asked me for anything. I'll see what I can do. I'll call you back in a few minutes, Jorge. But you be damn sure that you don't mention that name ever again. It could get me and you both killed," she ordered as she broke the connection.

Depressing the switch hook, Villanueva made another call. This one was to the Sergeant Major at the 4th of the 10th. This time the phone was answered in two rings.

"Sergeant Major Smith's office, Private Summers speaking." answered a military sounding voice.

"This is Sergeant Major Villanueva at 4/20, get me Sergeant Major Smith, ASAP." he ordered as he tossed the grenade into the air and caught it.

"Smith." answered a brisk voice.

"Joe, Jorge here. Is my Lieutenant around there?" he asked, hope in his voice.

"I don't know. Aint my job to keep track of your Lieutenants."

"It's important, Smitty." Responded Villanueva.

"Call you backing a minute." Said Smith as he hung up.

It was only five minutes, but the wait for the return call seemed like hours to Villanueva.

"According to the A Company First Sergeant, that Lieutenant, and two NCOs from the 2nd platoon left here about two hours ago heading out to the range where Lieutenant Larson got killed. Haven't seen them since." came the laconic answer.

"Joe, I need to ask a favor of you," said Villanueva as he tried to keep the fear out of his voice.

"Name it."

"Is that chopper we sent this morning still there?"

"Yep. It's sitting out on the pad. I think the pilots are in the mess hall."

"Put your best armed fire team on it and go get that Lieutenant. Tell them to drag him back if they have to, but I want him in my office in less than an hour. Give your people live ammo and tell them to be prepared to shoot to kill."

"Is it as serious as that?" demanded Sergeant Major Smith.

"Yes. Please, Joe, as a favor to me, don't let another promising young officer die over this," he begged.

"Done." snapped Sergeant Major Smith as he slammed down the phone.

Later Smith was proud to be able to say that he had that chopper in the air, with a fully armed fire team, in less than ten minutes. The fire team was lead by Sergeant First Class Swanson, one of the most experienced NCOs in the Battalion. His orders were to bring back the Lieutenant, alive and in one piece. The Sergeant Major made it very clear that anyone who tried to stop them was to be considered expendable.

The chopper pilot put that helicopter at tree top level and with the throttle open full, he made damn good time on the flight toward the .50 caliber range. Breaking from his tree top-level flight path, the pilot soared over the Range Control shack at about five hundred feet. On the hilltop, he could see a parked jeep and three figures clustered around it. After another sweep to make sure that there were no potential hostiles, the pilot gently touched down less than thirty feet from the jeep. Swanson and his fire team were on the ground, running toward the jeep, almost before the skids came to rest.

Lieutenant Jennings raised his eyes and watched in surprise as the Huey came roaring over his head to touch down only a short distance away. He was even more surprised when an armed fire team came bursting from the chopper and ran toward him. The big, burly NCO in the front was coming straight toward him.

"Wonder what's up?" said Muldoon, "That's Swanson in front, probably the best NCO in the Battalion."

As Bill watched, the four riflemen took positions on the ground around him. The big NCO stopped in front of him and sketched a half salute.

"Lieutenant, we have orders to return you to Battalion, as soon as possible." he stated, his eyes peering at the Range Control shack below.

Swanson's mind was moving quickly, as he thought he detected some movement as they had flew over the range, but he decided he was wrong. Still, he felt uneasy standing on this exposed hilltop. He didn't know what was causing his uneasiness, but the Sergeant Major made it clear that if the Lieutenant didn't come back, then Swanson shouldn't come back. Swanson planned on going back.

Finally, his nerves got the best of him; he was positive that something was not right about the area. Quickly he hustled the Lieutenant and the two NCO's toward the waiting helicopter. They could come back for the jeep later. In Vietnam, Swanson had lost the index finger on his right hand and whenever he was in danger or a tenses situation, he found that his missing finger would begin to hurt. He had learned to pay attention to the phantom pain, it was seldom wrong. It was throbbing like a toothache now.

Buckling himself into his seat, Swanson tapped the Lieutenant Colonel, the senior pilot, on the shoulder. "Get us out of here. Quick!"

In a surge of power that almost cost Bill his breakfast and caused even Hughes to experience vertigo, the helicopter literally leapt for the safety of the sky. Swanson's keen eyes surveyed the terrain beneath them. With half his attention he heard the co-pilot talking on the radio. He failed to notice that the message disturbed the young Captain.

Phong Lei was one of the most highly paid assassins ever trained by the CIA. He had stalked his target carefully, but hadn't counted on the arrival of a fully armed fire team. As he had waited for the best shot to present itself, he had kept low as he crouched in the deserted Range Shack watching the soldiers on the hilltop. Measuring the distance with his eyes, Lei knew that it was a long distance for a good shot, but with his especially adapted AR-15 he was prepared and confident that he could kill all three. As he watched, he saw them doing something with the old wrecked jeep. He couldn't hear what they were saying, but from their actions, intuitively, he knew that they had found something. He didn't know what they had found, but if they had found anything at all, they had to die. He pulled his radio from his pocket and keyed the transmit key.

"1 this is 2." he said into the speaker, his eyes riveted on the figures on the hilltop.

"This is 1, go ahead." came the answer.

"I have them in sight. The Lieutenant appears to have found something in the wrecked jeep." he reported, his eyes never leaving the group on the hilltop.

"Where are they now?"

"Still on the hill, clustered around the jeep."

"When they come down the hill, kill them and dispose of the bodies in the jungle." came the orders.

"Understood." said Phong Lei as he put his radio back into his pocket.

Raising his rifle, he began to carefully sight in his scope. Meticulously, he placed the cross hairs on the face of the Lieutenant. At the same time, he kept watching the Lieutenant in his cross hairs as he tried to read the Lieutenant's lips. He could tell that the Lieutenant was excited about whatever he had found. All three were looking intently at something the Lieutenant held in his hand.

Slowly Phong Lei began to tighten his finger on the trigger. At the last second he had to abort his attempt as the helicopter came roaring over the Range Shack. Lowering his rifle, he watched the helicopter drop down on the hilltop and disgorge several armed men. Puzzled, he lowered his rifle, dropped down out of sight and pulled out his radio.

"1 this is 2." he said softly into the microphone.

"This is 1" came the prompt answer.

"There has been a complication," he reported as he peered out at the helicopter.

"What complication?"

"A military helicopter just landed and several armed men on board are picking up the Lieutenant," he reported.

"This may change things. Do you believe he found anything?"

"That is affirmative."

"Could you tell what he found?"

"No. It was small enough he held it in his hand, but I couldn't see it."

"Very well, break off contact, we will turn the mission over to Victor One. Bravo Oscar will pick up the pieces." came the response.

Phong Lei rose slowly from his hiding place as the helicopter lifted off, leaving the second jeep sitting forlornly on the windswept hill. Impassively, he stood and watched as the helicopter flew off to the north and Fort Davis. He wouldn't want to be in their shoes, they were all going to die.

Hughes again found himself tapped in limbo, forced to sit and watch the 4/20 Sergeant Major.

Sergeant Major Villanueva was as jumpy as a cat on a hot tin roof. He kept starring at the telephone willing it to ring with all the power of his mind. He was concentrating so hard, that when the phone did ring, the sound startled him. Coming out of his reverie, Villanueva leaned forward and literally snatched the phone from its' cradle.

"Yes." demanded Villanueva.

"You owe me big time for this one, Jorge." snapped his caller, obviously still upset, but with her sultry voice restored.

"Mallory, I have to know. It is extremely important. What is Project Resurrection?" he demanded rudely.

"Jorge, you have no idea what you are asking me." she complained, the fear coming across the line.

"I know that you owe me." he responded, "If not for me you would have been out of business a long time a go. Probably in prison by now."

"You don't have to tell me what I owe you. But you have no idea the danger I put myself in by just talking about this. If anyone knows I talked to you about this, we will both be killed."

"What is the project?" he demanded softly.

"It is a top secret project run under the auspices of the National Security Council. Before you ask me, I couldn't find out what the project was specifically about. However, I did get the information that I think you want."

"Did the Project have anything to do with Lieutenant Larson's death?" demanded Villanueva.

"Be careful, Jorge. You are getting off into dangerous waters," she warned.

"Mallory, did it have anything to do with the Lieutenant's death?" he repeated.

"Yes, it does appear that it had everything to do with his death." she answered hesitantly.

"Yes. Tell me!" he prompted, his knuckles white with the strain of his grip on the grenade.

"Well, it's tied in somehow with a CIA project called Operation Paper Clip. Do you know what that Project was about?"

"No, tell me." he demanded, whipping the sweat off his forehead with the back of his hand.

"Well, Paper Clip was a program run by the organization that replaced the OSS, and that later became the CIA. At the end of World War II, the Agency was recruiting all the ex-Nazis that they could find that would help the U.S. in the upcoming cold war. The people who designed and ran Operation Resurrection were originally scientists who trained and worked under Hitler and were recruited at the end of the war b y Operation Paperclip.

Certain of the individuals involved in the program found that the funds available to them for research were not considered sufficient to carry out the program as originally planned. Therefore, it was felt that another funding source was needed to supplement the funds available. This other source of funds was the drug trade."

Mallory paused and he knew she was picking her words carefully.

"The CIA/Nazi drug Syndicate has been using the Canal Zone as a central staging area for their shipments for over thirty years. The shipments are handled from the Atlantic side. Before you ask, I will not tell you how. Due to some bungling on the part of a major drug courier at Fort Davis, who is now deceased as a result of a most unfortunate accident, Lieutenant Larson discovered some very solid evidence of what was going on. No one knows what he found, but it is apparent that he found enough to realize that he was on the verge of a major drug bust. Nothing would have probably come of this as the Military Police would have made a show of investigating and then it would have been back to business as usual, but one of Larson's men was killed and he believed it had something to do with the drugs.

My source says that it is believed that the Lieutenant followed up and apparently found out enough to know that what he had found was only a portion of a larger scheme. Whatever Larson found led him to this Project Resurrection. My sources know that Larson went to the Criminal Investigation Division of the Military Police with the information. There was a leak and as a result he was killed."

"What else?" he asked softly.

"Now the next part of this is strictly classified information that I have no right to have. However, one of my more highly placed sources likes to indulge in pillow talk after sex. He's told me bits and pieces that have allowed me to put all of this together.

I found out that Project Resurrection is based at a big red-bricked facility near Fort Sherman, Kito Research Facility. Arthur Kennedy, the Deputy Director of the project and the head of security discovered that there had been an unauthorized entry into the facility. Kennedy checked and somehow discovered that Larson and two of his men had made the entry.

My sources believe that they had entered to get information that would tie the drug trade to the facility. Before you ask, I don't know what they found, but when Kennedy reported that there had been a breach of security and told them what information had been taken, it threw certain agencies of your government into total fits. That is supposed to be the reason for the termination of the Lieutenant.

As for your new Lieutenant, he was targeted this morning by one of the most deadly assassins in the world, Phong Lei."

"Oh, God." breathed Villanueva. "Who gave those orders?"

"I don't know ad don't want to know. That's it, sport and good by. I'm getting out while the getting is good. All debts between us are canceled," she said as she broke the connection.

In another of those weird dream switches, Hughes found himself back inside the helicopter.

Lieutenant Colonel Jimmie Macklin, the command pilot, was enjoying his job. A pilot's job couldn't be beat, especially a military pilot. But something about this mission didn't feel right. He glanced back toward his passengers and couldn't help but notice the unusual tenseness among the armed personnel on board. He had known Swanson for several years and it took a great deal to spook that man. It was disconcerting to see that the big man was certainly spooked. That knowledge made him fly even more carefully than usual. It also made him do something totally out of character, he decided to radio back to base. It was then that he discovered that he had been so concentrating on what was happening that he had failed to notice that he had no radio contact with his base, or any place else for that matter.

Keying his intercom, Macklin spoke to his copilot as he continued to scan the ground.

"Hank, the radio's out. We'd better make tracks back to Fort Davis." he said checking his fuel gauge.

"Don't think so, Colonel." came the laconic reply.

Snapping his head to the right, Colonel Macklin found that he was looking down the barrel of a service .45 held in his copilot's right hand. The automatic was held close to his chest so that the passengers were unable to see it.

"What the fuck are you doing?" demanded the Colonel as he half-turned in his seat.

"Just obeying orders, you stupid shit. Release your controls, I'm flying this bird." ordered his copilot.

Having no choice, Macklin released his controls and set back in his seat. At the same time, his left hand was releasing his seat belt. When the copilot's eyes flicked toward the ground, the Colonel dove at him, wrestling for the gun. As the pilots struggled over the weapon, the aircraft began to swerve and climb almost straight up. The passengers were thrown against the rear of the craft. Macklin began to pound at his copilot's hand holding the rudder causing the helicopter to begin to drop toward the ground.

Swanson realized that if something weren't done shortly, the helicopter would crash. Having been in one crash in Vietnam, he had no desire to be in another. Fighting against the centrifugal force that threatened to pin him to his seat, as the chopper spun wildly around, Swanson unfastened his seat belt and crawled forward, trying desperately to separate the two pilots.

There was the sound of a shot, Macklin slammed back against the door on his side of the craft and the copilot turned to bring his pistol up at Swanson. Luckily for Swanson, the copilot's aim was handicapped by his seat belt and shoulder harness. Swanson drew back his right hand

and slammed his fist against the copilot's jaw. His eyes glazed over and he dropped the pistol.

Turning to his left, Swanson tried to pull Colonel Macklin upright in his seat, but then noticed the ground coming up at them fast.

"Crash positions. We're going down," he yelled at his companions, as he tried to wedge himself between the seats.

Almost before anyone could move, the helicopter dropped low enough to hit the top of the jungle canopy. With it's forward movement stopped, the helicopter dropped like a rock, the blades still turning. In spite of his training, Corporal Arnette panicked and, jerking off his seat belt, he jumped for the closest tree limb. He hadn't counted on the still turning blades slicing through both the tree limb and his body. It was a horrible way to die.

Tumbling over and over as it fell through the canopy, the helicopter finally slammed into the ground nose first. The tail rotor tangled in the canopy overhead. The only sounds were the hot metal expanding, the gurgle of the aviation fuel as it spilled from the ruptured fuel tanks of the chopper and the various sounds made by the frightened animals that ran wildly in every direction. The impact was so severe that it even affected Hughes, who once again found himself staring at the ceiling of his bedroom.

In a fully lucid moment Hughes found that he was covered with sweat. He had thrown the cover off and was lying curled up in the bed. His wife's sleeping form was pressed against his back. He noticed that she was recovered, he could also feel her nightgown was back in place. He was torn between the thought of his wife's infidelity and the dream adventure.

His first thought was to get up and take a shower and forget the haunting dreams. Unfortunately, Hughes finally had to admit to himself that he was hooked on the story. He felt a burning desire to find out what had happened to Lieutenant Jennings. Closing his eyes, he mentally willed himself to return to the dream. He felt elated when before his eyes, he saw the jungle began to re-materialize.

Swanson was the first one to regain consciousness. Since his seat belt had been released before the crash, and he had been crouching behind the pilots' seats, he had been thrown clear of the site. Luckily, instead of being crushed by the wreckage, or being sliced by the wildly spinning blades, he had come to rest in a tangle of branches about thirty feet off the ground, relatively unharmed. He was groggy, and sore but basically unhurt. Closing his eyes until his head quit spinning, he finally felt good enough to make his way to the safety of the ground. At first his legs buckled, but he finally he was able to stagger over to the smashed chopper, looking for survivors.

His first glance showed him that, if they were lucky, the pilots were both dead. The nose of the chopper was smashed almost flat against the ground. Painfully, he climbed up the side of the chopper and pulled himself into the passenger section of the craft. Both members of his fire team who had been sitting on the left side of the craft were dead; their necks appeared to be broken. Sergeant Casey was alive, but unconscious, but bleeding profusely from his head.

Gently, he unfastened Casey's seat belt and lowered the NCO to the ground. He paused for a moment trying to place a peculiar smell that seemed to permeate the area. He glanced over the side and saw the stream of liquid that was running down the side of the chopper. Looking up and finding the source of the stream of liquid, he saw that the liquid was aviation fuel, dripping from the ruptured fuel tanks. He'd have to move fast, before some spark from the super-heated metal of the engine started a fire.

Carefully making his way around to the other side of the passenger compartment, Swanson saw that from the way blood was pouring out of Muldoon's mouth, he had some serious injuries. Swanson shook his head sadly, he was sure that Muldoon probably wouldn't last the night. Swinging over to the other side of Muldoon, he released Hitchcock, one of his own fire team members and lowered him to the ground. The last person he checked was the Lieutenant who was coming around even as Swanson worked to get him to the ground.

Dropping to the ground himself, Swanson began to drag those he had rescued away from the crash site. He knew that sooner or later, something would ignite the fire that was waiting to happen. Then it hit him, he wasn't surprised at what had happened, but he knew enough to know that the Sergeant Major had apparently expected something like this. When the bad guys showed up, he wanted to be far from this place. He walked over and sat down by the Lieutenant who was holding his head in his hands. Blood was trickling down his face from a gash on the side of his head.

"Lieutenant, we've got to get out of here," said Swanson as he laid a hand on the Lieutenant's back.

"Sure, Sarge." mumbled the groggy officer. He tried to stand and immediately fell again.

"Hold on, L.T." soothed the Sergeant as he pulled the officer up by one arm. Firmly, he held the young officer until his head cleared. When he was sure that the young officer wouldn't immediately fall on his butt again, he let him go. The Lieutenant seemed to be fine.

Leaving him to his own devices, Swanson walked over to where Sergeant Casey was moaning and holding one leg. He dropped down beside him and laid a hand on his arm.

"Just lie, still." He said as he took a piece of rag and wiped much of the blood off the injured man's face. The head injury wasn't serious. The leg injury appeared to be more serious.

"Casey, how's it hanging?" he asked as he pulled Casey's hands from the site of the injury. He could see blood seeping through the fabric of his patient's fatigue pants. Gently, Swanson pulled out his

Gerber survival knife and sliced the pants near the wound. Peeling back the material, he winced when he saw a fragment of bone sticking out of the torn skin. Casey wasn't going anywhere.

Looking over at his rifleman laying on the ground, he saw that Hitchcock seemed to be coming out of it slowly. He looked down at Casey and patted his arm.

"Don't go away, big guy. I'll be back in a moment," he said as he got to his feet and walked carefully back to the crumpled aircraft.

He studied the upended helicopter for several seconds before making his way back to its' side. Holding his breath, he once again scaled the side and pulled himself back into the passenger compartment. Carefully, he examined Muldoon and found that, as he suspected, the NCO was already dead. He moved around cautiously, feeling the precariously balanced wreck sway as he moved. Finally, he found what he was looking for, the big first-aid kit and released it so that it fell to the ground.

Swanson was no medic, but he was fairly well trained in first-aid, so his treatment of Casey's injury was more than satisfactory. In an hour, he had the NCO sitting comfortably by a small fire, several dozen C-Ration cans stacked by his side, as well as two five-gallon canteens of water. Though it hadn't been said, they all knew that Casey was going to have to be left at the crash site until help could be sent back from the Post.

"Well, my man. That's about all that I can do for you," said Swanson as he stood up and stretched his sore back.

"You going to leave me here?" asked Casey as he shifted his leg to a more comfortable position by the fire.

"You think you're up for a walk in the woods?" Swanson grinned as he studied his patient.

"Nope." Casey leaned back against his makeshift pillow. "Just asking is all. I'd just as soon sit here all warm and comfortable until you all come back and get me."

Swanson looked over at the Lieutenant who was leaning against a tree, looking at the crashed helicopter. His mind seemed to be a million miles away. Swanson walked over to the young officer and tapped him on the shoulder.

"Uh, yes, Sergeant." said Bill as he turned away from the wreck site.

"Lieutenant, you and I need to talk," he said, placing himself squarely in front of the pale young man.

"Uh, sure. What do we talk about?" asked the Lieutenant as his troubled eyes watched the Sergeant lying by the fire.

"We just damn near died and it has something to do with you. Now I want to know what the fuck is going on!" demanded the angry Sergeant First Class as he grabbed the Lieutenant by the front of his uniform.

"I'm not sure, Sergeant. I honestly am not sure I know what's going on." said the Lieutenant as he meet the angry Sergeant's gaze calmly.

Slowly Swanson's temper calmed and he released his grip on the Lieutenant's collar.

"Well, I've got a hot news flash for you, bud, somebody wanted you dead and were willing to risk crashing a chopper to do it. The Battalion Sergeant Major sent us to rescue you. Now someone needs to rescue us. Furthermore, in case you didn't see what happened the copilot shot the command pilot. This is not a normal occurrence.

Now, I know that I have no idea what this is all about and none of the others knew or had anything worth dying over. So it has to be you and whatever you were doing on that range today. That's why the Sergeant Major sent an armed fire team out to get you."

Bill pursed his lips and put his hands on his hips.

"I was ordered to investigate the training accident that you all had last week."

"Lieutenant Larson's death?" interrupted Swanson as the two began to walk back toward the fire.

"Yes, that's the one," agreed Bill, "Sergeant Casey and Sergeant Muldoon were afraid to talk to me in garrison, so it was decided that we would drive out to the range. After all, sooner or later I would have to come out and look at the jeep."

"Make's sense, I guess." offered Swanson.

"We never really got a chance to talk before you arrived, but I did find this embedded in the back of Larson's seat cushion." Bill said as he dug the lump of copper covered lead out of his shirt pocket and held it out to the Sergeant.

Swanson took the lump from the Lieutenant and held it up to the light.

"Looks to me like it's a .45 round. So what?" he said as he looked back at Bill.

"Just this, Sergeant. If Lieutenant Larson was shot accidentally with a .50 caliber machine gun while on the range, then what was a .45 round doing embedded in his seat, right about where his chest would be?" said Bill as he took back the bullet. "It's my belief that he was shot and killed before the accident. I suspect that he was dead before the .50 caliber rounds were fired at him. In other words, I think he was murdered, probably by whoever drove him that day or at least with the driver's knowledge."

Swanson stopped and whistled softly to himself.

"God, if you're right, then this could be a real mess. If you could find that bullet so easily, then why didn't the Criminal Investigation Division investigators find it? I know that several of them went out to that range and spent the better part of a day investigating the scene, or so they said. Sounds to me like it was a half-assed investigation."

Bill dropped down to sit by the fire and leaned back on his elbows.

"The thing that puzzles me is how the killers were able to react so fast. We found the bullet less than ten minutes before you landed. I couldn't really tell what happened, but it looked to me like the copilot already had his instructions before you even got here. That means he had to receive the instructions to kill the pilot prior to leaving the Post."

"Not necessarily, LT. Those choppers had more than one method of communication. The co-pilot could have gotten the word to do what he did in a dozen different ways. Only thing I can figure is that there was someone watching you and reporting back, probably by radio." He paused and stared at the fire for a moment, "I don't know what or how it happened, but I do know one thing. We've got to get that bullet back to Sergeant Major Smith."

Swanson raised his voice and looked over at Hitchcock, who was methodically cleaning his M-16.

"We're going to have to get a move on if we're going to get to Fort Davis by dark. We're probably ten or fifteen miles away from base. Casey can't come with us, his leg is too bad. For some reason, Lieutenant, everyone wants you back in garrison as soon as possible. So we walk cross country."

Bill nodded and got to his feet, brushing at the seat of his tattered khaki trousers. For a moment he swayed, the world spun around him, but quickly his head cleared and he gestured toward the Sergeant.

"Ready when you are." he said as he walked past Swanson to kneel beside Casey.

"Sergeant Casey, you going to be O.K.?" he asked in concern.

"Shit, Lieutenant, I've had hurts lots worse than this one. 'Fore you know it, I'll be back running these jungle-covered hills. But for now, I get to rest. You go on and tell them what you found. That's the most important thing." the NCO replied as he studied the young Lieutenant's face.

Nodding, Bill got to his feet and looked over at Swanson.

"Well, Sergeant, I have no idea where we are in relation to the Post. If you do, please lead the way," he said as he glanced one last time over at the wrecked helicopter.

"Follow me, Lieutenant." The NCO picked up his own M-16 from the ground and tossed another over to the Lieutenant. Turning he headed off across the clearing.

Lieutenant Jennings and Private Hitchcock shouldered their weapons and followed along behind him. Bill's last sight was of Casey snoring peacefully beside the small fire, and then he was into the jungle, straining to keep sight of Swanson. Within ten steps his khaki uniform was soaked with sweat and his low-quarters beginning to rub a blister on his right heel. Then suddenly, Swanson vanished.

Startled, Bill ran forward and saw that the Sergeant had started to make his way down an almost vertical hillside into a ravine that cut across their path. With a weary sigh, Bill began to work his way down that same hillside.

Hughes' perception continued to hover over the scene of the crash. He was puzzled as to why he was remaining in one spot, as the only thing to be seen was the snoring Sergeant Casey. It was clear that Casey was enjoying his enforced rest. In spite of the pain in his shattered leg, it was nice and peaceful laying in the clearing and dozing quietly. If he had running water, he would be perfectly happy to stay here for quite some time.

Suddenly Hughes and Casey both were startled by a noise. Casey painfully straightened as he was pulled from his doze by the sound of voices and the thunk of a machete cutting into the underbrush. It would appear that he was going to be rescued sooner than he had anticipated.

"Help!" he yelled as he struggled to turn over and spot his rescuers.

"Help! Over here." he yelled again as he struggled to sit up so that he could be seen from the crash site.

His next yell froze in his throat as he got a look at the file of men that came out of the trees. Instead of the familiar green camouflaged uniforms worn by U. S. troops, he saw that these men were dressed in solid black, with blue berets. Over their faces they wore black mesh, which effectively concealed their identity. While half of the column surrounded the crashed chopper, several of them came to stand around Casey. After a short conference, one of them left the crash and walked over to Casey.

"Where is Lieutenant Jennings?" rasped the new comer, leaning over the reclining Sergeant.

"Who the hell are you?" demanded Casey as he edged back toward the M-16 lying in the grass behind him.

Taking the time to steal a glance around him, Casey saw that his weapon was missing. Looking back at the man towering over him, Casey began to feel uneasy. The guy kept giggling all the time he was edging closer to the wounded soldier. When he was close enough to Casey to touch him, the masked man pulled a large gleaming knife from a sheath on his belt.

"Let me ask that question again." he said as he knelt down beside Casey's injured leg.

Mercifully, Hughes was instantly transferred to the location of the jungle group.

Swanson paused when he heard piercing screams echoing over the jungle. Instinctively, he knew who was making those tortured sounds and cursed. Someone was going to pay for this shit and pay big, he swore to himself. Hughes silently agreed with the big NCO.

CHAPTER ELEVEN

Hughes was now hovering in an office he didn't recognized. He did recognize General Goodrich and it was very clear that Major General Goodrich was in an unbelievable rage. It wasn't bad enough that he had one dead Lieutenant on his hands, but now it seemed that he had two dead line officers and possibly two other aviation officers, one of who was a God Damn field grade. It was unbelievable, at this rate; his entire command would be dead of unexplained causes in no time.

"What the fuck are you people doing? How many of my young officers are you folks going to kill before this mess is over. Where's my damn helicopter?" he demanded of Lieutenant Colonel Green, who stood in front of the General's desk.

"General, I sent that young man over there to bail your ass out of a problem you asked me to help you with. I had absolutely no idea that something would happen to him. As for the chopper, all I know is that it has failed to report back. We don't know that it's crashed and I don't know if Jennings is dead." objected Green as he folded his massive arms and glared back at the enraged General.

"We were very careful to make sure that he was chaperoned the entire time he was to be at Fort Davis by two NCOs. An hour ago he was to be picked up by chopper and returned to Fort Clayton. To insure that he would be safely returned, an armed fire team was on board the chopper. Now the Lieutenant, the two NCOs, the armed fire team and the chopper are all missing. That is all that we know." explained Green patiently for the hundredth time.

"Oh wonderful, a third NCO and a fully armed fire team gone who are dispatched at the totally unauthorized request of your Sergeant Major! To make matters worse, without any command authorization they draw live ammo and then simply vanish. An armed fire team in direct violation of standing orders regarding when live ammunition can be issued." Goodrich's temper took control and he swept his in-box off his desk onto the highly polished floor. Green simply ignored the outburst.

Finally calming down, Goodrich began to think.

"Green, is this some more of your Brotherhood shit?" he demanded as he jumped to his feet and glared his rage at the big Colonel. "You people seem to forget that I am in command of this Brigade. I don't want any of you Brotherhood characters running off half cocked."

Green shook his head decisively.

"General, I've checked with everyone all the way to the Pentagon. None of the Council of Twelve has any knowledge of these happenings. The Brotherhood does have some independent operations running, but none of them would have any impact on what has been taking place."

Dropping down into his desk chair, Goodrich struggled to bring his temper back under control. Having seen such displays of temper before, Green merely stood and watched calmly as the General composed himself, swung his chair around, grabbed up his phone and dialed a two-digit extension.

"Get Sergeant Major Ashe in here."

The two senior officers simply sat and starred at each other as they waited for the Brigade Sergeant Major to arrive. Shortly, there was a timid tap at the door.

"Enter!" yelled Goodrich, as he got ready to ream out his senior NCO.

To their surprise, it was not Ashe who came in the door, but the rather pretty Specialist 4th Class that worked as the Sergeant Major's clerk.

"Where's Ashe?" demanded the General.

"Uh, sir, he had to leave." stammered the terrified clerk, tears in her eyes.

"Leave, for what reason?" demanded the irate General.

"Sergeant Major Villanueva, sir, he had to leave because of Sergeant Major Villanueva." she managed to stammer between her sobs.

"What the flying fuck are you talking about?" bellowed the totally exasperated General, throwing his desk calendar across the room in his frustration.

First his Colonels were sending off Lieutenants who managed to get themselves lost; Sergeant Majors were sending out armed fire teams without permission and now his Brigade Sergeant Major had disappeared. He vowed to himself that some heads would roll over this one. Green, however, seemed to sense what the girl was going to say. Before she even opened her mouth, he closed his eyes and dropped his head.

"He's dead, sir. Sergeant Major Villanueva is dead," she finally managed to gasp before collapsing limply to the floor in a dead faint.

Major General Goodrich looked like he was going to have apoplexy. He was so overwhelmed that he could only make little gasping noises in the back of his throat and wave his arms as he fell back into his chair. Green looked at him and slowly shook his head. Taking a deep breath, Lieutenant Colonel Green very carefully put his fatigue cap firmly on his head and marched out the door, carefully stepping over the unconscious girl on the floor. His driver already had the jeep started and waiting outside the door to Brigade Headquarters.

"Fort Clayton! And break the speed laws." snapped Green as he jumped into the waiting jeep.

Private Barney Ross had been Lieutenant Colonel Green's driver for almost a year. Generally the only thing the Colonel ever said to him was 'slow down'. Now he was being told to move it and move it he did. They took some corners on two wheels, shot through intersections and passed everything on the road. The Colonel said not a word, but merely held onto the dash with both hands. Glancing at the Colonel's grim face from the corner of his eye, Ross was sure that there would be hell to pay before this day was over. When they arrived at the entrance to Fort Clayton there were five Military Police and two Pan Canal Police cars hot on their tail. Green ignored them completely.

Ross was forced to let the Colonel out just inside the gate to Fort Clayton, the Military Police road blocks wouldn't let them get any closer. A Pan Canal cop dashed over to block the Colonel's path, but Green simply picked him up by the collar and threw him to one side. The rest of the pursuing cops wisely gave the Colonel a wide berth. The entire Battalion must have been standing around watching the firemen battle to put out the fire that was raging in the Battalion Headquarters. As they noticed their Colonel striding purposefully toward them, the crowd parted and let him through. He came to a stunned stop at the curb. Almost the entire front of the Headquarters building appeared to have been blown out from the inside. Where the Sergeant Major's office had once been was now just a massive hole in the corner of the building. Green's legs buckled and he dropped down to sit on the curb in front of the ruined building. He couldn't believe what had happened.

Hughes' perception or dream self suddenly left the scene of the fire and found himself hovering inside what were obviously a set of private quarters. His confusion was relieved when he saw Julie Jennings walk into the living room. Julie was happily humming and cleaning her new home. She was determined to surprise Bill when he came home that night.

When Bill's new military sponsor and his wife, Lieutenant Fred Peterson and his wife Glenda, came by the new quarters to see her, she asked them to help her coordinate with the furniture division to have enough furniture delivered to let them stay in their new house that night. After stopping by the warehouse to pick out her new furniture, they had taken her by the Post Exchange to grocery shop. It took over three hours to run these few errands and return her to her new home. When they finally left her, Julie was working happily in her empty quarters. The furniture truck was due any time.

She was on her knees scrubbing the commode when she heard a knock outside. Pulling off her rubber gloves, she wiped her hands on a towel as she walked to the living room. Through the glass louvered door she could see a slim dark haired young lady waiting on her front porch. Curious, she opened the door and stepped onto the porch.

"Yes, can I help you?" she asked politely, brushing some loose strands of hair from her face.

"Yes, I am here to conduct a final check of your quarters before the furniture is delivered." the young lady said with a smile as she slipped past Julie into the quarters.

Feeling a little annoyed at her visitor's pushiness, but aware that the military did things differently from the real world, Julie followed her back inside and closed the door. Looking at her clipboard, her visitor began to pace off the dimensions of the various rooms. After watching her for a few minutes, Julie went back to her cleaning. She had barely gotten started again when there was another knock at the door. Muttering to herself, Julie peeled off her gloves and started toward the door again. As she walked past the young lady from Housing, something hit her on the side of her head and the lights went out.

Dropping her clipboard to the floor beside Julie's unconscious form, the bogus Housing Representative grabbed Julie's wrists and slowly drug her unconscious body back into the bedroom. Swiftly she rolled Julie over on to her stomach and, pulling a set of handcuffs from her purse, fastened the unconscious woman's wrists together. She then shoved a small rag in Julie's unresisting mouth and, pulling a roll of wide masking tape from her purse, she tore off a long strip and plastered it securely over Julie's mouth. Closing the door to that bedroom, the imposture walked out to the living room, opened the front door and greeted the postman who stood impatiently on the porch.

"I believe that these are Lieutenant Jennings' quarters," said the Postman as he dug into the large brown leather bag he had hanging from one of his shoulders.

The pretty dark-haired woman smiled back at him.

"Sure are, I'm his wife, Julie," she said with a dimpled smile.

"Well, nice to know you ma'am." he said as he handed her several envelopes and a small package.

"Thank you, sir." she replied, watching him walk back down the walkway.

With the smile still on her face, the young lady stepped back into the quarters and shut the door. She glanced at the letters as she tossed them to the floor and made a small sound of triumph as she quickly tore the wrappings off of the package. As they had suspected, Larson had put what they were looking for in the mail to his best friend. She dropped the small notebook into her side pocket and opened the door to the bedroom. She saw that the unconscious woman was beginning to stir. She had rolled over onto her side and was struggling against the cuffs, making muffled sounds against the tape across her mouth.

With a look of regret on her pretty face, the bogus Housing Representative pulled a gaily-decorated scarf from around her neck and knelt over Julie. Swiftly, she rolled Julie back onto her stomach, threw one leg over the semi-conscious girl and sat heavily on her back. Moving so fast her movements were a blur, she wrapped the scarf around Julie's slender neck twice. Leaning her weight back, she pulled the scarf tight. As her air was cut off, Julie began to gasp weakly. The bigger woman then began to tighten and loosen the scarf, causing Julie to buck and struggle for air. From her expression, the killer enjoyed her work.

Finally, tiring of the game, the woman held the scarf tight around Julie's neck until she quit moving. Placing her hand beneath Julie's long hair the killer felt for a pulse. She found none. When she was assured her victim was dead, the woman returned the scarf around her own neck and stood.

Reaching in her pocket for the key, the killer removed the handcuffs. She rolled the dead girl over onto her back and pulled her into a sitting position. Slowly, she removed Julie's blouse and unfastened her bra. Lowering her torso, the killer then removed Julie's shoes and pants, leaving her in just her panties. Rolling her over onto her stomach, the Killer quickly used the masking tape to tightly bind her wrists and elbows together. Pausing, she experienced a moment of regret as she viewed the lovely body, so beautiful and so dead. Slowly, she spread Julie's legs apart and finished setting the stage.

From her purse, the lovely assassin pulled a used rubber, filled with sperm. She untied the top of the rubber container as she reached down and pulled Julie's cunt lips apart. Quickly, she forced the sperm from the rubber into and onto Julie's cunt and upper thighs. Finally, satisfied with her work, the killer stood and stretched. Looking around, insuring that she had overlooked nothing, she slipped out the back door. What was to have been a happy home was now a house of death. Had Hughes been able to cry, he would have at the death of so lovely a woman.

Given no time for mourning, once again Hughes found his essence transported to the group in the jungle.

Swanson and his companions were moving as fast as they could in the rapidly falling darkness. Since the Lieutenant was not familiar with the jungle, they were forced to move slowly to accommodate his state of physical conditioning and the thick undergrowth. Swanson broke the trail and Hitchcock made sure that Bill didn't fall too far behind. Finally, however, after several hours of walking, Bill had gone as far as he could and after they had forded two shallow rivers that left his low quarters and socks soaking wet, they were forced to make camp in a clearing on the banks of a third river.

Normally, Swanson would have preferred a cold camp, but due to the fact that the Lieutenant was wearing khaki's, which were certainly not suitable dress for jungle operations, Swanson built a small fire. After wringing out his socks and putting them and his shoes out to dry, Bill lay by the fire exhausted, until Swanson stuck a C-Ration can of pork and beans under his nose. Normally, Jennings detested C-Rations, but in this particular instance, he would have eaten a horse. His stomach reminded him that he had eaten nothing since breakfast.

Finishing his pork and beans, Bill washed them down with several swallows of water from one of the canteens. Sitting back against a nearby tree, Bill began to take stock of his situation. The three of them had covered what seemed like a hundred miles since the crash, but he knew they hadn't gone far.

"Well, Sergeant, how far have we come?" he asked, as he folded his arms around his knees.

"About three or four miles, I guess. You have to remember in Panama there is straight-line distance and there is ground distance. The difference can be a surprising amount of distance. For example, from where we crashed, it's about ten or twelve miles Fort Davis. However, on the ground it's actually closer to twenty miles, most of which is up and down."

They all started as they heard a crash in the jungle to their right. Bill reached over and pulled his M-16 closer. He was uneasy and wished he could be as calm about the rigors of their situation as were Swanson and Hitchcock.

"Rest easy, Lieutenant. That's nothing but a Hollow Monkey or some such creature," laughed Hitchcock as he tried to make himself comfortable on the hard ground.

"What's a Hollow Monkey?" asked Bill glancing at the dark jungle around them.

Swanson grinned and eased his own long frame back against a small hillock.

"Well, Lieutenant, a Hollow Monkey is a monkey that stands about four and half feet tall. It usually runs in packs and is very territorial in nature. I've heard stories about patrols walking into Hollow Monkey areas and being spotted by a pack of the little devils. They aren't particularly dangerous, but they do have one habit that distinguishes them from other monkeys."

"What's that?" asked Bill curiously, fascinated by the story.

"They will shit in their hand and throw the shit at the last man in the patrol. It can make for some pretty funny situations," answered Swanson with a chuckle.

The fire had begun to die down and the darkness was reclaiming the jungle clearing. As long as they didn't make a move, Bill was unable to pick out the location of his companions.

"Don't forget what happened to Lieutenant Martin's platoon last week." said Hitchcock from the dark.

"What happened?" asked Bill, as he felt his muscles begin to relax.

"There was a Battalion size operation last week. A Company had been assigned to train in Area Mosquito." began Swanson as he shifted to get more comfortable. "That's an area where we do training for the Jungle Operations School. There are neither roads nor any other ways in or out but by sea or by air. A Company was dropped in by air and each Platoon operated in its own area. Larson's platoon drew the mission of occupying a hill at the far end of the area, overlooking the sea. Lieutenant Martin's platoon drew the assignment of patrolling the central valley.

The first night, his people were tired and all were rather lax on security since the aggressor force wasn't due to be dropped in until the next morning. I got this story from Sergeant Crosby, Lieutenant Martin's

Platoon sergeant. He had put two of his newer people on guard and they were both trying not to fall asleep. One was armed with an M-60 and the other with an M-16. Now you know that when we use blanks, we have these big red blank adapters screwed on the end of the barrels of our weapons. The M-60 has a huge bright red adapter, in the firelight it flickers.

It's a well-known fact that bright things fascinate Hollow Monkeys. This night a Hollow Monkey was sitting in a tree near where the sentry was patrolling with his M-60. The reflection of the firelight off of the blank adapter caught the monkey's attention. The sentry walked under the tree where the monkey was sitting and the monkey simply reached down and grabbed the M-60 out of his hands.

Now naturally, this freaked out the poor sentry who had only seen this big hairy hand come out of the dark and grab his weapon. Deciding he had other places to be, the sentry went running through the camp screaming like a banshee. Lieutenant Martin jumped to his feet in time to be knocked ass end over teakettle by the panicked sentry. Unfortunately, when Martin got hit, he fell head first into the campfire and caught his hair on fire.

When Sergeant Crosby woke up, he saw Martin rolling around on the ground beating at his burning hair. He rushed over to help the Lieutenant put out his burning hair and realized that the entire platoon was in an uproar. He tried to restore order and managed to get things quieted down. Then he sees this monkey come strolling into camp, apparently attracted by the smell of the stew that they had left heating for breakfast. The strange part was that the monkey was carrying the machine gun just like he had seen our people do it, with the butt plate braced against his hip. His finger happened to be in the trigger guard. Behind him he was dragging a long belt of blank rounds, still attached to the gun.

The other sentry thought the platoon was under attack and he started blasting away with his M-16. Not knowing what was happening, the rest of the Platoon started blasting away again, in every direction, with every weapon that they had. At this point they had total chaos on their hands, but Martin brought it under control. Of course, that was after he got the fire in his hair put out.

Crosby told me that it was almost a rout and most of the troops, the Lieutenant included, still had no earthly idea who was attacking them. Then the funniest thing happened. The Monkey was apparently startled by the firing and instinctively tightened his grip on the M-60. Somehow he pulled the trigger. So he opens up and fires almost the entire belt attached to the machine gun. Lieutenant Martin had his back to the monkey and was so startled when the monkey started firing that he actually crapped in his pants.

All the commotion had the monkey so terrified, especially when the M-60 he was holding went off, that he had a heart attack and keeled over backward with his finger still on the trigger. Lieutenant Martin had to be medivaced out of the area with third degree burns to his scalp, which is why he now wears a crew cut, and of course he had to change his britches. Oh, and incidentally, Crosby said that he was laughing so hard at the chaos that he wet his own pants."

Swanson waited until the laughing died down and then kicked some dirt over the fire. "Now go to sleep. We've got a long day ahead of us."

Basking in the heat still generated by the coals of the fire, Bill drifted off to sleep. When he next opened his eyes, it was dawn; he was looking at the business end of an M-16 held by a black suited man wearing a blue beret. He started to jump to his feet but his captor reversed his weapon and slammed the stock of the weapon against his jaw. He fell into darkness.

Hughes was again hovering in Goodrich's office.

General Goodrich sat quietly, looking at the stark black letters on the report in front of him in shock. This little escapade had cost him one helicopter, four officers, three NCOs, and four enlisted personnel. Other casualties were one Battalion Sergeant Major dead, most of the Battalion staff of 4/20 dead or in the hospital and that lovely little Julie Jennings, the Lieutenant's wife, dead, apparently a murder victim in her own quarters. The C.I.D. claimed that the killer hadn't left a single clue but that t had definitely been rape since the killer had left sperm all over the girl's body. It was unbelievable that his Brigade should have been made to look so completely inept.

He raised his eyes to look at the three colonels in front of him. His three Battalion Commanders were as shaken as he was by all that had happened. It was just simply unbelievable. He had no idea how to handle it.

"Well, gentlemen, we have to make a statement, not only to higher headquarters, but we've got local media and one or two national representatives here. If we don't handle this just right, we're going to look like fools. Suggestions?"

It was Colonel Green who acted as the spokesman for the senior members of his command.

"I suggest that we just ignore it and it'll go away," he said.

General Goodrich shook his hand slowly.

"I wish I could believe It.," he said as his eyes searched the faces of his officers, "but we have to make some type of statement."

Green leaned forward and pointed a finger at the General.

"General, I speak for the Brotherhood in this matter and this is the way it will be handled. Steps have already been taken to make sure that there will be no inquiries from the media. Those national media representatives who are here are being recalled," he said firmly.

That pretty much ended the General's meeting. He handled it just the way that Colonel Green had directed and it worked. General Goodrich finished his tour peacefully, to be reassigned to a desk in Washington D.C. All of the senior Brotherhood members involved in the escapade went on to bigger and better things. Later that day, an unmarked Leer Jet left Howard Air Force carrying a very important person back to Washington D.C. He was satisfied that the secret operations being conducted in the Panama Canal Zone would continue unmolested.

Hughes was suddenly brought into full wakefulness as his bedside alarm rang long and hard. He awoke with a feeling of satisfaction that he had finally gotten to the end of the dream, but puzzled that what he had seen seemed to be so familiar. But that night had left him with many more questions than it had answered. Not the least of which was whether or not his wife was having an affair. The next question was what it all meant. He would have to ponder on it.

PART TWO

HELL IN SESSION

CHAPTER TWELVE

THAT SAME NIGHT

PHOENIX, ARIZONA-SHERATON HOTEL

The huge garish sign in the richly furnished lobby of the Phoenix Sheraton announced that Senator Hyman Schwarz was having a fund-raising dinner in the main dining room. Some of the very wealthy that arrived in their gleaming limousines followed the directions on the sign and headed for the closed doors to the main dining room. Others sniffed as if there was a bad odor in the hotel as they went in the other direction toward the bar. One thing about the senior Senator from Arizona, he definitely generated public reaction.

As one of the most controversial members of the United States Senate, Hyman Schwarz was a national institution. He had first been elected at age 60 as a conservative Republican and now at age 80, he was still running, still the favorite son of Arizona. The liberals hated him. At the same time, Senator Hyman's controversial nature aroused a lot of anger from the general public toward himself and his programs. As probably the best-known conservative in the Senate, his mere appearance at the podium would bring horrendous hissing from the visitors' gallery. Hyman loved the attention of the demonstrators, but his security people feared for his life.

On this warm Arizona night, Hyman Schwarz was having another one of his famous fundraisers. After all, even though he was now a multimillionaire, he never liked to spend his own money for any reason. These fundraisers were known nationwide for the antics committed by some of the attendees, for they were actually very much like stag parties. The booze flowed like water and there were rumors about topless dancers and other adult 'entertainment'. Everyone knew about Hyman Schwarz, he was an institution.

By 7:30 P.M. the room was full of the wealthy and the famous, the doors closed and guarded by both Phoenix police and Schwarz's own security personnel. The party was in full swing. Seated at the table in the front of the room were the invited dignitaries. At the center of the table, of course, was the good Senator Hyman Schwarz; to his right were Congressman Lester Adder, Circuit Judge Oscar Putnam and Moultrie Anderson, a big campaign contributor. To the Senator's left was Sheriff Buster Kildare, Governor Martin O'Hara and Lyle Prescott, scion of the super rich Prescott Beer family. Even though many of these people had appeared on magazine covers and television often enough to have gained some national prominence, on this night there were no cameras allowed at this particular event, too many important people might be embarrassed.

Senator Schwarz leaned over to the Sheriff, pulling back slightly at the bad breath that emanated from the police officer's huge mouth. Biggest mouth I ever saw that didn't have a hook in it, thought the Senator, suppressing a shudder.

"Did you spring Daisy Miller and her girls for this one night?" asked the Senator with a leer as he reached for his first toddy of the evening.

Sheriff Buster Kildare grinned and burped, running one of his blunt fingers inside his lower lip to search for a piece of food. He was already showing the effects of the punch, which was sure strong this year.

"Sure did, Senator. She and all her girls are waiting in the next room as the main entertainment of the evening." he said in a whisper, getting closer to the Senator than the Senator cared for, "you gotta try that new girl of hers, Doris. She's got a superstructure on her better than any ship I ever did see."

Senator Schwarz nodded without answering; he had noticed that new girl and planned on making her his private stock for the evening, or maybe longer. Daisy Miller was probably the most famous madam within two hundred miles of Phoenix. She and her girls had been a tolerated institution in the area for as long as Schwarz had been in the Senate. Wanting to make sure that this fundraiser was spectacular in every respect, and since he secretly knew that he would probably not live out the upcoming term, he had asked Daisy to furnish the entertainment for the evening.

Unfortunately, Daisy had wanted to charge more than the Senator wanted to pay, so he had arranged for his good friend Sheriff Kildare to raid Daisy's place of business and arrest her and all of her girls. The bail was set, by another of the Senator's good friends, Judge Putnam, at such a level that there was no chance that Daisy could raise the money quickly enough to get back in business anytime soon. Then, just when it seemed obvious to all that Daisy was going to jail for prostitution, the deal was offered, if Daisy furnished the entertainment for free to Senator Schwarz's fund raiser, all charges would be dropped. Daisy knew when the fix was in and happily agreed.

Schwarz was ecstatic over the turn out for this fundraiser. He had managed to get people to attend who had never showed an interest in politics before. He was especially proud of getting Oscar Windsor, the biggest real estate man in Phoenix, to attend.

In previous years, Windsor had always politely declined, to the point that Schwarz asked some of his political friends in the State to do a background check on the man. Many of Schwarz's backers supported him, not because they liked his politics, but because they liked the fact that he didn't reveal the dirt he seemed to have on them. They had reported back that Windsor's background was absolutely clean, what they could trace of it. The main things were that Oscar had more money than Midas and a lot of political clout. Schwarz was confident that Windsor's support was easily worth ten thousand votes.

With the exception of his good friend, the Vice President of the United States who was involved in a campaign trip for the President in California, all of Schwarz's closest friends and backers had come for this fundraiser. It was good to be a Republican. He was a shoe-in for this election, even without the rigging of the ballot returns always conducted by his good friend, Macy Bloom, head of the Board of Elections.

As he exchanged comments with the other men at the head table, his eyes traveled over the room. He could see that all of his guests were having fun and most were feeling no pain, even the few females among them were enjoying themselves. He kept a special eye on Mr. Windsor who was quietly sipping a drink and seemingly staring off into space. He'd make sure that Daisy singled him out for special attention. That would help him loosen up.

Looking over at his senior administrative assistant, Angela Ortega, Schwarz motioned for the meal to be served. While the waiters and waitresses were running around serving the guests, Porter Watson, his campaign manager came to lean over his chair.

"It's your best year ever, Boss." he said in a low voice as he pulled a folded paper out of his pocket.

Still smiling at his guests, Schwarz leaned back and spoke out of the side of his mouth.

"What's the take?" he asked as he caught the eye of Windsor and lifted his glass in a toast to the real estate mogul. Windsor smiled back, and then paused to take his cellular phone from his pocket and hold it to his ear.

"Five million and change. About twice what we expected by this point in the evening." exulted his manager as he showed his candidate the sheet of figures. "After your "join the party" speech, we should be able to double that figure tonight."

After this bit of information, Schwarz was in seventh heaven, he was a certainty to be re-elected and after the election, he would use the left-over campaign funds for that new house he wanted in Zurich with maybe a little to spend on that new girl of Daisy's. Life was good, even at his somewhat advanced age. All that would be needed to make this a perfect night would be a roll in the hay with one or more of Daisy's best.

When he was assured that all of his guests had been served their food, Senator Schwarz stood and lifted his glass.

"My friends, I want to thank you for coming tonight. Once again, I ask for your support in my efforts to bring a conservative balance to the Senate. With your help we can continue our never-ending struggle for truth, justice and the American Way."

With that innate talent he had for knowing how to work an audience, Hyman continued his supposedly impromptu speech, playing on the emotions of his slightly drunk guests until they were ready to carry him back to Washington on their shoulders. Since this was his last fund raiser before his retirement, he decided that he was going to go for broke, he was going to try and raise a record ten million dollars in one night, a record that would stand for a long, long time.

"Folks, campaigns like mine are expensive to run. I know you have given a great deal of your time, money and support to my campaign over the years, but I need more, much more. If our campaign to bring decency and morality back to this great nation is going to succeed, then we will need you and your friends to give until it hurts. I, therefore, ask you who will be the first to stand up and be counted. Who will be the first to join our Legion of Decency?"

On a roll now in his call for his vision of a new future for America, Hyman Schwarz reached behind him for the basket that he always kept beside his chair for unexpected donations.

"Who will be the first to step forward and put his all behind a campaign for a new morality for this great nation?"

To Schwarz's total delight, the first man on his feet was Oscar Windsor. For a moment, Windsor seemed to sway, appearing unsteady on his feet. For a moment, Windsor just stood rubbing the nub of his missing right index finger before starting to make his way to the head table. Schwarz's greedy eyes locked on the wealthy real estate magnate as he made his way toward the head table.

The applause was deafening as his peers congratulated the new-comer's patriotic fervor. That and the knowledge that with a new sucker in their midst, the bite on each of them would be a little less. Nodding his head in recognition of their gratitude and support, Windsor stopped in front of the beaming Senator and reached inside his coat. No one noticed that Windsor's eyes were looking everywhere except in front of him.

Schwarz was already anticipating the large number of zeros he would see on the check he knew was forthcoming. He was a little sur-prised that the previously apolitical real estate man was the first to stand. But, it did appear that Schwarz had managed to convince Windsor that he should offer his full support, he was proud to see that he hadn't lost his touch.

But Windsor wasn't reaching for his checkbook; in fact, his proposed donation wasn't quite what Schwarz had in mind. What Windsor pulled out of the inside of his coat was not his checkbook, instead, he threw back his jacket and pulled up a cut-down Colt AR15- 9 millimeter, fully automatic, assault rifle that had been held under his coat by a strap over his shoulder. Schwarz's eyes bulged out of his wrinkled face as he looked at the hard-featured face of Oscar Windsor.

"You and your kind are what is wrong with this country. Here's your donation, Senator," said Windsor as he pulled the trigger of his assault rifle. On full automatic, it took mere seconds to totally decimate the people sitting at the head table. Most amazing of all, was that with the sophisticated silencer attached to the weapon, for several seconds, no one in the audience knew that anyone had been shot.

Witnesses later said that Windsor never altered his expression as he emptied the 30 round magazine into the dignitaries in front of him. Pressing the magazine release, he dropped the expended magazine to the floor and inserted another. Spinning around, he began to spray the crowded room with 9-millimeter rounds, making sure that he first dropped the security guards who were dashing toward him, clawing for their weapons.

To make maters worse, several of the waiters dropped their trays and pulled out automatic pistols. They began to fire into the struggling mass of humanity clawing for the lobby doors. Bleeding from two head wounds, Milt Siggerson, the billionaire oil man from Tucson pulled his own 9 mm from his hand tooled hip holster and fired back at the waiters. He nodded in satisfaction when two of them spun around and collapsed. There were other weapons in the room, but their owners were busy running for the door, trying to survive.

Sheriff Kildare, who bragged that he always carried a .44 magnum even in church hit the floor and stayed there. He never moved throughout the entire incident, though later he made a great show of, modestly of course, telling the press of his own heroics. No one dared mentioned that in the course of his heroics he has soiled his pants.

Lieutenant Louis Lazard of the Phoenix Police Department had left the dining room to make a telephone call, so he didn't see the beginning of the carnage. He always hated these functions and spent as little time as possible in attendance. The first he knew about a problem was when Eva Elias came stumbling through the dining room doors and fell to the floor. Hotel personnel came running from every direction to check on the fallen woman, after all, she owned over thirty percent of the land around the city.

She was babbling incoherently and pointing toward the dining room, when Lazard got to her. He had no idea what she was talking about, but he recognized the stains on her arms as being bloodstains so he was alerted that something was wrong.

"What's wrong ma'am? Are you hurt?" he asked, kneeling beside the sobbing woman.

"All those poor people!" she sobbed, "he's killing them."

Getting to his feet and pulling his service revolver, still uncertain about what was happening, he glanced over at the Concierge.

"Pierre, call Police Headquarters and tell them there is a problem at Senator Schwarz's fund raiser." he said as he dashed across the lobby and jerked open the doors to the dining room. He was almost trampled by the stampede of the rich and famous.

Struggling against the flow, like a Salmon swimming upstream, Lazard fought his way into the dining room. It took but a moment for the experienced Lazard to size up the situation. Staying low, he dove into the room into the shelter of an overturned table, coming up beside a bloody body that had earlier been a prominent local businessman. Slowly, he peered around the edge of the table and saw Windsor changing magazines in his assault rifle. Seeing his opportunity, he jumped to his feet.

"Police, drop your weapon!" he demanded.

Windsor's answer was to swing around and point his weapon at the Police Lieutenant, triggering a burst of lead. Two of the renegade waiters began to flank him, firing at him. Spinning, Lazard snapped off a shot at the one on his left, feeling satisfied when the terrorist flipped over backward, falling limply to the floor. Hearing a noise behind him, Lazard whirled around and froze, his eyes riveted on the weapon pointed at his head.

"Say good by, pig." sneered the skinny waiter in the ill fitting uniform, slowly placing the barrel of his weapon against Lazard's forehead.

There was a shot and Lazard flinched, waiting for the pain. To his surprise, the waiter crumpled and almost fell on him. Glancing to the side, he saw Siggerson wave at him from the floor, his own pistol clutched in his bloody hand.

"Get him, boy!" yelled the oil man weakly, motioning toward the head table.

Clutching his pistol in the correct grip, Lazard dove to his right, Windsor's hail of bullets shredding the table behind which Lazard had crouched. From his position on the floor, Lazard snapped off a shot, hitting Windsor just above the right knee. The assassin fell to one knee as the wounded leg buckled.

"Drop your weapon, man. This is the police. You're surrounded, you don't have a chance," he yelled at the real estate man.

Seeing that his opponent had no desire to surrender, Lazard popped up and fired his revolver three times at the Real Estate man, satisfied when he saw his target crumple to both knees.

Glancing around cautiously, Lazard saw only one of the phony waiters still living and he had been wrestled to the ground by some of the bolder diner guests. Slowly, he got to his feet and walked toward Windsor, never taking his pistol off the target. He reached the wounded man and slowly knelt beside him. Reaching out one hand, the Police Lieutenant pulled the smoking assault rifle out of the limp hands of the assassin.

"Get up!" ordered Lazard as he laid one hand on Windsor's shoulder.

Instead of obeying Lazard's order, Windsor slowly keeled over backward. Eyes staring, face expressionless, he fell limply to the floor. Lazard could tell that he had hit him twice, both times in the chest, but he didn't see much blood. He glanced around as he heard the door creak open, he could see the worried face of the Hotel Manager looking in at him.

"Call an ambulance," he ordered as he looked around the room at all of the bodies. "Actually, call several of them."

CHAPTER THIRTEEN

Phoenix, Arizona

Several hours later, Lazard was still trying to piece all of his bits and pieces of information together. Nothing he found seemed to explain Windsor's actions. As soon as he had gotten things under control at the Hotel, he had immediately dispatched a squad car out to Windsor's massive country estate located outside of Phoenix.

Since the estate was outside the city limits, the first officer on the scene had been Deputy Sheriff Clay Ponder. His car lights showed that the tall gates were closed. Riot shotgun in his hands, round in the chamber, he cautiously approached the gates. He could see nothing moving. There were no lights showing in the compound.

"Where's the gate guard?" he muttered to himself.

He was unsure what to do when the second sheriff's car came screeching to a halt beside his own car. He breathed a sigh of relief when Lieutenant Kyle Taylor walked over to stand beside him, flashlight in hand, the beam pointed toward the ground.

"What's going on, Clay?" he asked quietly, his eyes constantly moving.

"Got here only a minute or two ago, myself. Ain't nothing moving in that place. Usually one of the rent a cops is in that little guard shack over there." Ponder said pointing with the barrel of his shotgun.

"Well, standing here isn't getting us anywhere." returned the Lieutenant.

Walking forward, Taylor flashed his light on the gate before he reached through the bars of the main gate and pulled the bolt back, the gate slowly swung open. The two officers stood on the threshold of the estate and intently stared into the darkness. Nothing was moving and not lights were to be seen. The only sound was the wind rustling the leaves on the many trees lining the driveway.

Finally, transferring his light to his left hand, Taylor opened the snap on his holster, before walking slowly over to the guard shack. Pausing at the door to the shack, he peered around the doorframe, his light flashing around the little shack. He froze when he saw a pair of legs. From the uniform pants, it was clear that they had found the gate guard.

"Clay!" he called, his light still illuminating the body. "Over here."

Ponder came up behind him, still clutching his shotgun.

"Find something?" whispered the deputy, his eyes never leaving the darkness.

"Go back to the unit and call for back up and an ambulance."

"What'd you find?" asked Ponder trying to peer over the Lieutenant's shoulder.

"The guard, now get back to your unit and call for backup," repeated Taylor.

"Uh, right, yes sir, Lieutenant," stammered Ponder as he almost ran back to the dubious safety of his patrol car.

Carefully, so as not to disturb the crime scene, Taylor moved forward to crouch over the dead guard. The body was lying on its side, partially on its face. Taylor gently rolled it over and saw the guard had been shot at least three times, twice in the chest and once in the face. There was no question that the guard was dead. Moving his light around, Taylor noticed that the guard's side arm was still snapped into the holster. He'd never had a chance.

Taylor backed out of the guard shack as Ponder returned.

"Several more sheriff's units on the way and a half a dozen Phoenix city units responding. We're ordered to check the house."

Taylor nodded, flashing his light up the winding driveway. He could see no one moving.

"Ponder, you follow me in your unit, but go slowly. You see anything move, you sing out."

"Uh, sure thing, Lieutenant."

Returning to his unit, Taylor flipped on the mounted spot light and, pulling around Ponder's unit, he began to slowly drive up the winding drive. He was getting more and more uneasy the further he drove toward the house, as he swiveled his spot light to cover as much of the area as possible, but he continued to find the place deserted. He could see the massive manor on top of the hill, illuminated by only the moon above. Still he could see no movement.

Suddenly, he jammed on the brakes as he spotted a dark figure lying in the drive. He snatched his microphone from the seat beside him.

"Hold it, Ponder. There's someone lying on the ground at the curve, I'm leaving the unit to check it. Stay alert."

Dropping the radio mic onto the seat, he oriented the spotlight toward the house so that it would illuminate the body and anything or anyone that might be moving on the well-manicured lawn. Easing his revolver from his holster, Taylor open his door and exited the unit. He crouched beside the car, staining his ears for any sound and his eyes for even the faintest movement. He heard and saw nothing.

Still crouched over, Taylor darted in front of his unit into the shelter of the trees alongside the drive. Pistol ready, he carefully placed his feet, being careful to step on nothing that would alert any possible watchers. He paused and dropped to one knee a few feet from the body.

From his position, he could tell that the body was that of a woman. She was lying face down in the driveway, wearing the uniform of a housemaid and he could see several dark spots on the back of her dress, obviously bullet holes. Easing forward until he was crouching next to the still form, he rolled the body over on to her back. Even in the reflected light from the spotlight, he could tell that she had died with a look of horror on her face. The right side of her head was also a mass of dark blood, making it clear that after being shot in the back someone had made sure that she was dead with a head shot.

Glancing around nervously, he slowly eased back from the body and started back to his own unit, crouched down low. Passing his own unit, he circled around to the rear of Ponder's car and came up to the driver's window. Crouched low, he paused with one hand on the door of the second unit.

"It's a woman," he panted, "she dead."

He waited for a response from the deputy sitting in the idling car, but he made no response. Puzzled, Taylor rose to his feet and placed a hand on Ponder's shoulder, releasing his hold when the Deputy fell forward, his face hitting the steering wheel with a hollow thunk.

Opening the car door, Taylor leaned over and pulled the body back upright. Ponder's eyes were open, staring. A trail of blood ran down from the wide cut in Ponder's throat. He's hadn't known what had hit him. Even worse, Taylor hadn't heard a thing.

Jerking back in horror from the bloody sight, Taylor spun around to face a tall figure wearing a black stocking mask. Diving to the side, he raised his pistol, but it fell from his suddenly nerveless fingers. Taylor sprawled on the ground dumbly contemplating the two red-rimmed holes that had silently appeared on the front of his starched uniform shirt. His last sight was of the masked figure seeming to dematerialize in the darkness.

Lazard was sitting quietly at a table just inside the dining room, jotting down notes for a preliminary report, trying, in his own mind, to make some sense of what had happened. Jeremy Washington, Lazard's assistant came over and dropped into a nearby chair. His ebony face shown in the brightly lit room.

"Lieutenant, I've got the report on the Windsor home. It's not good."

"Well, I'm waiting." the Lieutenant observed not looking up from his notes.

Washington referred to a small black leather notebook held in one hand as he spoke.

"The first officers on the scene were a Sheriff's Department Lieutenant and a Deputy. They radioed back a report that the rent a cop that usually manned the gate was dead. Instead of immediately sending backup, Dispatch ordered them to continue on to the house. About halfway up the drive, they apparently stopped to examine the body of a dead housemaid, whose body was lying in the middle of the drive. She has been tentatively identified as that of Felicity Martin, age 22. She has worked for the Windsors for about two years.

When the second wave of units arrived, about twenty minutes after the last contact with the initial units, they found that the Deputy, identified as Clay Ponder had been murdered by having his throat cut while sitting in his car. The Lieutenant, Kyle Taylor had been shot twice in the chest and was lying on the ground beside Ponder's car. His own service revolver was clutched in his hand, but he hadn't gotten off a shot.

The officers continued on to the house to find a scene of carnage that equaled if not surpassed that here at the hotel. According to the reports in so far, all of Windsor's immediate family, except for his wife, Catherine Barnard Windsor, are dead, shot down as they had apparently been starting to have dinner. Scattered over the grounds of the estate were the mutilated bodies of the rest of the household staff."

"My God!" came a choked voice from behind Lazard. "This is impossible!"

Lazard twisted in his chair to see the Mayor standing behind him, surrounded by a small army of political aides. It was obvious that this news came close to sending the Mayor off the deep end. He had spent millions of taxpayer dollars advertising Phoenix as the safest spot to live in the country. In one night, the murder rate of the state went from one of the lowest in the nation to the uncontested highest.

"Lieutenant, what's going on here?" demanded the Mayor, his hands shaking to the point of being very noticeable. "How can something like this happen in Phoenix. Why didn't you stop this massacre?"

"Mr. Mayor, at the moment, all I know is that at least a dozen terrorists have killed or wounded over a hundred of Phoenix's wealthiest citizens. One of the terrorists, probably the leader of the terrorist team at this hotel, was Oscar Windsor."

If the Mayor had looked ill before, at this news his eyes bugged out of his head.

"Man are you mad?" he demanded, "Oscar Windsor is a multimillionaire. He couldn't have been one of the killers. Do you know how much he donated to my political campaign? Why this could be a major blow to my reelection campaign if word got out that one of my major contributors is a killer. You've got this all wrong, it can't be true!'"

At that moment Carl Arnoldsen, chief of police came bustling over to the table. The mayor immediately rounded on him before he could say a word.

"I don't know what type of police department you are running here, Chief, but some of the richest citizens in this town are dead and this lunatic accuses Oscar Windsor of being one of the killers. I want this idiot off the case. If he's that stupid, he doesn't have a snowball's chance in Hell of solving this case. Hell, the Keystone Cops could do a better job than has been done here thus far!"

The Mayor paused, overcome by the thought of millionaires killing each other in his town, and the need to take a breath.

"Hell man, Oscar Windsor donated a million dollars to my last election campaign. The very idea that such a find upstanding citizen could be a cold blooded killer is preposterous."

At that point Sheriff Kildare, his uniform shirt bloody and torn, came bustling up waving his arms wildly.

"I'm in charge now, Lazard. You and your people are not needed any more as this hotel is on the edge of the city; it's actually in my jurisdiction as the chief law enforcement officer in the county. I'll have this thing solved in two shakes of a lamb's tail. So you and all of your traffic directors get the hell out of my crime scene!"

"Shut up, you bozo!" snapped a harsh voice from nearby.

The entire group turned, as one, to see Milt Siggerson shrug off two paramedics and come steaming over to the table. He had bandages from his neck to his waist and was obviously in a lot of pain.

"Now see here Siggerson," blustered Kildare, "I'm sheriff of this county and I'll ——————"

"If you don't shut up you'll be back tending bar at one of those road-side dives you spend so much time in. You bumbling ass, you know about as much about criminal investigation as a goose does about rocket science," snapped Siggerson.

Siggerson turned and towered over the Sheriff.

"Kildare, this Police Lieutenant is the only reason that I and many others are alive. While you were hiding under the god damn table, worried about getting your fat ass shot off, this guy was risking his life protecting the citizens."

"I wasn't hiding under the table," yelled the red faced Sheriff, fully aware of the lobby full of reporters silently watching the exchange, "I was trying to protect the Senator with my own body."

"Bull shit!" snapped the angry oil man, "Hell, man, half the folks in that room could have hidden behind your fat body. Besides, the Senator was lying some ten feet behind where your fat body was quivering. As for you protecting him, he was shot so full of holes, that he looked like a piece of Swiss cheese.""

Without waiting for an answer, Siggerson swung around to face the Mayor and Chief of Police.

"I want both of you jackasses to get this straight. I will repeat what I said before, this man here," he said, putting one bloody hand on Lazard's shoulder, "is the only reason that I and many of those other poor souls in that room are alive right now. With no thought of his own safety, he and he alone entered that room against at least a dozen killers.

If either of you have any thought of taking this man off the case or letting this worthless piece of shit you call a sheriff get involved in this matter, I'll make two phone calls and have the god damn FBI in here investigating not only this incident, but some of the corruption and graft that you people make such good use of. Now what's it gonna be boys?"

The Mayor looked ridiculous with his mouth hanging open. Kildare tried to look fierce. The Chief of Police was sniffing the air, a puzzled look on his face. He leaned over and looked behind the Sheriff and grinned.

"Now see here, Siggerson!" began the Sheriff, his pudgy fists on his broad hips.

Carl Arnoldsen tapped Kildare on the shoulder.

"Buster, what's that on the back of your pants?" asked the Chief of Police, trying hard not to grin.

A puzzled look on his face, Buster Kildare felt the seat of his pants with one hand, then, a his face beet red, he clapped both hands to his rear.

"Uh, I'll get back to you on this." the Sheriff stammered, backing toward the front entrance of the hotel.

"See here, Kildare!" began the Mayor, "Where are you going? Are you going to let this man talk to you like this?"

Kildare paused in his retreat, both hands still clamped tightly to his rear.

"Uh, Mr. Mayor, I'm going to continue the investigation in my own way. Uh, I'll get back to you."

With that he backed away from the group, spun and dashed for the front door. Lazard caught sight of a dark spreading stain on the seat of the chief's khaki pants.

"My hero." said Police Chief Arnoldsen with a grimace, dismissing the Sheriff with a wave of his hand.

"Milt," Arnoldsen continued turning to the raging oilman, "don't worry, Lieutenant Lizard is in complete charge of this investigation and he has the full backing of the department."

"Damn straight he is!" returned Siggerson, " and if there is anything he needs that this cheap ass city won't or can't give him, then I'll given him a blank check. Now take your politically appointed asses back down town and let the boy work."

Arnoldsen turned to Lazard.

"Louis, keep in touch. We'll have to hold a news conference as soon as we can."

He turned to the Mayor.

"Mr. Mayor, let's go and let the boy work in peace."

"But————" began the Mayor, but stopped at the look on the face of Siggerson.

"Mayor, get out before I kick your butt back to that selling shoes like your daddy!" snapped Siggerson.

For a moment it looked like the Mayor was going to cry, but then finally he quietly, he followed Arnoldsen across the lobby, his gaggle of aides trailing silently along behind him.

Lazard glanced at Siggerson with a lifted eyebrow.

"This is a strange town." he remarked.

Siggerson grinned and slapped Lazard on the back with his good arm.

"I owe you one boy. A big one. Get this thing solved and then look me up. I got a job for you if you want it."

Turning on his heel, the big man strode off toward the ambulances bellowing for medical attention.

Lazard turned back to Washington who had stood quietly during the duel of the political titans. Washington's mouth had been hanging open while his head moved back and forth like he was watching a ping-pong match during the exchange. Now he favored his superior with a grin.

"I guess this is why you get the big bucks, uh?"

Lazard just shook his head, all the while wondering what the hell had happened to his peaceful city, and began to issue his instructions.

"Get a forensics team out to the Windsor mansion to examine all of the bodies. Coordinate with the sheriff's office to have an ambulance and a joint task force investigation team sent out to pick up the latest corpses to grace the City's morgue.

Oh, and what about Windsor's wife?"

Washington shook his head.

"There's no sign of his at the Mansion. I've put about a notice to all units to find her if possible."

Lazard nodded and rubbed his face. God he was tired.

"Good, keep me posted."

Spinning on his heel, Washington left to look for a phone.

Piece restored in the hotel lobby, Lazard finally resumed his seat. He was pleased to note that sometime during the confusion someone had been kind enough to place a cup of coffee beside his notebook. It promised to be a long night.

As Lazard sat at one of the blood-splattered tables sipping a cup of coffee and checking his notes, he totaled up the butcher's bill. At the Hotel, alone, there were over thirty dead and a hundred of the area's wealthiest were injured. Doodling on his pad, Lazard tried to figure out what to do next. His reverie was interrupted as his assistant, Jeremy Washington, came over to him again.

"Windsor is at the hospital under heavy guard. I managed to get a good set of prints off of him before the ambulance took him away, boss. Whatever happened to him, Windsor is definitely out of it now. He seems to be totally comatose," said Washington as he glanced around the room with a slightly dazed look on his face.

Lazard sighed deeply and rubbed his tired eyes. "Did they sedate him?"

"No, sir." responded Washington. "He's like a zombie, doesn't blink, and doesn't react in anyway to anything."

"Well, send the prints out to the F.B.I. just for the hell of it. It'll at least make us look like we're doing something. Hell, we know who he is, but you never can tell what a full check might turn up. He might have a record of some kind. These rich folks sometimes have very unusual pasts," he said as he stood and stretched, still rattling off orders.

"Seal off the dining room and keep the guys taking statements. I'm going to headquarters to start preparing a report for the brass. There's apparently going to be press all over this from all over the country nosing around. All statements come from me, you got that?"

"Sure do, Lieutenant. Better you than me." responded Washington with a smile.

"Jesus, why did this have to happen on my beat?" Lazard groused as he headed for the door, pulling on his sport coat as he entered the ornate lobby.

A thought hit him and he stepped back into the bloody dining room.

"Oh, by the way, any news on Mrs. Windsor yet?" he asked Washington.

Washington very decisively shook his head.

"No sign of her yet, but the team is still searching the mansion and we have units checking all of the hotels and restaurants in town. I've also alerted the airlines and trains. We should get a report soon if she was registered on any of their flights or trains."

Lazard nodded and started back out the door.

"Man the press is gonna have a field day with this." he muttered to himself.

Lazard was right. The press played the story up big. Schwarz had been a big name nationally and always made it a point to leak information to his favorite reporters. This shameless manipulation of the national media resulted in the press making him a household name. As a result, Phoenix became the host to several hundred reporters from all over the world. Each of them demanded a private interview with Lieutenant Lazard and the Mayor. The Mayor, who harbored aspirations of national office after his term as Mayor, ordered Lazard to cooperate fully with the press. This became the most reported murder investigation in history.

One of Lazard's continuing complaints was that his department was more concerned with public relations than investigations. He had been informed that the Mayor was talking the position that Windsor had been over-worked and simply snapped. He was insisting that it be found that Windsor had been insane at the time of the shooting. There was no way that the Mayor of Phoenix was going to admit that a sane assassin had been allowed to get close to a public figure. Such an event could kill Phoenix's convention business.

Lazard wasn't so sure that Windsor had been insane. Everything he had seen in that dining room led him to believe that the assassination had been very carefully thought out in advance. The Mayor was bringing so much pressure to bear on the Chief that he had gotten to the point that he was spending more time justifying his manpower requirements than he was conducting his investigation. This was soon to change.

It would be late the next day before the biggest bombshell of all was dropped in Lazard's lap. He had been in his office, preparing his preliminary report when Washington crossed the busy squad room and knocked on his door. Without looking up, Lazard waved for him to enter. As was customary, Washington walked over to stand by the Lieutenant's desk waiting to be acknowledged. Reaching the end of the paragraph he was working on, Lazard straightened up from his paper, removed his glasses and dropped them on the desk, then reached for the paper cup sitting in the midst of his cluttered desk.

"Watcha got, Jeremy?" he asked as he took a long drink from his cup of, now cold, coffee.

"Well, I've received an F.B.I. report on Windsor's fingerprints. You're not going to believe this," he warned as he handed the paper to his superior.

Giving his subordinate a quizzical glance, Lazard took the paper in his left hand while he picked up his reading glasses and placed them back on his face. Washington watched his expression as his superior read the report. He knew that Lazard understood the true meaning of the report when he cursed and dropped his head.

"God damn, what else can happen in this investigation?" he demanded of the air. Lieutenant Lazard's shoulders slumped and he leaned forward, resting his weight on his elbows planted solidly on the desktop. Visibly shaking himself, Lazard picked up the F.B.I. report again and studied it carefully.

"Are you sure about this? I mean, are they sure about this?" demanded the harassed Lieutenant waving the report toward his assistant.

"Positive, Lieutenant. In fact, the F.B.I. agent in charge of the local office said if you had any questions to call him. His number is on the bottom of the report."

He looked up at Washington, his eyes wide in disbelief.

"Did you read this carefully, Jeremy? You got any idea what this will do to the investigation?" he demanded as he continued to wave the report in the air.

"Yes, I did, that's why I took the liberty of calling the number on the bottom of the report. They verified it. In fact, they informed me that they have a team of agents on the way here now. It seems that they want to talk to him as badly as we do."

Lazard just sat and looked at the report in total disbelief. He had no idea how he was going to break this bit of news to the powers that be. The press would have a field day with it. The Mayor would probably have coronary arrest, and would be as disbelieving as he was. How in the world could a man commit these murders when the man who did it was supposed to have been dead for over fifteen years? Shit, he should have taken his vacation; he could be on a quiet riverbank fishing instead of investigating this circus.

Instead he was going to have to go before the Chief and report that one of the wealthiest people in Phoenix and a man who had just helped kill dozens of Phoenix's most prominent citizens was already a dead man.

CHAPTER FOURTEEN

Thursday, DECEMBER 23RD-11:45 A.M.-12:05 P.M., FEDERAL BUILDING, New York City

At approximately 11:50 a.m., a large white limousine with darkly tinted glass pulled up to the curb outside the New York Federal building. The uniformed chauffeur got out and moved to open the back door of the car. Reverently, the driver helped four middle-aged men wearing turbans and Middle Eastern robes exit the car. Immediately, the four were mobbed by reporters, microphones shoved eagerly into their faces.

"Sheik Sadir, what are your feelings at this moment?" yelled a NEWSWEEK reporter as he shoved a small microphone toward the Sheik's face.

"Sheik, did you or any of your followers kill Marty Cosack?" shouted a young lady also carrying a microphone, this one with the ABC logo stamped onto its side.

The largest of the brightly robed men, a 6'5" former pro basketball player born Kareem Dennis, who, after his conversion to Islam, now called himself Sheik Abu Thaer, stepped forward and raised his arms for silence. Like magic, the babbling reporters immediately fell silent.

"I am the spokesperson for the Sons of Allah and its spiritual leader, Sheik Muhammad Hussein Sadir. Sheik Sadir wishes it known that neither he nor any of his followers had anything to do with the death of the reporter, Cosack."

"How do you explain the last message left by Cosack naming one of the Sheik's followers as his killer?" interrupted Marvin Leob, the small dark intense man who was a well-known feature writer for the New York Post, and had managed to worm his way to the front of the pack of reporters.

Abu Thaer glared down at the 5'6" Leob and growled something under his breath to the smaller turbaned man standing slightly to his rear. When Leob failed to wither under his angry glare, Sheik Thaer raised his arms again to stop the new bombardment of questions ignited by Loeb's question.

"While we do not recognize the authority of your earthly government, My Master, Sheik Muhammad Hussein Sadir wishes it made known that he has voluntarily come in answer to the demands of the Federal Bureau of Investigation. Sheik Sadir believes that the truth will relieve all suspicion from the Sons of Allah. That is all he has to say at this point."

With that, Sheik Thaer, helped by four Deputy U.S. Marshals began to clear a path through the mob of reporters for his leader Sheik Sadir, and two of his ever-present security men to use to enter the Federal Building. The driver of the Sheik's limo moved to stand by the trunk of his car, totally ignored by the reporters who were pressed against the glass front doors of the Building. Two members of the New York Police Department helped by two of the Deputy U.S. Marshals stood in front of the glass doors, blocking the reporters from entering the building.

Just inside the entrance, waited four F.B.I. field agents. Quickly, they patted down the four for weapons and then led them through the metal detectors. At the elevator bank two other Agents, whose job was to escort the Sheik's party up to the F.B.I. Office, waited. The elevator was packed with the Sheik's party and the two F.B.I. agents assigned to ride up with the Sheik and his men.

When the elevator doors opened, Sheik Thaer led the way to the reception area of the floor wide office. Waiting for them was a party of six well-dressed men. Sheik Thaer stopped two feet from the leader of the group to wait for his party.

"You should be honored that my master has consented to speak with representatives of your despotic government. Sheik Muhammad Hussein Sadir has come out of the great goodness of his heart to answer your questions," intoned the big spokesman as he raised his arms.

The senior member of the reception committee, Robert Grossman, United States Attorney for New York held out his right hand toward Thaer.

"I wish to thank you for your cooperation in this matter. I wish you to assure the Sheik that I am sure that we can clear this matter up in just a few minutes," he said to Thaer, as he waited for the expected hand-shake.

Sheik Thaer crossed his arms into his robes, and studiously ignored the U.S. Attorney's offered hand. He did not even favor the U.S. Attorney with so much as a glance; instead, his eyes seemed to be fixed on the large clock at the far end of the reception room. Grossman continued to hold his hand out for some few seconds before dropping it and nervously clearing his throat.

"We believe that physical contact with your people will contaminate us," growled Thaer.

Mr. Grossman colored slightly, and turned his gaze toward Sheik Sadir.

"Yes, well, once again, I wish to thank you for coming, Sheik Sadir. I am sure that you understand the necessity of this meeting. If—."

"Who are these others?" growled Thaer, as he swung one tree trunk-like arm to indicate the people standing behind Grossman.

Robert Grossman started for a moment and then flushed slightly.

"Oh, yes, forgive me for my lapse of manners, Sheik. This is Martin Abbot, head of the New York Office of the Federal Bureau of

Investigation." He indicated the slightly built man standing to his left rear.

"Pleasure to meet you, Sheik Thaer, Sheik Sadir." murmured the F.B.I. chief as he pursed his lips thoughtfully.

His greeting was rudely ignored.

The U.S. Attorney indicated the uniformed man to his right.

"This is Chief Arnold Blitzen, Deputy Chief of Police of the New York City Police Department."

Sheik Sadir continued to stare straight ahead, eyes riveted on the clock, saying nothing, no expression on his taciturn face. Thaer nodded coldly at each introduction, all the while glancing around the reception area. He could see through an open door into the agent's work area in front of him where at least twenty F.B.I. personnel were busy just on the other side of the wall.

After a long moment, Thaer refocused his stare on the group in front of him. He noticed an individual leaning against the wall to the rear of the group. He seemed to be staring at Thaer, himself, in great amusement. For a moment, Thaer was sure that he recognized the man, and the feeling gave him a moment of unease.

"Who is that?" interrupted Thaer, raising one huge tree truck like arm to point at the man standing to the rear of the reception committee.

"Who?" queried Grossman as he glanced around, "Oh, that's Bernard Kahane, a senior field investigator with my office."

"Hello, Mr. Washington. Whose your friend?" asked Kahane, amusement evident in his voice as he began to walk toward the big man.

Thaer drew himself up to his full height and almost roared his answer. "I am Sheik Abu Thaer, spokesman for the Sons of Allah and this esteemed personage is Sheik Sadir."

"Bullshit! Your name is Kareem Dennis and you're from Queens," snapped Kahane, as he came to a halt no more than a foot from Sheik Sadir.

"Kahane, what are you doing?" demanded Robert Grossman, grabbing his subordinate's arm. "You are offending our eminent guest Sheik Sadir."

"Stopping you from making an ass of yourself, Boss is what I am doing. You've been had, whoever that guy with Dennis is, he's definitely not Sheik Muhammad Sadir." shot back Kahane, never taking his eyes off of the big black spokesman for the Sheik's party as he jerked his arm from his boss' grasp. "I know the real Sheik Sadir from way back. He's actually an old carnival magician name Henry Osborne who I arrested numerous times for fraud or some other con game and this ain't him."

Immediately, all eyes turned toward the figure purporting to be Sheik Sadir. Sheik Thaer simply stood with his mouth open, apparently speechless. His only movement was his eyes darting toward the wall clock.

Martin Abbot glanced toward the two agents standing at either side of the elevator doors and motioned toward the still silent Sheik Sadir. In unison, the two Federal Agents came up to the Sheik and grabbed his upper arms. This action seemed to shake Sheik Thaer out of his shock.

"Sheik Sadir, or whoever you are, you have some serious questions to answer." Stated Grossman in a firm voice.

"You dare to lay your unclean, infidel hands on Allah's spokesman?" he demanded in total outrage, as he seemed to swell in his righteous anger.

"Oh, can it, Dennis!" snapped Kahane, as he took a step to the side, leaning back against the receptionist's desk, "The game's over, where's the real Sheik Sadir?"

Before anyone else could say a word, the man masquerading as Sheik Muhammad Hussein Sadir effortlessly shrugged off the two federal agents and crossed his arms inside his robes. This action enabled the Sheik to make the two metal plates strapped to his wrists come in contact with each other. In turn, this had the effect of making a complete circuit, with the same result as pushing the plunger on a detonator.

The agents at the entrance to the building had checked all of the Sheik's party for conventional weapons and even had them go through a metal detector. What the searchers did not find out was that the fake Sheik Sadir was wearing a Kevlar flak vest, as did the real Sadir. However, this particular vest had been modified to remove the protective padding and replace it with twenty pounds of a newly developed concentrated plastic explosive and hundreds of small metal pellets. The fake Sheik was in effect a walking time bomb.

Two seconds after the metal plates made contact, the signal reached the actual detonator. The explosion of that twenty pounds of plastic explosive totally blew out the entire floor. For all practical purposes, the New York F.B.I. Office ceased to exist at 12:02 P.M.

The forty or so reporters on the sidewalk in front of the building knew something was wrong when the force of the explosion blew the glass out of the windows of the floor that housed the F.B.I. Office. The crowd on the sidewalk was showered with glass, concrete, pieces of desks, walls and people. Utter chaos reigned. Flames shot out from the building for hundreds of feet.

As if things were not bad enough, at the moment the explosion erupted, the Sheik's limo driver jerked open the lid to the trunk and two black clad, masked men carrying H & K MP-5 sub machine guns sprang to the street. Wildly, the two began to spray 9-millimeter rounds at anyone in sight. Their first rounds slammed the police and Deputy Marshal guards back into the glass front of the building. Their bloody, broken bodies shattered the glass doors. The crowd of reports scattered and ran in all directions, but most were cut down in a hail of bullets.

When at last no one moved in the area around the Federal Building, the two terrorists jumped into the open rear of the limo and the driver sedately drove away from the curve. He didn't want to break any speed laws.

Thursday, DECEMBER 23RD-11:58 a.m.- ONE POLICE PLAZA, New York City

There was a great deal of hustle and bustle around One Police Plaza, the Police Headquarters for the New York Police Department. Almost a small city in and of itself, on this day, the complex housed approximately twenty thousand people, when you counted police personnel, prisoners and civilian visitors. The idea of anything being able to destroy such a large complex in the middle of one of the world's largest cities was totally unthinkable.

New Yorkers, as a whole, are a very jaded people. They have seen everything, from the commonplace to the bizarre, so it takes something very unusual to really get their undivided attention. For this reason, the mob of Moslem demonstrators waving protest signs as they toward One Police Plaza really didn't excite anyone, only the tourists really paid any great attention. Even the police patrols that saw them coming did nothing more than shake their heads and radio in a report.

Though as jaded as the rest of the City, the New York Police are still one of the most efficient paramilitary organizations in the world. By the time the protest mob reached One Police Plaza, there was a riot control force of forty SWAT trained officers waiting for them in the center of the complex. It was assumed that the protesters would mill around for a few hours and then disperse.

When the mob reached the center of the Plaza, the commander of the Police Unit, Lieutenant Emile Kozinsky, stepped forward and raised his right hand for them to stop. With his left hand he put a bullhorn to his lips.

"I must ask your group to disperse," he said forcefully as he blocked their path, "You do not have a permit to march. You are breaking the law. If you disperse now, we will not arrest anyone. If you do not, we will begin to arrest anyone who remains."

The leader of the marchers, Sheik Ali Hussein, stepped forward to meet the Lieutenant.

"I am Sheik Ali Hussein, assistant to his most reverence Sheik Sadir. We have come to demand justice for our people. You agents of the Great Satan have oppressed our people for too long. We want the persecution of Sheik Muhammad Sadir to end at once."

Lieutenant Kozinsky looked the Moslem cleric up and down for a moment and then raised the bullhorn again.

"Once again, I must ask you to disperse." he said to the crowd. "You are breaking the law."

"Is this your last word?" asked Sheik Hussein in a very mild tone of voice.

"Yes." answered Lieutenant Kozinsky, as he locked eyes with the Cleric.

Sheik Hussein bowed his head and turned toward his followers.

"My brothers, it is time to do Allah's will," he yelled as he folded his arms across his chest.

With that, Sheik Hussein spun around, his robes billowing out around him. He raised his right hand, which now held an automatic pistol. Jerking the trigger, he fired his first shot directly into Lieutenant Kozinsky's face.

"Death to the Great Satan!" shrieked the Sheik as he waved his followers forward.

As Kozinsky fell backward into darkness, he could distantly hear the sounds of a pitched gun battle. He didn't see his forty men being literally overrun and butchered by the gun and knife-wielding mob that rolled across the plaza. He didn't see the hundreds of armed reinforcements that joined the hollowing mob. He also didn't see the butchery and violence that enveloped the entire complex as the armed invaders stormed into all the buildings of the complex.

In what should have been the safest place in the City of New York, the howling mob committed the most brutal atrocities of rape, mayhem and murder. The attackers were able to do the impossible, simply because no one in their right minds believed that it could be done, so no one was prepared for such an attack. Hussein and his followers simply overwhelmed the officers on duty and quickly emptied the cells in the holding area. Those officers and civilian employees assigned to One Police Plaza were hunted down and exterminated.

The New York Police force lost its entire command structure in the space of the next two hours. Additionally, some two hundred and fifty dangerous violent prisoners were released into the streets armed with weapons and uniforms stolen from the arms rooms of the New York City Police Department.

CHAPTER FIFTEEN

The City of New York is one of the largest single areas of human habitation in the world. According to legend, the Dutch purchased the Island of Manhattan from the Indians for a paltry sum. Of course, many think that the Indians that sold the island pulled off the first real estate scam to take place on the island, since other Indians claimed that they really owned the island. The weather is too cold in the winter and much too hot and humid in the summer.

Originally, New York City was called New Amsterdam by its' Dutch founders, but after a small war, the British captured it and renamed the place after the Duke of York. The City has been the site of battles in several wars. During the American Revolution, the British made it their main headquarters and staging area, the Harbor being the main anchorage of the mighty British fleet. Washington made several efforts to take the City, but failed.

During the War of 1812, again, the British showed a fixation for the area of the City, though this time they were not able to take it. They did destroy Washington D.C., however, which seemed to have no major effect on the country as a whole.

During the American Civil War, Southern sympathizers, called Copperheads, fomented revolt in the North that eventually led to the New York City draft riots of 1864. The riots became so bad that U.S. troops needed for the battlefields were sent into the City to fight pitched battles with the armed mobs. Even against trained combat soldiers, the citizens of New York managed to hold their own. The fighting eventually became a matter of the soldiers have to clear rioters of out of each street. Combat troops were tied up for weeks.

Today, New York City is literally, the financial and informational center of the civilized world. Almost all news is transmitted over the U.P. and A.P. wires which have their headquarters in the City. Wall Street controls over 80 percent of the financial transactions in the entire world. The destruction of this City would cause major damage to the international financial structure. A prize worthy of the greatest efforts to conquer. Numerous terrorists groups were constantly studying how to disrupt the City. None had succeeded.

THURSDAY, DECEMBER 23-11:45 A.M.—ROCKEFELLER CENTER, New York City

Carter Davis Hughes was a man in a hurry. He was late for his luncheon date with his wife and kids. He had not been a very good father this year, it was only two days before Christmas and he had not yet taken his kids to see Santa. Today, he would rectify that oversight. He was taking the rest of the day off and going Christmas shopping with his wife and kids. He had decided to put the matter of his wife's infidelity behind him until after the 1st. For his children's' sake, he would pretend.

Locking the door of his office, he almost sprinted for the open elevator.

"Coming back?" yelled the receptionist as she spotted Hughes charging past her desk.

"Nope, gone for the day." he yelled back as he made a hopeless dash for the closing elevator doors. He just caught a glimpse of someone entering ahead of him.

"Hold that elevator!" he yelled.

He could have saved his breath, as the individual on the elevator apparently ignored his yell. Just as he reached forward to hold the elevator doors open, they closed in his face. He just caught a glimpse of long red hair, impossibly long nylon covered legs and the brightest green eyes he had seen in a long time. Swearing under his breath, he pushed the button, bouncing on his heels with suppressed energy as he nervously ran one hand through his longish curly brown hair. The Paramount Publishing Building had, without a doubt, the slowest elevators in the City, he thought to himself.

Lately, he had felt somewhat depressed, always concerned with the dreams that haunted his sleep. Today, however, he felt like a heavy burden had been lifted from his shoulders. Allowing the dream to play out, as his psychologist friend had suggested, had affected some type of healing allowing him to sleep the rest of the night without interruption.

Finally, with a bang, the elevator doors furthest from him opened, shaking him from his reverie and he stepped inside. Pushing the button for the ground floor, Hughes crossed his fingers and hoped that he had an express not a local elevator. For once, the car dropped straight from the 11th floor to the first. Bursting from the car, he jogged to his left and down a flight of stairs to the marble lined passages that ran beneath the Rockefeller Center Complex. He glanced at his watch and noticed that it was five minutes to twelve. He never liked to be late when he had a lunch date with his wife.

As Hughes passed one of the entrances to the New York Subway System, he was rudely jostled aside by a group of dark complexioned, coarsely dressed men who came spilling through the subway turnstiles, each carrying a medium sized rolled bundle under an arm. With an annoyed glare at the rude group, Hughes quickly forgot them and continued on toward the American Festival Cafe, his fast pace quickly out distancing them.

By all rights, he should have beaten them to the restaurant, but as he passed the BLAKES Restaurant, he was spotted by the manager who was a long time friend of his and who wanted to talk. For several minutes he was caught in conversation. The rude group that had come from the subway silently passed him by as he talked. There was something odd about the group that disturbed him, but Hughes was too preoccupied to pay much attention.

Noticing that he was now late for his meeting with this family, Hughes finally said good-bye to his friend and hurried on his way. Pausing for a moment at the newsstand at the corridor junction, Hughes purchased his kids' favorite chewing gum as well as cough drops for himself. Catching sight of himself in a gleaming brass plate on the wall across from the newsstand, he paused to take stock of his appearance.

As usual, his dark conservative cut suit was immaculate, though he meticulously found some lint to remove. He noticed that his dark red tie was slightly askew and straightened it. One last check and he felt relatively satisfied with his overall appearance, but at 6'1" and two hundred twenty pounds, he knew that he should probably lose some weight. After all, Martha was continually pointing out that he had gained several pounds since they had married. He had to grin at his reflection, for some reason, she always had the effect of making him feel like a teenager going out on his first date whenever he had to meet her out in public.

Another glance at his watch showed that he was several minutes late for his luncheon meeting. Trying to make up for lost time, he hurried down the corridor to his left until he came to the glass wall that separated the American Festival Cafe from the main corridor. Scanning the crowd he quickly spotted his wife and kids sitting near the outside windows, engrossed in watching the ice skaters spinning around the ice rink.

Hughes followed their line of vision and for a few seconds, he watched a beautiful young lady executing some rather professional moves out on the ice. In spite of her unusual grace and beauty, for some reason, movement to the left of the rink attracted his attention.

Suddenly there was a loud explosion that literally rocked the underground shopping area. So violent was the explosion that dust and ceiling tiles dropped onto the people below. Everyone froze where they stood and looked around in confusion. A second equally loud explosion rocked the area, cracking windows, knocking over displays and generally causing the beginnings a panic in the holiday crowds. What Carter didn't know was that each explosion has been a large hijacked airliner full of holiday travelers crashing into one of the World Trade Center Towers.

Glancing up worriedly scanned the crowd across the rink looking for the source of the explosions. The crowd moved in confusion as twin pillars of thick lack smoke began to fill the air to the south. As sometimes happens when you scan a crowd of strangers, Carter singled out one man. This man was acting a little strange, instead of looking for the sourced of the explosions, this man kept his eyes glued to the skating rink.

Carter continued to watch in puzzlement, unable to take his eyes away from the man as he was joined by another man who had been standing to the left of the rink on the stair landing that led up to the sidewalk level. The new comer seemed to be struggling with a long, narrow piece of equipment. With a start, Hughes recognized what the man was trying to use, it was a Light Anti-tank Weapon (LAW). The small, but powerful, warhead of such a weapon could take out a tank, much less the double paned glass of the restaurant.

Frantically, he looked around for one of the Rockefeller Center Security Guards, but, as was the usual case, he could see none. The two that usually patrolled the area were lying in pools of their own blood in the men's room nearby. What he did see were the shabbily dressed men he had seen coming out of the subway earlier. They were now scattered around the area, holding their bundles across their chests, as they scanned the panicked crowds. Though he had no definite clues, for some reason, one thought came to Hughes' mind, "Terrorists."

Spinning around, Hughes looked back at the man with the LAW. He seemed to be aiming it across the Ice Rink directly at Hughes' wife and kids who were frozen in fascinating watching the pillars of smoke that were filling the sky. Wildly, Hughes began to yell and wave his arms as he ran along the gently curving corridor toward the entrance of the restaurant fighting his way through the crowd.

"Martha, get down! Watch out!" he yelled as he frantically pounded on the glass as he searched for a way into the glass-enclosed restaurant.

He could see his wife looking around in puzzlement, miraculously, she had somehow heard his voice, but over the noise of the frightened holiday crowd, she didn't understand what he was yelling. In confusion, other diners, as well as the numerous people hurrying through the hall looking for the closest exit, simply stared at him as if he was insane. They seemed to be totally ignoring everything but him.

Before he can make them understand the danger, one of the roughly dressed men scattered around the corridor slammed into him. The blow, added to Hughes' own momentum, caused him to ram head first into one of the columns that supported the roof of the passage; he collapsed in a heap at its base. Helplessly, he continued to yell as he watched, as if in slow motion, the rocket leave the tube and cross the rink, to explode against the glass outside wall of the restaurant. Instinctively, he threw one arm across his eyes.

The rocket hit the glass wall of the restaurant that bordered on the ice rink. Upon contact, the rocket exploded, sending glass shards flying in every direction. From the corner of his eye, Hughes watched the beautiful skater that had been the center of attention sliding loosely across the ice, leaving a trail of blood behind her. Following right behind the explosion came the sound of automatic weapons fire.

Hughes was terrified almost out of his mind; at first he tried to curl up into a fetal ball. A sane part of his mind was concerned about his family. Raising his head, Hughes could see that their table was over-turned; there was no sign of his wife or children. To his right, one of the terrorists was firing through the shattered glass wall into the restaurant; expended shell cases were peppering the area around him, bouncing off the concrete floor. Frantically Carter pulled himself up against the near-est wall.

Cautiously looking back into the shattered restaurant, Hughes saw his wife and children pulling themselves out from underneath their overturned table. By some miracle, they seemed unhurt. He yelled to them to stay down, but in the chaos and confusion, he knew in his heart that they didn't hear him. Somehow, his son, Jason, seemed to sense that his father was near. Spotting Hughes lying on the floor in the corridor, Jason yelled and began to run to him. Martha, her hair in disarray, and her dress torn, screamed and dragging her daughter, began to chase after her son.

As if leading a charmed life, all three made it across that deadly kill zone, almost to him, but then the unthinkable happened. The terrorist standing near him, stopped to reload his weapon and the movement of Hughes' family attracted his attention. Slamming the new magazine into place, he calmly stitched the three from waist to neck. They fell in a jumble, less than ten feet from where Hughes was lying, helpless.

Across the City, a group of twelve men sat around a large oval dark wood table in a very richly furnished conference room. The room was in darkness; only one lamp was lit in the center of the table, throwing out a pool of light. On the wall behind the man at the head of the table hung a large painting of George Washington, illuminated by a small light attached to the bottom of the portrait.

All in the room sat silently, watching the big man who sat silhouetted against the light of the portrait behind him. None of the Council had ever seen him outside the dark room, none knew his identity. Beside the leader's right hand sat a phone. It had never rung before, but on this day, they all impatiently waited on it to ring. They had been sitting in the darkness for the last hour waiting for a message. It had not yet come. Finally, when the tension had mounted to almost unbearable levels the phone rang suddenly. The shrillness of the sound caused several of the men at the table to start. One dropped his

The leader grabbed up the handset and put it to his ear. He listened for a long time and then silently hung up the phone. For a long moment he simply sat, making no motion or sound. Finally, he looked slowly around the table.

"Gentlemen," he said ponderously, his voice low and deep "The second American Revolution has begun. Thus far our strike teams have been unusually successful. The FBI Office has ceased to exist and One Police Plaza has been overrun by mobs, most of the officers on duty are dead and the prisoners have been released. Ten minutes ago teams of our people commandeered flights from Regan Airport and are turning them toward their targets. One has been crashed into each of the World Trade Center Towers and one has hit the Pan Am Building. The City is in a panic."

Something inside Hughes snapped, the normally loving, kind father was filled with a killing rage. Some deeply buried part of his psyche was released, turning the humorous Insurance Executive into a highly trained killer. Scooting along the floor toward the terrorist, Hughes rolled onto his stomach, braced his hands on the floor, locked his legs and swung his body counter clockwise, so that his locked legs struck the terrorist standing near him in the back of his knees. When Hughes' legs impacted, the gunman's legs were swept out from under him, his back slammed hard against the marble floor, knocking the breath from him.

The weapon discharged harmlessly against the ceiling, knocking loose chips of plaster, which rained down on them. The terrorist moaned weakly and tried to turn onto his side toward Hughes, still holding his UZI.

Rolling onto his back, and spinning around so that he was lying beside the fallen terrorist, Hughes rammed his right elbow down into the exposed throat of the fallen killer. The terrorist dropped his weapon, grabbed his damaged throat and began to hack and cough. His heels began to drum on the floor as he slowly suffocated, his throat crushed by the blow. Hughes grabbed the fallen weapon and, using the dying terrorist's body as cover, he began to fire at the scattered gunmen.

His first bursts knocked two of the terrorists from their feet; they died with looks of total shock on their faces. He looked quickly around for other targets, but before his eyes, the body littered corridor slowly faded away, his senses reeled. When his vision cleared, he was looking at a jungle-covered riverbank. Instead of coarsely dressed terrorists, he saw a black clad figure wearing a Blue Beret step from behind a tree and raise an M-16 to fire at him.

Wildly, he fired his M-16 at the black clad figure in front of him. With an almost physical jerk, Hughes was snapped back to the present by the sound of his borrowed UZI erupting lead death in his hands. He saw another terrorist being knocked spinning by his fire.

Hands shaking, Hughes lowered his head to the cool floor, forcing himself to breathe slowly, he was totally disoriented by his visions. It seemed that his dreams were now invading his waking hours. This was definitely not the place to lose his mind, at least not yet. Around him, for a moment, all sounds stopped. All he could hear was moans and screams of pain from the wounded. Pulling himself back together, he searched the pockets of his first victim for more ammunition.

His movement brought a reaction from two terrorists hidden in an alcove by the escalator. Both popped out of their temporary sanctuary and each fired a burst at the American. Both riddled the corpse of the dead terrorist that served as his cover. When Hughes did not return fire. Believing that he was out of ammunition, or dead, both broke cover and charged toward him. Seeing his opportunity, Hughes raised up. His return fire sent them crashing to the floor. Two more down.

Smoothly, as if practiced at such maneuvers, Hughes shifted to his left and snapped a shot toward a movement he saw in the newsstand area. The move saved his life as a bullet chipped the floor where he had been laying. Rolling over onto his back, Hughes fired along his own body at two men who had been crouching to his rear. Both went flying backward, their weapons discharging harmlessly into the air.

Then with a sensation like that of watching a movie, Hughes found himself back on his jungle riverbank. There was gunfire and explosions all around him. He looked for Swanson, but couldn't find him in the smoke.

"Swanson should be organizing covering fire," Hughes thought "Where is he?"

Frantically, Hughes searched the area for the big figure of the Sergeant, but he saw no one. He seemed to be totally alone.

Slowly the riverbank dissolved and Hughes found himself back in the Rockefeller Center. He was huddled against the corridor wall, partially sheltered by a post, his face covered with sweat, as tremors ran through his body. Slowly, he pressed one arm across his eyes. He had been looking for Swanson, but who was Swanson? Swanson was in his dream, why did he think of him now? He had also never been in the army so why was he having delusions about combat?

For a moment, he actually had no idea where he was, or even who he was. Who is Swanson, he thought to himself again? There seem to be two personalities in his mind, each occupied a different space, both were concerned with survival. Closing his eyes tightly, Hughes concentrated on not seeing the riverbank. He prayed that he wasn't on the riverbank. Slowly, opening one eye, he was gratified to see he was still in the body-strewn hall.

More movement by the newsstand to his right attracted his attention. Automatically, his weapon began to track the movement. After a second Hughes' eyes focused and he saw that the movement was actually an armed man moving slowly behind a rack of magazines. Suddenly, the man jumped and ran, he seemed to be trying to escape by making a break for the main corridor that led deeper into the complex. Snapping a shot at him, Hughes was savagely satisfied to see his target go cart wheeling off his feet into the Electronic Boutique's display window.

The second terrorist, the leader of this particular group, huddling in the cover of the newsstand cowered in the shelter of a bookrack watched his companion die, praying to Allah that the infidel didn't see him. In all of his planning for this most holy of missions, he had never dreamed that his team would be cut down around him, one by one.

Ahmad Sidah, a ten-year member of Hizbellah, had been extremely proud to be chosen to be the group leader of this particular team. He and all of his men were thoroughly trained killers. They had all survived the hell of Syria, Lebanon, assaults on Israel and dozens of terrorist attacks on unarmed civilians. Now they were Allah's warriors in the Jihad to destroy the Great Satan. He had been among the first to volunteer to help bring the war to the American homeland. He had hoped to command one of the suicide teams sent to crash a plane into some famous landmark, but each must serve as Allah willed.

Here in America where most people depended on police protection and did not carry weapons, he had been so sure of success that he had been bragging to everyone about the large number of American devils that he would personally kill. Now most of his men were dead, he had wet his own pants in fear and the timetable was totally off. He had no idea what to do at this time.

He raised his head and cringed back as the bookrack above his head shook violently from a hail of bullets. Whoever had that weapon was a professional; his men had been no match for this single American killing machine. Ahmad put his head back down and concentrated on not fouling his pants any more than he already had.

Seeing two of the killers from the corridor break and run toward the safety of the outside, Hughes scrambled to his feet, and dove into the shambles of the restaurant. Keeping low, he literally scuttled across the floor to the shelter of an overturned table. Looking around the edge of the table, he spotted the two killers slipping and sliding as they tried to run across the center of the ice rink, trying to avoid the bloody bodies littering the ice. On the landing of the stairs that led from the ice rink to the street, the terrorist who had fired the LAW was laying down covering fire for his comrades, the bullets adding to the shambles inside the restaurant.

When the gunman that had fired the Law stopped to change magazines in his weapon, Hughes raised himself to his knees and returned fire, his first burst slammed into the chest of the terrorist, he fell forward to topple over the railing down onto the ice. When the two running killers saw their friend cut down, they tried to redouble their efforts to escape, but could only slip and slide as their efforts were frustrated by the icy surface. At his leisure, Hughes knocked the legs out from under both. Their blood began to stain the ice beneath them.

Hearing the sound of glass crunching behind him, Hughes spun around and pulled the trigger on his weapon. He was startled to hear it click on an empty chamber. He had made the potentially fatal mistake of running out of ammunition in a firefight. Raising his eyes, he found himself looking up the barrel of an UZI held in the capable hands of a stony faced Arab. Strangely, the smell of urine filled the air.

Hughes laughed to himself that the last smell he would ever smell was someone else's urine. Taking a deep breath, he braced himself for death, his own useless UZI falling from his hands to the littered floor before him.

Ahmad Sidah sneered at the figure kneeling before him. It was right that this man should die on his knees. On their knees was where all

American devils should be before a loyal servant of the one true God, Allah, thought Ahmad. Tightening his grip on his weapon, the Arab prepared to pull the trigger, but at the last second he hesitated, he realized that he knew this man. He was— he was—, but how did he get here; he had last seen him at the training base in Iran. For a moment Ahmad lowered his weapon.

"Carter, my friend, what are you doing here? Why are you killing my men?"

Resting his right hand on the glass-strewn floor, Hughes was winded. When he saw his captor slightly lower his weapon, he swept up a glass fragment and propelled it like a dart toward the terrorist's face. Unfortunately, the terrorist had time to jerk his head back and the glass only sliced his right eyelid. Slowly the terrorist raised his left hand to his face, it came away covered with blood.

The terrorist looked at his bloody hand and then back at Hughes, an expression of surprise on his swarthy face. His features hardened again and he gripped his UZI with both hands.

"Die traitor!" he snarled as his finger tightened on the trigger.

Hughes braced himself for death once again. The shot that echoed through the room was deafening. Hughes sagged back, waiting for the pain.

"Where's the pain?" Hughes thought to himself.

He was puzzled that he didn't feel any different, only tired and dead inside. He looked down at his chest, expecting to see blood, but he saw nothing other than the blood smears and dirt he had picked up crawling around on the dirty floor.

Puzzled, he looked up at the terrorist, who was still standing before him, face expressionless. The UZI was still pointing straight at Hughes' chest, the killer's eyes glaring at him. But slowly, the terrorist fell to his knees, the UZI fell from his suddenly limp hands. Like a great tree that has been chopped down, he slowly toppled forward to land on his face on the cluttered floor. It seemed that he tried to rise twice, but finally, he lay completely still.

It was several minutes before Hughes could tear his eyes away from the dead terrorist, but he finally raised his head. Behind where the terrorist had stood, Hughes could see a very disheveled, red haired young lady crouched beside an overturned table. A very large automatic pistol was clutched in her small right hand.

"Hi." she said with a lopsided grin on her makeup-smeared face. "Are you all right?"

Still slightly disoriented, Hughes took a moment to realize that the young lady had shot the terrorist rather than the terrorist shooting him. Suddenly overwhelmed by exhaustion, Hughes fell back into a sitting position, the realization that he hadn't been shot just beginning to penetrate his consciousness. The world around him began to spin, from the edge of his vision, darkness started to close in on him. He felt himself falling back against a nearby table.

His next sensation was of strong arms pulling him back upright, his head pushed between his knees. Strong hands began to massage his the back of his neck.

With a groan, he opened his eyes; it wasn't a dream. He had prayed that the entire event was a terrible dream, but when he opened his eyes, there were dead and dying all around him. He pulled back and looked at the owner of the hands massaging his neck. He saw that it was the girl with the long red hair. The one that had saved him. He started to speak, but then out of the corner of his eye, he spotted the bloody body of his wife. Pulling away from the girl, he rolled onto his stomach and, using his forearms, began to crawl toward her body. Beyond her, he could see the bodies of his two children.

He finally pulled himself into a sitting position beside his wife's body and tried to gather her up into his arms. To his despair, he didn't have the strength. Finally, he pulled her head into his lap and reached out to gather the small bodies of his children into his arms. He had his family back together one last time.

His grief was broken by the crack of a gunshot. He raised his head to see the girl peering around a table into the corridor beyond. She had just fired at a target. Sensing his movement, she looked back at him.

"I hate to interrupt you, but some of those guys are still out there. I'd suggest that we get out of here."

Hughes was having trouble focusing his attention on the meaning of her words. He knew there was danger, but he was strangely content to sit beside his wife's dead body. His family had never been apart in life, and he saw no reason to be separated from them in death. Even her infidelity, if it was real, was forgiven. He just wanted her back. He would just beside her and wait to be killed. For a moment, he was back on that jungle covered riverbank, a big man kneeled to his left.

"Make a run for it Lieutenant. I'll try to hold them off."

He turned toward the speaker and saw Sergeant Swanson kneeling behind him. He understood the words that Swanson had used, but he couldn't comprehend what Swanson wanted him to do. Shakily he reached out toward the Sergeant.

"She's dead, Sarge. My wife is dead."

Swanson shook his head, slowly.

"Dead's dead man. There's nothing you can do for her now. In this world you got to look out for your own ass, LT. I'd suggest you move it."

Shakily, Hughes reached out to grab Swanson's arm.

"Help me get my wife to safety." he pleaded.

Slowly, the riverbank faded away and Hughes was looking out at the bloody ice skating rink. He was reaching out at nothing. The girl came over to kneel beside him.

"Who're you talking to?" she asked in a gentle voice, looking around the cluttered room, "Whose Swanson?"

Visibly Hughes shook off the madness that threatened to envelope him.

"No one," he mumbled hunching even closer over his wife's dead body, "My wife is dead."

Gently, but firmly, she pulled Hughes away from his wife's bloody body.

"We've got to get out of here," she said again trying to pull him to his feet. "Or you'll be dead as well."

Tenderly he laid the bodies of his children down beside his wife and folded her arms around them. Martha had died trying to save them; he had failed them by living.

When Hughes finally stood up, she grabbed his hand and literally dragged him out of the shattered restaurant. She paused at the alcove that protected the escalator up into the General Electric Building. Satisfied that it was safe, she pulled Hughes onto the escalator and they rode it up to the street level. At the top of the escalator, she paused, and looked around carefully.

Slowly, she approached the revolving door to the street. Reaching out, she spun the door and ducked as a bullet ricocheted down the street. Keeping low, she ran back to where Hughes sat dazedly against a column. She dropped down beside him.

"Can't go that way," she said to him as she craned her neck to peer out the door.

With great effort, he turned his head toward her.

"Who are you?" he asked slowly and carefully, as if English was not his native language, his eyes filled with a great deal of pain and hurt.

Shifting her pistol to her left, a smile on her grimy face, she stuck out her right hand.

"Addie Vandemeyer, pleased to meet you."

For a long moment he simply stared at her outstretched hand, like he didn't know what to do with it. Then he slowly engulfed it in his own larger hand. Instead of shaking it, he just sat and held it, gently.

Finally, Addie pulled her hand away. She didn't know what was wrong with this guy, but he obviously had a real problem. More importantly, she had heard the Terrorist she had shot call him by name. That was of definite interest. As an investigative reporter for NBC, she was constantly under pressure to produce new and more important stories. If her suspicions were correct, this guy could represent the biggest story of her life.

"What's your name?" she prompted, digging in her purse for more ammo for her pistol.

"Carter, Carter Hughes." he responded absently, his head leaning against the cool marble wall.

For a long time they set silently against the column.

"I'm with NBC." she said, "and you?"

"North American Insurance." he responded in a dull, listless voice, his eyes closed.

"That woman that you sat beside, was that your wife?" she asked softly.

He nodded slowly, "Yes, we have, uh, no, we would have been married five years next week."

She gently touched his arm.

"I'm sorry," she said.

It was hard for her to know what to say. He sat as if he did not hear her. She could tell from his blank stare that his mind was a million miles away.

For his part, Hughes was back on that jungle covered riverbank, fighting that long lost battle over and over again. It was so real for him, he watched as the two men with him were overwhelmed by black uniformed figures. He sat frozen watching the battle rage around him. Suddenly, he jumped as he heard a female voice speak to him and a hand touch his arm.

"Mr. Hughes, It's time to go."

Frantically, Hughes looked around him, searching for the owner of the voice. Slowly, his vision began to blur again, the sounds of the raging battle began to fade from his ears. With a loud groan, he put his hands over his face and tried to block out the scene. He felt someone trying to pry his hands from his face and found himself being studied by a pair of lovely green eyes. He was back with Addie Vandemeyer.

"What did you say?" he asked her in confusion, looking around wildly for the jungle foliage.

"We need to get out of here. I looked out the door and the police and terrorists are still slugging it out," she repeated, "I won't feel safe until we've gotten to my office."

"You go," he said in a monotone, "I have to wait for Martha."

"Mr. Hughes, don't you remember? You wife is dead. She died downstairs." Addie said gently, standing and pulling at this arm. "We have to go now."

Obediently, he got to his feet and looked around the lobby, it seemed deserted. However, through the revolving door, he could see the body of a police officer lying outside on the sidewalk. The young lady was right, it was obviously better to be safe than sorry. He turned toward her to see her hold an UZI out to him.

"You seem to know how to use this, so you'd better have one," she said seriously.

Slowly, he took it from her and mechanically checked the magazine. When he looked up at her there was a new purpose in his gaze.

Addie didn't quite know what to make of her companion. He was a man of surprises, he looked in control but she half suspected that he was on the verge of flipping out entirely. She just hoped that he didn't have that UZI in his hands when he lost it. Shrugging, she turned and led the way back over to the stairs and down into the passages below.

Once on the lower level, she led the way along the passages until they reached the escalator up into the center area of the General Electric Building near the NBC elevators. Pausing briefly at the top of the escalator, she darted across the open expanse of hall to the safety of the elevator bank. Hughes ran easily along behind her. Addie reached out and pressed the up button. Impatiently, they waited for the car to arrive, and then at the same instant, they both piled inside at. Sighing in relief, she pushed the button for the twentieth floor and leaned back against the wall.

Silently they rode up in the car, until it arrived at her floor. As the door opened, they found themselves facing several large shotgun carrying security guards.

"Hold I, guys." Said Addie, holding out her hands to show that they were empty.

Luckily, the guards recognized Addie and allowed the two off of the elevator. Hughes started to relax in the midst of the guards, but to his surprise, Addie spun around and yelled.

"Grab him."

Instantly, Hughes was overwhelmed by the hulking guards, disarmed and pinned to the floor, his UZI jerked from his hands. By the time he realized what was happening, it was too late to fight. Giving in to the inevitable, he relaxed and allowed himself to hauled to his feet and hustled into a nearby office. He was shoved inside and the door locked behind him. It seemed that he had survived one battle only to lose another.

Chapter Sixteen

Hughes was locked in the office, but he was really too numb to care. He dropped into the desk chair and leaned back against the headrest. He was exhausted both emotionally and physically. His wife and children were dead. The true impact of that statement now hit him hard. He leaned forward and dropped his head into his hands, his body racked by great sobs.

In his mind, he was pulled back to that jungle covered riverbank. This time he saw himself lying on his back, looking up at a large blonde-haired Caucasian dressed in solid black fatigues, wearing a blue beret. His boot was pressed against Hughes' throat. Then, to his amazement, Hughes heard a door open. His mind couldn't determine how there could be a door out here in the jungle. Feeling his control starting to slip, he closed his eyes and tried to concentrate on where he really was. Instead of seeing the big blonde man, he found himself looking at a familiar young woman.

For the first time, his thought process returned to close to normal. Initially, he had no idea who she might be. She was small, probably no more than five feet tall, her hair was long, thick and red, hanging down to her waist. Even in his stunned state of mind, he noticed that she was very, very well proportioned. Regretfully, he had to admit to himself that he had no idea who she might be.

"Look," she began as she sat down across from him, "Mr. Hughes, I'm sorry for having you thrown in here, but I didn't know whether to trust you. You say you are an insurance man, but I just watched you take out a dozen trained terrorists. Then in the next breath you seem to be losing it mentally and I didn't want you to go crazy with an UZI in your hands."

"You are?" he asked slowly, massaging his temples with his thumbs.

She paused for a moment; her large eyes searched his swollen tear streaked face. It seemed to disconcert her when he made such an unexpected response.

"Vandemeyer, Addie Vandemeyer." she prompted, "Remember, I introduced myself earlier. After I saved your ass in the restaurant."

For a moment, he didn't remember anything, but then vaguely, he recalled someone by that name. They were sitting somewhere, leaning against a column.

Silently, he nodded. She studied him for a long time, before trying another approach.

"Besides, I wanted to check out to see if you were really who you said you were. For all I know, you could have been a terrorist, yourself."

Slowly, he nodded.

"I understand. I really don't blame you." he responded in a low, flat tone of voice.

Addie nervously jumped up and walked around the room to finally perch on the edge of the desk, her stylishly short blue dress riding high up her well shaped legs.

"Listen, I checked you out as well as I could. I talked to a Scott North at North American."

"My boss." returned Hughes in that same low, flat tone.

She nodded. "Yes, he confirmed that you were on the level. Actually, he spoke very highly of you. So I guess you can be trusted."

He shrugged as if he really didn't care.

She pensively studied him closely. As if writing notes for a news piece, she described him in her mind.

"He is a tall well proportioned man," she thought to herself, "well over six feet in height. His longish dark wavy hair fell over his high forehead. He had handsome features, wide shoulders, and narrow waist. She guessed he would weigh about two hundred and twenty pounds."

Under other circumstances, she thought to herself, she could be very attracted to this man.

She didn't know how to get him to open up, so she took the direct approach.

"Listen, that terrorist I shot, it was clear that he knew you. Who was he?" she asked, her eyes intently watching him. "I think I have the right to know. Did you know him?"

There was a big story here and she wanted it.

For a long moment, Hughes just sat and stared at her. He was searching his memory for the man she was taking about. At first he had no clue as to whom she meant, but then he had a mental picture of a shabbily dressed man pointing a weapon at him. Something about him—Hughes' mind groped for the rest of the thought. Then, he remembered, the man with the gun had fallen forward, a woman—this woman in front of him, had shot him. As if this one memory had opened the floodgates, more memories began to come to him in waves.

He remembered the battle, his wife and children shot down before his eyes. His own furious battle with the terrorists. The final memory was of the face of the terrorist, for a split second, he almost knew the man's name. His name was—It was—Ah———. Ahmad, his name was Ahmad, and Hughes knew him because——because——then he lost the memory. Slowly he shook his head.

"I really don't know who he was. Perhaps I just looked like someone he knew."

Addie knew, as well as she knew her own name, that Hughes knew more than he was telling. She just didn't know how to get it out of him.

She was looking for something else to say when Hughes asked a question.

"I'm afraid I can't by that, Mr. Hughes." She responded, "I heard him. He called you by name."

"Well, that's the only answer you're going to get from me." he snapped, "I have no idea what that man was."

"O.K., O.K. Calm down." She said in a soothing tone of voice.

For a long moment he set quietly, looking at the ceiling. She also sat and watched him with those big green eyes. Finally, he broke the self-imposed silence.

"Can I use a phone?" he asked softly, his eyes dull, dead.

She reached across the desk, spun the phone around and punched in an outside line. Hearing a dial tone, she handed him the phone.

He took the receiver and slowly punched out a number. He leaned against the desk until the phone was picked up on the other end.

"Renaldi Enterprises." said a cool professional female voice.

."Howard Renaldi, please."

Addie jumped at the name. Why would this man call one of the richest men in the country? There was more to this Carter Hughes than met the eye.

"Whose calling?" asked the voice.

"Carter Hughes, his son in law." he responded.

The professionalism of the voice broke for a moment.

"Oh, Mr. Hughes, I didn't recognize your voice, this is Carla Morgan. I'm so sorry. Just a moment, I'll put you through."

In seconds Hughes heard the deep voice of Howard Renaldi.

"Carter my boy, are you O.K.? Where are you?" he demanded. "All hell seems to have broken loose out there."

"I'm fine, Howard, a little shaken up but generally fine. I'm in the NBC building. I wanted to tell you— I mean I felt that I should tell you—I mean." he broke off, unable to continue.

Addie reached across the desk and took the phone from his hand.

"Mr. Renaldi, this is Addie Vandemeyer of NBC. Your son in law is safe here. He called to tell you that, well," she paused, "There's really no good way to tell something like this, but he wanted to tell you that terrorists killed your daughter and her children."

She heard a sharp intake of breath.

"Are you sure?" the man on the other end of the line asked quietly.

"Yes sir. I saw it happen. Your son in law tried to save them, but he didn't have a chance."

She listened to him breathe loudly into the phone for a few moments. Finally, Renaldi's famous iron self control reasserted itself.

"Thank you for telling me, Miss. When I heard the news that something had happened at the Rockefeller Center, knowing that my son in law worked near there, I called his office. They told me that he had gone to meet his family for lunch. I rushed several of my security personnel over to the restaurant, but they seemed to have arrived too late. They reported back that the place was a shambles with bodies lying all over the place. Then when the news about the rest of the disasters hit the airwaves, was almost frantic."

Addie sighed deeply, all the death amidst the opulence of Rockefeller Center. She glanced at Hughes who again had his head in his hands.

"I don't mean to tell you how to do things, sir, but I would recommend that you have someone look at your son in law. He's taking this very hard."

"Thank you for your recommendation. They were very much in love. I'll have my doctor look at him. In fact, I'll have two of my security people come get him."

"That's not necessary, sir. I've already arranged for two of our people to take him home."

"I recommend that they be very careful. According to my men there are running gun battles taking place all over the city. It's not safe on the streets. There are many police, but the street gangs are having a field day."

"I'll make sure they are careful." She responded, "But if I may be so bold, there are a couple of points that I want to clear up if I can."

"Such as?" Howard Renaldi asked.

"Has you son in law, to your knowledge, ever been in the middle east?"

Howard Renaldi didn't answer for a long moment.

"Why do you ask such a question at a time like this?"

"I don't know. Something happened that just brought up the question." she responded.

"Well, if you must know, to my knowledge, he hasn't been out of this country since he has been married to my daughter. Before that I wouldn't have any way of knowing."

"Do you know anything about his military training or if he was ever in the army?" she asked.

"Hmmmmm, no I don't. I don't think that he was ever in the Army, but I don't know for sure." he responded.

Addie contemplated asking several more questions, but she had an intuitive suspicion that she wouldn't get anywhere. She didn't know why but she didn't believe that Renaldi was telling her the truth. She was sure that anyone who married a Renaldi would be checked out back to conception.

"Well, thanks a lot." said Addie, "Don't worry, we'll get him home. Oh, one other thing that I'm sure he would want to know."

"What's that?" Renaldi asked cautiously.

Glancing again at Hughes, she cupped her hand over her mouth and the lower part of the phone receiver.

"Can your people arrange to claim your daughter's body and that of her children?" she asked in a low voice.

"Rest assured, young lady, instructions have already been given to do that." he responded gravely. "Please tell Carter that I'll have my doctor come by his apartment as soon as it is safe to travel the streets."

With her thanks, Addie hung up the phone. She wasn't sure what it was that made her worry about Hughes, probably, the same feeling she would have had for a sick puppy. As big as he was and as deadly as she had seen that he could be, there was something really helpless about this man.

There was a couch against one wall of the office and with a lot of urging, she was able to get him across the office and stretched out on the couch. He lay back with his left arm across his eyes. Gently, she loosened his tie and removed his shoes. From a closet, she removed a light blanket and covered him. Almost before she had him fully settled, he was asleep.

Quietly, she tiptoed across the office trying not to disturb the sleeper. What she didn't know was that while his body aped the signs of sleep, his mind was wide-awake. In fact, in his mind, he was locked in a bamboo cage, being tortured by numerous laughing black clad men. A small portion of his mind was marveling at the extreme reality of the dream. Slowly, the dreams of last night and the events of the day had begun to unravel some very complex mental programming within Hughes mind. Like two lumps of clay, the two personalities that had long existed in his mind, unknown to each other, began to merge to create a larger, tougher single personality.

Addie couldn't see any of this inner working. She only saw a man pushed close to the end of his rope. With a small, sad smile on her face, she cut out the office lights and stood for a few moments watching him sleep.

Gently, Addie eased out of the door, pulling it closed behind her. She turned to find Moses Gardner, photographer and probably her best friend in the world waiting for her in the hall. One of his easy grins split his dark skinned face.

"Well, now I've seen it all. Girl, I've seen you bring in and nurse injured birds, sick pups and even, that time in southern Iran, a sick camel, but this is a first even for you. I've never seen you even look at a man twice and now you're playing Florence Nightingale to this one."

Addie blushed slightly, and then flared back.

"Moses Gardner, I'll have you know that he just saw his wife and kids killed in front of him and then almost single handedly he wiped out their killers. He was like Rambo the way he blasted back at them. I'd say at one time he was a trained commando or maybe Green Beret. So—"

She paused at that point, leaned against the wall and rubbed her chin slowly.

"So you decided to adopt this Manhattan Rambo and nurse him back to health?" he finished, half question and half statement.

"Hush, I'm thinking," she snapped.

Gardner, recognizing that look, groaned to himself. She was going off on one of her tangents; it had all of the signs.

"Do you still have that friend of yours at the National Security Agency?" she asked.

"Yes, you know I do." he returned with a tired sigh. "What is it you want to know."?

"Howard Renaldi just told me that this man was never in the Army to his knowledge. You know that before he could have married Renaldi's daughter the old man would have known everything that there was to know about him. In an hour, I want to see a copy of his military file. I want to know exactly who Carter Davis Hughes is, besides being the son in law of the rich and powerful Howard Renaldi."

Moses whistled slowly, "Renaldi. Whoa, girl if you tweak Renaldi's nose, he'll buy this network just to have the pleasure of firing you. That man has more political connections and more money that anyone else I know."

"Oh, piffle," she snapped back at him. "Who can fault me for merely looking for information?"

Moses slowly shook his head, but he knew he was fighting a losing battle. Mumbling to himself, he walked down the hall to his office. He navigated through a real maze of stacks of photos and cameras to drop into his chair.

Addie went straight to the newsroom. She wanted to know what was happening. To her delight, the anchor waiting to go on the air was Cyrus Wentworth.

"Addie." Wentworth exclaimed in delight, leaning forward to hug the reporter.

"Cyrus, glad to see you." She said enthusiastically returning the hug. "What's happening out there?"

His face fell as he sadly shook his well-coiffured head.

"Ah, Addie, it is utter chaos. The north tower of the World Trade Center is in flames, tens of thousands are probably dead. The rescue units are converging now. There are gun battles all over the city. One Police Plaza is in flames, hundreds are dead. Escaped prisoners run the streets. The New York Stock Exchange is in flames, the traders killed as they began the trading day. I never thought I would see things like this in America."

Addie knew that it was bad, but she didn't know it was that bad.

"The police? Maybe the Mayor should call the National Guard."

"Many of the police are dead at Police Plaza. According to the latest reports, a lot of the patrol units are on fire, the officers dead in the street."

"The Mayor?" asked Addie again.

Wentworth shrugged.

"Gracie Mansion was in flames according to the last reports. The guard detail is mostly dead. No one has seen the Mayor since this morning."

"I guess we're in deep shit." Observed Addie in a classic understatement.

An hour later, Addie came back to check on Hughes. With her she had a local Doctor who had stopped in to see a friend on the NBC staff and been trapped in the building. Addie gently shook Hughes' shoulder. Groggily, he pulled himself back from a large white cage filled room to New York City. Slowly, gently she helped him sit up straight.

"Mr. Hughes, this is Doctor McGuire. He's going to look over your injuries," she said slowly to the disoriented man.

Under Addie's expert supervision, Dr. McGuire checked Hughes over thoroughly. The various cuts and bruises were treated and then he prescribed some sedatives for his new patient. Finally, Dr. McGuire finished his exam and closed his bag.

"Well, Mr. Hughes, you are a very lucky man. According to Miss Vandemeyer, you have spent your afternoon playing John Wayne and by all rights you should resemble a large piece of Swiss cheese. I now prescribe rest, sleep and a good meal."

He handed Hughes a card.

"If you have any problems, then I suggest you either see your local doctor or call me."

Hughes tiredly nodded in response. He was sleepy again; he could barely keep his eyes open. Addie let the Doctor out and then called for the security guards waiting outside in the hall.

"Guys, can you take Mr. Hughes to his apartment?"

"Sure," responded the senior guard, "for him, anything."

"It's a war zone out there, guys," warned the doctor as he packed his instruments into his bag. "I suggest you take extra care."

"You know it, Doctor. We plan on tiptoeing in the shadows," responded the senior guard.

Gently, they helped Hughes to his feet and transported him down to a well-guarded automobile. Hughes was almost asleep most of the time, but he was alert enough to know that the streets were both deserted and silent. Here and there fires burned, several dead firemen and police lying in the street showed that there were still dangers. The only people out seemed to be lying in the streets and hanging motionless from crashed cars. New York City was a city living in fear of the next attack.

As Addie had asked, the guards escorted Hughes all the way to his apartment door. Fumbling, his hands seeming to belong to someone else, he pulled out his keys and entered the darkened room. For a long time he just stood in the dark and leaned against the door. This would be the first night he had spent in New York without Martha. She had not only found the place they called home, but she had lovingly decorated each room.

Slowly, he wandered around in the dark, finding the furniture with his outstretched hands. Eventually, his rambling path led him into the room he dreaded the most, their bedroom. Martha's smile had always lit this room so that he had subconsciously considered it the brightest in the house. Now she was gone, her sunny smile would be seen no more. Still fully clothed, he fell across the bed, pulling the bed spread over him as he fell into a deep, troubled sleep. As he laid silently, Matilda, forgotten for the moment came to stand in the doorway. Her dark eyes intently studying the man, as he lay in troubled sleep.

Across the City, in that plush, richly furnished conference room, a tall swarthy complexioned individual was standing before the twelve who sat around the table. The overhead lights were turned off, throwing the room into a darkened pit. There was one table lamp lit. That lone light was so oriented that the faces of the men at the table were in darkness. The only fully discernible thing in the room was the picture of George Washington on the wall across the room from the man standing before the table.

"How did such a thing happen?" demanded one of the men sitting to his left.

Hadji Hindawi, terrorist leader, member of the Supreme Council of the Hiz Ballah, knew that if he said the wrong thing, he was only minutes from his own death. He had been so sure that there was nothing that could have gone wrong with his plan for the attack on the Rockefeller Center Restaurant, but something did. How that one man could have taken out ten of his highly trained freedom fighters was beyond belief.

"I don't know," returned Hadji with a shrug, "something seems to have set him off early. Unfortunately, his target was our people and not those planned."

"Did anyone know that his family would be present?" asked another of the seated men. "Could their deaths have triggered something? Damaged the programming?"

Another present responded to that question.

"Highly unlikely." came a suave voice from the darkness, "His programming was such that only the key words should have released his, shall we say, alternate personality."

The man who sat quietly at the head of the table slammed one hand down on the table. It resounded throughout the room like a pistol shot, gaining the attention of all present.

"Well something happened to him. While we were totally successful in removing the threat to us at the Federal Building, we have lost ten of our best men in what should have been a very minor operation. What should have been another outstanding victory for our forces has now been neutralized, in fact turned into a fucking disaster, as a result of one our own weapons gone awry."

He paused for a long moment. No one in the room dared breath a word. The leader was in a foul mood and his word could mean their death.

"Hadji," he continued, "you will take steps to move up the plans for the assassination. However, more importantly, you will take that young man into custody, immediately."

"At once, RAVEN."

The Doctor cleared his throat and spoke again.

"And Hadji, be careful with our "Comrade". Handle him gently. He is not to be harmed."

Hadji tried to pierce the gloom and see the face of the one he called the Doctor, but could only see his hands that rested on the table. On the Doctor's right hand was a large gold ring, topped by what looked like a family crest. On the left wrist, the terrorist could just barely make out what looked like a large gold Rolex.

"Naturally, Doctor."

"What if he has actually turned against us?" asked a figure to the left of the leader. "Is such possible?"

All eyes were turned toward the shadowy figure at the head of the table. When he sat silent, they all waited patiently. Finally, he spoke again.

"Doctor, in your 'considered' medical opinion, is there a chance that he could have turned against us? Is there any possible way that he could be our enemy?"

The right hand left the circle of light on the table to rub against the unseen face. For long moments the Doctor sat silently.

"I don't think so. Remember, that as advanced as medical since is, the human mind is really a mystery. However, you must remember that the mind control program first developed by our German friends during World War II was refined and finally brought to full developed by a Canadian psychiatrist for use by the American CIA.

The CIA has used this system of brainwashing, if you will forgive the term, since the 1950's. The Red Chinese and the North Koreans used this type of mental programming to break the minds of American Soldiers. There has never been a complete failure of programming in all that time. It is my opinion that his programming is still intact. This situation at Rockefeller Center is, I firmly believe, an unfortunate aberration."

"I hope you are correct, Doctor." responded the man at the head of the table. "For all our sakes, you had better be. If something has gone wrong with the programming, this man could be a deadly loose cannon."

He paused for a few seconds as if collecting his thoughts.

"There is a new factor." he began, "My sources inform me that an NBC network investigative reporter by the name of Addie Vandemeyer, has shown some recent interest in the background of our "Protégé". It would be unfortunate for all of us if she should find out more than is good for her to know."

"I will take care of Miss Vandemeyer," said the man sitting at the leader's right.

Raven turned his head slightly to glance at the man that had spoken.

"Good. But she is not to be hurt. If word should get out that we had intentionally harmed a reporter, we would lose the ear of the media and it is important to our plan. I believe that this finishes our business this evening.

Hadji, you have one more chance. If you fail us again, it is better that you do not survive the failure. Better to die a martyr than a failure."

Hadji bowed and left the room. He was seething at what had been said by those infidels. He was a Prince of the Royal Blood; he was not to be spoken to like a lackey. He would get his revenge, but now was not the time. These individuals were financing his war against their own countrymen. For now he would take their insults.

The one light in the conference room snapped off as, one by one, the other members of the council left the room. Soon only the leader was left sitting in the darkened room. For several hours, he simply sat in the dark, smoking a large cigar as he contemplated the future. It was all coming together. Soon, very soon, he thought, he would have more power than any man in history. When that happened, he would no longer need the support of the Brotherhood or the mystery man behind the conspiracy.

CHAPTER SEVENTEEN

Hughes pulled himself out of his stupor and began the long, painful trip toward full wakefulness. Groaning, he threw off the bedspread, rolled to the edge of the bed and fell to the floor on his knees. For long moments he wasn't able to remember anything other than simple things like his name. He tried to stand but instead fell back to his knees.

Painfully, he crawled across the thick carpet to the cool tiled floor of the bathroom. Grabbing to the sink, he pulled himself to his feet and stumbled into the shower. He turned on the water and let it run over his face. Slowly, he began to feel better, more in control of himself. Leaning his forehead against the cool tile, he began to peel his dirty clothes. He blindly threw them out of the shower to lie in a pile on the bathroom floor.

For at least a half an hour, he stood and soaked his battered body under the hard spray. Listlessly, he soaped his hair and his skin until he felt his knotted muscles begin to release under the warmth of the water. Finally, he tired of the shower and turned off the spray. Wiping his face, he stepped out into the cool air of the bathroom and began to slowly towel off.

Physically, he felt better, but mentally, he was still felt numb. He couldn't believe that his wife and kids were dead. They were gone, as if they had never existed, but he could reach out and touch the shower curtain that Martha had picked out, the knickknacks that she had used to decorate the bathroom. He just couldn't bring himself to admit that she was gone. Like a marionette whose strings had been cut, he dropped to the floor, his towel clutched to his chest. Great sobs shook his body. A sound in the doorway alerted him that he was not alone. He looked up to see Matilda. He'd forgotten about her. The children's nanny-but he had no children-now.

"Mr. Hughes, we need to talk."

Addie Vandemeyer was not having a good morning. With the deaths yesterday of so many of NBC's field reporters, she had been pressed into service covering the explosion at the Federal Building. She wasn't averse to covering a story involving death and murder. It was the sheer viciousness of the previous days attacks that bothered her.

Her main problem, however, was that she was totally pissed at her own network. The Executive Vice President of the News Division, Arthur Teicher, had called her into his office when she had arrived at seven that morning. She had been out prowling the deserted streets all night looking for stories. She had returned dead tired, planning on sleeping in his office for a couple of hours then getting back out on the streets.

The last thing she had expected was being summoned into the presence of the Great Man as the rest of the staff called him. He had been in a meeting with Peter Novak, Assistant Operations Manager when she arrived at his office. She had nothing against Teicher, but she absolutely loathed Novak.

"Addie, I want you to drop everything else and dig into this bombing at the Federal Building."

"But, sir," she protested. "I have a lead on the terrorists. I met a man, yesterday, Carter Hughes; he knew one of the terrorists. I want to follow up on Hughes."

At that point, that prissy little upstart, Novak had stuck his big mouth into the middle of the discussion.

"That's the very thing you can't do, Miss Vandemeyer. I received a call from Howard Renaldi personally yesterday. He wanted to make sure that there was no mention of any of his family in our reporting of the incidents of yesterday. He is naturally grateful for your help to his son-in-law, but he wants our involvement with Mr. Hughes to end there. This Hughes is his son-in-law, and is much to busy to take time to talk with you."

Under her glare, Teicher looked decidedly uncomfortable. "I'm sorry, Addie, but we need you on this Federal Building bombing. I have been instructed to tell you that if you value your job with this network, you are to report on the Federal Building bombing and nothing else. Other reporters have been assigned to cover the other attacks. We really have no time for your personal investigations."

She had been so angry that she had tears in her eyes as she stormed out of the office. What made it even more infuriating, was Novak's self-satisfied smirk. One day, she promised herself, she would wipe that asinine expression off his fat little face.

It was a major effort, but she turned her mind back to her present assignment. The authorities were not yet willing to call the explosion at the Federal Building a terrorist attack, and yet there were no other explanation that made any sense. It would be simply too much of a coincidence for an accidental explosion to take place at the exact moment that a suspected leader of a terrorist organization was being interviewed. Then there was the additional evidence of all of the dead reporters. Rumor had it that nine-millimeter wounds had killed them all. Why all of the secrecy, she wondered?

Slowly, Addie picked her way through the debris surrounding the Federal Building, a cameraman following in her wake. Naturally, the bodies that littered the area in front of the building had been collected by the coroner's office, but the mystery remained. What really happened, what caused the explosion? There seemed to be absolutely no witnesses.

Finally, after considering what little information she had been able to collect, Addie had to conclude that it would take better heads than hers to solve the mystery of these killings. She turned to the cameraman following close behind her.

"Jim, why don't you go on back to the station? I think we've gotten all that we can get for the time being," she said, shading her eyes with her right hand.

Jim Corralson dropped his video camera from his shoulder.

"You sure? I mean, we've shot only a little film."

Addie shrugged eloquently and waved one slim arm at the pockmarked front of the Federal Building.

"I don't know about you, but I don't see anything else we can shoot. The inside of the building is off-limits and guarded, the dead have been hauled away and no one wants to talk. So, hot shot, what do you suggest we shoot?"

"Hey, I don't know what we ought to be doing, after all, you're the star reporter. I'm just suggesting that we may have wasted a trip if we don't get more than we've already collected. Besides, I hear that it took some powerful strings being pulled to get permission to put the news van on the street, what with the curfew and all."

Addie sighed and let her shoulders slump. "Sorry, Jim, I'm just a little edgy right now. Why don't you go on back, I'll poke around a little more and talk to people in the neighborhood. I have my car here and I'll be in later."

"Sure thing, Miss Vandemeyer. I'll tell Mr. Petrie you'll see him later about the story."

She should really be scouting around for any information regarding the terrorists, but all she could think about was Carter Davis Hughes. All of her instincts told her that he knew far more about what was going on that he was admitting. But at the same time she believed him when he said that he didn't know anything more than what he had told her. She couldn't figure him out; she couldn't decide what to think of him.

"Poor guy," she murmured to herself, "having to watch his entire family being shot down before his very eyes. No wonder he was out of it."

Shaking herself out of her daydream, Addie turned and started for her car. She had decided to go by the Coroner's office and see if anything had turned up from an examination of the bodies found in the F.B.I. office. As she walked toward her car, Addie's eyes constantly scanned the area; the street was deserted.

"Psst, hey you." she heard.

"Hey, over here." came the voice again.

After looking around the entire area, Addie decided that the voice was coming from a large trash container sitting on the edge of the parking lot. Cautiously, she strolled over to the dumpster and raised the lid. She had been expecting to see someone inside, but she was surprised to see two blue eyes staring at her out from beneath a tangle of black hair.

"Hey, lady, you want to get me killed? Drop the lid," demanded the figure half- buried in the garbage.

Startled, Addie let the lid fall shut. Casually, she turned to lean against the side of the garbage container. Of course, even her sainted deaf grandmother would think it somewhat odd that she was talking to a garbage container.

"Who are you?" she asked quietly, scanning the street. She could see a pair of heavily armed officers patrolling the grounds of the damaged Federal Building. To her relief, they paid no attention to her.

"That's not important," came the quiet voice from the dumpster, "are you one of them reporters?"

"Yes, I am. Did you happen to see what happened here yesterday?"

"No, I weren't here yesterday."

"Oh. Well, what do you want?" she asked, digging in her purse for her notebook.

"It ain't fer me. I got a friend who was here yesterday. He wants to talk to a reporter."

"I'll talk to him," she offered as she tried to appear to be casually waiting for someone.

"He wants to talk to one particular reporter. What's yer name?"

"Vandemeyer, Addie Vandemeyer."

"I thought you was her. You look just like he described."

"Who is this HE, you keep talking about?" she demanded, spinning around to glare at the trash container.

"Not so fast. I've got to be careful. I've got to take you to him, he can't come to you."

"Why can't he come to me? If he's worried about protection, NBC will protect him. Have him meet me at my office." she said firmly.

"Can't." returned the voice and, for the first time, the superior attitude of the person in the dumpster appeared to falter, "He's hurt bad. He may not last the day."

Addie made an instant decision.

"O.K. take me to him." she said, feeling the comfortable weight of the pistol in her purse.

"Get in your car and back it up beside this dumpster. Won't do for anyone to see us together, they might follow us back to him."

"But—"

"Just do it, lady. If he dies before we get back or if they find him before we get to him, then you won't get nothing. Besides, if someone spots you talking to this here oversized garbage can, they might be moved to investigate and we can't have that."

Quickly, Addie returned to her car, started and backed up by the dumpster. She turned to try and see who got out of the garbage container, but was surprised when the door was immediately jerked open and a small figure literally dove into the passenger seat of the car.

"Drive, lady. Make sure no one is following."

Immediately, Addie drove out of the parking lot and headed to the right. She made several turns and doubled back more than once; as near as she could determine, there was no one following her. In fact hers' appeared to be the only car on the street, other than the ever-increasing number of armored vehicles that were appearing on the scene. She looked at her watch, it was a little after noon, curfew was at six p.m. Apparently, the mayhem of the previous day worked better than a curfew to get people off of the street. She could feel the fear in the air.

"All clear, sport. There's no one following. Now what it this all about?"

"Head for the east side, 32nd street."

Obediently, Addie navigated through the empty streets of New York City until she arrived at East 32nd street.

"We're here, now where?" she asked as she looked cautiously around.

"See anyone?" asked her mysterious companion.

Again Addie carefully studied her surroundings.

"Nope. All clear."

"O.K. As soon as you can, pull over and park this heap. We go the rest of the way on foot."

Obediently, Addie pulled her car over against the curb. She prayed that her companion was on the level. After all, this could be an elaborate setup for a rape or murder, but she had long ago learned to trust her instincts. Those instincts told her now that she was onto something big.

To her surprise, when her new companion joined her beside the car, she discovered that the voice belonged to a young girl who, she judged, was probably in her teens. The girl appeared to be about 5'3" and was dressed in a brown coat and pair of dark pants a couple of sizes too big. Over those black curls was pulled a floppy black hat. She reeked of the garbage dumpster.

"Follow me," she snapped as she darted across the street.

Gritting her teeth, Addie darted after her guide. For several minutes they wove a complicated course through alleys and deserted courtyards.

Quite frankly, Addie had long since lost track of where she was when they arrived at the rear entrance of a nondescript apartment building.

"In here." said her guide, pulling open the door.

Silently, Addie followed the woman down a narrow hallway to a flight of stairs. On the first landing, a hand signal from her companion brought Addie to a halt. As quietly as possible, the youngster knocked out a complicated tattoo on the door.

"Who's there?" came a quavering voice through the door.

"It's me, Bet."

The door opened and Addie was almost jerked into a dingy apartment by a strong pair of hands. Before she could catch her breath, she was spun around, expertly frisked and dropped into an overstuffed chair.

The next thing she knew, she was looking at the business end of a .45 automatic held in the capable looking hands of a middle-aged woman. Bet was rummaging through Addie's purse.

"What do you—-?" began Addie.

"Shut up." hissed her captor, as she pushed a strand of dishwater blond hair out of her eyes.

"But—."

This time, the woman with the gun almost climbed on top of her prisoner, her own rage-contorted face only inches from Addie's.

"I said hush, bitch, or I'll splatter you all over this apartment." she growled.

Addie glanced at Bet who was now digging through Addie's wallet checking her I.D.

"It's her, Miranda. This is her driver's license, says that she is Addie Vandemeyer." said the younger girl, shoving Addie's driver's license in front of the older woman's face.

Suddenly, the woman thrust the gun toward the young girl. "Here, Bet, watch her while I check with him," she said, continuing to clutch Addie's identification in her hand.

Bet took the gun and dropped down on the coffee table, the barrel never wavering from Addie as the older woman crossed through the living room and into a bedroom.

For a long period, the two just sat and looked at each other. In this light, Addie could tell that the girl was a little older than she had first thought, the short black curly hair actually a wig, as some platinum blonde strands of hair were now hanging down in the girl's eyes.

Addie began to study the room. It was a typical New York apartment living room, relatively small, the furnishings not expensive, but serviceable, though most had seen better days. The couch had a few tears in its' fabric, stuffing was beginning to force its way out through threadbare areas. The carpet was old and worn by hundreds of feet over the years. There was a faint odor lingering in the air, but she couldn't determine what was making the odor. Finally, Addie broke the silence.

"What's this all about?" she asked.

Her captor sat silently, totally ignoring Addie, her young smooth features totally blank.

"It's her, Bet," said the older woman, relief in her voice.

Silently, the younger girl stood and pocketed the gun. Addie relaxed and stood up.

"In here, he's waiting."

At the urging of the older woman Addie stepped into the dimly lit bedroom and the door was pulled closed behind her leaving the room in almost total darkness.

At first her eyes had trouble adjusting, not only were the shades drawn, but also the curtains were pulled tightly together. Uncertain what to do, she stood just inside the doorway until her sharp ears detected a slight movement from the bed.

Slowly, she felt her way across the room. "Hello?"

"Addie." Rasped a faint whispery voice, "I'm glaaaad you came. I wasn't sure that I could wait long enough to see you."

"Who are you?" questioned Addie.

A weak laugh came from the darkness. Slowly, she moved toward the sound of the voice, her arms feeling ahead of her. Finally one of her hands touched a lampshade. Feeling along the length of the shade, she found a dangling chain. She pulled the chain and flooded the room with weak light. She had to blink a couple of times to adjust to the light, and then found herself looking at something directly out of her wildest nightmare. She was looking at a totally ruined human body, so damaged that it was a miracle that life still remained.

"Oh, my God," she breathed.

"Addie my girl, I'm so glad to see you, again."

"Who—-?" she began in a choked voice.

Another weak laugh came from the ruined figure on the bed. "Forgot me already have you girl? Well,—-" he was interrupted by a fit of coughing.

"We've got to get you to a doctor." protested Addie.

The bandaged face turned toward her.

"No—no. Addie you must listen. I don't have much time. It's me, Bernie Kahane. I need to tell you what I know about what is going on."

Addie dropped to her knees beside the bed. When she had first been assigned to New York years ago, she had covered the crime beat. Bernie had been one of her first sources of information inside of the established law enforcement agencies and the reason that she had broken so many big stories in this city. Then they had become more than just friends, it had been one of her few serious love affairs.

If she had stayed, they would have probably married, but she got the offer of an assignment in Saudi Arabia to cover Desert Storm. It had been a tough choice between her career and her personal feelings. After Desert Storm had been an assignment in Iran, then she had gone undercover in Iraq. Time had just sped by; she wouldn't be in New York now if she hadn't been recalled to take part in a television special on terrorism.

She smiled as she remembered that Moses used to refer to her and Bernie as a major item before her agreement to accept the assignment to Saudi Arabia. She remembered how big, strong, but tender Bernie had been. Now she wanted to cry, it was devastating to see him reduced to this shell. She gently laid her hands on the man lying on the bed.

"Bernie, what happened? Who did this to you?"

Drawing a deep breath, Kahane blindly groped for Addie's hand. She could tell that he really couldn't see her. One eye was totally bandaged and the other was so swollen that it appeared to be closed. She couldn't help but wince as her hand felt the stubs of his ruined fingers through his makeshift bandages.

"Satan———-Satan is among us." he gasped.

She thought he was delirious and tried to get him to lie still.

Then in a clear, normal sounding voice he began to talk to her.

"Remember, this Addie: Yea though I may walk through the valley of the shadow of death I will fear no evil for I am the meanest son of a bitch in the valley. Don't forget this Addie. Promise me you won't forget!" he begged.

Addie leaned over the dying man.

"I promise Bernie. I promise I won't forget it."

She thought for a moment that he was gone then he weakly moved one hand.

"Look for the man with one blue eye and one green eye. He is the key," gasped Kahane as he arched his body in pain. He fell back against his pillow and lost his tenuous grip on consciousness. Worried, Addie placed her fingers against his neck, the pulse was extremely weak. Each beat of his fast-weakening heart seemed to be his last.

Addie leaned her head against the side of the bed. Bernie obviously knew more than he told her. All he had said merely left her another riddle—why would Bernard Kahane, a professed atheist, want to quote scripture at a time like this? Who was the man with one blue eye and one green eye? How was she to find this man? God—she was totally out of her depth.

As she knelt there holding Bernie's hand, she felt him quiver and jerk. The fingers momentarily tightened and then he was still. Frightened, she got to her feet and ran to the door. "Come quickly, do something."

The older woman ran into the room and leaned over the body, taking his pulse. After a few moments, she sighed, crossed his hands over his chest and pulled the sheet over his face.

"He's gone." was all she said to Addie as they both wept quietly.

CHAPTER EIGHTEEN

Cutting out the light, leaving the dead man in the darkness of the stuffy bedroom, the woman led Addie back into the living room. While they'd been in the bedroom, the younger girl had made coffee and now, as the other two rejoined her, she poured three cups and carried them to the table. With a wave of her hand, the older woman motioned Addie to take a seat.

"Sorry about the gun and all, Ms. Vandemeyer, but Bernie said I should be extremely careful." she pushed a loose strand of hair behind her right ear.

Addie's legs just seemed to give away and she dropped gratefully into one of the chairs at the table. Things were simply happening too fast. She had to begin to make some sense out of these events.

"Who are you two?" she asked quietly, feeling the weariness flood over her.

The older one shrugged her shoulders. "Well, not that it is really important, but I'm Miranda Ochoa and this is my" here Miranda paused slightly, "friend, Betty Connors."

Addie silently sipped her coffee as she considered the best way to approach the matter. Carefully sitting her cup back on its saucer she glanced at the bedroom door.

"How do-did- you know Bernie?" she asked.

Miranda looked for a moment as if she might finally start to cry. Her almost masculine Hispanic machismo appeared to drop away, leaving her hurt and vulnerable. Betty slipped quietly out of the room into another bedroom.

"Bernie was a good man, he helped us when no one else would."

Miranda toyed with her cup.

"You see, Betty and I are very close, actually, we're more than friends. We're——"

Miranda couldn't seem to decide how to describe the relationship, so Addie decided to help her.

"You mean that you're lovers?" she asked gently with a small smile.

Miranda smiled her thanks and nodded.

"Yes. We had been arrested in a setup at one of the local clubs that cater to couples like us. I'm thirty-five but Betty was only seventeen at the time. I was threatened with prosecution for statutory rape unless I helped some crooked cops set up a politician for blackmail. I didn't want to, but I also didn't want to lose Betty and I sure didn't want to go to jail, myself. They even threatened to turn her over to the juvenile authorities if I didn't help."

Miranda paused as Betty returned to the room, a changed girl. The black wig was gone and the platinum blonde hair was combed out so that it fell to the center of her back. Instead of the baggy clothes, she was wearing a skimpy halter-top that emphasized her unusually large chest and a micro mini skirt that exposed most of her long slim legs. Addie had to admit that Betty was a beautiful young lady by anyone's standards. Miranda held out a hand to the younger girl and Betty pulled a chair close to her and they held hands.

"Not knowing who to turn to," continued Miranda, "I asked around and was advised to go to Bernie. After all, he was a top investigator with the U.S. Attorney's office. He helped us and kept our names out of it. He was a good man. I hope whoever did this——"

Miranda's control finally gave way and, putting her hands over her face, she began to cry silently. Betty pulled her close, while Addie patiently sipped her coffee and waited for Miranda to regain control of herself.

"I'm sorry." she said, rubbing her red eyes, "I'll miss him."

"We all will, Miranda." Addie said reaching across the table to touch Miranda's hand.

"He was a good friend to me when I first came here."

At this point Betty took up the story. "Bernie felt that normal police wouldn't be able to do anything with the information he had discovered. He thought an investigative reporter would be the best one to follow up on his info."

One thing continued to bother Addie. "How did you know to look for me at the Federal Building? It was only by chance that I went there today."

Betty smiled. "I have a "client" who works in your office. I called her and she found out where you were supposed to be today. When I got there, I spotted you and your partner with the camera doing some filming so I decided to crawl into the dumpster and wait for you to come back to your car."

Suddenly Betty wrinkled her tiny nose and laughed.

"Boy, did it smell inside that thing. I'll be forever getting the odor out of my hair."

Addie nodded slowly as she considered the information she was hearing; so far it made sense.

"What happened to Bernie? I mean how did he wind up like this and what is he doing here instead of in a hospital?"

Miranda shook her head and, placing her elbows on the table, she leaned forward. "We don't know everything, just what he was able to tell us when we first got him here. But apparently, he was in the F.B.I. Office yesterday when that Sheik fella turned himself in. Only it wasn't the real Sheik. Then he said something about a bomb going off.

Bernie said that he knew something was wrong from the start. About the time the bomb exploded, he threw himself behind a desk. Only the bomb was so powerful it blew up everything on the entire floor. Bernie was caught in the fire that the bomb started, literally cut to pieces by splinters."

"Did anyone else get away?" gasped Addie.

This time Betty shook her head, her long strands of hair billowing around her pert face.

"Bernie said that as far as he knew he was the only one to get out. He called me at my workplace and he asked me to come get him. I'm a table dancer at a nightclub near 42nd street. I took a break and drove to the address he gave me. I found him lying in an alley. I could tell he was hurt bad. I tried to get him to the hospital, but by then all hell had broken lose and in the panic, it was impossible to get anywhere near the hospital. Besides, he asked me to bring him here, so I did."

"But why would he want to come here and not keep trying to go to a hospital?"

Miranda sighed and leaned forward even further.

"I am—or was, a registered nurse. Bernie knew that I was fired from my job when my employers discovered my alternative "lifestyle". But he also knew that I could at least help. But he refused to allow me to call anyone until he had a chance to talk to you."

Addie ran one hand through her long thick hair. "Why would Bernie do such a thing? He had to be in great pain, I would have thought that he would want to go to a hospital."

"Well he gave me the impression that he was actually trying to hide the fact that he was still alive. He never said so, but I got the feeling that he knew something important, but he was afraid to tell me."

"Did he have any notes or books or tapes with him?" asked Addie as a sudden thought hit her.

Betty shook her head decisively.

"Nope. His clothes were almost torn off of his body when I found him. He didn't have anything with him."

"Did he say anything to you about who did this?" asked Miranda.

Addie forlornly shook her head.

"I'm afraid not. The only thing he did was quote a line of so-called scripture to me."

"Scripture? Bernie!" laughed Betty.

Addie grinned weakly, "I thought it was rather strange myself."

"What did he say?" asked Miranda curiously.

Addie thought for a moment to make sure she had it straight, then said. "Yea though I walk through the valley of the shadow of death I will fear no evil for I am the meanest son of a bitch in the valley."

Both her listeners laughed when she finished. While the quote did have its basis in the Holy Bible, it had been given a definite new twist. All were silent for a few minutes, each busy with their own thoughts, when Betty's face suddenly brightened.

"I've heard someone else say that."

"Who say what?" asked Addie.

Betty flipped another annoying strand of her long fine hair out of her face.

"That quotation Bernie said to you. I've heard someone else say that."

Addie began to get one of her premonitions.

"Who, Betty? Who have you heard say that?" she demanded eagerly.

"Well, I'm trying to remember," returned the flustered girl.

"Was it on television?" quizzed Miranda.

Betty thought for a long moment, before shaking her head. "No, it was somebody I was talking to. And it was just recently!"

Addie gritted her teeth in frustration. It was all she could do not to go around the table and shake the information out of the girl. Slowly, she began to take deep breaths in order to calm down. She knew that anger wouldn't help Betty to remember; in fact it might only make things worse. She definitely didn't want to alienate these two.

She decided the best thing to do was not to pressure Betty and hope that she remembered where she'd heard Bernie's words before. It might be a lead. At this point she had everything to gain and nothing to lose. So Addie rummaged in her purse and found one of her business cards.

"Well, think about it and if you can remember, call me. Here's my card," she said as she handed it to Miranda.

CHAPTER NINETEEN

FRIDAY, 3:00 P.M.—LINCOLN TUNNEL, New York City

Transit Police Lieutenant Arthur Dumfrie was in a terrible snit. He had twenty of his best men, in his mind the elite of the Metro Transit Police, guarding all of the approaches to the Lincoln and Holland Tunnels. No one was going to do any damage to his tunnels as long as he had anything to say about it. Dumfrie knew that he had everything well in hand and he certainly didn't need some snot nose rookie New York City Policeman telling him how to handle his job, and the worst insult was that the kid was Irish to boot. Everyone knew that Irish cops were all drunks and lazy.

Dumfrie angrily stalked along the walkway that ran along the inside of the Lincoln tunnel. His destination was the center traffic observation booth. His big black face was beginning to run with sweat as he entered the oven like tunnel. Through the glass wall of the booth, he could see that snot nose kid, Police Lieutenant Shamus O'Rourke sitting comfortably, idly watching the cars go through the tunnel. As if he didn't have enough problems with traffic control on the tunnel approaches, he is sent for, sent for mind you, by a snot nose City Cop who shouldn't even be in the tunnel area. Well, he'd give him a piece of his mind.

As Dumfrie approached the booth, which was almost halfway though the tunnel, he could see, standing outside the booth, seemingly oblivious to the heat and noise, his own assistant, Jim Mulligan, leaning against the railing watching the cars past beneath him, apparently lost in thought. Dumfrie snorted in outrage. Was everyone losing their mind? Why wasn't Mulligan watching that bastard from the City so that he didn't fuck anything up? As if Dumfrie didn't have enough problems, he'd have to straighten out his own people after he told the snot-nose kid who was in charge.

As Dumfrie arrived at the booth and reached for the doorknob, he barely heard Mulligan over the traffic.

"Something is not right, Artie." shouted his assistant.

This brought Dumfrie up short.

"What?" he yelled.

Mulligan motioned for Dumfrie to follow him. When they were a suitable distance away, Mulligan put his mouth close to Dumfrie's ear.

"There's something not right about that Cop," he repeated to his superior.

"What are you talking about, Jim? What's not right?" snapped the annoyed Dumfrie.

"I was talking to him and if he knows anything about tunnel security, then I'll eat my hat," asserted Mulligan.

This news just added fuel to Dumfrie's already raging temper. Trust the city to send a total rookie to do a man's job. It takes special training to know how to protect a tunnel from terrorist assault. Dumfrie looked at the bumper-to-bumper traffic filling the tunnel to his right. Traffic had been this heavy since the attacks yesterday and was getting heavier by the hour.

After all that had happened in the City, most of the population was trying to get out while the getting was good. Unfortunately there were only four major exits from Manhattan Island. The main one seemed to be the George Washington Bridge, then there were the Lincoln and

Holland Tunnels to New Jersey or the Mid-town Tunnel to Long Island. If any of those four were damaged or destroyed, the ensuing backup of cars would probably gridlock the entire city.

Snorting again in total disgust at the mess and confusion in his tunnels, Dumfrie turned his back on his subordinate and stalked back toward the observation booth and the snot-nose kid lieutenant he could see sitting placidly inside. Reaching the door, he jerked it opened and crossed the booth in two steps. Towering over the City Policeman, Dumfrie came to his full six-foot-seven inches and used his best command voice.

"What the fuck are you doing in my area?" he demanded. "You think I can't handle my job?"

The Police Lieutenant, Shamus O'Rourke, idly looked the big Transit Cop up and down before rising from his seat to his full six-foot-two inches, his uniform hat held in both hands.

"Well it's like this, my bucko, we can do this the easy way or the hard way."

"Do what?" roared the enraged Transit Lieutenant.

"Why, destroy the tunnel, of course."

That response totally shocked Dumfrie into complete silence. For a moment, O'Rourke's words simply didn't register in Dumfrie's mind. Why would anyone want to destroy his beautiful tunnel? When the words finally did penetrate his brain, Arthur Dumfrie made a grab for his sidearm. O'Rourke simply shot him with the small .38 automatic concealed in his uniform hat. The bullet hit him almost exactly between his bulging eyes. Dumfrie's body fell straight back like a great tree falling.

Tossing his smoking hat onto the countertop that ran beneath the window of the booth as he returned to his chair, O'Rourke pulled his radio from his belt pouch and pressed the talk button.

"Are you there, me bucko?" asked O'Rourke.

"Here, sir." Came the crisp military-like response from his second-in-command.

"Do It," he ordered.

With a sigh of great satisfaction, Lieutenant Shamus O'Rourke, aka Shamus O'Toole of the Irish Republican Army, on loan to the HizBellah unified command, placed his radio beside his hat, leaned back in his chair and put his hands behind his blonde head. In ten minutes, this great wonder of engineering would be rubble. He loved it when a plan came together.

What O'Rourke didn't know was that Jim Mulligan had been watching through the window and had seen him shoot Dumfrie. Now Mulligan was running hell for leather toward the Manhattan side of the tunnel to summon help for his boss. He was relieved to see the blue of a beat cop directing traffic at the entrance to the tunnel. Vaulting the railing from the walkway to the street, he dodged cars to reach the traffic cop.

"Hey, my boss was just shot by a fake police lieutenant." he yelled frantically, pulling at the officer's arm.

The cop looked at Mulligan quizzically as he continued to try and direct traffic.

"What've you been drinking?" asked the Cop with a tired grin on his face as he pulled his arm away from the frantic Transit Cop.

Mulligan grabbed his arm again and literally pulled him from the street toward the tunnel's mouth.

"Aint been drinking a thing, man. I'm serious; my boss has been murdered by a guy who said he was a police lieutenant sent to help us. You gotta help."

The two were forced to stop by an enclosed panel truck that partially blocked their way into the tunnel. After that truck moved forward, Mulligan raised his hand to stop the car following the truck so that he and the cop could cross the lane and climb over the railing onto the walkway that ran along the left wall of the tunnel. Once on the walkway, both began to jog into the tunnel.

Pausing outside the observation booth, Mulligan pulled his sidearm and motioned for the cop to get ready. When he saw the cop pull his own weapon, Mulligan jerked open the door and almost dove into the room. The fake Police Lieutenant was still sitting back in his chair and Dumfrie's dead body was still lying just inside the door.

"Hands up, mister, you're under arrest for murder," snapped Mulligan!

Ignoring Mulligan's drawn gun, the Lieutenant glanced toward the Cop.

"Ah, Tommy, is everything under control?" asked the Lieutenant in a calm voice.

"Of course, Mr. O'Rourke." returned the Cop in his militarily precise voice.

Realizing that he was in deep shit, Mulligan tried to spin so that he could cover both of them. Unfortunately, he couldn't turn faster than Thomas Nelson of the European Red Army Faction could pull the trigger on his police issue .38 special, which he now held in one firm hand. The bullet threw Mulligan back against the glass separating them from the traffic-filled tunnel before he fell forward across Dumfrie's body. No one in the cars momentarily stopped in front of the booth noticed anything out of the ordinary. They were all concentrating too much on escape from the Island that they now considered as a death trap.

Nelson holstered his revolver and glanced out the door along the tunnel to his rear. He was relieved to see the panel truck inching its' way toward his location. Pulling the door closed, he turned back toward his commander.

"At this rate the truck should be here in about fifteen minutes."

Shamus O'Rourke nodded his blonde head in satisfaction. His plan was working relatively smoothly. Soon, the island that was New York City would be cut off from the outside world.

"Excellent. Then in approximately eighteen minutes we should be making our escape into the sewers. Go back and check the entrance, make sure that there are no last minute problems."

Obediently, Nelson left the booth and made his way back along the walkway to a metal door set into the tunnel wall. Taking a large blade knife from his belt, Nelson worked the blade under the edge of the door, pried the lock open and crawled inside. Once inside, he glanced into the inner chamber and saw that the opened manhole cover was still leaning against the wall, the ladder was in place and the flashlights were sitting beside the door. All was in readiness.

Crawling back out of the maintenance doorway, Nelson stood and straightened his uniform jacket. A former Major in the South African Army, he felt that there was no need for sloppiness even when wearing the enemy's uniforms. He now noticed that the panel truck was almost even with him, at this rate, they would have to evacuate in about eight minutes. Turning, he walked briskly back to the observation booth.

"Almost here, sir." reported Nelson.

"The escape route?" queried O'Toole without taking his eyes off of the crowded roadway.

"All is ready. Everything is in place."

The Irishman nodded again, preoccupied with watching the cars passing in front of his position. It was hard for him to imagine that soon all of those cars would be buried beneath tons of rubble and if the bombers were very successful, the sea would be pouring into the tunnel. O'Rourke stood and carefully placed his damaged uniform hat on his head. Turning to his second-in-command, O'Rourke motioned toward the door.

"Well, my friend, time for us to go."

Slowly, the two uniformed individuals walked along the pathway toward the Manhattan side of the tunnel. The panel truck that they were so interested in was slowly but surely inching its way to the required position. O'Rourke's plan was really a stroke of genius. The driver of the truck and his helper were unknowing accomplishes in what would be the crime of the century. The employees of the moving company thought they were moving a wealthy individual's furniture to a warehouse in New Jersey. In reality, the "furniture" was a thousand pounds of plastic explosive packed with white phosphorus and thousands of small metal pellets. Once the truck reached the preplanned position, the explosion would be ignited. When the explosion happened, the white phosphorus would begin to burn anything it hit and the metal pellets would be thrown in every direction with the force of a bullet.

As he and Nelson stood on the walkway, O'Rourke began to assemble several pieces of metal in his pocket into a very serviceable rifle. Carefully, he loaded a single .22 round into the chamber and took careful aim. As the truck passed his position, he gently pulled the trigger. The bullet went straight and true, striking the panel truck driver in the left temple.

As the driver fell against his companion, he pulled the steering wheel to the right. The truck swerved to crash into a large Lincoln Town car. The car's horn began to blow and the passenger in the truck tried to crawl across his partner's body and escape. Nelson fired once with his handgun and the helper fell from the door of the truck to lie on the hot pavement.

Turning, O'Rourke and Nelson jogged away from the building chaos to the maintenance door in the wall. Nelson pulled open the door and stood aside allowing O'Rourke to precede him. Once safely inside the inner chamber, O'Rourke pulled a device that resembled a garage door opener from one of his many pockets.

"Are you ready, Tommy, my bucko?" he asked.

At Nelson's silent nod, O'Rourke pushed the single button on the device in his hand. A second later, the very ground on which they sat trembled and the walls around them began to crumble. Rapidly, the two slid down the ladder into the sewers below; while in the tunnel above them hell was in session. Hundreds of New Yorkers who had believed escape was a few minutes away were left to die beneath the inrushing water of the river above.

CHAPTER TWENTY

FRIDAY: 4:30 P.M.- Washington D.C.

Richard Armiger turned from his wet bar, a drink in his hand, looked at the five people seated in the room and allowed himself a slow smile. After spending a morning with that idiot of a President, it felt good to be with people who were dedicated toward reaching an achievable goal and placing America on the right road to the future.

The President had called in his closest advisors to discuss ways of handling the current crisis in New York City. Armiger had attended as an assistant to the National Security Advisor, Admiral Samuel Zemfelt. The main topic of discussion had been the continuing emergency in New York and it had quickly degenerated into a verbal brawl between the White House Chief of Staff and the Directors of the F.B.I., CIA, and the Attorney General. Each blamed the other for failing to anticipate such a major disruption n the normal operations of the financial capital of the world. Though he had worked to cause the confusion that affected the Oval Office, Armiger really hadn't believed that it would result in this much disarray.

The White House blamed the C.I.A. for not knowing that terrorists were planning such as an attack and the F.B.I. for being so easily out maneuvered by the fake Sheik. The C.IO.A. Director had yelled back that if the White House had not cut their funding so drastically then they would have had the international infrastructure to discover such a plan before it was carried out.

The meeting had degenerated into a shouting match.

Armiger went back to join his guests.

"Is it true that Middle Eastern terrorists are in control of one of the largest cities in the world?" demanded Senator Dan Rostow, as he helped himself to a sandwich from a tray at his side.

Armiger grinned as he took a sip of his drink.

"Well, they aren't in total control, Senator, but they are definitely having an impact."

"What's coming out of the White House?" asked Senator Frank Lopez

Armiger's grin got bigger as he went over to sit in one of the big leather chairs with the Senators.

"The President has no idea what to do. Eastman, the Chief of Staff, is using the emergency to solidify his power over the old man. Naturally, none of his advisors can agree on what to do about the situation. The White House blames the C.I.A. and the F.B.I., and C.I.A. blames the White House. Naturally, in this atmosphere, nothing was accomplished. No decisions have been made. " he responded as he reached over for a sandwich.

"What are the chances of the President ordering troops sent in to restore order?" asked the eighty-five-year-old, Supreme Court Justice Higgins, as he leaned forward resting his weight on his silver topped cane.

Armiger shook his head as he tossed off the rest of his drink. "That possibility was discussed, but Eastman vetoed it. Said it would make the President look like he was too quick on the draw. He urged a negotiated settlement. There was only one problem with his suggestion."

"And what was the one problem, young man?" asked Justice Higgins curiously. He was the only one of the group who didn't drink.

"There have been no demands out of the terrorists. We have no idea who to negotiate with." he laughed as he used tongs to drop ice cubes into his glass.

"Since the terrorists are suspected to have been involved in totally destroying the F.B.I. Office in New York, the Director of the F.B.I. was in favor of full scale invasion. The Attorney General was also livid about the death of the forty members of the National Press Corp waiting outside the Federal Building for an interview with U.S. Attorney Grossman regarding the capture of Sheik Sadir and, naturally, the death of the United States Attorney for New York."

"Grossman's dead?" interrupted the last member of the group, Salvatore DeNero.

"As a doornail. According to the investigation report, you would have to use tweezers to recover the body," replied Armiger, as he resumed his seat.

"Then things are proceeding on schedule?" asked Higgins as he pulled himself to his feet. Like most of the current Supreme Court Justices, he had been appointed over fifteen years ago and owed no loyalty to the current administration.

Armiger nodded emphatically.

"Yes, as we planned, the assassination of Schwarz and his major supporters in Arizona has created a power vacuum that is causing a scramble among the major players who should be concentrating on the terrorist situation. In addition to the deaths among the F.B.I., there were attacks on Rockefeller Center where they shot down God knows how many innocent civilians. At about the same time as these first two attacks, a mob almost totally destroyed One Police Plaza and the City's Emergency Operations Center."

"What's Mayor Dalton doing about this?" he asked.

"Not much." furnished Armiger. "The President's furious, but the Mayor of New York is in Europe on a goodwill tour."

"In Europe! That's priceless, I'll bet that mental defective in the White House is furious" laughed Senator Rostow, slapping his leg in glee. "New York City is being blown to bits and the Mayor's in Europe!"

As they were laughing among themselves, the phone rang. Armiger excused himself and, crossing to his desk, he answered the phone. They all had their ears cocked to listen to his conversation, but Armiger said nothing. Finally, he thanked the caller and hung up. It was obvious that he had momentous news.

"Well," began Armiger as he returned to his seat, "That was the National Security Advisor. He was fit to be tied, but he wanted me to know that at approximately 3:45 p.m., there were several massive explosions in the Lincoln tunnel and a few minutes later in the Holland Tunnel and Midtown Tunnels. The tubes initially acted like the barrels of a large cannon and channeled the force of the bombs in either direction pushing everything before it. There were cars at either end of the tunnel that were thrown over a hundred feet. Pedestrians walking as much as two hundred feet from the tunnel mouth were killed. The water above crashed through the roof and drowned those not killed by the explosions.

The President is so upset that the Chief of Staff thought that he was going to have a stroke. He firmly believes that bombing can solve the problem, but he can't figure out whom to bomb.

The press reports say that there is no real way to know how many were in the tubes when the explosion took place, but the traffic was bumper to bumper going out of the city."

He looked up at his guests.

"Due to the catastrophe in the tunnels, the Island is almost isolated. Only the George Washington Bridge is left."

Armiger picked up his glass and raised it. "Gentlemen, if things continue as they are going, then the Brotherhood will have no choice but to step in and save the country from total anarchy. A grateful nation will put our man into office. "

With satisfied nods, the group raised their own glasses in a toast.

CHAPTER TWENTY-ONE

FRIDAY- CHRISTMAS EVE- 5:00 P.M.- AN APARTMENT ON 5TH AVENUE

Carter Hughes slowly moved around his apartment, fixing himself a small meal. This would be the first thing that he had eaten since breakfast the day before. Sandwich and coffee cup in hand, Hughes opened the door to his balcony and carried his dinner out to eat among the flowers his wife had loved so much. It wasn't much, but it made him feel closer to Martha.

Placing his sandwich and cup on the table, he dropped into one of the padded deck chairs. Crossing his legs, Hughes idly watched the one or two cars traveling on Fifth Avenue. Across the way, he could see a few people moving through Central Park but there were only one or two pedestrians on the sidewalks. On the whole, it seemed to him that the City died at the same time as his wife.

Groaning, Hughes ran one hand across his broad face. He was still groggy; he really hadn't had much sleep the night before. He dreamt of death and violence, but surprisingly not the death of his wife. He had been in a jungle firefight. It seemed as if he knew the people he had been leading, he couldn't recognize any of the faces that he had seen flash before his dream self.

His mind seemed clearer today. As if his interrupted torturous sleep had performed some repair work in his shattered mind. Rationally, Hughes was aware that he would have to go seek some sort of professional help. He felt like he was two people living in one body, he was having the sensation that he was looking out through someone else's eyes. Hughes ran one hand nervously through his curly hair. He was having what appeared to be memories of events and places that he had never experienced.

He looked up as Matilda came out onto the terrace to join him. He still didn't know what to make of what she had told him.

"Good morning, Mr. Hughes."

"Good morning, I think, Matilda. Though I don't know what's so good about it."

She shrugged and took a seat across from him.

"We probably don't have much time. So I'll be quick. Fifteen years ago, my God daughter was murdered in her home in the Panama Canal Zone and her husband vanished. My husband was a detective with the Dallas Police and he took time off to investigate. The Military Police not only could not solve the case, but were also completely uncooperative. When the Military authorities closed the case, my husband took time off from work and went to the Panama Canal Zone to conduct his own investigation."

She paused and looked across the street toward the apartment building across the way. She was quiet for so long that Hughes became impatient.

"Well, did he solve the case?"

For a moment, he didn't think she had heard him. Finally she sighed and leaned back against her chair.

"No, Mr. Hughes, he was unable to solve the case. Her husband, a Second Lieutenant in the Army also disappeared at about the same time and was presumed dead."

Hughes paused with his cup halfway to his lips.

"Was his name Jennings."

Matilda allowed herself a small smile as she stirred her coffee.

"Yes it was."

"Then the wife would be Julie?"

"Yes."

Hughes shook his head in total frustration. How did he know this, the dreams had to be just that, dreams.

"This is just crazy. I didn't, don't, know the people. How could I know their names?"

Matilda looked at him for a long moment.

"Is there something wrong, Mr. Hughes?" she inquired.

"No. No, it's just that I have dreamed about these people for some time. I don't know how to explain to you what has been happening."

He paused for a long moment, at a loss for words how to explain to this woman that he was afraid to fall asleep for fear that he would find himself living another man's life.

Matilda looked at him for a long moment as if weighing what she wanted to say.

"Mr. Hughes, I am going to tell you something that you will find hard to believe. Your wife and a Dr. Bremer have been conducting some kind of experiment on you. I don't know the particulars, but I suggest that you look under your mattress."

He looked at her for a long moment.

"Are you serious?"

"Go see for yourself Mr. Hughes."

He got up and went quickly to his bedroom. He pulled the pillows off the bed and stripped the bed coverings back. All he saw was the mattress. Perplexed, he shoved his right hand underneath the mattress. To his utter amazement, he felt the outlined of a square item. Grabbing the side of the mattress he manhandled it off the bed and onto the floor. There under where he would normally sleep, he saw a very complex device. He grabbed it and ripped the box from its base. Full of conflicting emotions and hundreds of questions he carried the box back onto the terrace. He found the one, he failed to notice the one bolted under the bed, the one that gave an electronic alarm to the apartment across the street that faced his terrace.

In the darkened apartment across the way a buzzer sounded. A shadowy figure flipped a switch and the apartment was filled with the sounds of the conversation in the Hughes apartment. He leaned forward and pressed a switch on the phone console.

"Yes." Came a voice from the speaker.

"He has found the programmer that was placed in his bed."

"This was unexpected. How could such a thing have happened?"

"The Nanny told him. It would appear that she is one of the opposition."

"If you are certain, eliminate her. For him to find out the truth at this stage could be disastrous."

The connection was broken.

Hughes dropped the box onto the table in front of Matilda.

"How did you know?"

She shifted in her seat and looked steadily at him.

"How do you expect, Mr. Hughes? I was a servant. You rich folks look at servants like pieces of furniture. I watched the two of them use that item on you night after night. These walls have ears and I listen."

He stared at the box like it was a snake.

"Wh—what is this thing? I mean—what does it do?"

Matilda shrugged and picked up the box, studying it intently.

"What does it do? I'm not really sure. I suspect it programs your mind in some manner."

"Program? What do you mean program?" he stammered.

She tossed the box back on the table, its' broken wires spreading out from it like Medusa's hair.

"I don't really know for sure, Mr. Hughes. But I will tell you this-very little of what you believe is real it actually as it seems. Remember that."

He just sat and looked at her in perplexed silence.

"Who are you Matilda?"

She smiled, somewhat sadly he thought.

"I am a member of a small group that means you well. When my husband died, I came into a bit of money and, having no children, I set out to solve the mystery of what happened to Julie and her husband."

"What does this have to do with me?" he asked slowly.

"We, by that I mean those of us who tried to solve the case, managed to get records showing everyone who showed up on the official census of the Canal Zone during that time frame. Your name showed up as being a patient in Gorgas Hospital at the time."

Hughes grimaced and shook his head.

"Then I am afraid your records are wrong. I have never been in a hospital and I have certainly not been in the Panama Canal Zone."

"Mr. Hughes, you must forgive me my little deception. In following up on the names listed as being in the Canal Zone at that time, yours attracted considerable attention. I was selected to try and get close to you and see what you knew. You advertised for a Nanny and I asked for the job."

Hughes was struggling to colleted his scattered thoughts. Slowly he sipped his coffee.

"Why would my name attract that much attention? There was well before I became Howard Renaldi's son-in-law?"

Matilda smiled her small smile once again.

"For a very simple reason Mr. Hughes. You see according to the records from the U.S. Military, you died on the operating table at Gorgas Hospital on December 3, 1975."

His attempt to sort out his confused thoughts was interrupted by the ringing of his telephone. Slowly, he rose and entered his apartment, carefully pulling the sliding door closed behind him. Actually the last thing Hughes wanted was to talk to anyone else.

"Hello?"

"Mr. Hughes?" answered a suave voice.

"Yes, who is this?"

"I'm so sorry to bother you, Mr. Hughes, this is Dr. Simon Bremer. I'm your father-in-law's doctor. He asked me to come by and check on you. Would seven this evening be convenient?"

Something about Dr. Bremer's voice bothered Hughes, but he couldn't think of any real valid objections.

"Uh, Dr. Bremer, I appreciate my father-in-law's concern, but I'm fine, really."

"Well it can't hurt to give you a check up, Mr. Hughes. So I'll see you at seven." said Dr. Bremer as he hung up the phone.

Hughes stared at the receiver in his hand for a long moment. He really didn't want to see anyone but, well, it was probably just as well that he had an examination. Dropping the phone back onto its cradle, Hughes began to aimlessly wander around the apartment. He was restless; he had the feeling that something was about to happen. Finally he went back out on the terrace. Matilda was sitting where he had left her.

"So tell me more about when I died." He began.

Matilda didn't respond, just sat and stared at him with a totally blank expression. Slowly Hughes leaned forward ad placed a hand on her shoulder. In response, she toppled forward to lie face down on the table. He rose to stand over her and saw the spreading blood stain on the back of her dress. Before he could think, Hughes dropped to his knees, using her body and the table as a shelter from the sniper that had targeted the terrace.

"Shit!" he swore, "Another body. What'll I do with this one?"

Addie Vandemeyer entered her office and snapped on the lights. It was almost seven and she had been up since three that morning. She was beat; it had been a very trying day. After she had left Miranda and Betty, she had continued her interrupted trip to the City Coroner's Office; it had been a dead end. She dropped into her desk chair and leaned back, depositing her purse on the credenza behind her. It felt good to be sitting down for a change. She was heartsick over the death of Bernie Kahane; he had been a good friend.

Bending over, Addie rummaged in a small refrigerator under her desk and found an unopened diet soda. She figured that she might as well get comfortable. She was probably going to have to spend Christmas Eve in her office since the curfew went into effect an hour ago. She opened the can and slowly poured the soda into the only clean glass she could find, carefully wiped out with a slightly soiled Kleenex.

She was totally lost in her own world when she happened to glance at the door.

"Who are you?" she asked in surprise.

The tall, slim man leaning in the doorway straightened and walked into the office.

"Ms. Vandemeyer?" he questioned.

"Yes, and I ask again, who are you?"

"Detective Martin Kincade. New York Police." he said, holding out his hand to her.

As Addie shook his hand, she was thinking fast. What could a cop possibly want from her? She had already given her statement about the terrorist attack to police earlier.

"So what can I do for you, Detective?" she asked cautiously.

Pulling out a notebook, Kincade leaned up against the wall. "Yesterday, you were involved in the incident in the American Festival Cafe." he began, making it a statement and not a question.

She nodded slowly.

"That's no secret. I believe that it was mentioned on last night's news program as well as the early news this morning. And I also gave a statement to the Police about it this morning."

"Uh, yeah that's right. But I still have to do a follow-up report." he replied.

She sat back in her chair and folded her arms under her breasts. "So, ask your questions."

She was puzzled at her reaction to the Detective. She had always been a good judge of people and she felt that there was something not quite right about him, but she couldn't put her finger on it. She was going to watch her answers.

"I believe that you met a Carter Davis Hughes."

Her internal alert was operating on full, how did he connect her to Hughes since Mr. Hughes had not been mentioned at the demand of Renaldi?

She nodded.

"Yes, his family was killed in the restaurant. He took a gun away from one of the terrorists and killed several of them."

Kincade wrote something in his notebook.

"I see. How did he do this? Did he shoot them in the back, or face them head on?"

She looked at him quizzically.

"Going to try and make a case against him for murder?"

For a moment Kincade looked at her in surprise.

"Uh, no, of course not. Uh, well, its just part of my report to get the full story."

She sniffed and leaned forward in her chair.

"Well it would seem to me that you have the story. Unless you have more questions for me."

He fumbled with his notebook for a moment, not meeting her eyes. Then finally, when she just sat and waited for him to speak, he looked at her.

"Well, I guess that wraps up what I need to know. Uh, did Hughes tell you anything about his background?" he mumbled.

She shook her head. "Nope."

"Well, thanks for your time, Ms. Vandemeyer. Bye." he said as he backed out of her office.

She sat looking at the door for several minutes before picking up her phone and dialing for the security office.

"Security Office. Sanderson speaking, how may I help you?"

"This is Addie Vandemeyer," she said.

"Oh, yes. How are you doing Ms. Vandemeyer? This is Melvin."

She was lucky to get a friend for a change.

"Oh Melvin, good to talk to you again. I need to know something."

"Sure," laughed the voice on the other end, "anything for you."

"Did you admit a New York City Police Detective named Kincade to this area, tonight?"

Melvin was adamant. "Ms. Vandemeyer, first, my orders are to let no one into the area unescorted, and I obey my orders. Secondly, I haven't let anyone on the premises since two o'clock this afternoon. This building is sealed up tight."

"Well, Melvin, I have a news flash for you. This so-called detective left my office no more than ten minutes ago."

"Which way was he headed?" asked Melvin.

"I really couldn't tell, but he appeared to head toward the research department."

"Thanks, Ms. Vandemeyer, we'll get right on it."

Addie spun her chair around to grab her bag and join the search when she noticed the large manila envelope hidden by the bulk of her purse. She picked it up and saw her name scrawled across the front in Moses Gardner's distinctive handwriting.

Settling back in her chair, Addie slowly broke the tape seal and opened the envelope. She slid the papers out onto her desk and began to thumb through them.

"Good old Moses," she said to herself. "He came through again."

What Moses had left her was a full report on Mr. Carter Davis Hughes prepared by the National Security Agency. She had to admit that it made very good reading.

"Let's see," she murmured. "Carter Davis Hughes, born hmmm, that would make him 41. Entered Reserve Officers Training Corp and was commissioned in 1971. Service in Vietnam."

She noted with interest that he had served in Saigon with the Company E, 20th Infantry. That, from research she had done for another article, was a unit used for long-range recon patrols. So she was right, he had been a combat veteran. That could explain his combat reflexes in the battle with the terrorists. But for some reason, she was sure that there was a great deal more to be known about Mr. Carter Davis Hughes.

She started to close the file when she noticed a post-it note stuck to the back of one of the top sheets. She peeled it off and held it under the light.

Addie,

This is the file from my buddy at the NSA. There is only one problem; it's not worth the paper it's written on. I called a friend who was with Company E, 20th Infantry in Nam at the same time Hughes was supposed to be there. He is positive that there was never a Lieutenant Hughes with his outfit. He did say that a lot of CIA types were assigned to the 20th on paper as a cover for cross border missions. I might also point out that there is a discrepancy on the age, I don't think the guy you brought into the building was 41, mid thirties tops. I've got some feelers out for any word on

Hughes. Also notice that there are no fingerprints in the file. This is an unusual oversight; one requirement that was never violated was the placing of a fingerprint card in each military record.

See you later,

Moses

Addie sat and held the note for a good long time considering what she had read. She knew that her inner sense hadn't steered her wrong. There was much more to Mr. Hughes than it appeared. She got as far as the door before she changed her mind. Cautiously, she glanced out into the well-lit hallway. She didn't see a soul.

Just to be on the safe side, Addie closed and locked her door before returning to her desk. She dropped back into her chair and jerked open her top desk drawer. Pawing through the crap she at last found what she was looking for, her personal telephone book. Quickly she flipped though the pages. Maybe, just maybe, he could supply the missing part of the puzzle.

Pulling the phone closer to her, Addie slowly dialed the number from her phone book.

"Marker." A deep male voice answered after three rings.

"This is Addie Vandemeyer. I want to speak to John Voynich. It's an emergency," she said.

"I don't know who you're talking about. There is no John Voynich here," replied the deep voice. "You must have the wrong number."

"Tell John that I'll tell about the salami incident on national television if he doesn't call me within ten minutes." she said in a perfectly serious voice.

"But—-."

"Bye." she said sweetly as she hung up the phone.

Grinning hugely to herself, Addie leaned back in her chair and, in a rare fit of girlishness lifted her feet and spun her chair around in a circle. By her clock it was exactly eight and a half minutes before her phone rang.

"Hello?" she said sweetly.

"Damn it, Addie, what the hell do you think you're doing?" demanded the voice on the other end.

"Hello John, it's good to hear your voice again," said Addie with a smile on her face.

"Yeah, right." her caller snorted, "what do you want this time?"

"John, I've got a problem."

"Don't you always?" he interrupted.

"I'm serious, John. In case you've missed the news lately, someone is trying to level New York City and doing a damn good job of it."

"So I've heard," he responded. "But remember my area of operations is Europe."

"John, I was in the American Festival Cafe, when the terrorists attacked. All but one of them was killed by an Insurance Man named Carter Davis Hughes."

"Who killed the other one?" asked Voynich.

"I did but that's not the reason for this conversation." she snapped back at him.

"O.K., calm down. I was merely admiring your marksmanship."

"O.K. John. But this is very serious. I seemed to have stumbled over something very odd."

"Such as?" he asked, interested in spite of himself.

"Well, this is just between you and me. But a bogus New York Detective who appeared to want to inquire into what I knew about Mr. Carter Davis Hughes has just visited me. By the way, a guy named Kincade wouldn't be one of yours would he?"

"Describe him." ordered Voynich.

After hearing the description, Voynich was silent for a few seconds and then spoke to someone on his end. He didn't answer the question.

"Go on." he said briskly.

"Then I ran a background check on Mr. Hughes and discovered that his military record appears to be incorrect."

"So?" asked Voynich, "Almost every military record I have ever looked at has incorrect information in it."

"But this is different." persisted Addie.

"Different, how?" asked Voynich, the interest in his voice gone.

"He was allegedly assigned to Company E, 20th Infantry in Saigon. Only problem is a man who was there at the same time as Hughes was allegedly assigned to the company says that Hughes was never there. Then there is the little matter that in one of my investigations I found out that your people used Company E as a paper trail cover for cross border operations."

"So what do you want to know?" asked Voynich cautiously.

"Was Hughes CIA?" she asked flatly.

"You know I can't tell you that!" he objected.

"John, there are people dying all over this city. Someone who is not what he seems is investigating the only man I have seen that is effective at stopping these killers. I'm afraid to step outside my door for fear I'll be shot and you don't want to tell me anything."

" John," she pleaded, "you're the only one I can turn to for help. Please."

"Well," he began, "damn it Addie, I ought to hang up on you now. Every time you call me I get in trouble. Damn." he muttered. "Well, all right, this one last time. What's this guy's full name and social security number?" demanded Voynich.

Addie dug through the papers on her desk looking for the copy of Hughes' DD214 form that Moses had included in the file. Quickly she found it.

"His name is Carter Davis Hughes, SSN # 432-35-9369."

"O.K. It'll take me a couple of hours to look up this information. Where'll you be?"

"Well, since there is a curfew that started over an hour and twenty minutes ago, I suppose I'll be in my office."

"Call you." he said and broke the connection.

Addie dropped the phone back onto the cradle and sat making some notes. She could see several possible explanations for some of the puzzles, but at the moment, she was beginning to get a headache.

Probably, she thought, her headache was due to the fact she hadn't had anything to eat today. She stood and stretched her tired aching muscles. Impulsively, she decided to walk down to the employee's lounge and see if any of the vending machines had anything edible that wouldn't be poisonous. She dug in her purse for some change, jerked open her door and stepped into the hall. That was the last thing she knew until the floor came up and hit her in the face.

CHAPTER TWENTY-TWO

Very much against his better judgment, Carter Hughes answered his door at seven that evening. He had to admit that Dr. Bremer was very prompt. The man at the door was relatively small. He was polite and oozed charm.

Perhaps he had misjudged the good doctor, mused Hughes. After all, perhaps his intuition was off the mark after watching his family die in front of him. He trusted Howard Renaldi and if Howard felt that this doctor was the man for him, and then he should just keep his mouth shut and be a good little patient.

Awkwardly, Hughes stood with the Doctor in the entry hall.

"Why don't we sit down where you are comfortable and I'll examine you," suggested the Doctor.

"Oh, sorry. Right this way." said Hughes as he led the way into the living room.

Once Hughes was settled on the couch, Dr. Bremer opened his medical bag and began to pull out his instruments. Swiftly and surely, Dr. Bremer had him remove his shirt. Finally, after a thorough physical examination, he allowed Hughes to put his shirt back on and pulled a chair close to the couch.

"Well, Mr. Hughes, how do you feel?" asked Dr. Bremer as he took hold of Hughes' wrist to check his pulse.

"Fine, I guess. I'm just a little at sea after what happened to —my— family." Hughes found that he still choked up when he tried to talk about it.

"There, there." soothed the Doctor, "Loss is hard to accept, but eventually you will adjust."

After once again making sure that Hughes was comfortably settled, Bremer bustled around the apartment turning off all of the lights except the one directly over the couch. Hughes watched intently to make sure he didn't look in any of the other rooms. Wouldn't do to have the good doctor find Matilda sprawled across her bed like a side of beef. Finally satisfied with his lighting arrangements, Bremer returned to, again, resume his seat near Hughes.

"Physically, you seem to be fine, but \now for a last test. Lean back and relax." he instructed his patient as he unbuttoned his well-cut jacket.

As directed, Hughes leaned back against the couch and tried to relax. His eyes were drawn to the gleam of light from the big gold Rolex that Dr. Bremer wore on his left wrist and the reflection from the gold signet ring on the Doctor's right hand.

"Now Mr. Hughes, you will listen to my voice. You will hear nothing but the sound of my voice," said the Doctor in a very low, monotone voice.

Slowly, as he listened to the soothing voice of the Doctor, Hughes began to drift off to sleep. When he realized what was happening, Hughes tried to snap the spell that was being woven, but he was still physically tired and depressed. By the time he began to fight, he was too far-gone. Several minutes later, Dr. Bremer had put Hughes into a full hypnotic trance.

"Mr. Hughes, I am going to count to three, clap my hands and say the phrase, Three Blind Mice. When you hear that phrase, you will cease to be Carter Davis Hughes, insurance man and will revert to your original identity of Captain Illai Noyotivik, assassin. Do you understand?"

"I understand." intoned Hughes.

Even as he spoke, Hughes struggled against the compulsion to follow the instructions. He was fully alert, but had absolutely no control over his actions.

"One, two, three" said Bremer as he clapped his hands. "Three Blind Mice."

Dr. Bremer watched Hughes' reactions keenly as Hughes straightened and his features seemed to harden.

"Mr. Hughes can you hear me?" asked Bremer softly.

He received no response from the man on the couch.

"Captain Noyotivik, can you hear me?" asked Dr. Bremer.

"Yes, I hear you," returned his patient.

Dr. Bremer was elated. The programming still worked. The incident at the restaurant was just a fluke, as he had believed. Carter Davis Hughes was now mentally and emotionally Captain Illai Noyotivik, the perfect weapon, programmed to be the perfect assassin, now under Dr. Bremer's total control.

"Captain Noyotivik, from this point forward you will obey my every command. Do you understand?" asked Dr. Bremer.

"Yes, I understand." answered the man who now thought of himself as Noyotivik.

"You will rise and come with me," instructed Bremer as he got to his feet.

Obediently, Noyotivik came to his feet and stood waiting for further instructions. Dr. Bremer beamed at his patient like a proud father.

"Follow me," he said as he led his patient toward the door.

Like an automaton, Captain Illai Noyotivik marched across the room and followed Dr. Bremer into the hall. As they reached the elevator, the door across the way opened and one of Hughes' neighbors stepped out, his left arm loaded with trash for the incinerator. He stopped when he saw Hughes.

"Carter, how're you holding up? We heard about your wife," he said sympathetically.

Noyotivik/Hughes said nothing but stared straight ahead.

"Carter, it's me, Sammy Cohen. Carter?" he said putting his free hand on Hughes' arm.

Finally, Hughes moved to shake Cohen's hand away.

"You dare to lay hands on a member of the Spetz Netz?" roared Noyotivik/Hughes swinging around to face his former friend and neighbor.

Quickly Dr. Bremer stepped between the two.

"Quietly my friend. Now is not the time." he said to Noyotivik/Hughes.

He turned suavely toward Sammy Cohen. "I am sorry, but Mr. Hughes is my patient, I am Dr. Bremer. He's suffering a severe psychosis as a result of the death of his wife."

Cohen who had cowered back against the expensively wallpapered wall, away from the commanding figure of Hughes now relaxed.

"I quite understand, Doctor," he said. "Is there any chance he will get better?"

Dr. Bremer shrugged his well-padded shoulders.

"Who can say? He's had a great shock, and is having delusions. Hopefully, we can bring him back to normal."

At that moment, the elevator doors opened and Dr. Bremer steered his patient into the empty car. The last thing Sammy Cohen saw of his neighbor were the hard features of a total stranger. Cohen shook his head sadly, Mrs. Hughes had been such a pleasant, pretty young thing and the two kids were angels.

Addie Vandemeyer was aware, first of all, that she was in the dark. She could feel a rocking motion and she still had a splitting headache. She tried to bring her hands up to hold her aching head and discovered that they were tied behind her. She became more aware of her surroundings by the moment and realized that she was lying face down on the floorboard of a speeding car. It seemed very dark because she was wearing a blindfold.

Struggling, she tried to sit up, but found that she was so wedged in the floor that she couldn't free herself. To make matters worse, a well-manicured female hand came into her range of vision below the edge of the blindfold and cupped her chin. The movement was accompanied by a puzzling musical sound.

"Well, my pretty, I see that you're finally awake." cooed a low female voice.

Addie jerked her head away from the hand and slumped back to the floor. She rested the right side of her face on the gritty surface and tried to think. The last thing that she could remember was leaving her office to go to the employee's lounge.

"Oh, oh." said the female voice, "There's a police car over there."

Addie was suddenly hopeful. Anyone caught merely being on the street during curfew was supposed to be arrested. She prayed that the police would stop the car and rescue her.

"Not to worry, Malika. That's one of ours," said an amused male voice. "Besides we're here."

The car carrying Addie suddenly slowed and swung to the right. She could tell from the echo that they had entered an underground parking garage. She rolled back onto her face as the car angled downward. She could tell that they were now below ground level. Suddenly the car slowed and then braked to a stop.

The driver and his passenger exited the car and slammed their doors. Addie started to relax, when the car door at her head was jerked open. Seconds later, someone opened the one at her feet. Two hands slipped under her shoulders, while someone else grabbed her feet. She felt herself being lifted onto the seat.

Addie then felt herself being pulled into a sitting position and she gratefully slumped back. The hands at her shoulder released their grasp, but the ones that had been holding her ankles began to travel up her long smooth legs toward the edge of her short skirt. To her embarrassment, Addie realized that her skirt had ridden up her thighs.

"Kincade!" snapped the female voice; "This is neither the time nor the place for that."

The phony police detective, thought Addie.

"Malika, when are you going to learn that this job has certain fringe benefits?" questioned a laughing voice from Addie's left.

In spite of his comment, the phony police detective took his hand off of her legs and grabbed Addie's left arm. She knew, however, that she was going to have a great deal of trouble with that man before this was over.

At the insistent pulling of Kincade, Addie scooted across the seat and cautiously put one foot onto the ground. She was well aware that her scooting had forced her short skirt even higher on her legs. At Kincade's urging, she left the car and stood cautiously beside it, unable to see anything because of her blindfold. Addie stood indecisively, she was afraid to move for fear of falling, but then felt someone tugging on the cloth over her eyes. Finally, it fell away, blinding her with the light from the bare bulbs set in the ceiling.

She discovered that her captors were, as she had already known, the phony police detective Kincade, and a woman she had never seen before. The newcomer was about 5'4", with long silky dark hair, her skin dusky. With every move of the woman there was a musical tinkling, caused, Addie now saw, by the great number of bracelets that she wore on both arms.

"Miss Malika, would you pull my skirt down for me?" asked Addie hopefully. If she could establish a rapport with the woman, it might prove useful in escape.

Malika stepped back and looked Addie up and down, a slow smile crossing her face.

"Actually, my dear, I think your ensemble is very fetching. If anything, I think the skirt might need shortening again." Malika said in a low throaty voice as she reached one well-manicured hand over to pull the edge of Addie's skirt an inch higher on the reporter's already totally exposed legs.

"Much as I would like to see you two have a "session", I think the boss is probably waiting for us," offered Kincade.

"Perhaps you are right, Kincade." answered Malika turning her gaze toward the man.

Then she looked back at Addie. "But you and I will have some time together later, my dear."

Taking Addie's arm, Kincade led her toward the elevator, Malika following along behind them. Wildly, Addie's eyes searched the underground parking garage, hoping that she would see someone to help her. Unfortunately, the garage was deserted. Then they entered the elevator and the door closed.

Addie pressed herself against the back of the car. Her mind was working rapidly, there had to be some way to escape. She had been in a lot of tight spots in her life, but she had always been able to think her way out of them. Unfortunately, she had no idea what to do at this point.

CHAPTER TWENTY-THREE

FRIDAY EVENING- CHRISTMAS EVE- 10:45 P.M.- Washington D.C.

This particular meeting of the group came as a surprise to the members of the secret enclave. The President had called a meeting of his National Security Advisors to make them aware of some new developments in the emergency. Actually his Chief of Staff Oliver Eastman had run the meeting. When Armiger returned to his home, he found that the members of the group was waiting for him.

"So what's so important that you have to get me out of bed?" demanded Justice Higgins, as he banged his cane on the floor.

Before answering, Armiger opened his briefcase and pulled a slim file folder from inside. He laid it on the desk in front of him.

"This just came in, sir. It's from a group that calls itself the Revolutionary Command For the Freedom of Oppressed Peoples," said Armiger as he opened the folder.

"What's this make so far, twenty crackpot groups who have claimed credit for the mess in New York?" asked Senator Dan Rostow.

"Twenty-two, actually. But this one is different." returned the National Security Assistant.

Higgins glanced up at younger man with a quizzical look.

"So what's different?"

"This one talks about some details of the bombing of the F.B.I. Office that we never released to the public." he answered as he passed a copy of the Terrorist's note around the group.

"So," mused Rostow, "By mentioning the details, this letter proves it's the real thing. So let's see what our friends have to say."

So saying the Senator turned his attention back to the letter in the folder. Slowly, he read it through the first time and then, in disbelief, he read it a second time.

"But, these demands are ridiculous!" sputtered Rostow. "The President can never agree to this. It would be treason on his part."

"That's exactly what his 'loyal' advisors told the President. In fact, Eastman was very adamant. He said, and I quote 'You can't agree to these demands and still remain President, but it is my opinion that if we do not agree to their terms that they will utterly and totally destroy New York City and kill over three million people.'"

Higgins paused and looked at Armiger.

"Eastman said that?" he asked in surprise.

For a long moment, the members of the group simply looked at each other, but then one after another they began to smile. Things were coming together nicely.

PART THREE

THE SPECTOR

CHAPTER TWENTY-FOUR

Dr. Bremer hustled Noyotivik/Hughes through the lobby of his building and pushed against the outside doors only to discover they were locked.

"Doorman!" he yelled, looking around the lobby angrily.

"Just a minute. Keep your shirt on. I'm coming," responded a voice from behind the doorman's stand.

In a few minutes a white-haired old man came shuffling out into the lobby, fumbling to button his coat across his paunch.

"Open these doors," ordered Bremer glaring at the old man.

"Can't do it," answered the doorman, shaking his gray shaggy locks, "there's a curfew in effect. Orders are the doors stay closed until six a.m."

Dr. Bremer stepped close to the old man and pushed a finger into his chest.

"You see that police car sitting out there?" he asked jerking his head toward the doors.

The doorman glanced out and saw a city police car idling at the curb.

"I do." he returned drawing himself up to his full 5' 1" with great dignity, "all the more reason not to open those doors."

"Well" said Bremer, making a major effort to contain his anger, "that car is waiting to take me and this man down to police headquarters. This is a witness that the police is needing downtown."

"Well——-" began the old man, visibly uncertain as to what to do. "I guess—"

With an oath, Dr. Bremer grabbed the old man's arm and hustled him over to the doors. Tapping his foot impatiently on the tile floor, Dr. Bremer watched as the little doorman fumbled with a big ring of keys attached to his broad leather belt by a chain. Mumbling to himself, the old man looked carefully at each key and finally pulled out one and held it up.

"This is the key." he said, a satisfied smile on his face.

"Well use it, damn it." snapped the Doctor as he impatiently waited while the old man bent down to open the locks in the bottom of each door.

The moment the lock turned, the Doctor bulled his way out of the building with Noyotivik/Hughes close behind him. Conscious of the old man's eyes on them, Bremer stood back for Noyotivik/Hughes to precede him into the waiting police car.

"To the apartment, quickly." snapped the Doctor, as soon as he had his patient safely in the car.

Nodding, the officer behind the wheel pulled away from the curb and sped off into the night, lights and siren going. Bremer sat back against the seat, smiling to himself, very satisfied with the way things were going. He was sure that RAVEN would be very happy with the way that Bremer handled the abduction of Hughes.

Bremer looked over at Hughes, or to give him his current name, Captain Noyotivik. Noyotivik was staring straight ahead, no emotion showing on his broad face. As big as he was, it was no wonder that he could do the feats of strength that Bremer had read about in his file. This would be the ultimate weapon to break the spirit of the American people. Like a specter in the night, Noyotivik would conduct a reign of terror such as never been experienced before.

On two wheels, the car swung into 66th street and started across Central Park.

"It's sure easy to drive in this crazy city when the streets are deserted like this." laughed the cop in the passenger seat, looking back at his passengers in the rearview mirror.

"Yeah, wish it was always like this." grunted the driver, flicking a glance over at his partner.

The driver laughed.

"Yeah, took a major disaster to make the streets safe for driving in this city."

The first cop turned around and looked over the seat at the passengers in the back. "So this is the big guy everyone's been waiting for?"

"Yes," answered Dr. Bremer with pride, "Captain Illai Noyotivik."

"Don't look like much to me." grunted the driver, inspecting the big man in the rearview mirror.

"He could snap you in half like a twig." sniffed Dr. Bremer in disdain.

"Well sometime we'll have to see about that," returned the driver, grinning at his partner.

"Can't much of a tough guy if he couldn't even keep his family from being blown away." mocked the driver, laughing at Hughes in the rear view mirror.

Dr. Bremer started to flare up at the cop, but stopped when he felt Hughes begin to move forward in his seat.

"What— did— you— say?" asked Hughes hesitantly in a soft, flat voice, peering intently at the laughing cop.

"I said, you jackass, that if you're such a high-powered hit man, why did you let the Arabs off your wife and kids?" repeated the cop, sticking his face closer to Hughes.

"My wife? Kids? What are you talking about?" asked Hughes in a more normal tone of voice.

"What's happened to my wife and kids?" he asked, a puzzled expression on his face.

Sensing something had possibly gone wrong with the programming, Dr. Bremer tried to intervene and grabbed Hughes by his arm. For a moment, Hughes glanced at the Doctor and then, effortlessly, he pushed the Doctor across the seat, before turning to the cop who was taunting him.

"What did you say?" he asked politely, flexing his hands.

"I guess he's deaf as well as wimpy," the Cop in the passenger seat said to his partner. "I said, you deaf idiot, that you fucked up and got your family killed. You couldn't even protect your own family and you're supposed to be such a hotshot," jeered the cop, looking at his buddy for support.

With cobra-like speed, Hughes' right hand snapped up and grabbed the cop by the throat, his thumb pressed deeply in the skin beneath his chin. Slowly, Hughes' fingers began to tighten, as the cop's eyes bulged further and further out of his head. He totally ignored Dr. Bremer's futile attempts to pull his hand off of the guard.

"Noyotivik, let him go," yelled Dr. Bremer, as the guard's face began to turn purple.

With an oath, the driver slammed on the brakes and brought the speeding car to a stop. He turned and swung a big left hand at Hughes' head. To his surprise, Hughes showed no sign he had even felt the blow. The driver drew back his fist to hit him again, but Hughes beat him to it by striking out with his own left. The blow connected with the point of the driver's chin and knocked him senseless.

With a last squeeze, Hughes finally released his hold on the jeering cop, who grabbed at his discolored throat and fell back against the door wheezing for breath. Dr. Bremer sat with his mouth hanging open, senses stunned by the violence and quickness of the attack. Even though he was aware of how dangerous Hughes or Noyotivik was, Dr. Bremer really had no first-hand experience with the type of mayhem that a man like Hughes could produce.

As his escort recovered sufficiently to continue the trip, Dr. Bremer sat back in the corner of the car and began to reconsider what he and his unknown colleagues had really created. Bremer considered himself a highly civilized man, no, a superior man. A superior man never resorted to violence. Now, here he was assisting the commission of unbelievable violence and death in his home city.

"Where did I go wrong?" he asked himself, as his pensive eyes studied the big man beside him.

Dr. Bremer had agreed to join the Revolutionary Council in order to get power and money and he had to admit that the fringe benefits of being one of the leaders of the new revolution were outstanding. But he was starting to believe that all of the death and destruction were too much cost for too little return. To Bremer everything was a business transaction. He really wasn't sure that he was getting enough for his involvement.

Seeing his escort recovering themselves, Bremer leaned forward and lightly tapped the driver on the shoulder. "Now, if we may continue."

With one last glare, tinged with grudging respect, the driver put the car back in gear and pulled away from the curb. Hughes' anger subsided and he was sitting slumped in the opposite corner of the seat, staring out the window at the passing scenery. Bremer watched Hughes in concern. He wasn't certain what had set Hughes off, but something had certainly caused a reaction. As near as he could remember, the Noyotivik personality hadn't been married, so why would the mention of Hughes' dead wife bother Noyotivik? In fact, Noyotivik was simply a false identity created to be used to channel Hughes' violent nature. He would have to check with some of his colleagues. The plans were too far along to have anything go awry now.

"Noyotivik, are you O.K.?" asked Bremer.

"Fine." snapped the big man, not bothering to look at Dr. Bremer.

For a long time Bremer watched his companion closely, then satisfied, he leaned back against his seat. Almost time for the second phase of the plan.

Moses Gardner hustled along the hall toward Addie's office. She was-n't going to believe what he had found. Moses was excited; he was mov-ing so fast, he was almost running. Uncharacteristically, her office door was closed. Impatiently stopping in the hall, the Photographer knocked and waited. He glanced down to see several coins lying on the floor out-side her door. He knew that she had to be there, since she couldn't go home due to the curfew. He frowned to himself when his knock brought no response. He tried the door. It was locked. His eyes nar-rowed, this was definitely out of character for Addie. She never locked her door.

"Hey." came a yell from back down the hall. "You! Freeze!"

Moses spun around to see Melvin Brown, head of security hurrying toward him, gun drawn.

"Oh, it's you, Moses."

"Mind putting that away?" Moses indicated the gun.

Brown smiled grimly as he looked down at the gun, held tightly in his right hand. "Sorry, Moses, but we seem to have a breach of security. Several folks have reported unauthorized people in the building," he said, holstering his pistol.

"Whom'd you expect to find here?" demanded Moses as he leaned against Addie's office door.

"Thought you might be that guy that Miss Vandemeyer reported," returned the Security Chief.

"Who was that?" asked Moses curiously.

Melvin shrugged his broad shoulders. "Some guy pretending to be a Police Detective came around asking her questions."

Moses suddenly had a horrible thought.

"Melvin, Addie's office door is locked and I can't find her. You know as well as I do that she never, never locks her door. I'm worried about her; can you open the office for me?" he asked.

Melvin rubbed his stubble-covered chin with one calloused hand. "Well, it's definitely against regulations to open someone else's office."

he began, "but since it's you, and you and her are so close, I guess its o.k. Besides, if something has happened to her, I want to know it."

He reached in his pocket for his ring of passkeys.

"Hurry." pleaded Moses.

Fumbling with the huge ring of keys, Melvin checked key after key until he found the one he was after.

"This ought to do it," he said, sliding the key into the lock and turning the doorknob.

The moment the door opened, Moses pushed past Brown and burst into the room only to skid to a complete stop. The place had been ransacked; papers were thrown on the floor, drawers dumped upside down, couch cushions thrown onto the desk. Moses didn't start to breath again until he assured himself that Addie's body wasn't stuffed under her desk.

"My god." breathed Melvin. "What happened here?"

"Call the front and see if anyone left the building with her!" ordered Moses as he righted her desk chair and dropped into it.

Melvin jerked his radio from his belt. "Central this is Unit 1."

"This is Central."

"Bill, did anyone enter or leave the building within the last thirty minutes?" he asked.

"No. The place has been completely dead. Even the street outside is completely deserted."

"Thanks. Out."

Melvin hesitated a minute and then brought the radio back to his mouth. "All units, this is Unit 1. There are one or more intruders in the building. They may have kidnapped Addie Vandemeyer. I want all floors, elevators, stairways and every out-of-the-way place in this damn building checked and then rechecked. I want you guys to seal every exit until further notice. I want to know the name of every person in the building."

Returning the radio to his belt, Melvin looked back at Moses.

"Don't worry, we'll find them. They couldn't have gotten out of the building."

Moses nodded and watched Melvin bolt from the room, reaching for his pistol again. Addie was well thought of by the staff. He knew that Melvin would kill anyone who hurt Addie. With a sigh, Moses started to get back to his feet.

"If Addie is missing, I would do better trying to find her than sitting here." he thought to himself.

As he was pulling the door closed behind him, the phone rang. Thinking it might be Addie; Moses pushed the door open and almost dove across the room.

"Hello!"

"Miss Vandemeyer, please." said a deep male voice.

"She's not here. Can I take a message?" Moses rounded the desk and slid back into the chair.

"Who is this?" asked the voice suspiciously.

"Moses Gardner, a friend of hers."

"Moses, John Voynich here."

For a moment Moses' face was creased with a smile and he began to relax. He hadn't seen John since Beirut and if anyone could help find Addie it would be John.

"John, good to hear from you again. How's things?"

John snorted.

"Addie has, as usual, stirred up a hornet's nest for me. Where is she?"

"Addie's disappeared, John," said Moses quietly.

"What!"

"We were both stuck in the building as a result of this curfew. She'd been working on a story for tonight's late news. We'd decided to meet in the snack bar, but I was late getting there. I had news for her and instead of waiting around I came to her office and found it locked.

I met the Security Chief who told me that we have intruders in the building. Her office was ransacked, her papers are scattered all over the floor. It looks like someone grabbed her as she left her office. There's even some change lying on the floor. Building security is searching high and low for her now, but I think she's gone."

"Anyone see anything?"

"Well, shortly before it happened, it appears that she notified security that a phony New York City Police Detective came to her office and tried to ask her some questions. My guess is that when she wouldn't answer, he kidnapped her. I don't know how he could have gotten her out of the building, but it looks like he has."

"Yeah, when OI talked to her earlier, she asked me about someone, I think his name was Kincade."

Voynich paused for a moment.

"That's not good, Moses. As big a pain in the ass as Addie can be, it's not like Addie to drop out of sight intentionally and not let someone know. But it may actually tie into what she called me about."

"What did she want, John?" Moses Gardner's big hand threatened to crush the receiver.

"She asked me about a former Army Officer named Carter Davis Hughes. She wanted to know if he had been C.I.A."

"Yeah, that's the guy who killed the terrorists in the American Festival Cafe. She brought him up to the office. Turned out he is Renaldi's son-in-law. So, was he C.I.A.?" questioned Gardner.

"No, not according to our records. I checked the main computer data base at Langley and found absolutely no reference to a man by that name being an agent. However, we did find an army officer by the name of C.D. Hughes, who was assigned to the 193rd Infantry Brigade. He was a decorated combat veteran with two tours of duty in Vietnam. Wounded several times in the line of duty.

I ran a thorough check on him and found out that he is supposed to still be in the military. His current assignment is Embassy duty in London. We checked and found out that he is not assigned there and apparently never has been. So we started to back check and found out that a man by this name died at the Gorgas Hospital in the Canal Zone in 1975.

There was nothing unusual that we could find in his records, other than this; it would appear that he was assigned to the 4th Battalion, 10th Infantry in the Panama Canal Zone. Now about the time he was there, some very unusual things took place."

"Well, what happened?" asked Moses, his curiosity aroused, in spite of his concern for Addie.

"I don't know completely yet. There were some unexplained deaths, but the matter was covered up very completely by the Brigade Commander. So far, we haven't found anyone willing to talk." replied Voynich, his voice tinged with regret.

" Piecing what little bit we do know together, it would appear that several officers and enlisted personnel died in unusual circumstances. It could have well been murder. We are still trying to put the rest of the pieces together."

"Well," shot back Gardner, "whoever he is or was, this Hughes guy is hell on wheels when the chips are down. The press is calling him the Manhattan Rambo and from what Addie tells me he fits the bill. He took care of those terrorists that attacked Rock Center in short order."

"So I've heard."

"Any other information?"

"Well you're not cleared——" began the C.I.A. man.

"Damn you and your clearances. Addie's gone, John. Remember, she saved your ass in Baghdad last year. So, talk to me."

"O.K., cool your jets, big guy. There's not a great deal of concrete information, merely supposition. But here goes."

Voynich paused and Moses could hear some pages being turned.

From what we could find out, this Hughes was a mysterious duck. He was assigned to Company E, 20th Infantry, in Nam, but never reported for duty. Instead he was immediately sent out into Cambodia. He ran 24 successful cross boarder missions in Vietnam. There was some talk that he was psychotic, he liked to kill and inflict pain. Around the mid 1970s, he was apparently assigned to the Panama Canal Zone. After Panama he seemed to be assigned to one classified project after another. In mid-1983, he suddenly resigned his commission. Shortly after that, he married the only daughter of Howard Renaldi.

Then six months later, (this was in 1983, remember) a controlled asset we were running in the Middle East sent word that several of the more radical terrorist groups were banding together. They had a program of terror that would cost them millions and take years to put together. Now these crackpot groups have made threats against us for years, but this one was different. The information that came to us was that the group had the secret backing of wealthy Americans.

According to other independent sources, there were some Americans seen in Baghdad who were supposed to be working with the terrorists. We got photographs and prints but were never able to identify the people. Allegedly, one of them was a world-class assassin known only as the Specter. Prior to this he had never been photographed, so we had nothing to check his picture against. We later learned that the Specter had been sent north into China in some type of exchange training program.

In return for the Chinese helping train the Specter, they supposedly received several million dollars in cash from some secret Swiss bank accounts. By the time we traced the money to the bank accounts, the accounts were closed, the records and destroyed and the Bank Officers who had opened and controlled the accounts had either disappeared or were dead. We still haven't figured out who was ultimately behind the operation. After this last piece of information, we lost track of the Specter.

However, later we managed to at least get on his trail through assets in China and found information that led us to believe that the Specter went to the Soviet Union for what we might call an advance degree in assassination. That's it." finished Voynich.

Moses made a sound of disgust. "Don't you spooks ever talk to each other?"

"What do you mean?" asked Voynich in puzzlement.

"I mean that the N.S.A. has a bit more on our boy."

"Like what?" he demanded.

"Seems that they were able to follow him closer than your "assets". According to my source, in Panama Hughes is supposed to have had something to with an operation called Operation Resurrection. Only there is something very peculiar about this."

"Such as what?' demanded Voynich.

"One of my friends is with the State Department, part of the team allowed access to K.G.B. files last year. He didn't want to talk about it, but he finally said that he remembered the Russians had their own program called Operation Resurrection. Rumors he heard in Russia had it that the project was being run in conjunction with a similar American effort.

According to him, Operation Resurrection was shrouded in mystery. However, he had an idea of what was involved since he was one of those analyst working on what the K.G.B. laughingly called termination programs."

"Does that mean what I think it means?" asked Voynich.

"It means that the project may have been designed to train assassins to work for the K.G.B.," returned Moses.

"Damn, a journalist knows this and the C.I.A. doesn't. What a way to run a railroad." objected Voynich.

He muttered to himself for a moment, apparently making notes, and then came back on the line.

"What do you mean that the program may have been designed to train assassins? Doesn't your source know what the project was about?" he demanded.

"My buddy claims that the information on Operation Resurrection was released on a need-to-know basis only. Due to the shakeup in personnel in the Soviet Union, lately, there was no one available that knew much about it. Unfortunately, when he started asking questions about the program, his Russian guide freaked out and kicked the matter upstairs. The few records that existed vanished." reported Moses.

"Did he tell you anything else on your "need-to-know" basis?" asked Voynich sarcastically.

"Only that all records regarding Project Resurrection were missing. The only reference to it was the label on an empty file folder."

"O.K., I'll bite. What did the label say?"

"It said 'Project referred to the Pasdaran'." answered Moses.

"Pasdaran!" exclaimed Voynich.

"Yes. Do you have any idea what that is?" demanded the photographer.

"I certainly do. Pasdaran is a word that is used to refer to the Islamic Revolutionary Guard. It means, Moses, that the program was probably turned over to Iran, that someone wanted the matter kept so quiet that they cleaned up their back trail. It also means that there is an outside chance that your Carter Davis Hughes, if he was involved in this program, is probably an extremely violent, heartless killer."

" Addie, where are you?" groaned Moses in despair.

As soon as John Voynich hung up, he sprang into action. Voynich was Deputy Assistant Director of Operations for the Special Operations Command, a super secret intelligence force that operated under special authorization of the President. In his position, he had a great many resources at his disposal. He had the power to commit men and money to any project that he desired. At the same time, he was a very shrew campaigner who knew the importance of clout in sorting through red tape in time of emergency.

Collecting his notes, he left his office and went down the long walnut paneled hallway to enter the office of his boss, James J. Hall, Assistant

Director of Operations. Hall was finishing some dictation to his secretary, Mary Longworth, when he saw John enter.

"Well, what brings you out of your cave before midnight?" he asked cheerfully.

John crossed the thick carpet to sit in one of the red leather chairs in front of Hall's large gleaming desk.

"I've been talking to a friend of a friend in New York."

Hall nodded gravely as he toyed with a paper clip.

"I'm fully aware of the chaos there. Today, the President ordered the F.B.I. and the C.I.A. to commit whatever assets to New York that are needed to get a grip on things. I would take a hand, but the Director of Intelligence has specifically told the President that he didn't want any of the "Black Agencies" involved. He thinks we get in his way."

His Boss shook his head sadly.

John nodded, distracted. "Sir, as serious as the situation is there with the terrorists, I think we've got something more important to look into."

Hall's bushy eyebrows always shot up when he was interested in something. On occasion, his eyebrows almost disappeared into his hairline. Silently, he motioned for John to continue.

"I have a friend, Addie Vandemeyer."

He broke off and grinned in spite of himself.

"You may be aware of her?" he finished with an innocent expression on his ruddy face.

Hall grimaced ruefully at the recollection of his one meeting with the female reporter.

"Let me guess, you two to have decided to get married and she wants me to give her away; right?"

John shuddered with distaste and mentally granted the first point to his boss. He had to admit that Hall was fast on his feet.

"Not likely, that would be like trying to saddle a tornado. But, to more important matters. She was in the American Festival Cafe at

Rockefeller Center when the terrorists attacked. She dove for cover and had a front row seat to the entire event. An insurance man named Carter Davis Hall took a gun away from one of the terrorists and proceeded to wipe them out. Addie said that he seemed to be mentally out of it, but he was functioning well enough to get the best of some very dangerous radicals.

She called me and asked for confirmation that Hall had been C.I.A. during his military time. I checked and what I found doesn't make any sense."

"Such as?" asked Hall as his eyebrows began to descend toward their proper location on his broad face.

"First, she did some investigating on her own with his current employer. According to North American Insurance Company, Carter Davis Hughes was 37 years old last month. He joined them in 1985. He is married to a Martha Renaldi, the boss' daughter and has two kids."

Voynich paused at this point and glanced up at his boss.

"That is, he was married and did have two kids."

Hall frowned, but said nothing, continuing to play with his paper clip.

"His wife and kids were killed by the terrorists. Anyway, she asked me to look this guy up. I did a normal record check and at first found no records, so I called the St. Louis records storage facility. Hughes was never a member of the C.I.A., nor any other intelligence outfit that I could find. We were ready to quit looking when we noticed something peculiar."

"Such as?" prompted Hall, spinning the paper clip in his hand.

"First, the birth dates didn't check out. According to his military 201 file, Carter Davis Hughes should be about 46, the one Addie found, so to speak, has just turned 37. I double-checked the social security numbers and they match, so this should be the same guy."

"That all?" asked Hall softly.

Voynich shook his head.

"Not at all. Second, the fingerprint card was missing. We questioned the clerk in charge of this section and he assured us that it should have been there.

Third, the 201 file shows that Hughes was wounded several times in Nam. We pulled his medical records and found that he should have stiffness in his right arm. According to Addie, this guy she met was hell on wheels. They are calling him The Manhattan Rambo. He outfought and killed a half a dozen of those killers. She made no mention of any stiffness.

Lastly, the picture is missing from the file. We have absolutely no way to determine if this Hughes in New York is the same man whose file we have."

Hall sat quietly and played with his paper clip. He leaned back in his chair and studied his ceiling for a long while before looking directly at John.

"So what does it mean?" Hall asked quietly, resting one arm on his desk.

"By itself, nothing. However, her photographer, Moses Gardner apparently has contacts of his own. He found out that the National Security Agency knew a few things that the C.I.A. doesn't know about this guy. First, he was assigned to Panama in the mid 1970s, about the time some very weird things apparently happened. After this assignment with a regular line unit, he was suddenly detached to classified projects for the remainder of his military career."

This definitely generated interest in Hall.

"What classified projects?" he asked in his soft voice, as a pen suddenly appeared in his hand.

Voynich flipped to another page in his file. "I don't have all of the names, but the last one is the most important. It was called Operation Resurrection," he said looking back at his boss.

"What was the subject of Operation Resurrection?" asked Hall.

"I don't know, but I do know that the Russians also had a project by this name. The most interesting thing was that rumors in Russia maintained that the Russian Project and the American Project were working together on some matter," replied John with a shrug.

James J. Hall rose to his full 5' 7" height and took a turn around his lavishly decorated office. First he straightened the picture of the President that hung behind his desk, then he strolled over to the concealed bar, John knew all about, and fixed himself a small whiskey sour. Slowly, he stirred the drink, sipped it, and then stirred some more. Finally he walked back to his desk and almost elegantly resumed his chair.

"John, I don't care what it takes, I want the full file on Project Resurrection on my desk within twenty-four hours. I also want to know what Hughes' involvement in this matter is," he said, as he sipped his drink.

With those simple instructions, James J. Hall pulled a folder out of his in-box and began to read, totally ignoring his subordinate. Taking the hint, Voynich hurried back to his own office. He had a lot of work to do.

CHAPTER TWENTY-FIVE

Addie was hustled into the elevator and watched as the button for the twelfth floor was pressed. They stood and waited for the elevator to arrive at its destination. With a muted bing, the elevator slid to a stop and the doors opened. Malika grabbed Addie's upper arm pulled her close enough to whisper, "One sound and it'll be your last." she promised as she shoved her pistol into Addie's side.

With a push from her captor, Addie was propelled out of the elevator into the dimly lit hallway. The phony police detective walked slowly in front of them, his right hand in his jacket pocket, clutching his pistol. Addie was praying that someone would come out into the hall and see them, but the doors all along the hall stayed firmly shut. All too soon, Kincade stopped before one of the apartment doors and rang the bell. Addie's heart sank even further as the door jerked open, light spilling out into the dimly lit hallway.

Roughly, Malika shoved Addie into the apartment. The toe of her right shoe caught in the rich Persian carpet causing her to fall heavily to the floor, the side of her face coming to rest on someone's embroidered slipper. She struggled to get her legs under her and sit up, but the unseen person lifted his leg and, with the flat of his foot, pushed her back to the floor.

"So who do we have here?"

"The reporter, you Highness." said Kincade.

"Ah, so this is the famous Addie Vandemeyer."

The man leaned forward to rest a hand on Addie's head. For what seemed like hours to Addie, he rested his hand on her head and his foot on the middle of her back. Then he straightened to his full height and removed his foot. Addie immediately struggled to pull her exposed legs under her and rise to a sitting position, her wrists tied behind her. Jerking her head to swing her long hair out of her eyes, Addie defiantly glared up at her captor.

He was a tall, muscular man of Middle Eastern extraction, in his mid-forties, dressed in the fashion of his homeland. His hair was dark, as were his eyes. A pencil-slim moustache adorned his upper lip.

"Who are you?" she demanded, trying to get to her feet.

He smiled down at her haughtily, as he reached out one hand to push her back to the floor.

"I am Prince Abu Adein Hadji of the Royal House of Iraq."

"Well," she laughed, "another camel jockey."

Price Hadji's face darkened and he raised his hand to hit her. Addie tensed. For a long moment, he stood with his hand in the air. Then a smile crossed his face and he lowered his arm.

"A woman with spirit. I like that." he said.

He considered her for a long moment then looked over at a mountain of a man standing against the far wall of the room.

"Otto, take her!" ordered the Prince.

At the Prince's command, the big servant reached down and picked Addie up from the floor as though she weighed nothing. In spite of her struggles, Otto, followed by Malika, carried Addie out of the room into one of the bedrooms. Walking over to the large bed in the far corner, Otto simply dropped Addie's bound body so that she bounced from the mattress to collide with the wall. In a flash of her long legs, she pulled herself back into a sitting position on the bed.

Malika, with a malicious grin on her dark face, roughly pushed Addie back onto her back and jumped on her to sit squarely on Addie's lower chest. Malika quickly forced her neck scarf into Addie's mouth and secured it with a piece of twine Otto handed her. Then Malika rolled Addie onto her stomach and shifted her weight to the top of Addie thighs while Otto expertly tied Addie's ankles.

After satisfying herself that Addie was safely secured, Malika crawled off her captive to stand beside the bed. Rolling Addie back over onto her back, Malika captured her face with one hand.

"You and I have an appointment, my dear. I, for one, am going to enjoy it," she said before allowing Addie to jerk her head away from the imprisoning hand.

Laughing loudly, Malika turned and left the room, Otto following close behind, clicking off the lights as he left. Then the door shut and Addie was alone in the dark. She rolled onto her side, curling into a ball. She felt helpless and alone, as tears trickled from her eyes.

Dr. Bremer and his companion were driven to the front door of the Apartment Complex in style, as befitting a man of Dr. Bremer's importance. The doorman at 155 West 68th Street was sitting in the lobby reading a magazine, expecting no one due to the curfew. Naturally, he was confused and surprised when he saw a police officer banging on the glass doors, but he rushed to unlock the door.

"Dr. Bremer for Prince Hadji."

"Yes, sir." Reaching around the counter to the telephone, the doorman punched out the number for Prince Hadji's suite. After several rings, the servant answer.

"Dr.——Dr. Bremer to see the Prince." stammered the doorman.

"Send him up." came the quick response.

"Elevator is to the right," offered the doorman, but Dr. Bremer had already led his companion in the proper direction.

Making a face, the doorman returned to his book and didn't bother to glance up as the police car pulled away. It didn't make any difference to him who did what to who. He was quite content just to sit and read.

Dr. Bremer and Noyotivik/Hughes exited the elevator on the twelfth floor and went immediately to the door of apartment 1235. Bremer rang the bell and waited impatiently for a response. Otto slowly pulled the door open.

"Yes, sir. Please come in.," he said.

Dr. Bremer pulled Noyotivik/Hughes inside and they followed Otto into the living room. Prince Hadji rose from the couch where he had been enjoying some tea. "Ah, Bremer, my friend, you are welcome in my humble home." He indicated the couch across from him.

"Please, my friend, have a seat."

With a sigh, Dr. Bremer dropped onto the offered couch.

"Prince Hadji, may I present the long awaited Captain Illai Noyotivik?"

Prince Hadji nodded slightly without taking his eyes off of Noyotivik's face.

"Is he one of us, my friend?" inquired the Prince.

Dr. Bremer nodded.

"Everything is under control, Prince. Captain Noyotivik has assured me that he is firmly committed to our 'movement'."

"Excellent, excellent." beamed the Prince. Prince Hadji, elegant as always, sank back into his position on the couch and brought his cup to his lips. Even as he sipped his tea, the Arab continued to stare at the "Captain." Placing his cup carefully back onto its saucer, Prince Hadji turned to Dr. Bremer.

"We have a mission planned for tomorrow. Will Captain Noyotivik be able to take part?"

"Certainly," assured Dr. Bremer, "I think you will find him quite helpful."

Prince Hadji nodded.

"Very good. Then all is ready for our biggest 'incident' to date," he said.

Dr. Bremer turned to Captain Noyotivik.

"Illai you will obey the commands of Prince Hadji, in my absence. Do you understand?" questioned Bremer.

"Yes. I understand." intoned the Captain in a flat voice.

"Excellent." applauded the Prince.

"Have you solved the problem of the inquisitive reporter?" asked Bremer in concern.

Prince Hadji beamed at his guest. "But of course. Shall I show you?" He rose again to his feet. Leaving his guests for a moment, the Prince walked down the hall to the bedroom holding the prisoner. Stopping in the hallway, the Prince turned to Malika, who was sitting in a chair beside the door.

"Prepare our guest for display. Then have Otto bring her to the living room." he commanded.

Malika rose gracefully and bowed almost to the floor. "With pleasure, my Prince." she said.

Addie had almost drifted off to sleep, when the lights came on. Groggily she rolled onto her back and looked over at the door. She saw Malika and Otto come in, Malika carrying several leather items in one hand and a bottle in the other.

"Well, my dear, it is time. His Highness, Prince Hadji has commanded that you perform for him and his guests." she said.

Addie made a rude noise in her throat and rolled over onto her side.

Malika only laughed as Addie heard her drop the leather items in her hand to the floor. After a few seconds of low voiced instructions to Otto, Malika took the top off of the bottle. A peculiar aroma filled the room.

Addie couldn't really tell what would make such a smell, but she wanted no part of it. With a rapid movement she rolled over so that her back was to the wall and she faced her tormentors. She was in time to see Malika soak a cloth with the liquid from the bottle. Suddenly, she remembered what made that type of aroma, chloroform.

Malika handed the bottle to Otto and approached the bed, the cloth held out to her side.

"Cooperate and you'll enjoy it. I promise." she cooed to her prisoner.

In answer, Addie tried to push herself even closer to the wall. Malika continued to close the distance, slowly putting one knee on the bed as she began to crawl toward Addie. Addie's eyes stayed glued to the white cloth clutched in Malika's left hand.

Suddenly, Addie tried to kick out with her bound feet, but Otto was quick enough to catch her ankles. He flipped Addie onto her back and pulled her into the center of the bed. Malika quickly sprang up to sit on top of Addie's struggling body. Quickly, she brought the chloroform-soaked cloth down over Addie's nose and mouth. It only took a few involuntary breaths for Addie's movements to slow down and gradually stop as she became unconscious. Malika sat up with a satisfied look on her lovely face; she would definitely enjoy preparing this one for the Prince.

Swinging her legs over, Malika was helped to her feet by Otto. Under his gaze, Malika rolled the unconscious reporter over onto her side, unfastening and removing the gag. In its' place, she pried open Addie's mouth and inserted a large rubber plug, which she secured around Addie's head with two straps. Addie was now securely gagged.

Grabbing Addie by her long red hair, Malika hauled her into a sitting position. Pushing her forward, Malika lowered the zipper on the back of the one-piece blue dress. Grabbing the front of the garment with her right hand, Malika released Addie's hair and let her fall back, literally peeling the clothing off the upper part of Addie's body. Her breath heavier and more rapid, Malika grabbed a handful of Addie's material where it was bunched at her hips and begin to work the dress down the reporter's unconscious form. When Malika straightened, Addie's clothes held in her hand, the reporter was wearing only her black high heels, a black garter belt, stockings, pale blue, bikini panties, a lacy bra and the black leather gag.

Malika pulled Addie back into a sitting position by her hair. With a flick of a finger, she slid Addie's bra straps off of her shoulders and jerked the unconscious girl's arms out of her bra straps. Only the snap of the bra kept her full breasts covered.

Then Malika rolled Addie onto her stomach and reaching across her body, grabbed her right wrist. Expertly, Malika fastened a large, heavy leather cuff, with a dangling ring, onto the girl's right wrist. Quickly she repeated the same movement with Addie's left wrist. Taking both of Addie's cuffed wrists in her hands, Malika twisted the two dangling rings together so that they hooked. Addie's wrists were very firmly tied together behind her back. Pausing, Malika gently ran her hands over Addie's soft smooth back, reaching around to slid her hands under the bra to cup her full breasts.

"The Prince is waiting," reminded Otto.

She looked at Otto with a smile.

"Otto, your soul has no romance."

Malika removed the high-heeled shoes and rolled Addie's stockings down her long smooth legs, tossing them aside once they were removed. Then she took off the garter belt. This left only the pale blue bikini panties. Malika was pulling at the panties when the door flew open. Kincade stuck his head inside and snapped.

"His nips are impatient. He said to bring the girl as she is."

With a grunt of annoyance Malika grabbed a bigger handful of the panties, but Otto knocked her hands away.

"Malika," he rumbled, "The Prince said now and he means now."

Swearing under her breath, Malika grabbed the ankle cuffs from the floor and quickly strapped them on Addie followed by a large leather collar. Once she snapped a leash onto the collar the slave girl costume was ready. By now, Malika's mouth was actually watering she wanted the prisoner so badly.

Angrily, Malika grabbed Addie's legs and pulled them around so that they hung off the bed. Dropping to her knees, Malika carefully fitted Addie's black high-heeled shoes back on her bare feet. Using the leash Malika pulled the unresisting girl back into a sitting position for third time. Finally, Malika pulled an ammonia capsule from her pocket and broke it under Addie nose. As soon as the pungent smell penetrated Addie's nose, her head began to jerk. Soon her eyes fluttered open.

"Ummmmm." she said.

Malika pulled Addie to her feet.

"Get ready, girl. You are going to perform for his highness."

Addie began to fight against her bonds. Drawing back her left hand, Malika slammed her fist into Addie's mid section. Retching into her gag, Addie sagged to her knees. Once again, Malika pulled her back to her feet and pulled Addie's face close to hers. "Unless you obey, you will suffer more pain that you ever believed possible." threatened Malika.

To emphasize her threat, Malika again drove her left fist into Addie's defenseless mid section. Addie dropped to her knees like a rock, as she wretched into her gag. This time when she was pulled back to her feet, Addie cooperated. Satisfied with the appearance of docility, Malika pulled Addie out of the bedroom and down the hall. In the distance, Addie could hear men talking.

When Prince Hadji glimpsed Malika in the doorway, he broke off the conversation and motioned her into enter the room. Obediently, Malika pulled Addie along behind her. Otto and Kincade stopped at the door. Under the Prince's watchful eyes, Malika led Addie around the room. Addie's temper was seething, but she was totally helpless. No matter how she strained her muscles, she couldn't free her wrists and the gag was impossible to spit out.

Noticing Addie's struggles, Prince Hadji smiled slightly, this was one with spirit. "Bremer, my friend, I trust you know a superb specimen of femininity when you see it. During my years as my country's ambassador to France, I learned some new techniques for instilling a submissive attitude in those women that I desire. You would do well to watch and learn."

Dr. Bremer made no comment, but his eyes never left the captive woman as she was paraded around the room.

Finally, Malika came to a stop in front of the Prince. The Prince rose and slowly circled his captive; he was very impressed by what he saw. She was small, but her figure was superb. Her legs were some of the best he had seen, as his eyes roamed from her full, firm thighs down to her slim well-muscled calves. He could imagine the treasures that those pale blue bikini panties were concealing.

He came to a stop in front of her and motioned to Malika. Obediently, she stepped behind Addie and unfastened Addie's bra, allowing it to fall to the floor. Jaded as he was, after having so many women, even the Prince had to catch his breath when he saw the superb firm, full breasts that graced Addie's chest. With something approaching reverence, the Prince reached out his hands and cupped her left breast in both of his cool hands.

Dr. Bremer actually envied the Prince having such a woman at his disposal. The reporter was a truly beautiful woman, one he would have been glad to call his wife. However, now she would spend what little remained of her life as a slave to the Prince. From the look on the Prince's face, Bremer knew that it was an even bet that she'd end up drugged, in a steamer trunk, shipped back to the middle east

The man who now thought of himself as Captain Illai Noyotivik watched the performance with puzzlement. He seemed to know this girl, but he had no idea who she might be. He was sure that she had recognized him. He had a sudden memory of her pointing a gun at him. Then over this girl's face, he saw the face of another woman, her eyes wide open, in fear. Next there was the quick memory of a woman and two kids being shot down by a man dressed in scruffy clothes.

He was brought back to the present when Dr. Bremer, elbowed him in the side. "Wouldn't you like a piece of that?" whispered the Doctor, indicating Addie's barely covered backside.

"Uh, yeah. Sure." he responded mechanically.

"Are you o.k.?" asked Bremer in concern.

"Sure, just a headache." returned Noyotivik, as he quickly took a sip of his rapidly cooling tea.

With a searching stare at Noyotivik, Bremer turned his attention back to the slave girl in front of them. He had never felt such desire for a woman as he did Addie Vandemeyer.

Noyotivik/Hughes, like his two companions just sat and watched the performance, but instead of thoughts of sex, his were darkened by blood, screaming women and gunshots.

Taking a deep breath, Prince Hadji dropped his hands to his sides. There would be time tonight for pleasure of the flesh, but for now he had things to do for his cause and for Allah. He looked at Malika.

"Take her to my bed room and secure her, then return here for instructions." he commanded with an imperious gesture.

Malika curtseyed low. "As you command, my Prince."

Conscious of all the eyes on her captive, Malika led her on one more circuit of the room. Addie had quickly learned to cooperate or be strangled by the leash and collar. In spite of the fact that she seethed when the Prince fondled her breasts, Addie was biding her time until she could figure out a way to escape. In the midst of her anger and humiliation, she was stunned to see Carter Hughes sitting here as an honored guest. Especially since he made no effort to help her. She couldn't figure out what was happening.

Several times as Addie was being led around the room, it seemed to Bremer as if Noyotivik/Hughes wanted to say something, but each time subsided. Bremer was very puzzled by this reaction; the Noyotivik personality was designed to have absolutely none of the softer feelings. In fact, the sight of an attractive female such as this one should have elicited erotic feelings in the assassin. If such feelings were being generated, they were well concealed. If he didn't know better he would say that Noyotivik was fighting the programming, but such a thing was impossible.

As Malika pulled on the leash, Addie wisely followed the older woman out of the room. She didn't have any idea what was in store for her, but she did know that in that room, she had absolutely no chance of escape. The last thing Addie heard was the Prince instruct his servant to call for the rest of the team. Then she was out in the hallway with Malika.

Malika was very prim and proper in regard to her captive until she had Addie out in the hall and was sure that the Prince was no longer watching. Once certain she couldn't be seen from the living room, Malika pressed the younger girl up against the wall and began to fondle her. Addie stoically took the manhandling in silence until Malika leaned over and began to suck on her left nipple. This act so repulsed Addie, in spite of herself, she grunted a loud objection.

As soon as she did it, Addie knew that she had made a mistake. There was no doubt that the men in the living room had heard her because all conversation stopped. Malika's face was like a thundercloud as she straightened up.

"Next time, bitch," she hissed as she drove her left fist into Addie's solar plexus.

With a groan, Addie crumpled. Not giving her a chance to recover, Malika jerked her along the corridor on her knees until they reached the bedroom door at the far end of the hall. Throwing the door open, Malika flipped on the lights and literally drug Addie into the room.

Malika drove her left fist into Addie's weakened mid section. As Addie started to collapse, Malika grabbed a handful of her hair and used her grip to literally propel her prisoner onto the bed that dominated the center of the room. Addie tried to roll away from her attacker, but Malika was on her immediately, pounding away at her in a fit of rage.

Finally, after what seemed like hours, Malika stopped pounding Addie's battered stomach and lay, spent, on top of her almost unconscious prisoner. Addie drifted off to sleep, roused again by Malika rolling her over and freeing her wrists.

Swiftly, Malika attached each of Addie's unresisting wrists to one of the bedposts. That done, Malika crawled to the foot of the bed and grabbed Addie's ankles. With a quick jerk, Malika straightened Addie's partially curled body and fastened her ankles to chains at the foot of the bed. When Malika finished, Addie was tied spread-eagle, her body defenseless. Malika sat back on the bed and looked at her work, with a satisfied expression on her face.

"You will please my Master tonight. But remember, after he is through with a woman, he gives them to me." she said with a wide smile.

CHAPTER TWENTY-SIX

After Malika had led Addie from the room, Prince Hadji instructed Kincade to call his men to assemble at once. Hadji walked over to the desk and pulled out some papers. Accepting another cup of tea from Otto, he returned to his seat. Taking a sip of his tea, Hadji's eyes again searched the face of Captain Noyotivik.

"Dr. Bremer, you are totally sure of your success?" questioned the Prince.

"Totally." returned the Doctor.

"Good." nodded the Prince. "As soon as my men are here, we shall do our final planning. I also think that it would be only fitting that your man be the one to pull the trigger."

"He is ready." assured Dr. Bremer.

The ringing of the doorbell interrupted their conversation. Through the open archway that opened into the hall, Bremer watched Otto answer the door. In a few moments he led eight conservatively dressed young men of varying races, into the room.

"I have them staying in another apartment that I own on this floor. I try to leave nothing to chance." said Hadji. Hadji motioned for the new comers to sit. Most chose to sit on the floor. Otto wandered the room making sure that each of the visitors had refreshments.

"Tomorrow, during the largest religious observance of the Infidel Christian Religion, we shall make our biggest strike of all. Our boldness will make a new page in revolutionary history. We will kill some of the most important leaders of the West and strike terror into the collective heart of the great Satan."

Hadji paused as a murmur came from his men.

"Now I will tell you the plan. Tomorrow at the Four Seasons Hotel, on 57th Street, the Israeli Ambassador to the United Nations, the Secretary General of the United Nations, the U.S. Ambassador to the United Nations and the French Ambassador, will be having a luncheon to discuss the ongoing problems in the city. . Immediately after the meal, they go to meet the senior Bishop of New York at St. Patrick's Cathedral. They will then attend a Special Christmas Mass praying for world peace. These gentlemen think it will help to show that they have no fear of the terrorists.

Team A, which is to be led by Shamus O'Toole, who will have Captain Noyotivik under his command, will go to the Four Seasons Hotel. Their job will be to assassinate the Israeli Ambassador and the Secretary General of the United Nations. Team B, your mission will be to assassinate the Catholic Bishop waiting at St. Patrick's. After the mission you will, as usual escape into the subways and regroup at the usual place.

Team A will leave here at 6:00 a.m. you will be taking the place of the morning shift at the hotel dining room. Team B will leave here at 10:00 a.m. you will need to be in position by 11:30. The Bishop will be arriving at approximately 12:20. I want him killed as he enters the Chapel.

Any questions?" he asked.

When there appeared to be no questions, Hadji stood.

"Wonderful, you may all return to your rooms until tomorrow. Captain Noyotivik you can accompany Team A and stay with them. Mr. O'Toole, you will brief Captain Noyotivik on his duties. Remember, he will fire the first shot."

"Certainly, sir, I will remember." responded the young Irishman, with a grin at his second in command, the grim Tommy Nelson.

"Good," nodded Hadji rubbing his hands together briskly, "Now to other matters."

While Hadji was talking to his men, Malika was impatiently pacing about in the hall.

She was expecting someone and that person was late. Finally there was a timid tap on the door. Malika fairly leaped across the distance to jerk the door open. On the threshold stood a slim young girl with platinum blonde hair.

"You're late." snapped Malika.

"I had to dodge police patrols all the way."

Putting a finger to her lips for silence, Malika took the girl by the hand and led her to one of the bedrooms.

"You shouldn't keep me waiting, sweetie. Malika doesn't like to be kept waiting," said the Arab woman as she hugged her friend.

"Now, into the bathroom with you and get ready." ordered Malika.

Obediently, the girl took her things and walked into the bathroom, pulling the door closed behind her. As the water ran, Malika envisioned the games of the evening before them. To her annoyance, there was a knock at the door.

"His Highness desires your presence." Otto said when she opened the door.

With a grunt, Malika followed Otto back into the living room.

Meanwhile, the blonde in the bathroom slowly opened the door and peered into the bedroom. Though the water had been running for several minutes, her platinum hair wasn't wet. She tiptoed across the room to the dresser and rapidly searched through the jewelry box, periodically pocketing pieces of jewelry. Satisfied that she had found everything worthwhile in Malika's room, the girl crossed quickly back to the bathroom and pulled the door closed.

Quickly, she stripped and stepped under the shower, scrubbing herself thoroughly. One thing she had learned, the Arabs wanted their women totally clean. Again and again, she rinsed her hair until it was squeaky clean before stepping out of the shower and toweling herself thoroughly. Wrapping the towel around her body, she reached out and opened the door to face a totally dark room. For a moment she was surprised, since she was sure that Malika's light was on.

She had not realized that the bath connected with another bedroom. For a moment she hesitated, torn between a desire to search the room and an even greater desire not to be caught. Discretion won out over curiosity and she started to close the door when she heard a groan from the darkness.

Returning to the bathroom, she frantically dug into her bag and came up with a small flashlight. Clicking on the light, the girl cautiously opened the door and flashed her light into the dark bedroom. The first thing she saw was a large bed. There appeared to be something wrong with the person on the bed. Then with a jolt she recognized the person as Addie Vandemeyer and realized that Addie was chained.

Quickly, the girl scampered across the room.

"Addie," she whispered, "I'll get you loose. Don't worry, I'll get you out of here."

Addie's only answer was to moan softly through her gag. Gently, the girl removed the gag and allowed Addie to slowly recover. As Addie chaffed her wrists, the girl jumped to the foot of the bed and released Addie's feet. Returning to the head of the bed, she grabbed one of Addie's arms and pulled her up, but almost dropped her again when Addie's knees buckled.

"Hold on, Addie." she said, "I'll get you out of here."

She helped Addie into the bathroom as quickly as she could, but froze when she heard Malika return to her room.

"Are you ready, my dear?" asked Malika in a lilting tone of voice, as she tapped on the door.

"Not quite, in a minute." said the girl, trying to sound as normal as possible, as she lowered Addie to the floor.

"Well, no need to hurry. My boss wants me to run an errand for him. It'll take me about a half an hour." she said.

"Sure. I'll be ready when you get back."

Both of the girls in the bathroom held their breath until they heard Malika leave and shut her door. When she was sure that they were safe, the girl dropped to her knees and began to rub and message the reporter, studiously ignoring Addie's unclothed breasts.

"Addie, it's me, Bet. Remember, you came to my apartment today?" she asked softly.

"Who—Bet. Oh, God, I hurt." moaned Addie as she rolled on her side and clutched her stomach.

"We've got to get out of here," said Bet urgently, "These people are the ones who killed Bernie."

It took some time, but finally Addie was fit enough to at least sit up without assistance. She was still forced to clutch her stomach. Malika had really worked her over. "How did you find me?"

"I remembered who used to say that thing Bernie told you. You remember that thing Bernie said to you, 'Yea though I walk through the valley of the shadow of death I will fear no evil for I am the meanest son of a bitch in the valley." she said with a grin.

"Who was it?" Addie asked curiously.

"Father Gotcha, the street preacher."

"Who?" Addie said in utter bafflement.

"I don't know his real name, but the kids on the street all call him Father Gotcha. He'll sneak up and grab a kid and yell, "Gotcha, are you saved? I found him this afternoon and he told me that Bernie had given him a package to hold. When I told him that Bernie was dead, he gave me the package. There were some books and notes inside; one of them gave this address.

That crazy old broad, Malika has been bugging me for weeks to come over and spend the night with her. I found her card in my purse a couple of hours ago and noticed her address matched the one in Bernie's book. So I decided to investigate."

"Good thing for me, you picked tonight," said Addie with a rueful smile as she pushed her way up the wall to a standing position.

"Where are the notes?" she asked.

"I left them with Miranda. I told her to hide them and I'd be back later. When I left, she was trying to call your office." said Bet.

Realizing that she was still wearing her slave girl outfit, Addie quickly stripped the leather cuffs and collar off with disgust. Throwing them on the floor, she followed Bet as the younger girl opened the door. To their horror, Malika was standing in front of them, her hand raised to knock on the bathroom door.

With a fierce growl, Addie shoved Bet out of the way, drew back and hit the bigger woman in the mouth with all her might. To Addie's amazement, the bigger woman's eyes rolled back in her head and she keeled over backward. Recovering from her surprise, Addie jumped on top of her tormentor and hit her twice in the belly. Malika only groaned. Addie was determined to take no chances and drew back to hit her again when Bet grabbed her arm.

"Addie, she's out. You knocked her out," the girl gasped in delight.

Cautiously, Addie backed off her fallen opponent, half expecting her to try and get up. To her joy, Malika really was unconscious. She started to merely tie the older woman up so that they could escape, but then she was struck by a thought and quickly began to undress her.

"What are you doing?" gasped Bet.

"Turn about is fair play," said Addie, "Get those leather things I dropped on the floor."

Grasping her plan, Bet giggled and ran into the bathroom. She returned with the cuffs, collar, and gag but also with another item Addie had not been forced to wear, a leather hood. So much for the fear that

Malika would be immediate identified and released. With Bet's assistance, Addie soon had the cuffs, collar, gag and mask on the older woman. Quickly, they hustled her into the other bedroom and, throwing her onto her back, chained her to the bed as Addie had been chained. If nothing else it might confuse things for a few minutes when Malika's boss came in expecting a woman.

Silently, they returned to Malika's room and searched for clothes for Addie.

"I can't very well wander the street in just my panties, can I?" she asked Bet with a grin.

They did find some loose pants and a blouse that were a reasonable fit. Luckily she still had her own shoes. Soon they were ready to try and escape. Addie slowly opened the bedroom door a crack and listened, she could hear the murmur of men's voices from the living room, but she heard no one in the hall. With a deep breath, she opened the bedroom door and, followed closely by Bet, tip-toed toward the front door. It looked like they might make it.

Slowly, Addie unlocked the front door and eased it open; a quick glance showed that the hall was deserted. Grabbing Bet's hand, Addie darted to her right toward the elevator. As they approached the last turn in the corridor, Addie's sharp ears heard two men speaking in Arabic as the elevator doors began to open.

Addie frantically looked around for a hiding place and saw the door to apartment 1234. A slim blonde woman stepped into the hall, seemingly oblivious to Addie and Bet. Not willing to chance meeting any of the terrorists at this point, she grabbed the blonde woman and forced her into her apartment. Bet was close on their heels and closed the door gently, and watched through the view port set in the door.

"I can't tell if they went to that Apartment or not, but they were definitely speaking Arabic." said Betty from the door.

There was little to say at this point. Addie was so relieved that she dropped into a nearby chair and lowered her head into her hands.

"Don't move." said a soft voice behind them.

Addie spun around and her heart sank as she saw the shiny pistol clutched in the blonde woman's small hand.

"Out of the frying pan and into the fire," she thought.

CHAPTER TWENTY-SEVEN

Miranda Ochoa was in a panic, frantic over Betty's safety. For the hundredth time, she kicked herself for letting Betty talk her into this crazy plan. Miranda was sure that Betty would do something stupid and get herself killed.

Looking at the stack of notes and books on the table, her fingers tightened convulsively on the phone as she continued to listen to the impersonal ringing. She had been trying Addie Vandemeyer's telephone number for what seemed like hours and was getting no answer. She wanted to get Kahane's notes to Addie as quickly as possible.

Frustrated, Miranda was ready to drop the phone back into its cradle when she heard someone lifted the phone at the other end.

"Hello? Addie?" Miranda said anxiously.

"Who is this? "

"Is Miss Vandemeyer there?" asked Miranda cautiously.

"Not at the moment, but I'm sure that she'll be back soon. Can I take a message?" a man's voice asked courteously.

"Who is this?" she asked again.

"Peter Novak, Miss Vandemeyer's boss." said the man.

"Well——I don't know." wavered Miranda.

"Even if she doesn't return, she'll at least call in for her messages. I could tell her to call you," urged Novak.

"Oh, that would be o.k," said Miranda with relief. "Tell her that Miranda called and I have what we were looking for. My number is 472-8288."

"Certainly. Anything else?" asked Novak politely.

"No, and thank you very much." said Miranda.

"My pleasure. Goodbye" said Novak as he hung up the phone.

Opening a reverse telephone directory, Novak began to look for the phone number that Miranda left. After several minutes, he grinned in satisfaction. Miranda Ochoa, 322 East 32nd Street, apartment 7B. He jotted the address down on a desk pad then reached into an inside pocket for a small phone book.

Assistant Operations Manager for the Network, Peter Novak had access to pass keys for all the offices. He was also an important member of the Revolutionary Council, in Addie's office carrying out his assignment; making sure that the staff of NBC found no information that could prove embarrassing to the Council. So far Novak felt that he had been very successful.

I was such a pity that he found it necessary to dispose of Melvin Brown earlier in the evening. He did so hate violence, but Brown discovered that it had been Novak who let the phony detective have access to the floor. Without his assistance Kincade wouldn't have had a prayer of getting past security. He was taking care of the last loose end by searching Addie's office to make sure that she had left no incriminating information behind.

A sound in the hall caused him to look up in concern. Turning his attention back to his personal phone book, he soon found the number he wanted. Quickly, he tapped it out on the phone console near his right hand.

"Otto, this is Novak. I need to speak to Prince Hadji, at once." he said.

"Sorry, sir, but the Prince has left word that he is to not be disturbed," answered Otto in his flat of voice.

"This is important, Otto, it can have an impact on Hadji's plans." Novak was firm.

"One moment, Sir." Otto put the phone down on the table.

Impatiently, Novak began to tap on the desk with a nearby pencil. He had a lot to do before morning and hated to be kept waiting. He dropped the pencil when he heard Prince Hadji's voice on the phone.

"Mr. Novak, what is so important that I am called from my friends?" asked Hadji impatiently.

"Bastard," thought Novak to himself.

"Hadji, I am in Vandemeyer's office. She just received a call from a woman named Miranda. This Miranda said that she had information that Vandemeyer was wanting."

"Most interesting." murmured Hadji. "Did she say what it was that Ms. Vandemeyer was looking for?"

"No, she wouldn't tell me," responded Novak, "but I do have her address."

"Just a moment." said Hadji, as he called to someone on his end. Novak could hear the sounds of a quick conversation in the background.

"Very good, Mr. Novak. Now what is the address?" asked Hadji.

"The number is 472-8288. Her address is 322 East 32nd Street, Apartment 7B," said Novak.

"You have done well." Hadji hung up the phone.

"Arrogant bastard!" swore Novak as he looked at the phone in his hand.

"Well, you do leave your ivory tower," said an amused voice form the doorway.

Novak jerked his head around to see Moses Gardner leaning in the doorway, his arms folded across his broad chest, cup of coffee from the snack bar clutched in one hand.

"Gardner, I, uh, I was looking for Miss Vandemeyer." stammered Novak.

Gardner's smiled widely, without humor.

"In her desk?" asked Gardner sarcastically.

"Uh, no, but I thought she might have left a note where she could be reached." he said in a low voice.

"Well." mused Gardner, "if you were looking for Addie, then who is Hadji?"

Novak's face turned white as a sheet. "W-w-what did you say?"

Gardner walked slowly into the room. "I asked you who Hadji was?"

Gardner towered over the slighter Novak. He grabbed Novak by his lapels and lifted the smaller man from his chair. "Who is Hadji?"

Gardner was so intent on getting his information that he missed seeing Novak's right hand slip into his right pocket. The first realization he had that Novak was armed was when Novak stuck a small caliber pistol in his stomach and pulled the trigger twice. The bullets staggered Gardner and he dropped Novak. The smaller man fell back into the chair and pressed his body back into the leather as Gardner fell to his knees, his head coming to rest in Novak's lap, as if he was praying to the Operations Manager.

Not wanting to get his conservative blue suit bloody, Novak reached out one trembling manicured hand and pushed Gardner's head away. The big man fell and sprawled loosely on the littered floor of the office. Trying to stay calm, Novak quickly returned his pistol to his pocket and rose to step carefully over the body. He was careful to use a handkerchief to close the door, just like he had seen in the movies. Left on the desk pad was the address 322 East 32nd Street, Apartment 7B.

Hadji handed the phone back to Otto and returned to his planning session. In a distracted fashion, he was aware that when he came back into the room, all conversation ceased. He gracefully lowered himself on the couch, deep in thought. The men around him respectfully kept silent until the Prince looked up at them.

"Mr. O'Toole, we seem to have a small problem. I would like you and your men to take care of it," he said calmly.

"Yes sir, and what might the problem be?" asked O'Toole, his eyes unreadable as he awaited instructions.

"That reporter, Addie Vandemeyer, she was looking for some information. It seems that a Miranda Ochoa found this information. I don't know what the information might be, but I want it," said Hadji.

Shamus O'Toole got to his feet and nodded his blonde head respectfully. "Certainly, sir. I'll go now."

Hadji raised one hand to stop O'Toole. "Not so fast, Mr. O'Toole. Enthusiasm for one's job is commendable, but there are certain minor details to keep in mind.

Miss Ochoa is expecting Miss Vandemeyer to come pick up the information herself. There may be a certain reluctance on her park to give it to you. I want you to be prepared to overcome this reluctance in the most expedient manner. Do you understand?"

Shamus O'Toole nodded his head, not taking offense at the Prince's manner. "I do, sir," he said simply.

"Very, well. Otto!" he called.

The massive Otto appeared immediately. "Yes your Highness?"

"Summon Malika." ordered the Prince.

"At once, your Highness." said Otto as he walked from the room.

Hadji turned his attention back to O'Toole. "I am going to have Miss Vandemeyer call this Miranda and tell her that you are coming to pick up the information."

Shamus looked puzzled for a moment.

"Begging your pardon, sir, but how are you going to get her to cooperate?"

"One of my men captured her this afternoon. She is even now a prisoner in another room. As to why she would cooperate with us, it has been my experience over the years that a good beating will change the attitude of most women."

Hadji looked around with a frown as Otto returned, alone.

"Malika is not in her room, sire. I have taken the liberty of checking the other rooms and I can't find her anywhere."

Hadji sat up to his full height.

"Is that reporter properly secured in my bedroom?" the Prince demanded.

"Yes, sir. I looked in on her and she is still chained to the bed," returned the servant.

"Well, never mind Malika now. She will return. Bring the reporter to me." he commanded, his face dark with rage.

"Malika will definitely be in for it when she comes back." thought Bremer with amused satisfaction.

In a few minutes, Otto came back into the room, leading the stumbling woman by the leash around her neck. Bremer noticed that Malika had taken the time to put a leather bondage mask over the girl's face before going on her own errands. He also saw that Otto had taken the precaution of binding her wrists securely behind her back.

Then something caught his eye. Bremer was certain that Addie was shorter the last time she had been in the room. Then with a shake of his head, Bremer told himself that he had to be mistaken.

In a haughty manner, Prince Hadji motioned for Otto to make the girl kneel before the Prince. With a jerk of the leash, Otto almost threw the girl to her knees. Looking around the room blindly, for the mask covered her eyes tightly, the girl began to try to talk through her gag.

"Silence!" roared the Prince as he nodded to Otto.

With no change of expression, Otto took the free end of the leather leash in one of his big hands and began to methodically lash the prisoner's bare back. Soon she was wriggling on the floor like a beached fish, sobbing lustily into her gag. At another nod from the Prince, Otto jerked her back onto her knees before giving her enough slack to regain her breath.

"Woman, you will do as I command!" ordered the Prince.

Again, she tried to talk around her gag, but only made unintelligible noises. Raising an eyebrow, the Prince looked again at Otto. Again the leash whistled through the air to connect with the wide smooth back of the sobbing reporter. This time, even the gag and the leather mask combined could not stifle the scream of pain and fear.

"I am going to have your mask and gag removed. You will not speak until spoken too. Do you understand?"

The kneeling woman frantically nodded her head, whimpering deep in her throat.

Satisfied, Hadji motioned toward Otto with one hand. Stepping forward, Otto's big fingers worked on the buckles securing the mask and the gag. Then with a jerk he pulled both of them off of the captive. Her dark hair covered her red, tear-streaked face.

Otto reached down and grabbed a handful of hair and jerked her head back.

"What outrage is this!" demanded the Prince as he looked down at the puffy face of the missing Malika.

"M-m-master, I am sorry," stammered Malika, "she got away. She had help, I couldn't stop her."

"Who helped her?" demanded the angry Prince.

"Well-" she began.

"Who helped her to escape, I asked you!" he demanded again.

"I asked a friend to come spend the night. She helped her," said Malika in a trembling voice.

"You dared to disobey me!" shouted the Prince.

"I wanted some company. I meant no harm, your Highness, but you wouldn't let me have the reporter," stammered the kneeling woman, cowering from the enraged Arab.

"I warned you to control your appetites. I warned you what would happen if you disobeyed me," raged the Prince.

He stalked around the room, the rest of the men making certain to say or do nothing to attract his rage toward them. The Prince came to stand in front of the cowering captive.

"Now, because of your stupid perverted sexual appetites, you have allowed her to escape. The one person who can ruin my plans is back on the street."

Thoroughly enraged, the Prince again stalked around the room. He came to a sudden halt and turned toward the group gathered around the couch.

"O'Toole, you and your men go to that address I gave you. Either get the information politely, or make sure that no one gets the information. A police car will be waiting for you at the front. Now, go." he ordered.

At a signal from O'Toole, three men followed after him, almost running in their desire to leave the Prince's presence. The Prince turned to the men remaining in the room.

"Yoshi," said the Prince to the young oriental team leader, "you and your team will begin a search of the neighborhood for that reporter. She can't have gotten far."

"What do you want done with her?" asked Yoshi respectfully.

"Kill her and anyone you find with her," said the Prince as he looked coldly at the kneeling, sobbing Malika.

Silently, Yoshi and his team left the apartment, leaving Dr. Bremer and his companion sitting quietly on the couch. Otto still stood solidly behind the sobbing woman. Prince Hadji stood angrily in the center of his richly furnished living room.

Slowly, the Prince regained control of his temper. "Otto, I believe it has come time to dispense with Malika's services," he said in his normal calm voice. He detested failure.

With a shriek, Malika scuttled across the floor to press herself against the Prince's legs. She pressed her red, puffy face against his slipper.

"Master, please, another chance, I beseech you."

With a sound of disgust, he kicked her away. "Otto! Even the sound of her voice makes my skin crawl."

Again Malika shrieked and tried to crawl to the Prince, who had returned to his place on the couch. This time, however, Otto grabbed the dangling leash and pulled her up short. He jerked her onto her back and put one knee on her lush breasts, pinning her to the floor. With a few sure, powerful movements, he gagged his struggling captive. When he allowed her back on her knees, she was unable to make more than a snuffling sound. Only her terror-filled eyes showed her feelings.

Again, Otto stood waiting for instructions, the cowering woman on her knees at his side.

"Otto, I believe it is time that you took out the trash," observed the Prince in his usual calm voice.

Without a word, Otto turned and began to march from the room, pulling the struggling woman along in his wake. She never had a chance to get to her feet, but scampered on hands and knees to keep up with her captor. Unfortunately, she fell onto her face before she had even left the living room. Bremer listened to the sounds as Otto pulled his captive down the hall by her neck. The slamming of a door ended all sounds from the hall.

The Prince calmly reached for the steaming porcelain pot and poured himself another cup of tea.

"Good servants are so hard to find. Don't you agree, Dr. Bremer?" the Prince observed politely, having studiously ignored all of the sounds from the hall.

"Uh, yes. I suppose that can be a real problem," responded the Doctor, hesitantly, his own cup of tea held in one trembling hand.

"At least this little episode has been a good object lesson to my men concerning the price of failure. Don't you agree, Doctor?" he observed with a small smile.

"Of course, Prince. Of course." he answered carefully.

From the corner of his eye, Bremer noted that Noyotivik/Hughes hadn't moved a muscle after Malika had been unmasked, but before that point, for this a split second, he had almost thought that his protégé was going to intervene. This was highly unusual behavior.

"Now where were we?" asked the Prince.

CHAPTER TWENTY-EIGHT

Addie carefully raised her hands and prayed that Betty would do nothing foolish. From the look in the blonde's eyes, she could tell that she would have no problem pulling the trigger. It had been a hell of a day. She was rescued from one problem only to dive right back into another.

"Both of you move slowly over to the couch and sit at each end so that I can watch you."

As ordered, Addie and Betty carefully crossed the few feet to sit at either ends of the couch against the right hand wall. A grand piano stood in front of the window that ran the full length of the far wall. The curtains were tightly closed so that the only light was from two table lamps. The apartment was not large, but it was comfortably furnished.

Addie's heart sank even further as she closely watched their captor. The woman was very professional in her way of handling her weapon. She never allowed anything to get in her line of fire. As Addie and Betty moved across the room, she continually shifted her own position to keep them covered, never giving them a chance to get close enough to get to her.

Once they were both seated on the couch, the woman pulled a chair from her dining room table and primly seated herself some fifteen feet from them.

"Now what's this all about?" she asked. "Who are you two?"

Addie sighed and cleared her throat. This was definitely one of those days.

"My name is Addie Vandemeyer, I'm an investigative reporter for NBC. This is Betty, uh."

"Connors." finished Betty, her eyes never leaving the shiny gun in their captor's hand.

"So?" asked their captor, studying the two girls in a distracted manner. "Why did you come to me?"

Addie was in a quandary. Living right next to those nuts, it was very possible that this woman was mixed up with her kidnappers. If she were one of them, then any lie Addie told her would be discovered in only a few minutes. Besides, she was positive that Betty wasn't experienced enough to help carry out any story that Addie could concoct off the top of her head.

If on the other hand, the woman just happened to live next to the kidnappers, but had nothing to do with them, then a lie might jeopardize her life as well as theirs. After weighing the factors, Addie decided to tell her the truth. Well, at least part of the truth.

"Well," began Addie, "it's a long story but, in a nut shell, I was kidnapped from my office and brought to the apartment across the hall. From what little I was able to hear, these guys are mixed up in the recent terrorist attacks that have plagued this city.

Betty managed to get in the apartment and rescue me and we were trying to get out of the building when we heard two men get off the elevator, you opened your door and we came in here."

"Yeah, and my name is Burton, I'm the President. Can't you cook up a better story than that?" she asked with a skeptical smile on her rather pretty face.

"It is the truth," said Addie quietly.

From the corner of her eye, Addie saw Betty nodding her head solemnly.

"Please believe us," begged Betty quietly.

For a moment, the woman looked undecided, then reached for the phone.

"Who're you calling?" asked Addie anxiously.

"A friend who might be able to help me decide what to do with you." returned the woman as she touch dialed. "Hello, Jim. This is Helen."

"Fine. Listen, I have a bit of a problem, can you come up for a minute? I need to talk to you about something. O.K., in about ten minutes. Good. See ya," she said as she hung up the phone.

In silence, the three women sat motionless and looked at each other. From time to time, they heard voices and footsteps as people came and went in the hall. However, none of the three women moved as much as a hair.

In time, it seemed like centuries to Addie, there came a knock on the door. Never taking her eyes off of her visitors, Helen rose to her feet, stepping toward the door. Her gun barrel never wavered. Without looking to check who might be outside, Helen turned the knob.

The man who entered was tall and fit. His skin was tanned so dark he reminded Addie of the old actor, George Hamilton.

"Well, what have we here, Helen?" he asked in surprise as he saw her gun and the two women on her couch.

"I'm not sure, Jim. These two forced their way in here. They seemed to be hiding from someone. Their story sounds wild." she said as Jim followed her back to her chair.

Jim stood beside Helen with his hands on his hips studying the two women sitting primly on the couch.

"All right, what's your story? Spill it," he demanded, glaring at the two defenseless women.

Again, Addie told her story, then was forced to answer a good many questions fired at her both by Helen and Jim. By the clock on the wall, they questioned her for the better part of an hour before Jim folded his arms across his chest and turned toward Helen.

"Well it's a wild story, but no wilder than the things that have been going on in this town. If they are right, we have a chance to nip this thing in the bud before it goes any further." he said.

"I find it very hard to believe."

The woman with the gun looked directly at Addie.

"What do you have to prove you are really Addie Vandemeyer?" she demanded.

Addie's shoulders slumped in defeat.

"Nothing. As I have told you a dozen times, I was kidnapped and then stripped almost stark naked. My clothes are somewhere in that lunatic's apartment. I was lucky to get out of there with a whole skin, much less letters of recommendation from the head terrorist." snapped Addie, angrily.

Pursing her lips, Helen turned her attention to Betty.

"How about you. You have any identification?" she asked.

Betty nodded and reached for her bag on the floor where she had dropped it.

"Not so fast, young lady. Back away and let Jim look for it." she snapped, her eyes taking on a hard glint.

Betty stopped, her hand inches from her bag. Slow, so as to not appear to be doing anything threatening, Betty sat back against the arm of the couch.

Jim came over, picked up the bag and carried it to the dining room table. Turning the bag over, he dumped the contents out and began to paw through it. Finally, he picked up Betty's wallet and flipped it open.

"Betty Connors, 322 East 32nd Street, Apartment 7B." he read aloud. "The picture on the I.D. card is hers." he finished as he turned away from the table.

Helen's brow was creased for a few minutes, and then she leaned forward.

"Addie, or whatever your name really might be, is there anyone at NBC at this time of night that can vouch for you?" she asked.

Addie thought for a moment and then shrugged.

"I really don't know. My photographer partner might still be there. We were both caught by the curfew."

She stopped in mid sentence as a sudden thought hit her.

"Melvin, Melvin Brown the security chief at NBC knows me. I can call him," she said excitedly.

"Correction. I can call him," said Helen.

Handing her weapon to Jim, Helen pulled the phone into her lap and called information. After obtaining the telephone number for NBC security, she broke the connection and began to redial.

"Security." answered a very serious voice.

"Yes, I need to speak to Addie Vandemeyer. It's very important," said Helen.

"I'm sorry ma'am but I'm afraid that she is not available. She has been sent on assignment to Paris."

"Oh? When did she leave?" asked Helen with a peculiar glance at Addie.

"Last night."

"Are you sure?" pressed Helen.

"Well I was just given this information by Peter Novak, Assistant Director of Operations for the Network."

"Do you know Miss Vandemeyer, personally?" asked Helen.

"No. That is to say, I've seen her, but I don't know her," said the voice on the phone.

"Is the security chief there? She asked.

"No, I'm afraid he is also unavailable." answered the guard.

"Is he still in the building?" she asked again.

"I'm afraid that I can not give out that kind of information. Who is this?" he demanded.

With a frown, Helen broke the connection and sat for a long moment holding down the button of the phone. Finally, she replaced the receiver and turned back to the group.

"Well, it seems that Addie Vandemeyer left for Paris on assignment, last night." she said, leaning back in her chair.

"What?" gasped Addie.

"Peter Novak, assistant Director of Operations for the Network."

"That's impossible. I would never leave for an overseas assignment with a story like this in New York." she almost shouted in frustration.

What could Novak be thinking? It was impossible that he would even make such a statement. She had known that he was a pompous idiot, but she had no idea that he was also a complete fool.

"How about the Chief of Security?" she demanded.

"Unavailable." she shot back studying Addie closely.

"God, now what?" muttered Addie as she swept her hair out of her face with one hand.

"I don't know how to convince you of who I am, you'll just have to take my word for it." groaned Addie.

"Alright." said Helen rising from her chair.

"I'm Helen Slater formerly an attorney with the U.S. Attorney's Office." she said as she offered Addie her hand.

"And I'm Jim Monteverde, private investigator." said Jim as he also offered his hand.

"But you believe me?" asked Addie incredulously.

Helen nodded slowly and she reclaimed her pistol from Jim.

"Yep. I don't know Addie Vandemeyer, but I do know her reputation. She has a solid reputation as a good investigative reporter. A professional reporter like that would never leave this type of story to fly off to Paris. I also saw the chaffing on your wrists which would tend to confirm your story about being chained up."

"Well now what?" asked Jim.

Addie mind was racing. "Can I use your phone?" she asked.

Wordlessly, Helen pointed toward the phone. Darting across the room, Addie dialed the number for her C.I.A. contact. Impatiently, she waited until someone picked up.

"Marker." said a bored voice.

"John Voynich and hurry." said Addie quickly.

"There is no—"

"Yeah, I know, there is no John Voynich at this number. Well get him anyway, this is Addie Vandemeyer." she snapped.

There came a series of clicks and then Voynich, himself, was on the phone.

"Addie where are you? Are you alright?" he demanded.

"I'm fine John, but I need your help."

"What's the story?" he demanded.

"First, I need you to check and see if this line is tapped." she said.

"What's the number?" he asked quickly.

When he had the number he hung up.

Addie stood impatiently by the phone, willing it to ring. Finally, it rang and she grabbed it up.

"John?"

"Yeah, the lines clean, but make it quick."

She outlined what had happened, including Novak telling security that she had left for an assignment in Paris. He listened patiently, interrupting only to get clarification on various aspects of her story. Finally, she had told him everything.

"Addie, this is serious. I need to make sure that you really saw Hughes in that apartment." he said slowly.

Though he couldn't see it, she nodded rapidly.

"I did, he sat right there on that couch and watched as that bitch parade me around the room almost naked. He didn't lift one single finger to help me."

Voynich gave a short laugh.

"Well don't blame him too much. He may not have been able to help you even if he wanted to do so. After something Moses Gardner told me earlier, I called some people at State, the NSA and even some friends in the KGB. Now Addie you have to swear to me that you will never repeat what I am about to tell you. You never heard me say this, do you understand?" he said earnestly.

"I understand, John. I promise."

"Alright, I'll trust you simply because I can't get anyone there to stop him in time. It appears that the man you call Hughes is not really Carter Davis Hughes. The real Hughes may or may not be dead. But we think that this guy may be an international assassin. We think he was sent by the Russians or the Iranians or somebody to be a submarine."

"A what?" interrupted Addie.

"A submarine." he repeated impatiently, "that's an individual who is sent to a foreign country to establish a deep cover. You never know that he or she is a spy until they commit some act. The Russians were very good at creating deep cover agents. According to what I found out, the Russians and we had something called Operation Resurrection. They were working in the area of mental programming, we think. At this point we really don't know what the hell is going on, or who is doing what to whom. Just don't trust this guy if you see him again. Promise me?" he demanded.

"I promise." she said earnestly. "Anything else."

"Shortly before the fall of the Soviet Empire, General Nicholas Romanoffsky, of the KGB had a diabolically brilliant idea. He worked out a deal with the Iranians for them to use the products of Operation Resurrection as part of their terrorist war against the west. He was smart enough to know that with glasnost, his government would never activate these walking bombs, so he smuggled them out of the country and destroyed the files. There was one set of files that he missed. We now know that Hughes thinks, or probably thinks that he is Illai Noyotivik, a hard liner red. The real Noyotivik was the best assassin that the Russians ever had. He was called the Specter because he was to slip in and out of secured facilities like a ghost. Of course, there is always the possibility that this is the real Specter. It's just totally fucked up.

Addie, if you see him, stay away from him."

"Is it possible to help him?" asked Addie.

"It's too dangerous to risk. For all practical purposes, at least for a while, Hughes is really Noyotivik and a very dangerous man. We are investigating more deeply."

Now listen, we have arranged for a counter terrorist force to be dropped into Central Park tomorrow morning. We are coordinating with the New York Police-"

"But you can't." interrupted Addie.

"Can't what?" demanded Voynich.

"Can't tell the police. I heard my kidnappers talking. Some of the police are on their side."

"Are you totally sure of that?" demanded the C.I.A. man.

"Positive." she shot back.

"Damn. Gotta go. Take care kid and if you ever mention the Salami Incident again, I'll turn you over my knee." he said, breaking the connection.

Addie dropped the phone back onto the cradle and turned around, she shrugged and dropped tiredly into the chair Helen had left earlier.

"Well you heard the call. Things are not good. A counter terrorist team was going to be dropped into Central Park in the morning, but unfortunately, they told the police about it. I happen to know that some of the police are involved with the terrorist. If he can't stop the drop, it'll be a blood bath." she said tiredly as she sprawled back in her chair. She was so tired.

"Can I use the phone? " asked Betty timidly.

"Certainly, help yourself." replied Helen.

Betty walked over to the counter and picked up the phone. Eagerly she dialed her home number. She smiled when Miranda answered.

"Hello?" said Miranda in a very tense voice.

"Miranda, it's Betty."

"Oh, Betty, I'm glad to hear your voice. Are you alright?"

"I'm fine. I'm with Addie and we're trying to get help." she reassured her friend.

"Well tell Addie, her friends are here to pick up those items," she said softly.

"What friends?" asked Betty, suddenly concerned for Miranda's safety.

"Those people Addie sent to pick up the papers." answered Miranda.

"Addie hasn't sent anyone to see you. I've been with her every minute since I told her about finding those things." said Betty in a frantic tone. "Miranda, get out of there."

Addie came over to join Betty at the phone.

"What's wrong?" she asked.

"Someone's at Miranda's" Betty whispered frantically she said as she listened intently.

In the distance, Betty could hear Miranda talking to someone and then there was a scream. The phone fell to the floor. She could hear the sounds of a scuffle and then the phone on the other end was gently hung up.

Betty's face seemed to crumple in on itself.

CHAPTER TWENTY-NINE

Slowly, Moses Gardner fought his way back to consciousness. He tried to get to his feet but the pain in his side forced him to lie back on the blood stained floor. As long as he didn't move, the pain wasn't too bad. If he ever got his hands on Novak, he'd squeeze the life out of the little weasel.

From his position on the floor, Gardner could see that long phone cord Addie liked dangling over the edge of her desk. Reaching out one long arm, he grabbed the cord and pulled. Inch by inch the phone console moved toward the edge of the desk. Finally, one last tug brought it crashing to the floor, just missing his head. He rolled over and pulled the receiver to him. One painful digit at a time, his eyes were blurring and he was having trouble making out the numbers, Moses Gardner dialed the number of his own office.

"Photo Center. Wilkinson speaking." said a bored voice.

"Wilkie," gasped Gardner, "I'm in Addie's office. Help me."

There was a stab of pain and Gardner dropped the phone. He sincerely hoped that Wilkie had understood what he had said. Otherwise, he was going to die her on Addie's dirty floor. At the edge of his vision, Gardner began to see tiny flecks of light. Then he drifted off into a world where there was no pain.

SATURDAY MORNING—1:30 A.M. —THE OVAL OFFICE, Washington D.C.

Richard Armiger walked out to his pool a drink clutched in one hand. The plan was working beautifully. Over and over he played back the scene in the President's Office in his mind. They had almost got the prick to sign the decree putting Richard Nixon's Executive Order, No. 11490 into effect. The next time it would work. Armiger eased himself into one of the pool side chairs and ran one hand over his sweaty face. He had known when he had manipulated himself into a position close to the President that he would be in the position to influence the big decisions. Now he was forcing the biggest of all decisions.

"Sir, you have to do it. You have no choice." Eastman had urged.

"It does seem the best of all the terrible possible decisions." The Secretary of State offered.

"But I don't like it!" snapped the beleaguered President.

"Mr. President. If you don't do it, there is every possibility that the death toll could run into the millions."

"I know."

"Mr. President," Democratic Congressman Brad Holling, Speaker of the House of Representatives had requested. "May I speak?"

"Please do. I need to hear someone who is unbiased."

"The possibility of a national emergency like this happening was foreseen back in the 1970's. That's why former President Richard Nixon signed Executive Order 11490. It was to allow the country to be able to face a catastrophe of this magnitude. Without this ability to react immediately, in my opinion, we will not be able to handle this current emergency." Congressman Holling volunteered.

Armiger smiled to himself as he remembered the nervousness of the ROCK, as his friends called the President. The lily livered bastard had left his chair to pace the office. Finally, he had stopped at the window and looked out over the White House grounds.

"If I put this Executive Order into effect, then I will become a virtual dictator, with total dictatorial powers. I will be only the second president in American History to have suspended the right of judicial due process and the first to rule without Congress. I do not relish that reputation," he had said over his shoulder.

The others in the room waited respectfully while the President stood looking out the window. Finally he turned around to sweep the group with his gaze.

"I thing that thing that bothers me the most is having to put Rex 84 into effect as well. That is nothing but a repeat of the type of imprisonment without trial that happened on the west coast during the early days of World War II to those of Japanese extraction. These camps you are urging me to erect or authorize are nothing but concentration camps. I really can't see the necessity of going this far."

"Mr. President, I am going to speak frankly. I was with him when President Reagan agonized over the decision to implement Rex 84. He finally decided that the welfare of the country was more important that his personal feelings. His proposed camps were and are to be merely a series of internment camps for holding suspected terrorists. You know as well as I do that these terrorists are taking advantage of our due process system to get around our laws.

You have to remember, that we are in the middle of a national emergency. We have chemical warfare attacks in New Mexico, gang warfare in Los Angeles, genetically engineered diseases running through various portions of our population, terrorist attacks in New York and the new threat of nerve gas being released in five major cities unless we surrender our national sovereignty and pay a ransom of five million dollars to this terrorist group.

If you don't have the intestinal fortitude to do what is required for the safety of this country, then I would suggest that you step down and allow your Vice-President to rule in your stead. This is a time when America needs a strong hand at the tiller."

The sweating President looked at Congressman Holling for a long time before he finally nodded his head wearily and returned to his chair. Sighing deeply, he picked up his pen and signed the two pieces of paper lying on his desk.

"Never has one man held such total power as I assume with these two signatures. I hope that I am able to handle it as I should."

For several minutes, he merely stared at the papers before him, his lips moving, but no sound coming out. Then, as if he had made a decision of great import, the President looked at the two men seated across from him.

"I have dated these two documents for the day after Christmas. If there are any other terrorist attacks, I will authorize the issuance of a proclamation declaring a national emergency and instituting Executive Order 11490," he had said.

Eastman and Holling looked at each other and smiled slightly, Armiger felt a warm feeling as they had both turned and looked at him. Holling had even favored him with a wink. Things were going according exactly to plan.

OFFICE OF JAMES J. HALL, SPECIAL OPERATIONS COMMAND

Seated around Hall's office were several of the senior members of his staff. Voynich had come up with such important information that he felt that this should be a team effort. After making sure that all of his senior staff was present, he turned the meeting over to John Voynich.

"Gentlemen, you have been familiarized with the situation in New York. I have some confidential sources in the city with whom I have been in contact with. One lead is a man named Carter Davis Hughes. Based upon the information I have received, I began to dig into the background of this Carter Davis Hughes.

Now the folders that you all have been given show all the information we have on this individual. It would appear that he served in our military. I had his 201 jacket pulled and studied in detail. In the process of this review, we have discovered is that the entire Military 201 folder for this man is bogus. There is not one piece of correct information in it. As far as we can tell, this man is not Carter Davis Hughes. Unfortunately, we have no idea who he is." Voynich paused as he opened another folder.

"Now after saying that we do know that one section of the file appears to have been correct. Hughes was involved with a classified research project called Operation Resurrection. Unfortunately, we can't find out anything about the program. It is important that we know what the project is about.

Our research department was able to confirm that Project Resurrection was a black project, authorized under Executive Order 54/12 signed by President Eisenhower in 1954. As you may or may not be aware, this Executive Order is itself classified but we know that it authorized a 'Black Budget' for technology. It also authorized the funds for the creation of a team of specialists to handle any required cover-ups.

President Eisenhower's Executive Order also called for the formation of a committee to oversee the funds. This funding organization was called Majestic 12 and was a committee formed under the National Security Council. I called a friend over at the National Security Council and he was very helpful until I mentioned Operation Resurrection. Suddenly, he couldn't get off the telephone fast enough. Now he won't even take my calls."

"John, I'll see the National Security Advisor tomorrow and request the records we want, personally." interrupted Hall, as he jotted some notes on a pad.

"And if he won't cooperate?" asked John, looking up from the folder in his hands.

Hall smiled thinly as he carefully laid his gold ballpoint pen on top of the pad. "Then that is a bridge we will cross when we get to it. Continue your briefing, John." he directed quietly.

"There is not much left. There are rumors of some deaths at Fort Clayton and Fort Davis in the Panama Canal Zone at about the same time that the false records show that our phony Hughes was stationed there. We have been unable to find anyone who was stationed there at that time. That's all," he said as he folded his papers and waited.

Hall sat a long time looking at his steepled fingers.

"John, you have done well with such limited information. Now here is what we will do. John, you will leave for the Panama Canal Zone immediately. I have a friend living there, his name is Ernest Causwell, and he was Station Chief of the Zone C.I.A. office there in the 1970s. See what he can tell you."

"Bill, " he said to one of the senior agents to John's left. "I want you to go over to see what is in our own records about Majestic 12. I seem to recall something about them a few years ago. It seems to me that it was something very bizarre. Check it out."

Hall sat silently again for several seconds before sitting upright in his chair.

"The rest of you are to investigate any possible connection between the Intelligence Community and the terrorists in New York. I will expect preliminary reports by this time tomorrow. That's all."

At that moment, a rather disheveled secretary came running to the room.

"It's terrible, it's terrible!" she blurted before collapsing in a heap in the doorway.

Hall was the first one to reach her side and help her to a chair.

"Clarisse, what's wrong?" he asked.

"A plane-a plane crashed." she sobbed.

"Crashed where?"

"It was on the news a moment ago. A airliner crashed into the C.I.A. headquarters, it's burning."

Voynich grabbed Hall's desk phone and began to dial. He had no doubt that what she had said was true. America was under attack.

NEW YORK

As soon as Betty collapsed on the floor in tears, Jim and Addie pulled her back to her feet and helped her over to the couch. Helen rushed to get her some water as Addie held her hand.

Betty wiped her eyes with she sleeve of her blouse and tried to control her sobs.

"Someone's there with Miranda. She said that the men said that they came from you. They seemed to know about the notes and things." gulped Betty.

"What notes are you talking about, Betty?" asked Jim as he rubbed her shoulders.

Addie swept an errant strand of her long hair from her face.

"Bernie Kahane was an investigator with the U.S. Attorney's office and a friend. He found out something important about these terrorists. He was injured and went to earth until he could get someone to find me. He wanted me to get his notes and see what I could do to stop the terrorists' plans. " Addie said as she tried to comfort Betty.

"Bernie. You knew Bernie? What was his last name?" Helen asked skeptically.

Addie looked at her and nodded.

"Yeah, I knew Bernie. His last name was Kahane. We dated some last year," she said.

Helen slapped the palm of her hand against her forehead.

"Stupid me. Now I know who you are. Bernie used to talk about you all the time. He and I used to have lunch together until I left to open my own private law practice."

Helen's face clouded over for a moment.

"Did you say he was injured?" she asked anxiously.

Addie's eyes spoke volumes.

"He's dead?" Helen asked weakly, as tears slowly slid down her face.

Addie nodded slowly, as her own eyes began to tear.

Betty shifted in Addie's arms and sat up.

"Please, we've got to help Miranda." she pleaded.

Jim went to the phone and began to dial.

"I'll get us a police escort," he said.

"But Jim, I told you that some of the police are in with the terrorists. I have no desire to be captured again," she said.

"Relax," grinned the detective, "I'm calling my old man. He's a Captain in one of the local precincts on the east side. If he can't help us, no one can."

Jim stood and listened to the phone ring until there was an answer.

"Prince Hadji's residence, Otto speaking."

"Dad," said Jim, into the phone. "Good to talk to you again."

"Who is this?" asked Otto

"Your son, Jim Monteverde, remember me?"

"Ah," said Otto, "just a minute."

"I'm fine. Listen, I need a favor."

There was silence until Prince Hadji came on the line.

"Mr. Monteverde?" he said.

"That's right, Dad, I need a police escort tonight."

"Are you trying to tell me something, Mr. Monteverde?" asked the Prince.

"That's right, Dad." said Jim, smiling at Helen who was literally staring a hole through him.

"Where are you?" the Prince asked.

"I'm at my apartment building." he responded.

"Is it possible that you have a stunning red head reporter named Vandemeyer with you? asked the Prince.

"I knew that you would understand," laughed Jim.

"I'll have one of my police cars at the door of the building in ten minutes." said the Prince.

"Be careful, Dad, according to at lady with me, I've heard that there are some phony police on the street tonight." responded the private investigator.

"So, she knows about that does she? Well, I guess we will have to dispose of her after all." said the Prince with regret.

"Fine, thanks, Dad." finished Jim as he hung up the phone.

He turned back to his companions with a smile.

"Dad said he would have a car at the door in about ten minutes. He's placing two of his best men at our disposal for the rest of the evening."

"Thanks, Jim. I really appreciate it." Betty laid her hand on his arm.

"Well I had better get changed." Helen headed toward her bedroom.

Suddenly she stopped and looked at Addie critically.

"If we're going to go racing around the town, you need some better fitting clothes. You and I are about the same size, so come along and I'll outfit you," she said.

"Great." said Addie with a giggle, "When you are as full chested as I am, you don't like to swing free."

It wasn't until they were in her bedroom and the door closed that Helen turned to face her.

"Addie something's wrong." she hissed.

"What?"

Helen pressed her ear against the door as she spoke

"Before I agreed to date Jim, I checked him out through the U.S. Attorney's Office. His father was on the New York Police force, but he was killed stopping a bank robbery five years ago. I don't know who he was talking to, but it wasn't his father."

Addie was dismayed. She felt trapped and had no idea what to do at this point.

Helen left her position at the door long enough to dig in her closet and toss Addie some jeans, underclothes and a loose blouse. At her urging, Addie quickly dressed in her borrowed clothes and prowled around the room looking for a weapon.

Seeing Addie dressed and guessing what she was looking for, Helen went over to her dresser and opened the top drawer. Reaching inside, she brought out a small derringer. "You've got two shots, make them count," she said as she opened the bedroom door.

Jim looked up and smiled as the two girls rejoined them. Addie was quick to notice that Jim now had Helen's pistol stuck in his belt. Helen made no comment, but went into her kitchen and poured herself a glass of juice. Swiftly she gulped her drink and then came back into the living room.

"Well, shall we go?" Helen asked as she opened the hall door.

"I'll go first," said Jim. "If it's all clear, then come quickly."

Pushing past Helen's slim body, Jim walked down the hall toward the elevator. His right hand was inside his jacket on the handle of Helen's pistol. Addie's nerves were stretched to the breaking point. She kept waiting for terrorists to spring out of the surrounding apartments and overwhelm them. The memory of her humiliation at the hands of Malika grated on her pride.

She was snapped from her musings by Helen's signal that all was clear. Leading Betty by the hand, Addie walked softly but rapidly down the hall. She rounded the corner to see Jim holding the elevator door open for Helen to enter. In less than a second she and Betty piled into the car and Jim allowed the door to slid shut. So far, so good.

"We're home free, now." said Jim as he punched the button for the first floor.

Silently, they rode down. All too soon, they arrived at the first floor, the door opening to reveal a completely deserted hallway. They left the elevator and walked along the hall to their left. At the entrance to the lobby, they stopped and Addie craned her neck to see the outside doors. The lobby was completely empty, the doorman was absent, but at the curb, she could see the front end of a police car. Slowly, she pulled back into the dubious safety of the hall.

"Place is deserted." she said. "I did see a police car at the curb."

"Dad came through." Jim said with satisfaction.

Helen just looked at him silently, her expression unreadable. Addie silently slid the derringer from her pocket to conceal it in her hand. Jauntily, Jim started across the lobby, waving for the women to follow him.

"Be careful, Addie. I really don't trust him," whispered Helen.

"I'll definitely be careful. That's my middle name," murmured Addie.

"Where's the doorman?" asked Betty as she looked around the lobby.

"Hmm, good question." said Jim in a puzzled tone of voice, his eyes scanning the empty lobby.

"But at least the police are here." he said indicating the police car sitting near the door.

Experimentally, Jim pushed against the outer doors. They were unlocked. He went outside to speak to the two people in the car. Leaning down to the passenger window, he carried on a long animated conversation with the officers in the car. Helen and Addie both kept checking the lobby behind them, while Betty was impatiently waiting to leave.

Completing his conversation with the police, Jim came back toward the doors, his face all smiles. Pulling open the door, he waved toward the car.

"Ladies, your carriage awaits." he said with a flourish.

Eagerly, Betty darted across the entry and literally dove into the back seat of the police car. Addie and Helen followed more slowly, with Jim bringing up the rear. At the car, Addie hung back, allowing Helen to get in the car first that was when Jim stopped her.

"Helen, honey, maybe we had better not all go in the same car. I can have Dad send another for us."

Helen lowered herself into the car before answering him.

"Why do you say that?" she asked mildly.

He shrugged and looked around.

"It's like putting all your eggs in one basket. I suggest that you and I go to the police department and explain what we know to Dad. He can do something with this information," offered Jim.

Helen got out of the car and put her arms around Jim's neck.

"Jim," she said looking up into his eyes, "you go tell your friend upstairs that I will do everything in my power to stop him."

Jim looked down at her with a look of total shock on his face. She could almost hear his mind racing to think of something to say. She stepped away from him and her pistol appeared in her hand, pointed at Jim's belt buckle.

"Jim, I know that your father died over five years ago. I don't know for certain who you called, but I suspect I know." she paused for a moment as he looked at her with shame filled eyes.

"I just want to know one thing. Why?" she asked.

Jim spread his hands and shrugged.

"Money. He promised me millions if I would help him gather information. I just gathered information."

Helen looked at him in disgust. "You would betray your own country for money?"

"If I hadn't have helped him, someone else would have. I wanted the money for us, babe. So that we could have a good life together."

Out of the corner of her eye, Addie noticed the officer on the passenger side tensing to spring out at the unsuspecting Helen. Whirling, Addie shoved the derringer in the officer's face.

"Don't move an inch or I'll blow you away." she said vehemently.

She didn't know whether it was the sight of the little gun or her threat, but the officer froze. Looking across him, Addie's eyes stabbed at the driver whose hand was inching toward his holstered pistol.

"You freeze too, bozo or your partner gets it," she snapped. Addie looked over the seat at Betty's white face in the back seat. "Betty, reach over the seat and take his gun."

Quickly, Betty leaned forward, reached over the seat and jerked the officer's pistol from his holster. Taking a cue from Addie's face, Betty took the pistol in both hands, pulled back the hammer of the revolver and placed the barrel against the Cop's right ear. Satisfied that the driver was preoccupied, Addie reached her hand through the window and pulled her captive's pistol from his holster.

"Out of the car, both of you. On this side." she ordered.

"Leave the keys!" she snapped to the driver as she saw his hand move toward the ignition.

Slowly, the two edged carefully out of the car on the passenger side to stand nervously on the sidewalk. Walking around them, Addie pulled their handcuffs from their belts and handcuffed them wrist-to-wrist around one of the pillars that held up the front of the building.

Waving goodbye to the two handcuffed cops, Addie walked back to the car. Helen was in deep discussion with Jim. Addie felt for the girl, for she had tears streaming down her face. She didn't want to disturb Helen, but she was well aware of Betty's anguish.

"Helen?" she said gently, "are you coming with us?"

"I am," she said very calmly.

"No, Helen. They don't have a chance, you'll be killed."

Jim reached for Helen's arm.

Turning slightly, Helen looked at Addie. At that moment, a shot rang out from the darkness of the drive; Helen staggered a couple of steps and fell against the car.

"Helen!" screamed Addie as two more shots came from the darkness.

Helen fell to her knees; blood streaked the front of her blouse. With great effort, she rolled around to face the direction the shots had come from. For a moment, a figure was silhouetted against one of the ground lights that illuminated the front of the building. Helen snapped off a shot and was awarded with a scream from her target. Jim tried to drag Helen toward the lobby door.

Helen pushed Jim away from her with one hand as she fired at another target; another black-clad form fell into the circle of light thrown by the building's security lights. All of Jim's pleading with her fell on deaf ears. Finally by sheer main strength, Jim managed to gather her up into his arms. As he tried to stand, a shot from the lobby entrance spun Jim around. With a look of shock on his handsome face, Jim reached a hand to his back and brought it away blood covered.

"No, he promised she wouldn't be hurt. He promised."

A second shot knocked Jim over onto his back, Helen landing on top of his body. Addie swung around to see Otto, the Arab's huge bald servant pointing an AK-47 at her. Dropping to one knee, Addie brought up her appropriated pistol and pumped three shots at the big German. He staggered and fell onto his ass, never letting go of his assault rifle.

"Let's get out of here!" screamed Betty from the back seat of the police car.

Addie could see where bullets had caused four spider-webbed areas on the back glass. As if to support Betty's plea, a bullet ricocheted off the hood of the car.

Torn by indecision, Addie dropped down by Helen and grabbed her arm.

"Let's go, girl. Lean on me." screamed Addie, as she tried to get Helen to her feet.

Helen turned a tear-streaked face toward Addie and shook her head.

"No, I want to stay with Jim. Besides, I'd slow you down." she said.

"Helen," begged Addie, "They'll kill you."

Smiling sadly, Helen pulled up her blouse to show Addie a gaping hole in her abdomen.

"Go. Don't worry about me." yelled Helen, weakly pushing Addie away.

Crying openly, Addie came back to her feet and emptied her pistol in the direction of the muzzle flashes. Sliding across the front seat, Addie put the car in gear and floored the accelerator. An armed terrorist jumped into the drive and began to pump bullets into the front windshield. Swerving slightly, Addie heard a satisfying thump as the bumper of the speeding police car sent his body went flying backward into the shrubbery.

Tears streaming down her face, Addie looked into the rearview mirror and saw that there was no movement in front of the building. Helen was lying on her back, Jim was down and both cops were sagging against the pillar. She pounded on the steering wheel in a rage, it was a set up and she shouldn't have just walked into it.

Fifteen minutes later, Prince Hadji, Dr. Bremer and Noyotivik/Hughes stood at the window of the Prince's apartment looking down at the figures sprawled on the concrete below. Terrorist that he was, even Hadji was shocked at the carnage that littered the sidewalk. His normally dark face was flushed, a definite sign of the level of his anger, he was in a killing rage. It was a major effort for him to restrain his murderous temper, when faced by incompetence. He couldn't believe that it was his own men who had foiled his plan to have the reporter killed far from his apartment building.

Now instead of a dead reporter, his most trusted servant had been carried upstairs with two gunshot wounds. Two of his pet police were now dead, caught in a crossfire after having been disarmed and handcuffed with their own handcuffs. To compound the problem, that detective who had been a rich source of information on both police and underworld activities was also dead.

He turned away from the window and glared at the young terrorist waiting patiently in the center of the room.

"Yoshi, where are your men?" Prince Hadji asked in a deceptively calm voice.

The Oriental terrorist gestured weakly toward the window, as he bowed.

"Sorry to report that they are dead, sire." he reported in an emotionless voice.

"How were they killed?" asked the Prince curiously.

"Two were shot and one was hit by the police car as the Americans left here." he responded.

Prince Hadji winced as he considered the damage to his plans caused by that Hell spawn of a woman.

"You mean that three women took out almost an entire team of highly trained freedom fighters?" he demanded in a voice of total amazement.

"Yes, sire." tiredly responded the Oriental, "the dead blonde woman killed one of my men almost immediately and wounded a second. We thought she was dead and after the police car left, we came out of the darkness. She had only been pretending to be dead and killed my second before I killed her. She was worthy of being Oriental, she was a warrior."

"Bah!" snapped the Prince.

The angry Prince walked back to the window and considered the night sky. Where would he get more men before the morning? He couldn't believe that one woman had caused so much chaos.

CHAPTER THIRTY

Moses Gardner's next sensation was of being lifted gently from his position on the floor. He opened his eyes to see that Wilkie had understood his message, after all. With his friend was an Emergency Medical Team, one of who, a rather pretty brunette, was in the process of taking his pulse as two others lifted him on a stretcher and started for the door. He saw two cops waiting outside the door and Peter Novak, one of the station big shots.

As he was carried out the door of the office, his eyes locked on Novak's face. There was something that he needed to say about that face, but he was so groggy with painkillers that he couldn't remember what it was. As the stretcher was carried past Novak, Gardner tried to shift to keep his eyes on the Assistant Operations Director.

"Just rest easy, big guy." soothed the woman holding his wrist. "We're taking you to the hospital."

"How is he?" asked a voice that Gardner was able to identify as Wilkie.

"Lost a lot of blood, but if there are no complications, such as infection, he should be fine in a week or so." answered a nice female voice.

In a rather dreamy, detached fashion, Gardner rested easily on the stretcher as they carried him toward the elevator. He was wondering if he could get the female tech's telephone number. Perhaps, he considered, it was time for him to stop roaming around the world taking pictures and settle down. Stranger things had happened.

When they paused to wait for the elevator, Wilkie's bearded face leaned into his line of vision.

"Mose, can you tell me who shot you?" asked Wilkie in concern.

"Wha?" asked Moses as he fought his way back from his dreamy state.

"Who shot you?" repeated his friend, slowly.

The drugs he had been given were forcing him to drift, off, but sudden he had one crystal clear memory. He saw, as if in slow motion, Peter Novak shoot him with a small caliber pistol. Aware that he was drifting off, Moses made a desperate grab for Wilkie's arm.

"Novak. Novak shot me. He's in with the terrorists," mumbled the wounded man as he tried to focus his suddenly uncooperative eyes.

Then the doors opened and the medical people rushed the stretcher into the elevator. Wilkie and the two police officers remained behind on the floor.

"Who is Novak?" asked Mitch Radigan, the senior member of the police team that had responded to the call.

Wilkie shook his head in confusion as he looked around.

"The only Novak I know is Peter Novak, the Assistant Operations Director for the Network. He's the guy with the suit that was with us a minute ago.

But it's ridiculous to think that he could be in with these terrorists, he's a rather important person here at the network." stuttered the Photographer.

"I remember him, he never said a word. He just stood and watched the medical techs," said Radigan.

"Where did he go?" questioned Scott Wolfe, the younger of the two police.

"I would guess back to his office in the executive section." answered Wilkie.

"Lead the way," offered Scott Wolfe, the younger of the two police.

Quickly the three walked along the deserted hallway toward the executive offices at the far end of the corridor. There was no real tension in the group until they saw the lights in the reception area snap off. Wilkie stopped and looked at his companions in puzzlement.

"This is the first time since I have worked here that those lights have been turned off. I usually work nights and those lights are always on." he said.

"Wait here, sir." said Radigan, politely, as he drew his sidearm.

Guns in hand, the two officers began to slow work their way down the hall toward   the now darkened office section.

They were within ten feet of the entrance when a shot rang out, Officer Wolfe bent forward and fell to his knees.

"Mitch," he groaned, "I'm hit."

Dropping to one knee, Radigan emptied his revolver into the darkened office. Quickly, the officer broke open his revolver, spilled the expended casing on the floor and reloaded using a speed loader from his pocket. Thumbing back the hammer, Radigan darted forward and flattened himself against the wall to the left of the doorway. Taking a deep breath, Radigan dove into the darkened room.

Wilkie braced himself for more gunshots, but the only sounds he heard were Wolfe's moans. Against his better judgment, Wilkie low crawled over to the fallen officer.

"You doing O.K.?" he asked softly, pulling him back out of the line of fire into a sitting position.

"God, it hurts." groaned Wolfe, as his head lolled back.

Wilkie pulled the young officer's hands from his mid section and winced as he saw the small hole that was regularly pumping blood. He pulled his handkerchief from his pocket and gently placed it on the young officer's wound.

"Keep the pressure on this." he said as the picked the officer's side arm from the floor.

Cautiously, he slowly edged his way toward the darkened doorway. Just as he reached it, there was the sound of a shot and the area was flooded with light. Peering around the doorframe, Wilkie couldn't see anyone, but he heard sounds from the office to his right. Bracing himself and holding the pistol in both hands, Wilkie darted along the wall to flatten himself at the edge of the office door, as he had seen the Officer's do.

As he was gathering his courage to spring into the office, he was relieved to see Officer Radigan come walking through the door. Seeing Wilkie flattened against the wall, the Officer gave him a slight grin as he holstered his gun.

"It's over," he said.

"What happened?" questioned Wilkie.

"That guy in the gray suit had a gun. I heard a sound in this office and caught him trying to destroy some papers. He grabbed for his gun and I had to shoot him," said Radigan tiredly.

"Better check on your partner," said Wilkie gesturing toward the hall.

As the Officer ran toward the hall, Wilkie cautiously stepped into Peter Novak's office. Crossing over to the desk, Wilkie stopped when he saw the dead body slumped in the desk chair. Novak was most thoroughly dead, with a large bloody hole in his chest. Glancing around the room, Wilkie noticed an open wall safe on the wall to his left, stacked haphazardly on the big walnut desk were numerous documents. Other shredded papers were lying scattered on the carpet.

Laying his borrowed pistol on the desk, Wilkie reached across and gathered up some of the items that Novak had failed to destroy. Doing his best to ignore the corpse sprawled in the desk chair, he quickly glanced through several of the documents, before he saw enough to make him read them more slowly. When Wilkie realized exactly what he was reading, however, he grabbed for others and quickly flipped through them. He totally forgot about the corpse and everything else.

Spinning around, Wilkie literally ran for the door.

"Officer! You have to see this," he yelled as he raced for the door.

At about the same time that Wilkie was making his great discovery, Addie was roaring through the night along 66th Street across Central Park. Betty had climbed over the seat in a flash of long legs and dropped into the passenger seat.

"Please, Addie, go faster!" she pleaded as her long, slim fingers clutched at the dash.

'Hang on, Betty." said Addie as she pressed the accelerator even harder, her hands clamped tightly on the wheel.

She tried not to look at the speedometer, aware that the needle was hovering at around sixty. Rounding the last turn, Addie saw the Fifth Avenue intersection dead ahead. Jerking the wheel to the right, Addie fought to control the fishtailing police car as she steered into the center land of Fifth Avenue. Gritting her teeth, Addie pressed the accelerator even harder; they had to get to Miranda before she died, too.

Prince Hadji sat calmly on his couch with his ever-present cup of tea clutched correctly in one hand, lost in thought. Dr. Bremer sat across from him, one Gucci loafered foot crossed across the other. He was leaning back in a most relaxed manner, his sharp features showing sardonic amusement.

"Could these unexpected casualties cause a problem with tomorrow's operations?" he asked the Prince.

Shaken from his planning, Prince Hadji took a slow careful drink of his cool tea before looking up at Dr. Bremer.

"Well, it has caused me to have to make some minor changes in my plans, but nothing that can't be taken care of." he paused and considered the silent Noyotivik/Hughes intently.

"Dr. Bremer, I wonder if we could talk privately?" asked the Prince.

Sensing that the reverses of the evening had shaken Hadji out of his usual superior attitude, Dr. Bremer was curious as to what he would say.

"I can do better than that, Prince," he said turning to Noyotivik/Hughes

"Illai," said Bremer, "Look at me."

Slowly Noyotivik turned his eyes toward Dr. Bremer. Pulling a bright crystal on a string from his pocket, Dr. Bremer began to swing the bright object slowly in front of his companion.

"Illai, my friend, your eye lids are becoming very, very heavy. Do you understand? You are becoming very sleepy," intoned the Doctor.

As Prince Hadji watched in amazement, the big man began to nod. In a very few minutes, the assassin was leaning back against the couch, apparently sound asleep. Just to be sure that he was asleep, Dr. Bremer leaned close to him and pried up each eyelid. Finally, satisfied, the Doctor turned back to the Prince.

"Now, we can talk in private." he said, with a smile.

"Amazing, absolutely amazing." said the Prince as he looked on in interest.

For the first time, Prince Hadji favored Dr. Bremer with a glance approaching respect. Very deliberately, he took another sip of his tea and returned the cup to its' saucer.

"Doctor, as you know, tomorrow's operations are very important. We can't afford to fail, for political, as well as personal reasons. As you are well aware, I am now three people short. It is very important that I thoroughly understand your protégé and how much he can be depended upon. It could make a big difference tomorrow," he said.

Dr. Bremer allowed himself to feel very satisfied. Finally, Prince Hadji was forced to ask him for a favor. This could definitely raise his standing with the Council.

"It is really quite simple." began Bremer. "This young man is completely convinced that he is Captain Illai Noyotivik, a member of the Russian Special Forces assassination team."

Prince Hadji nodded his aquiline head very slowly as he rubbed his chin with his right hand.

"Is there really such a person?" asked Hadji curiously.

Bremer looked over at the sleeping man beside him.

"Oh, most definitely. Captain Illai Noyotivik was and is one of the most successful assassins in the world. He has been so good at his profession that the British Intelligence Services began to call him the Specter. He comes and goes like a ghost in the night. In fact, this characteristic is his calling card.

It was the idea of the K.G.B. that a good assassin is born; training only improves the traits that are already ingrained. So ten subjects were chosen and through hypnosis and what the American's call brainwashing, they were each reprogrammed to believe that they were the Specter. This young man was the best of those ten. Noyotivik himself worked with them to make sure that they could and would act and think just like he would."

Now Bremer rose and went over to peer out the window at the night. With detached interest, he noticed that two police cars were now in front of the building. Four uniformed officers were wondering around, apparently investigating the carnage.

"Police out front." he observed to the Prince.

Absently noting the Prince's disinterested grunt, Bremer continued with his story.

"This man, an American Army Officer was indoctrinated with a new process through our operation in Panama. Under the cover of being assigned to several secret projects, he was sent to Iran, China and Russia for training. By the way, he was given all of the military training that Noyotivik himself had undertaken. Then he was turned over to the Russian Special Forces to act as a decoy when Noyotivik had to be away on special projects. Naturally, under glasnost, the Russian authorities were no longer quite so enthusiastic to terminate uncooperative dignitaries. The K.G.B. was ordered to account for all of the "special operatives", to include Noyotivik.

Approximately ten years ago, Noyotivik decided to offer his services to the highest bidder and went underground. A K.G.B. general, at about the same time decided that he didn't like his superior's politics, so he smuggled the false Noyotivik to your country in order to continue the revolution. I understand that the general himself met with an accident when he had a slight disagreement with your leaders."

Dr. Bremer paused for a moment as he searched his pockets for his cigarette case.

"I can assure you that this young man is now a completely dedicated killer. He is dedicated to whoever pays his fee. He believes that you have paid him several million dollars to assassinate five people. Tomorrow he will kill three of them. Then he will await your instructions to kill the other two. It is really quite simple. This procedure is even better than cloning. We totally control their minds."

Hadji's normally smooth forehead was creased as he gave his total attention to what was being said.

"But how could this man interact with the infidels for so long with out being caught?" he asked.

Bremer shrugged as he lit his cigarette.

"Quite simply," he said as be waved away a cloud of smoke. "Over the Noyotivik identity, another identity was placed, that of Carter Davis Hughes. So since he was "rescued" from Cambodia as a supposed P.O.W., he has actually been a mild mannered insurance man. The concept was brilliant."

Prince Hadji opened his mouth to ask another question, to be interrupted by the insistent ringing of a phone. Dr. Bremer pulled back his left sleeve and looked at his watch, it was 2:00 a.m.

"Doesn't he ever sleep?" commented the Doctor.

With a scowl, Hadji reached down to press a button on the bottom of the table sitting at his elbow activating a hidden speakerphone.

"Yes, RAVEN?" said Prince Hadji with a totally blank face.

"I am disturbed by the news of the death of several of your men. Have you lost totally control already?" asked the deep voice sarcastically.

"How did that bastard find out so quick?" murmured the Prince. "RAVEN, there have been certain, -'minor problems".

"You mean that your vaunted freedom fighters have been getting their ass' kicked. May I remind you that this is the second time that you have had your men shot down and then been unable to punish the killer," charged the voice.

"It will not happen again, Raven," maintained Hadji.

"Dr. Bremer, are you still there?" asked RAVEN

"Yes, RAVEN." replied the Doctor.

"Is our secret weapon ready?" asked RAVEN.

"Definitely. He will perform admirably," asserted the Doctor.

"I hope your part works better than have Hadji's people," rumbled the voice.

Dr. Bremer stole a quick glance at the Arab; his face was like a thundercloud.

"He will perform as required, RAVEN," said Dr. Bremer confidently.

"See that he does." snapped RAVEN, "As for you, Hadji, remember, it is better to die a martyr than a failure."

"I understand, RAVEN."

"I want that female reporter killed. Tonight."

"Even now, I have people looking for her, RAVEN."

"I have just received information that one of our council members was killed a few minutes ago. If you succeed tomorrow, you will take his place, Hadji." finished RAVEN as he broke the connection.

With an oath, the Prince angrily jabbed at the concealed button. "The sheer arrogance of that man." swore the Prince.

Coming to his feet, he turned on his guest.

"Tell me, Bremer, who is that fat pig?" demanded Hadji.

Bremer shook his head. "None of us know. I was contacted by a middleman and made an offer I couldn't refuse. I've talked to rest of the

Council; none of us have ever seen RAVEN outside that darkened conference room. He either works through messengers, by phone or while in a position that where his face can't be seen."

"But surely you know something about him." insisted the Prince.

Bremer contemplated the end of his burning cigarette. "I know that he is American. I know that he is someone of influence used to giving orders. He is wealthy, judging by the amount of funds that have been made available to fund this operation and I have realized one other thing." he paused.

"Well, what is this one other thing?" demanded the angry Prince.

"I have realized that he reports to someone higher up than himself."

Prince Hadji considered this information carefully. Used in the correct manner, it might be to his advantage.

"How do you know this?" he demanded.

"In one of our meetings, he let slip that he had received instructions to carry out a particular operation. In fact, it was in regard to activating Noyotivik at this particular time. He covered his slip quickly and carefully, but my job is to notice things like that. No, our mysterious RAVEN is not the man in charge."

Hadji nodded as the digested the fact that RAVEN might have a weakness after all. He had raged against his superiors when they had told him that he was to be assigned to work for an infidel. Prince Hadji had dedicated his entire life and fortune to the service of his cause. When his pleas had fallen on deaf ears with the leaders of the HizbAllah, he had even demanded and received a meeting with Hojat-ol-Islam Fazl-Allah Mahalati known as "the Incorruptible" since he put the revolution above all other considerations.

Mahalati had told him that all Islam was putting the greatest faith in Hadji to carry out this mission. If Hadji was successful, it would have the momentous effect of forcing the Great Satan to remove all support, militarily and financial from the State of Israel. Without the support of the Great Satan, Israel would not last a year. For such an outcome, Hadji had promised that he could put up with a great deal of the type of insults that he continually received from RAVEN.

However, when this was over and his homeland was free, Hadji had promised himself that he would have RAVEN assassinated. That is, he said to himself, if he could find out Raven's identity.

"Have you ever been allowed beyond the conference room with that damn Washington Shrine?" he roused himself to ask.

Bremer allowed himself a small smile. Hadji was referring to a most unusual obsession demonstrated by RAVEN; it appeared that he almost worshipped George Washington. He even conducted his meetings with an illuminated portrait of America's first President hanging on the wall behind him. More unusual, RAVEN never allowed any of his so called colleagues to see any part of his quarters other than that conference room.

Bremer had made major efforts to find out Raven's address, but so far he had been foiled. Every time there was a meeting, Dr. Bremer would be picked up in a limo with blacked out windows. When he was allowed out of the car, he was always in an underground parking garage facing an elevator. Inside the elevator there was only one button, which deposited the user in a reception area. The only door led to the conference room. It was frustrating, but Bremer relished the challenge. Somehow, someway, he was determined to find out the identity of the man who called himself RAVEN.

"No," he said in reply, "As far as I can tell, there is only one door out of that conference room and that goes back into the reception area."

Tiring of the discussion, Prince Hadji stood and stretched.

"Well, it is a puzzle. But, forgive me it is late and I am tired, my friend. I offer you the hospitality of my home. I will have Otto—." he stopped and frowned for a minute.

"Well, I will show you rooms for the two of you." finished the Prince.

Carefully, Dr. Bremer woke Noyotivik/Hughes from his enforce sleep and led the man along in the wake of Prince Hadji. Halting outside the door of the late unlamented Malika, Hadji turned to Dr. Bremer.

"Perhaps your friend would like to use this room. Its former occupant -er—no longer has any need for it," he said.

Dr. Bremer looked at his companion.

"Illai, you will stay in this room, until I come for you. Do you understand?" he asked slowly.

"I understand, comrade." he replied, looking straight ahead.

Dr. Bremer reached out and opened the door.

"Go inside, Illai." he ordered.

Obediently, the assassin walked inside the bedroom and shut the door. He heard the other two continue on down the hallway. Slowly, he paced the length of the room, seemingly just pacing, but in reality examining every inch of the room for camera or peepholes. Finally, satisfied that he wasn't being watched, he relaxed and a faint smile touched his lips.

"So they think they control me?" he thought to himself, "They might be surprised."

A sudden stray thought caught his attention. There was something important he should remember about George Washington. He knew that the name should mean something to him, but what could it be? As he tried to remember, he stripped off his jacket and shirt, slipped off his shoes and layback on the bed. His cold blue eyes were staring intently at the ceiling. He had to remember whom he had heard talk about George Washington. After long moments, his eyes closed and he fell into a restless sleep.

Chapter Thirty-one

SATURDAY, DECEMBER 25—2:00 A.M.-WASHINGTON D.C.

The Rusty Frog was a small restaurant that was definitely not on the must-see list of any tour guide of Washington D.C. In fact, this particular little hideaway was several miles outside the city limits of the Nations Capitol. However, it was very well known among the secretive set as a place where meetings could be held without a lot of people being the wiser. Raul Bakir, a former Palestinian gunrunner, Ethiopian slave trader, terrorist leader and international fixer was the owner, though these days he went by the name of Arthur Keman a supposed Israeli citizen. If you wanted anything from a gun to a sex slave, good ole Artie was the man to see.

According to the local ordinances, establishments such as his were to be closed by 2 a.m., though the beat officers did not rigidly enforce the closing time. More than once when they had tried to do so, they had found Senators and Congressmen entertaining Congressional pages, both sexes, or secretaries, again both sexes. After the last scandal, it was decided by the local police officials to be circumspect as to when they forced the Rusty Frog to close. Arthur, or Raul, knew enough to get a dozen Senators, of both parties, tossed out of office and in some cases, prosecuted for some serious felonies. However, everyone knew that good ole Artie would keep his mouth shut. It was good for business.

This night being Christmas Eve, actually Christmas morning, business was slow. There was only one guy sitting in the bar, who seemed to be intent on drinking himself into a stupor. Much as Artie hated to turn anyone out into the cold, all good things had to come to an end. Artie was tired and getting ready to close, in another twenty minutes he would throw out the drunk and go upstairs to bed. Some of his old wounds from his younger days were beginning to bother him. The way his back was hurting, the result of an attempt to kill him in Beirut he remembered, they were due for a change in the weather.

Slowly, and actually half heatedly, Artie was wiping down the long mahogany bar, when he heard the front door open. Glancing up, he caught a glimpse of a figure in trench coat and low pulled fedora crossing the dining room to join the drunk in the back of the restaurant. He wasn't sure but he thought, for a split second, that he recognized the newcomer. With a grin, he caught himself and went back to cleaning the bar. Even after all these years, he still had to remind himself that he was just a restaurant owner.

At his table in the back of the room, Clint Murchison was getting more and more depressed. Murchison had been waiting for over two hours for this meeting with his White House contact. There was much to be done and the fool had to be late. He was positive that something had gone wrong; FOX had never been this late for a meeting before. The message had made it very clear that FOX had to talk to him tonight without fail.

At fifty-five, Murchison had many regrets at the opportunities lost in his youth. Recruited by the C.I.A. out of a small college in Mississippi, the young man had been shunted around the world from hot spot to hot spot until he just happened to be at the wrong place at the wrong time. When the U.S. Embassy had been captured by the Iranians in the 1970's Murchison had just happened to be in Tehran on a mission to gather information.

Realizing what was taking place, Murchison had gone under cover and laid low until Hominy's undercover police had captured him. After some persuasion, Murchison had agreed to help the so-called students circumvent the protections on the safe in the C.I.A. station chief's office. Hominy had been ecstatic when he saw the prize that Murchison had delivered to him. The information had been well worth the two hundred thousand that Hominy had given him for his assistance.

As he poured himself another drink, Murchison laughed to himself. His superiors may have believed that he had done everything he could to help those in the embassy, but they never suspected that he had actively helped the terrorists. Unfortunately, his involvement had given these new terrorists something that they were now using to make him cooperate in this new venture. But the pay was good.

Money or no money, there was no amount that would be worth him getting caught. If his former employers found out he had been helping the terrorists, they wouldn't think twice about killing him. Murchison wanted to be around to enjoy all of that money he had stashed in Zurich. He promised himself that he would only wait another half an hour and then he was going to get good and lost. If FOX had been discovered, then Washington D.C. was not a healthy place for ex-C.I.A. agents. Murchison was almost praying that he could get the rest of his payment so that he could drop these people and get out of the country. After the attacks on the C.I.A. Building today, Washington was not a real healthy place. Security would certainly get tighter and he could be caught.

Stubbing out his twentieth cigarette of the evening in the cheap, black plastic ashtray, Murchison poured himself another drink of scotch, missing the glass with a good portion of the expensive liquor so that it formed a small pool on the table. Tipping back his head, he downed the drink and then looked around the room with bleary eyes. Suddenly, his eyes locked on FOX making his way across the room. His lips curled as he noticed the almost dainty way that FOX crossed the room.

Coming up to the table, the newcomer lowered himself into a chair across the table from Murchison.

"Are you drunk?" asked FOX in a soft voice, indicating the half empty bottle of 7-year-old scotch sitting on the table.

"No! I'm not drunk. I just had a drink or two while I waited," he said, making a major effort to focus his eyes on his companion as he reached for the bottle.

FOX shot out one hand and grabbed the bottle first, the light glittering on the massive gold ring on his left hand. The large purple stone in its center shimmering almost black in the garish light.

"That's enough of that," snapped FOX; "You'll need your wits about you for this."

"Well I've been sitting here for two hours waiting for you to arrive. As far as I knew, you might have been arrested and told all about me." Murchison protested.

FOX grunted.

"No one is going to arrest me. But I do have duties to perform that sometimes mean I have to be late for these meetings. Even if I am late, that's no excuse for you to fall apart and get drunk."

Murchison's eyes dropped to the cigarette burned table.

"Well, I don't like it." he said, "I don't like it at all."

FOX sneered at his companion.

"It really doesn't matter to me whether you like it or not. You have a part to play in our little conspiracy, small as it might be, and if you can't play it properly, then we will simply get someone else." snapped the figure in the trench coat.

Unfortunately for Murchison, he was not a happy drunk. When he over-indulged, his temper got touchy, he got mean.

"Well hot shot, you just get someone else. I'm not one of your little soldier boys just sitting around waiting to obey orders. I was serving this country when you were still in diapers." he said forcefully as his voice rose.

Fox hurriedly glanced around the room, but noticed that the bartender was the only one in the room.

"Keep your voice down, you fool!" hissed FOX.

Murchison fell silent but kept his eyes glued to the scotch bottle.

"I've got to get back, so I'll make this quick." began FOX, "I want you to go to Union Station. In locker 47, you will find a briefcase. Bring the brief case to the address you will find in this envelope."

Reaching into his coat, FOX pulled an envelope from the inside pocket of his coat and slid it across the table. Murchison immediate picked it up and put it in his own pocket.

Satisfied that his contact had the information, FOX rose and turned from the table.

"Hey, wait a minute," protested Murchison.

Silently, FOX turned and glared at the seated courier.

"My money? How about my money?" rumbled the seated man.

"In the briefcase. Look in the briefcase," answered FOX as he turned and left the restaurant.

As soon as his contact had left, Murchison defiantly reached for the bottle, poured himself a full glass and tossed it down. How dare that little upstart tell him what to do, why he'd half a mind to break him in half the next time they met. Finishing the drink, Murchison stood and swayed slightly. Why even a little drunk, he was twice the man that most were sober. Why, even Khomeni himself, had thanked him for his help at the embassy. He'd have to talk to the MAN about the respect he got from this little upstart.

Tossing some money on the table, Murchison staggered across the empty restaurant toward the door. Artie Keman watched the man weaving between the tables from under his heavy eyebrows. It didn't take a rocket scientist to figure out that he had just witnessed a drop. With all the unrest going on around the country, what he had just seen gave Artie a great deal of food for thought.

As Murchison left the restaurant and lumbered across the parking lot, he was totally unaware that he was being watched from a car parked by the road. In the passenger seat was FOX, the driver was a big man in a dark suit, his eyes covered with mirrored sunglasses even at this early hour of the day. In the shadowy back of the car, sat an individual of indeterminate sex. The aroma of Turkish tobacco filled the car.

"There he is." said FOX as they watched the obviously drunk Murchison who was having trouble inserting his key in his car lock.

"He has been a good servant in the past." rasped the voice from the back seat, " Are you sure that he has become unreliable?"

FOX swept the dark fedora off, peeled off a wig and shook out her long thick blonde hair. Turning down the upturned collar of the trench coat, FOX peeled off makeup to show herself to be a rather attractive blonde in her mid thirties. Pulling off the distinctive ring on her left hand, FOX reached across the seat and handed it to the unseen individual on the back seat.

"Definitely." she responded firmly, "He almost started a fight with me when I tried to stop him from getting drunker."

The figure on the back seat gave a deep sigh.

"He has been a good and faithful servant to the JIHAD for many years. It is a pity that he, like so many others of promise, have been ruined by the decadent living in the West." he paused for several seconds as he watched Murchison's car weave out of the parking lot. "Well, no matter, FOX, inform Kamala that after Mr. Murchison makes his delivery today there is no longer any need to keep him in our employ." he said.

"With pleasure." replied the young woman on the front seat.

As Murchison's taillights vanished in the distance, the shadowy figure on the back seat sighed again, deeply.

"John, you may drive me back to the City. There is still much to be done before noon."

Unable to restrain her curiosity, FOX turned toward the darkened rear seat.

"How goes the operations in New York?" she asked hesitantly.

At first she thought she would receive no answer, then she heard the unseen passenger shift on the leather seat.

"There have been some setbacks, however, if all goes well today we will still succeed."

"When do operations begin here in Washington?" she asked.

It surprised her, but intuitively, FOX was sure that she was being keenly studied from the darkness.

"It is sometimes not wise to asked too many questions, my dear," replied her superior.

Taking the hint, FOX fell silent and leaned back against the seat. She felt rather than heard the figure in the back seat move up behind her. As she expected, she felt a hand come over her shoulder and slide into her blouse, the fingers forcing their way into her bra to cup one of her large firm breasts.

"Soon you will know more my pet. But for now, the less you know the better."

Then a second hand grabbed a handful of hair, pulling her back for a deep kiss. The lips were soft, but the whiskers on the face of the man from the back seat scratched her face. For the thousandth time, she wondered who her mysterious superior might be. FOX had used all of her feminine wiles to try and wheedle information out of him, but had found that he barely reacted to her most seductive poses. It was very strange. She knew that he smoked cigars, actually the same specially made Cuban brand as the President. But she really wasn't sure what was real and what was for show when it came to this man. Why once after a meeting in the car, just as FOX had been ready to leave, she had detected the faint odor of Midnight Rendezvous, the same perfume favored by the First Lady.

Silently, the driver started the car and eased onto the main highway. Making sure not to catch up with Murchison's automobile, the long black Lincoln wove its' way back into the City using numerous side streets. At the Lincoln Monument, the car pulled over to the curb, just long enough to allow FOX to exit. Perplexed, she stood on the curb staring after the car that rapidly disappeared into the night. She caught sight of it just for a moment, or at least she thought it was the same car, but this one turned into the gate at the White House. Turning, FOX vanished into the darkness.

NEW YORK CITY

Addie brought the stolen police cruiser to a screeching halt in front of Betty and Miranda's building. Almost before she had the car stopped, Betty was out the car and racing for the front entrance. She was in such a hurry that she even forgot to carry her pistol.

"Betty! Wait for me." called Addie, but her friend paid no attention, vanishing into the building. Addie started to follow her, but paused long enough to stick a pistol in her belt and grab the riot shotgun from its rack in the front of the police car.

When she stepped cautiously through the front door, Addie could hear Betty literally pounding frantically up the stairs. If there was anyone still with Miranda, they were sure to hear Betty coming. Addie remembered that the apartment was on the third floor, so being sure not to make the stair treads creak with her weight, she began to climb the stairs. Above her, she heard Betty jerk open the door to the third floor, then nothing.

Addie paused, waiting for gunshots or screams from the third floor, but she heard nothing. Her nerves were stretched almost to the breaking point; she felt that if she didn't hear a sound soon, she would scream. On the landing below the last flight of stairs, Addie paused to wipe the sweat from her hands onto her borrowed jeans. Getting a good grip on the riot shot gun, she started up the last flight of stairs.

At the door to the third floor, Addie tried to look through the grimy glass set into the door. At first she couldn't see anything moving, but then she heard someone clear his throat. Easing open the door to the stairs, Addie peered out and saw a young dark skinned man in dark clothing leaning against the right hand wall about ten feet down the hall.

Racking her brain, Addie couldn't figure out how to get to the apartment without this guy spotting her. She watched quietly as he seemed to be enjoying his cigarette. Suddenly, she got an idea. Stepping to the right of the door, Addie partially covered her mouth with her hand.

"Help. Please help me!" she moaned in her best little girl's voice, her mouth pressed close to the door.

At first she thought he hadn't heard her, but then she saw the door begin to open. The first thing she saw was the barrel of his pistol as he began to ease through the door onto the landing. The guard was so intent on finding the source of the sound that he didn't even bother to check the area just inside the door. With a grunt, Addie brought the butt of her shotgun crashing down on his dark head. He never made a sound, but went head first down the stairs, his pistol falling to the floor at her feet.

Pausing to calm her nerves, Addie again had to wipe her sweaty hands on her jeans. Holding her shotgun in her right hand, Addie eased open the door to the third floor and peeked out, apparently there had only been the one guard. On tiptoe, she approached the door to Miranda's apartment and pressed her ear against the worn wood.

"Are you going to tell me?" she heard a male voice demand.

The only response she heard was a faint moan. Gritting her teeth, Addie backed up, pointing her weapon at the door. She was ready to pull the trigger when she had a sudden thought, what if one of her friends was on the other side of the worn wood? She could hurt them by mistake. There had to be another way into the apartment.

Lowering her shotgun, Addie turned to survey the hall. Noticing the window that overlooked the street, Addie was struck by a sudden thought. Trotting down the hall, she peered out the window, and confirmed that there was a relatively wide ledge that seemed to run around the building. She leaned her shotgun against the wall and as silently as possible, raised the window. Peering outside, she saw that the ledge was about eight inches wide, if she was careful, just wide enough for her to use as a way into the apartment.

Lithely, she jumped up onto the windowsill, reaching back inside to grasp her weapon by the barrel. Carefully, she stepped out into the ledge and began to inch her way along the front of the building. Addie had always hated heights, even on those assignments in the mountains of Afghanistan; she had been petrified of falling. Now, she was fifty feet in the air, only eight inches of crumbling concrete between her and the sidewalk. Holding in her fear, Addie took about a year by her estimation, to make her way to the edge of the building and painfully make her way around the corner. Pressing her body even closer to the rough brick, Addie turned her head to see the Promised Land. Outside Miranda's apartment was a fire escape.

As she neared the safety of that wonderful fire escape, a horrible thought came to her. What if, while she had been doing her Spiderman act along the ledge, the terrorists had left by the front, taking Miranda and Betty with them? Or even worse, what if they had killed the two women and then strolled merrily out of the front door? In spite of her fears, Addie began to move faster along the crumbling ledge, and finally reached out one trembling hand to grab the railing of the fire escape.

Almost weak with relief, Addie swung her legs over the rail and pressed her trembling body against the brick just beside the partially opened window of Miranda's apartment, her shotgun clutched to her chest. For the moment, she was unable to more than just try and suck air into her lungs. As her respiration began to return to normal and the roaring in her ears subsided, Addie heard voices and inched closer to the window.

Holding her breath, Addie crouched and peeked around the edge of the window. The apartment was trashed; papers and possession were strewn about the previously neat living room. It was difficult for her to see the entire room, without being seen, but Addie was determined to check on the welfare of her friends. To her relief, she finally saw both Miranda and Betty cowering on the couch. Miranda looked quite a bit the worse for wear. Her face was bloody and she was cradling her left arm against her chest. Obviously, her captors had been most insistent in trying to get information out of her. Towering over the two scared women were two large gun-carrying terrorists. Sitting rather primly in a chair across from the women was slim, well dressed young man, holding a small automatic pistol rather loosely in his right hand. Through the partially open window Addie could hear them talking,

"Now listen to me," he snapped as he leaned forward to rest his elbows on his knees. "I'm going to ask you one more time and then somebody gets really hurt. Now where are those notes you called the reporter about?"

Refusing to speak, Miranda met his gaze without flinching. Betty's arms encircled the shoulders of her friend and she only clutched Miranda tighter. The seated terrorist leader finally sighed and turned to the big sandy-haired man to his right.

"Jimmy, me bucko. It would seem that she needs some encouragement. Why don't you take her into the bedroom and 'convince' her to talk?"

The one called Jimmy grinned at the women on the couch. He stuck his pistol in his belt and grabbed Miranda's left arm in one of his big hands. That was the arm that Miranda had been cradling, so in spite of herself, Miranda groaned and allowed herself to be pulled off the couch.

"Take your hands off her!" shrieked Betty as she threw herself, kicking and clawing, at big Jimmy.

With a grunt, Jimmy back handed the slight blonde, and sent her flying across the room.

"Well done, my bucko." congratulated the seated terrorist as the big man began to drag Miranda across the living room toward the bedroom door. The third had rushed across the room and thrown himself on top of Betty.

Unable to watch any longer, Addie stepped in front of the partially opened window and racked back the slide on the shotgun, chambering a round.

"Let them go you bastards!" she yelled.

Jimmy threw Miranda from him and grabbed for his pistol, his coat billowing wide. With a roar, Addie pulled the trigger. The range was so close and Jimmy so big that she didn't miss. Her shot shattered the window, sending glass and splinters across the room. Jimmy fell back limply, his chest a red mess. The man on top of Betty screamed as his back was peppered with glass fragments. With a yell, the third terrorist fell over backward, scrambling for the hall door, frantically firing his pistol over his shoulder in the general direction of the window.

Addie was knocked backward by the recoil of the shotgun and almost toppled backward over the rail of the fire escape. Dropping the riot gun, only a wild grab for the railing kept the young reporter from making a quick trip to the ground. Pulling herself back onto the fire escape, Addie grabbed up her weapon and scrambled for the window. She saw the man who had been attacking Betty staggering around the room, clawing at his back in obvious pain. At first she was puzzled by his actions, but when he turned, she saw numerous large chunks of glass sticking out of his back.

She raised her rifle and aimed at the injured man, but paused as Betty, screeching at the top of her lungs, came up from the floor and kicked him squarely in the crotch, the man doubled over in pain.

Grabbing a lamp from the nearby end table, Betty brought it crashing down on his head. He collapsed to lay unconscious at her feet. There was no sign of the third terrorist.

Quickly Addie scrambled through the window, and, dropping her shotgun to the floor, she knelt over the fallen Miranda. Betty rushed over to the open door to the hall and pushed it shut. The third terrorist was nowhere to be seen.

Gently, Addie helped Miranda slide along the floor to the couch. It was obvious to her that Miranda's left arm had been dislocated. Her face was puffy and bruised, the flesh torn.

"Miranda, it's Addie. Can you hear me?" asked Addie softly as Betty came to kneel beside her friend.

Slowly, the fallen woman opened her swollen eyes. At first she looked at the two kneeling beside her in puzzlement, but then she recognized them.

"Addie, Betty, I knew that you would come. You got my message," she said weakly.

"What message, Miranda?" asked Addie, puzzled.

"I called your office earlier and left word with a Mr. Novak."

"Well no matter." Addie gently brushed Miranda's damp hair from her face. "What was the message?"

"Bernie's notes, we, Betty and I, found them." said Miranda, pointing weakly toward the bookcase. "Look over there behind those books."

"Why didn't you let them have the papers?" asked Addie, as Betty darted over to the bookcase. "There's nothing worth all this pain."

Miranda shook her head slowly and winced.

"Bernie wanted you to have them and he was my friend. You can do something with them to stop all of this killing. To me this was worth it." she said slowly.

Addie set back on her heels as Betty pushed a bundle of papers and two small notebooks into her hands. Quickly, Addie began to leaf through the sheets of Bernie Kahane's crabbed scrawling. Here and there she stopped to read a couple of paragraphs. As she began to get a full idea of what Kahane had written, she gasped in total shock.

"But—but" she stammered, "this is monstrous."

Forgetting everything around her, Addie crawled over to lean back against the front of the couch and began to read more intently. Kahane had managed to find out almost everything about the New York terrorist campaign. The only problem, she noticed, was that his superiors didn't believe him. She did have to admit that the entire concept outlined before her was outrageous. It was so unbelievable that she had to admit that a week ago she probably wouldn't have believed it either.

Gathering up the papers, Addie went over to the phone and dropped down into one of the old over-stuffed chairs. She pulled the phone into her lap and dialed the number for John Voynich, her C.I.A. contact.

"Marker." answered the same bored voice.

"John Voynich." she said as she started to flip through one of the small notebooks.

"There's no one———-oh, what the hell. Just a minute." he said as she heard the usual clicking sounds on the line.

"Addie! Where are you?" he demanded as soon as he came on the line.

"I'm fine, John, but what till you hear this," she said as she started to fill him in on the plan.

Shamus O'Toole ran along the hall in a panic, causing the neighbors who had come out into the hall to investigate the noise to jump back into the safety of their apartments. In all his years as a terrorist and hired killer, he had never been forced to run for his life. Now, at least two of his men were dead, and he had been forced to scramble from that room on his hands and knees like an animal. He had run for the elevators and then decided that the elevator would be too slow. He wanted to put as much distance between himself and that mad woman

as he possibly could. He paused to catch his breath and looked around
for Carson, the man he had left to guard the hall.

Things were not going well, he thought to himself in disgust, in fact
the entire operation had degenerated into a farce ever since the Prince
had gotten tangled up with that damn female reporter. He crashed
through the door into the stairwell and grabbed onto the railing as he
saw the body of Carson lying face down on the stairs. Kneeling beside
his fallen comrade, O'Toole tried to revive the unconscious man.
Noticing the way that Carson's head lolled, he looked closer and determined that Carson's neck was broken. With an oath, he dropped the
dead man and continued his mad dash down the stairs.

Rushing into the dingy lobby, O'Toole scrambled for the door. He
was getting himself to the airport and out of this crazy town before that
crazy female got him too. Racing out the main exit, O'Toole almost
leaped down the stairs to the sidewalk.

"Freeze!" demanded a female voice as a bright light silhouetted the
terrorist against the front of the building.

O'Toole stopped and swung around, bringing his pistol up. Three
shots rang out in the stillness of the night. O'Toole fell back against the
rough brick front of the building, his own pistol discharging into the
air. Once again, he made the attempt to bring up his own weapon, but
his strength failed him. He slumped to his knees and then fell forward
onto his face. His last sight was of three blue-coated pairs of legs coming
into the pool of light that surrounded him.

Guns drawn, the officers left one of their number with the wounded
man and the rest entered the building. Waiting for them in the lobby
was the sleepy super.

"Who turned in the call?" asked the senior patrolman.

"I did." he said, "There was a problem on the third floor, one of the
tenants reported yells and gunshots coming from one of the rooms. I'll
show you."

With an air of great importance, the pajama-clad super led the two officers up to the third floor. When they left the elevator, they saw the hall was full of people and the door to apartment 7B was standing open. When it was realized that there were two police officers present, an older woman with hair in curlers raised one trembling hand to point to the stairway door.

"Officers there's a dead man on the stairs." she wailed.

The junior of the two officers, eased open the stair door and cautiously peered around the edge of the door. He could see the bottom of a worn pair of shoes. Tensely, the officer edged onto the landing to see that the shoes were worn by a man sprawled on the stairs. From the way the man was laying, the Officer knew that he didn't have to check for a pulse. Turning, he rejoined his partner.

"Well?" questioned the senior cop, surrounded by numerous babbling women.

"One man. Dead." his partner replied.

At that moment, a disheveled young woman with long red hair looked out of Room 7B.

"In here officers." she said as she beckoned to them.

Carefully making their way through the crowded hallway, they took in the shambles of the apartment. There was one blonde woman lying on the floor, in obvious pain. A young blonde sat beside her, holding one of her hands. A third woman, the one that had called them, stood just inside the door.

"Am I glad to see you guys." she said with feeling.

The senior of the two officers, Glen Corbett, pushed his cap back on his head, put his hands on his hips and looked at her in perplexity.

"Now what went on here?" he demanded as he gazed at the shattered window.

"It's a long story, officers. I think you will find it very interesting. But, first, we need an ambulance for these two and do you know a Lieutenant Jackson?" she asked.

Corbett turned to his partner, Alex Cord and motioned toward the phone.

"Get an ambulance here as soon as possible and see if the Precinct can find Lieutenant Jackson," he ordered.

Satisfied that his orders were being carried out, Corbett turned back to the dirty-faced young women before him. "Now what's this all about?" he asked once again.

CHAPTER THIRTY-TWO

Prince Hadji normally rose each morning at seven o'clock. Never in all the years since he had become an adult had he allowed himself to disturbed before the appointed hour. On this particular morning, he allowed himself to be pulled from his sleep by the insistent ringing of the phone beside his bed. Glancing at the clock, he noticed that it was a little after five in the morning. He debated about ignoring the phone, but this was a special unlisted number, the one that was used by RAVEN. Composing himself, Hadji answered the phone.

"Yes?" he answered with great dignity.

"Well, you blew it again," snapped the voice of RAVEN.

"To what are you referring?" asked Hadji.

"O'Toole was killed by police about two hours ago. That female reporter killed one or two more of O'Toole's men and one was captured. You have failed miserably." accused the mysterious voice.

Hadji's hand tightened on the receiver until the plastic was in danger of breaking. It was only with great restraint that he did not flare-up at his accuser.

"Bah, this changes nothing. I will still carry out my mission today." he sneered at RAVEN.

"How," demanded RAVEN, " your men are dead. It will be several days before we can get a new crew into town."

"I still have your programmed assassin. I also have Kincade and two of the local scum and Bremer is here. I will carry out the mission with these," he asserted.

"Now listen to me, you desert idiot, you insufferable camel jockey. I want nothing to happen to Hughes. He is more important to this operation than your small plans. I have decided that I don't want you to use him for today's assassination. I want him moved to Washington today," ordered RAVEN.

"Bah. I spit on your orders, you infidel. I will report to the Revolutionary Council that you are placing personal feelings over the JIHAD."

"Why you gutless wonder. You have fucked this mission up since it started. I should have replaced you days ago," raged the voice on the phone.

With a sound of disgust, Hadji dropped the phone back into its' cradle and rose form his bed. It was time to get the mission underway. He had much to do to reorganize the entire operation. Jerking open the door to his bedroom, Hadji yelled for Otto, then rushed quickly into the bath. By the time, he had showered and dressed, the wounded Otto was waiting for him.

"How are you my friend?" he asked as he studied his servant's expressionless face.

"Fine, sir. It hurts, but I am fine," replied the stoic German.

"Good" praised his superior. "Would you be so kind as to have everyone staying down the hall, as well as Dr. Bremer join me for breakfast in thirty minutes? We will be eating in the dining room," he said as he turned toward his closet.

"At once, your Highness." replied Otto as he bowed and lumbered out of the room. His formerly solid step now a painful limp.

When Prince Hadji reached the dining room, he could tell by the sounds of talking and dishes clinking that the others had already preceded him. Regally, he swept into the room and took his place at the head of the table. With an annoyed twitch of his face, Hadji noted the very reduced size of the gathering.

"We have a slight problem." he began as Otto placed his breakfast before him.

"Due to certain er-unforeseen- happenings, we are reduced to the number of operational personnel you see before you. Therefore, I have been forced to change the plans we discussed yesterday." Hadji paused and took a long sip of the cup of tea Otto carefully handed him.

."First, as to targets, we will dispense with the Catholic Bishop at St. Peter's Cathedral. Instead, we will concentrate all available personnel on the assassination of the Israeli Ambassador and the Secretary General.

Mr. Kincade, you will lead the team inside the Hotel. You will keep the security personnel occupied so that Mr. Noyotivik can assassinate the targets. Once the primary targets have been hit, then you will withdraw to the car that will be waiting for you at the rear entrance of the Hotel on 58th street."

The Prince paused for a moment, a small smile playing on his face.

"Dr. Bremer, I talked to RAVEN this morning, he said that you were to assist me in carrying out this very important mission."

Dr. Bremer had just taken a large sip of coffee when he received this news. He almost strangled as tried to talk and swallow at the same time.

"You can't be serious!" he yelped between coughs. "I'm not an assassin, I'm a psychiatrist. I'm one of the Council, you can't really be serious."

Prince Hadji carefully kept his face empty of expression. "Raven felt that in this hour of emergency that all available personnel should be used to carry out this operation."

"What about you?" demanded the angry Bremer.

Prince Hadji waved his left hand at Dr. Bremer as he took another sip of his tea. "But of course, my good Doctor. I am going to be carrying out a most important mission of my own," he said.

Bremer sputtered and grumbled but finally he had to admit that he had no choice but to comply. He had no way to contact RAVEN so he had to trust the Prince.

"Very well." he finally said. "What do I do?"

Prince Hadji allowed himself a small feeling of triumph. His new plan was working perfectly.

"If you will all go with Otto, he will show you to the weapons room and brief you on the final details of the operation. Mr. Kincade, if you will please remain here for a moment. The rest of you are dismissed."

Obediently, the other four rose and followed Otto. Only Noyotivik glanced back at the Prince. He waited until they were into the hall, when Noyotivik spoke to Otto.

"I need to go to the bathroom," he said softly.

With a grunt, Otto indicated the bathroom to his left as he limped painfully down the hall toward the room containing the weapons. Noyotivik waited until they were all in the room, before he stepped softly to the dining room door and eased it open. Kincade had refilled his coffee and joined Hadji at the end of the table.

"Mr. Kincade, I have a job for you," the Prince was saying in his soft voice.

"Yes sir," Kincade answered respectfully.

"After Mr. Noyotivik has completed his part of the mission, it would be a pity for something to happen to him." the Prince said as he toyed with his teacup.

"Won't happen if I'm watching his back." responded Kincade with some pride in his voice.

"That is the point, Mr. Kincade," said the Prince. "I want something to happen to him. I want both he and Dr. Bremer to be casualties in this operation."

"Well." said Kincade, undecided.

"Mr. Kincade, let us understand each other. You are a greedy man. I am a powerful man, if Noyotivik is killed, I will be even more powerful.

If I am more powerful, then I can pay you more for your services. Do we understand each other?"

Kincade smiled and nodded firmly. "Certainly, your Highness. I will make sure that both die in the confusion."

Hadji smiled like a Cheshire cat. "Very good, Just make sure that they kill the primary targets first." he said holding up one index finger.

Unseen, Noyotivik eased the dining room door shut and rejoined the others. When he arrived, the wounded Otto was handing out the weapons and describing what was available.

"You will each be issued a nine millimeter handgun. The two outside men will also have satchel charges to toss into the lobby to cover the escape of the inside team. Check your weapons and make sure they are ready."

Noyotivik held his weapon loosely in his big right hand.

"Hotel security?" he said.

Otto nodded ponderously. "Naturally, there is very heavy security for this meeting. We have a man inside already. Your driver will deposit your weapons with this man who will return them to you once you are in the Lobby Lounge. You will each wear a white rose in your lapel. He will then slip you your weapons."

Falling silent, Otto stood and watched the four with him familiarize themselves with their handguns. When he was sure that even Dr. Bremer had become at least familiar with his weapon, Otto moved toward the door.

"What are those?" asked Noyotivik pointing at several small items on a table in the corner near the door. Otto glanced disinterestedly over at them. "Those are beepers that have been modified to fire nine millimeter rounds. You will not be using them this time."

As sharp as Otto was he never noticed the assassin scoop one of the deadly beepers into his pocket.

Hadji and Kincade were waiting for them in the hall. To Noyotivik and Bremer, he handed engraved invitations.

"The two of you will enter as very important persons, with Kincade as your security man. You are expected for the pre-luncheon reception in the Lobby Lounge. The other two will wait outside to cover your escape. Make sure that you watch for our man inside who will have your side arms.

But now, it is time for you to go. Your car is waiting downstairs," he said with a smile as he ushered his men out the door.

When the door shut firmly behind them, Hadji breathed a big sigh of relief. Now he could start phase two of his new plan. If he succeeded, then he, Hadji, would take RAVEN's place as the leader of the New York operations.

Addie Vandemeyer was feeling better than she had for days. As she sat in the office of Lieutenant Jackson at the 19th Precinct, she was rapidly jotting down notes of what she remembered from Bernie Kahane's records. Lieutenant Jackson was on the phone talking to some of few trustworthy senior officers left in the Department. Finally, to her relief, he hung up the phone.

"Well you were right about the fact that there were some turncoats among the police department. But they weren't all real cops. Unfortunately, it is still hard to determine how many impostors there are among us, since our central records facility and all our personnel records were destroyed when the mob burned One Police Plaza.

Apparently, as of this point in time, we are aware of about fifteen bad cops and another twenty impostors. You accounted for several of the bogus cops, and may I say that was some very good shooting," he said with a smile.

After a second his smile faded.

"But this morning, when it was expected that the counter terrorist force would drop into Central Park, our stakeout captured several very highly placed police officials waiting with another bunch of dirty cops to ambush the parachutists. One was a deputy police commissioner for God's sake. When word of this gets out, there will be repercussions that will reach all the way to the Governor's mansion."

Addie continued to jot down her notes as she thought of more points she had read in Bernie's diaries. She was still a little pissed that Jackson, on Voynich's orders she was sure, had immediately confiscated the papers from her. She understood the burning desire of the police to read them, but that was what Xerox machines were made for. They could have at least let her make a copy.

As if he could read her mind, Jackson favored her with a grin.

"Still pissed at me for taking those papers?" he asked.

Her answer was a glare that finally degenerated into a grin of her own.

"Yeah, you bastard. You could have let me read them all the way through."

"Well, we had to get them to our intelligence department as soon as possible so that we could try and figure out what that event scheduled for today might be." he said placatingly.

"Have you talked to the one that was taken alive?" she asked curiously.

Jackson nodded.

"We did this morning. He just kept asking for his lawyer. Wouldn't say anything else." responded the Police Lieutenant.

"Where is he?" she asked with an amused grin.

"What devilish idea do you have in mind?" he asked cautiously.

"Well it will definitely violate his Fifth Amendment rights, but what the hell," she said as she leaned forward and outlined her idea. After a moment he laughed and called for his sergeant.

Enos Ortega was a man in pain. That blonde bitch had really hit him one in the nuts. He tried to reach his right hand down to cup his injured members, but was stopped by the handcuff that held him to the bed. Swearing softly to himself, instead he cupped his balls with his left hand. God he had never had such pain. Since they brought him to the hospital that morning, he had been almost unable to move. Struggling to roll over onto his side, he found that even trying to move caused intense pain. He gave up, forced to ring for the nurse.

He heard the door to his room open behind him and someone approach his bed.

"Nurse, help me turn over on my side." he said in as firm a voice as possible, which wasn't that deep.

"Turn over yourself, you bastard," said a low female voice.

Ortega craned his neck and saw that his visitor wasn't the nurse, but the blonde bitch that had kicked him. Immediately, he knew that from the look on her face, he was in for trouble. Reaching out his left hand he fumbled around for the buzzer to call the nurse. Unfortunately, she beat him to it and ripped the buzzer from the wall.

"None of that, bud. You were a big shot last night, let's see how big a man you are today." She reached for his crotch.

"Guard, guard!" he yelled in panic. Surely the police guard at the door would hear him.

"Don't waste your breath, lover. I told him I would take care of you while he got a cup of coffee."

Her little hand gripped him firmly by his swollen testicles. The pain was so intense that he almost passed out. He was hurting so much that he couldn't even speak.

"I'll quit if you tell me what your boss has planned for today," she said in a wheedling voice.

Suddenly, he realized that this was all a set up to get him to talk.

"I'll never talk." he said in a funny high-pitched voice. "They'll kill me if I tell."

She looked sad and nodded.

"I understand, but I'll make you wish you were dead. I told the cop to take a thirty minute coffee break," she said as she tightened her grip.

For the next few minutes all activity stopped on the third floor of Lennox Hill Hospital as everyone listened to the very peculiar noises that came from room 5. It sounded kind of like a duck trying to sing. Even though Addie was responsible for what was happening, she was a little bothered by the thought that he was in such pain. But then she remembered the pain and suffering he and his friends had inflicted on the people of New York.

Finally the door to his room opened and Betty stuck her head out to beckon at Addie and the Lieutenant.

"He'd like to talk to you." she said with a grin.

The limousine pulled up smoothly in front of the 57th street entrance to the Four Seasons Hotel, just off Park Avenue. According to their invitations, the Christmas reception for the Secretary General and the three ambassadors was to begin promptly at ten in the morning. Luncheon was to be served at 11:00, so that those who wished to do so could get to St. Patrick's by the time that Mass started.

As soon as the car came to a halt, the two doormen marched smartly to the curb and opened the doors. Dr. Bremer alighted on the sidewalk and turned to wait for Noyotivik/Hughes to join him. Kincade got out of the front passenger seat and joined them. The other two had been let out of the car on the other side of Park Avenue. Leading the way, Dr. Bremer strode through the door held open by one of the doormen, but was stopped by two plainclothes security men just inside the lobby.

"Invitations?" asked one of the two security men in a firm voice as he held out his hand.

Dr. Bremer and Noyotivik both handed over the required documents. After their names were checked against a list, they were forced to submit to hand held metal detectors. Finally, they were allowed to proceed. Kincade began to follow them but was stopped, Dr. Bremer swung around.

"He's our personal security man assigned by Elite Security," said Bremer nervously.

To Bremer's relief, though carefully checking Kincade's identification, and running a metal detector over him for hidden weapons, Kincade was cleared to enter the hotel. The plan was off and running. In less than thirty minutes, the assassins were scheduled to begin their job.

The Four Seasons Hotel was the newest hotel in New York City. It was considered the height of opulence. Noyotivik looked it over in interest. Upon entering the front doors, a guest had to ascend five steps to a sunken lobby. If a guest continued straight ahead, and climbed five more steps, he could find the check in desk. However, if from that sunken lobby, one went either left or right, there were five more steps that led up to a corridor that led back to the 5757 Restaurant.

Dr. Bremer led the way to the right, but upon reaching the corridor, he continued up ten steps to the Lobby Lounge. The lounge area, probably thirty feet deep and fifteen feet wide, was filled with small tables and strategically placed sofas. The number of guests was small but growing. Bremer wove his way through the crowd to claim a table at the far end of the lounge, directly in front of the windows.

Bremer leaned over to speak to Kincade who had seated himself to Bremer's left.

"Do you see out contact?" he asked in a low voice.

Kincade glanced at the Doctor with ill concealed contempt.

"He knows who we are, that's all that's important. Now act natural before you give us away. That big guy over by the stairs is Emile Kassar, a MOSSAD officer assigned to head up security for the Israeli Ambassador. It is said that he can smell a plot against the Ambassador," whispered the gunman in a low voice.

Glancing past the rank amateur, Kincade studied the silent Noyotivik.

"What do you think about this? You've been silent since we left the apartment. Scared?" he taunted.

Noyotivik favored Kincade with a brief cold smile.

"Not so you could notice," he said in his flat voice.

"I wonder if you're as good as I've heard. After all you couldn't manage to save your wife and kids at the Rockefeller Center," he taunted again, his eyes watching for the Ambassadors.

"Young man," snapped Dr. Bremer in a low voice, " do not talk that way to this man. He is as dedicated as you to the outcome of this operation. "

Noyotivik merely stared across the table, no expression at all on his face. The Hughes persona was becoming more and more in control. Kincade looked over at his companions and laughed.

"All this whoop-de-do over this programmed puppet." he said indicating Noyotivik. "He's just so much cannon fodder. I don't care what you program this guy to do or think he did, but he's still just living in a fantasy world. It takes a real man to look someone in the face and pull the trigger," he taunted as he leaned back in his chair. Catching the eye of a waiter he signaled for a drink.

Dr. Bremer's face was flushed.

"You have no idea what you're talking about. This man for all practical purposes acts, thinks and believes that he is Illai Noyotivik. He has all of Noyotivik's characteristics, skills and most of his knowledge."

"Then he's as big a fool as you are, you old fart." laughed Kincade as he folded his arms and scanned the room. "He's still not real. "

Noyotivik came to his feet and walked over to stand behind Kincade. The seated terrorist started to swing his chair around so that he could face the target of his sarcastic attacks when Noyotivik reached down, grabbed Kincade's chin and jerked his head sharply to the right. Kincade went completely limp. From Kincade's actions, Bremer was certain that Noyotivik had just broken Kincade's neck.

In total shock, Bremer looked up at the man towering over him.

"Noyotivik, what is the meaning of this?" he asked. "This man was a friend."

The big man slowly turned and looked down at the ashen doctor.

"Dr. Bremer, I merely killed a worthless terrorist. I am also debating about killing you."

"Why?" asked the Doctor through trembling lips.

Noyotivik dropped back into his chair and leaned forward so that his face was close to that of the physician.

"For destroying my life; for taking my family from me. Whatever you bastards have done to my mind, it didn't work this time. I still know who I am. I still remember my dead family and I am going to get the man or men behind the attack."

Bremer was thinking fast. Something had corrupted the programming. He had to regain control.

"Captain Noyotivik, I am your friend." began Bremer, "I created you. Why would I want to hurt you?"

His creation smiled a cold smile.

"Dr. Bremer, I know far more than you realize. I partially woke up the other night. I saw you in my bedroom with my wife. I woke up later and discovered that you had fucked her body while you were fucking with my mind. You and the other bastards with you fucked up my life. Now it's my turn. I want to know how to find them."

Dr. Bremer slid forward in his chair as if to rise.

Hughes reached forward and pushed Bremer back into the chair.

"Tell me who you report to!"

Bremer smiled slowly and resumed his seat beside the Doctor.

"Oh, I think you will tell me everything I want to know."

He leaned over and took hold of one of Dr. Bremer's hands. Slowly he tightened his fingers until Bremer thought he could hear his bones creak. Unable to fight against the bigger man's strength, Bremer finally gave in.

"What-What do you want to know?" he whimpered as he unsuccessfully tried to jerk his hand away.

"Who gives the orders?" he demanded his piercing eyes glaring at the Doctor.

"I don't know. Really, I don't." he whined as he used his free hand to slip a chain from his pocket. On the end of the chain was a shiny coin. He raised his arm and began to swing the coin.

"Watch the shiny object." said the Doctor as he swung the coin before Noyotivik's eyes.

With a look of amusement on his face, Noyotivik, or rather Hughes leaned across the table and pried the chain out of Bremer's hand.

"Doctor, first of all, my name is Hughes, not Noyotivik. I do seem to have this Russian killer's memories, but I am definitely the personality in control. Secondly, you have exactly thirty seconds to answer my question. I won't ask it again," he said as he dropped the coin on the table.

Wetting his lips with his tongue, Bremer took another look at the hard features before him and decided that only telling the truth would get him out of this situation with a whole skin.

"His name is RAVEN," answered the Doctor.

Dropping his crushing grip on Bremer's hand, Hughes leaned back in his chair.

"Who is he?" asked the big man.

Bremer shook his head firmly. "I don't know." he said, "I've never seen his face."

"How does he give you your orders?" he asked.

"A limo picks me up and takes me to an underground parking garage, there is an elevator which we take up to a reception room. Behind the reception room is a conference room. RAVEN is always waiting for us, all the lights out except one that illuminates a picture of George Washington."

A memory tugged at Hughes mind.

"George Washington?"

Dr. Bremer nodded emphatically.

"Yes, George Washington. But not the picture on the one-dollar bill. It's a most usual picture; in this one he is wearing an apron and holding a trowel. That's all I know. This RAVEN seems to worship the memory of George Washington," whimpered the Doctor, sweat running down his face.

Hughes was suddenly struck full force by a thought of a visit he and his wife had made to an auction house a few years ago. He remembered that they had purchased a very unusual portrait of Washington. In this picture, Washington was wearing his Masonic regalia, an apron and a trowel.

"Tell me again, what was Washington wearing in this picture?" he asked softly, his eyes hardening.

Bremer looked at his face for several seconds before answering.

"He was wearing an apron, I believe it had something to do with the Masons." responded the Doctor, glancing over Hughes' shoulder at a waiter who was pushing a desert cart toward their table. Following his gaze, Hughes' face light up in a smile.

"Well it looks like the curtain is going up on our next act."

As Hughes suspected, the waiter pushing the desert cart was their contact. He halted the cart in front of their table, as if he was having trouble with the wheels. Bending down, as if to adjust the cart, he slipped three weapons out from under the long cloth that hung down to the floor and passed them to Hughes and Bremer. Hughes grabbed the one offered to Kincade.

"Thank you, my good man. But I don't think we will be having any desert just now." said Hughes as he grinned at Bremer.

Bremer was silent until the waiter pushed his cart to the next table.

"What are you going to do?" he asked.

"Why Doctor, you thought you had created a duplicate Specter, so that's what I will give you. From now on, I will live in the shadows and eradicate terrorists until I have killed them all." he said solemnly.

"But there are hundreds of thousand of-" he paused for a moment as if struggling with the concept." Us. You can never kill them all."

Hughes grinned slowly as he looked along the length of the lounge at the group moving in their direction.

"What does it matter?" he said, "I have lost everything I had, thanks to you and your friends. I can think of no better future than to pay you all back for the heart ache and suffering you've caused me."

Suddenly, as he spotted the Secretary General of the United Nations entering the Lounge, Hughes jumped to his feet, slid Kincade's gun across the table toward Bremer. As he had expected, Bremer instinctively grabbed the gun before it could fall into his lap.

"Security!" he yelled pointing at Bremer, "that man has a gun."

As he had hoped, his shout caused total chaos to erupt in the lounge. The personal security for the Secretary General and the Ambassadors quickly hustled their charges back down the stairs to the lobby. Other armed security guards came swarming from every direction, struggling to make their way through the crowd of screaming guests who were fighting just as hard to escape. Bending down so that he didn't tower over the others, Hughes was running with the crowd that was trying to escape.

Going out the 57th street exit, Hughes straightened his suit and walked back toward Park Avenue. Turning left, he quickly made his way to the corner of 57th and Park. Peering around the corner, he spotted the limousine waiting where Kincade had said that it would be. Both of the back up men and the driver were leaning against the rear of the car, smoking and joking.

Knowing that everyday activities are usually taken for granted, Kincade made sure that his jacket covered his pistol and turned the corner, beginning to stroll casually toward the parked car. The three terrorists were so intent on the 57th street hotel entrance that they paid little, if any attention, to anything behind them. As he discarded idea after idea for getting them away from the car, the New York Police suddenly helped him as a dozen cars came roaring in from both directions to screech to a halt.

The three terrorists instinctively moved forward toward the Hotel's entrance, two of them clutching the satchel charges in their hands. Taking advantage of the chaos, Hughes walked confidently around to the driver's side of the car, suddenly swung around, jerked open the door and dove into the car. As he had prayed, the key was in the ignition.

Watching the three in his rear view mirror, Hughes turned the key and heard the engine start smoothly. As he pulled away from the curb, the rear curbside door was suddenly snatched open and someone dove into the car in a tangle of skirts and long red hair.

Suddenly, he saw a lovely face in his mirror.

"Hi, guy. Glad to see you again." she said nervously.

CHAPTER THIRTY THREE

"What are you doing here?" demanded Hughes as he braked at the intersection.

"Well, I saw you steal this car and decided to follow you." she said.

"Why?" He struggled to regain control of the speeding limousine.

"I want the story of what happened to you," she said as she looked through the open partition at the swearing driver.

Slowing to a more sedate pace, he glanced at her in the rear view mirror.

"What do you know about what happened to me?" he asked her ominously.

"I know that you were kidnapped and hypnotized or brainwashed programmed by someone to be an assassin. But I don't think that they succeeded." she said.

"Why not?" he asked softly as he studied her lovely features in the mirror.

"I just don't. There's no particular reason." she responded.

He drove around in silence for a few minutes. Addie was facing forward, her chin resting on the rear of the driver's seat. Glancing at Hughes' profile, she pondered the man she thought she knew. He just didn't fit the idea of a hit man.

"Where are we going?" she asked.

He glanced at her in the rear view mirror. "You are going to get out and I'm going to go after the head terrorist," he said firmly.

"Let me go with you." she asked.

He shook his head.

"No, I can't. It's too dangerous." he snapped as he turned onto Lexington Avenue.

"Then I'll follow you. Listen." she said seriously, "I've been in battles and wars from Mozambique to Afghanistan. I know how to handle weapons. After all, I saved you didn't I?" she asked.

This brought him up short. She was right; she had saved his life. Perhaps she had earned the right to be in at the end. He made a quick decision.

"O.K. I'll take you along, but you have to do as I say." he said as he pulled over to the curb near the corner of 77th and Lexington.

"You got it, Kemo sabe," she said with a laugh.

"Then, let's go, Tonto." he said as he got out of the car.

"Where are we going?" she asked, trotting to keep up with his long stride.

"Subway." he said as he led her into the entrance to the downtown number 6 line.

Lieutenant Jackson was in a rage. He had no idea how he was going to explain to his superiors that he had lost the reporter. He had been against bringing her along, but gave in to pressure from his superiors when she threatened to expose the amount of Police Department corruption on the Network. He'd finally agreed, provided that she would agree to wait outside the danger area under what amounted to police guard. One minute she had been waiting with two of his men and the next moment she was gone. Of course, the two officers had been a little busy shooting it out with the three terrorists who had been standing in the middle of 58th street when their car had pulled away. He turned as Kossar came up to him.

"My people are safe. We have that guy cuffed and waiting for you," he said shortly.

Jackson shrugged as he followed the Israeli Security Chief into the Hotel. He just hoped that she was safe.

Due to the curfew, currently there was subway service only eight hours a day. Unfortunately, there was so much fear in the town that there were few subway personnel available to insure the safety of the passengers. For this reason, the gangs that used to prey on those citizens who roamed the city in the evening hours had decided it was safer to go underground. On this particular day, one of the most dangerous killers in the city, Sweet Daddy Grantham, a 6'4" ex-con, and three of his men had chosen to stake out the E Train as their special turf.

Hughes and Addie began their journey on the number six train until they arrived at the 51st street station. There they walked underground to the 53rd street station. Riding the escalator down to the E & F platform, they waited for the E train toward the destroyed World Trade Center. As the train raced toward the south end of the Island, they dropped down into the rather uncomfortable seats and relaxed. This was the calm before the storm. Hughes leaned back and closed his eyes, his arms folded across his broad chest. Addie pulled her notebook from a deep pocket in her jacket and began to make some notes.

Addie was first aware that they were in danger, when she heard the connecting door between the cars open. Glancing up she froze when she saw Sweet Daddy Grantham and his men come strutting up the car.

"Well, what do we have here?" asked Grantham, a leering smile on his big ebony face.

"Looks like some honkies found their way into our territory, Sweet Daddy." answered Johnny Daggers, his second in command, as he slid a long knife out of his left boot. Johnny Daggers liked to torture his victims before he cut them.

"Well, if they pay the toll, then there's no problem is there," said Sweet Daddy as his red streaked eyes lingered on Addie's trim figure.

"Why don't you boys run along and play before someone gets hurt?" asked Hughes, not even bothering to open his eyes.

"Why pretty mamma, who's this big talker you got with you?' asked Sweet Daddy, "Bet he's all talk. I thinks what you need is a real man, not this jive talking ass hole."

Glancing to his left, Sweet Daddy looked at Johnny Daggers and pointed at Hughes. Slowly, Johnny slid forward and reached out with his dagger toward the reclining Hughes. Addie covered her mouth with her hand as she realized that they intended to kill both of them.

Addie was frantically searching for some way for them to get help when Hughes reacted like a spring uncoiling. Addie knew that Hughes was dangerous, but even she had to gasp at the unbelievable speed demonstrated by Hughes as he grabbed Johnny's arm and snapped the young thug's wrist like a twig, He then shoved the squalling youth back against his two companion behind him. They all went down in a pile. Swinging around, Hughes grabbed the bigger Sweet Daddy by the throat with his right hand and applied pressure until the big black was forced to drop to his knees. This time, it was Sweet Daddy's eyes that reflected terror.

"Mister, we was just funning." croaked the terrified ex-con.

"Look out, Carter." gasped Addie as she saw the two unhurt gang members getting back to their feet. Without taking his eyes from Sweet Daddy, Hughes pulled a pistol from his belt and shot them both between the eyes. They were dead before they hit the floor.

At that moment, they felt the train begin to slow as it came to a station. As the doors opened, Hughes heaved the terrified Sweet Daddy to his feet and literally threw him out of the car. The doors closed and Hughes sat back down, ignoring the moaning youth and the two dead ones to his right.

"I don't know what to say." stammered Addie, "You killed them."

"Before you start a lecture about how misunderstood they were, let me point out that they planned to kill both of us." he said as he leaned back and closed his eyes.

'Yeah, I know, but it seems so—-vicious." she said.

"I am vicious, Miss." he said.

She turned to him and shuddered.

"Mr. Hughes, it would seem that you don't remember me. I am Addie Vandemeyer, remember? I saved your big ass at the Rockefeller Center. I shot a man to save you. So don't think about me as some liberal bleeding heart. You got me?"

"Thanks." was all he said.

She turned around and stared across the car.

"Where are we going?" she demanded.

"World Trade Center." he said.

"What do we do there?" she demanded.

Her only answer was a gentle snore. Carter Hughes was asleep.

Prince Hadji rode along in the silent limousine. From time to time, glanced at his watch as he felt under his robes to insure that his tracking belt was in place. They had been riding for over a half an hour. He knew that somewhere behind them, Otto was following. As long as the beeper attached to his belt continued to function, it was giving out a signal that could be picked up by the equipment that was in Otto's car. This time, Hadji was going to find and kill RAVEN.

Finally, he felt the car begin to descend and knew that they had arrived at the parking garage. Sure enough, after another few minutes up weaving, the car came to a stop. He heard the driver leave the car and then the rear door was opened. With great dignity, Prince Hadji left the car and followed the driver over to the elevator. He stepped inside and pushed the only button on the console. With a hum, the elevator began its journey upward.

With a hard smile, Hadji reached under his robe and pulled out a small caliber pistol. He broke the gun open and made sure, one last time that it was loaded. Satisfied, he pushed it back together and folded his arms into his sleeves, the gun clutched tightly in one hand. With a jerk the elevator stopped and the doors opened. Hadji stepped into the reception area and looked around, it was deserted. He walked over to the door to the conference and turned the doorknob; the door opened.

Pulling out his gun, Hadji stepped into the darkened room. There was a sound in front of him, the light on the picture clicked on, silhouetting a figure. Quickly Hadji fired two shots at the figure in front of him, and laughed as the figure fell back onto the floor. He had done it, he had killed RAVEN.

There was a sound to his rear that caused him to swing around. His eyes widened as he saw who was standing behind him.

"You, " he gasped "but—."

The figure standing before him pulled his cigar from his mouth and smiled.

"He was useful, pity you had to kill him," said the newcomer as he pulled a pistol from beneath his coat.

Belatedly, Hadji tried to bring up his gun. The man in the door simply shot him. Hadji fell back against the table and tried to raise his head. A second shot made sure that he would never raise his head again.

At about this same time, Hughes and Addie entered the front door of the financial tower at Number 7, World Trade Center. There wasn't much foot traffic in the cavernous building even though it was major subway and train stop for the southern part of the island. Walking quickly, they went over to one of the many elevator banks and waited patiently for one of the few working elevators to return to the lobby. When the doors opened, Hughes steered the Addie into the car and she watched as he pushed the button marked Renaldi Enterprises.

"Where are we going?" she asked curiously as she watched the floor numbers light up in the ascending elevator.

"See if I've put the pieces together properly." he responded as he stood stoically beside her.

"What do we do when we get there?" she asked nervously.

"Just follow my lead," he said, never taking his eyes off of the floor indicator.

With a musical chime, the doors opened and they found themselves in the reception area of Renaldi Enterprises. A pleasant young lady smiled up at them.

"Oh, Mr. Hughes, how nice to see you again." she said.

"Good to see you Marge, I'd like to see Mr. Renaldi." he said as he leaned casually against the counter so she couldn't see the gun stuck in his belt.

The Receptionist picked up her receiver and pressed two buttons, waiting patiently until someone answered.

"Janet, this is Marge in reception. Carter Hughes is here for Mr. Renaldi," she said into the phone.

In a second she hung up and smiled at him. "Go right on back, sir. He's waiting for you," she said indicating the door to their right.

Leading the way Hughes opened the indicated door and held it open for Addie. Together they went along a long corridor until they reached an even plusher waiting room. Janet Carter, a stunning red head and Mr. Renaldi's private secretary was waiting for them. She came to Hughes and held out her hands.

"Carter, I was so sorry to hear what had happened. We all loved her." said the lovely woman.

"Thank you, Janet. Is Howard here?" he asked looking over her shoulder at the door marked Chairman and beneath that it said Private.

Sensing his urgency from the tenseness of his body, Janet dropped his hands and turned to Addie. "And your name, Miss?" she asked politely, all efficiency again.

"Addie Vandemeyer of N.B.C." she answered firmly.

"Certainly, if both of you will come right this way." she said as she went over and opened a door marked Chairman.

Carter Hughes and Addie entered an unbelievably lavish office that in area was just slightly smaller than Addie's entire apartment. At the far end of the office, was the chairman's dark oak desk. The top of which was big enough to play table tennis. To their right and left were bookcases that covered the two walls. To their right front was a comfortable looking sitting area.

As the door shut behind them, Howard Renaldi got up from behind his massive desk and came across the office to meet them. Addie's reporter's eyes noticed that even though the Industrialist was dressed casually, his shoes were Gucci, his pants probably cost a thousand dollars, and his sweater was priceless, obviously hand woven. This man oozed money.

"Carter, my boy, how are you holding up?" Renaldi asked in concern as he motioned for them to follow him over to the sitting area near the windows.

"Just fine, sir." he paused for a second, "Please excuse my manners, sir. Howard, I'd like you to meet Addie Vandemeyer. She is a reporter for NBC and a friend. She's the one who saved my life at the American Festival Cafe."

"Why pleased to meet you Miss Vandemeyer." Renaldi said as he offered his hand. "Wait, I remember you, we talked the day that—-ah—-my daughter died. I want to thank you for saving Carter. Even though he is my son in law, he still means a lot to me."

"I was just glad I was able to help him," she said as she smiled over at Hughes.

Hughes leaned back in his chair and locked eyes with his father in law. Howard Renaldi wasn't a big man physically, he was actually short and stocky, but muscular. From nothing, Renaldi had clawed his way to the top to become one of the most powerful industrialists in the country. He was a man of supreme confidence; he had never lost to anyone. But at this moment, it was obvious to a trained observer such as Addie that Renaldi was a little afraid of his son in law.

Reaching into his shirt pocket, Renaldi brought out a cigar, unwrapped it and with a silver lighter from the table beside him, lit it. Throwing back his head, Renaldi blew a stream of aromatic smoke toward the ceiling.

"What can I do for you?" the Industrialist asked.

Hughes leaned forward and studied his father in law intently. Addie realized that this was a contest between two antagonists almost evenly matched in physical power and viciousness. She also knew that neither would back down.

"Where is that portrait of Washington in his Masonic regalia that Martha and I gave you last year?" he asked his father in law softly.

For a moment Renaldi looked puzzled, she could see his mind racing while he tried to think what Carter could be after.

"Why?" he asked curiously, puffing fiercely on his cigar.

"Let me see it and I'll show you. I wouldn't ask if it wasn't important," answered Hughes as he relaxed against the couch, his long fingers toying with the pager on his belt.

Renaldi shrugged and got to his feet, looking around the office as he stood.

"Well I think that it's hanging in Baxter Medford's office. He's got this thing about Washington, saw the portrait hanging in the study at my house and wanted to buy it. When I refused to sell, he asked if he could hang it in his office. I let him," said the older man as he walked to a door hidden behind a bookcase, on the wall to their right. He pressed a hidden button under the second shelf and a section swung back. Renaldi walked into a short, dimly lit passage and pressed against a flat metal plate set into the right hand wall, causing a section of wall to slide back. Following the industrialist, they walked into an office almost as large as Renaldi's.

Baxter Medford was a lifelong friend of Renaldi. They had done everything together, they had even married sisters, so Baxter was actually Hughes' uncle-in-law. He didn't know him that well, but he knew that Baxter was a very capable individual, not above taking an unfair advantage. He was also the President of Renaldi Enterprises or rather he was the late President of Renaldi Enterprises. For, lying sprawled back in his chair, with his arms hanging down was the body of Baxter Medford, a bloody hole in his head.

Clamping his cigar in his teeth, Renaldi ran forward to lean over his friend's dead body. Expertly, he felt for a pulse before straightening and shaking his head. Gently, he closed Medford's staring eyes and folded his limp hands over the dead man's chest.

"He was a good man," said Renaldi sadly turning to Hughes and Addie.

Hughes crossed the room and stood behind Renaldi, glancing curiously at the portrait of Washington. The answer hit him like a ton of bricks, he knew the truth. He knew who was behind the terrorists.

"It won't work, Howard," said Hughes in a sad low voice.

Howard Renaldi spun around and looked up at his son in law.

"What won't work?" asked the Industrialist blandly. "My best friend is dead and you're talking in riddles."

"Baxter was a ruthless son of a bitch. He would screw his own grandmother for a dollar, but he wouldn't go to the bathroom without asking you first."

"What gave it away?" asked Renaldi curiously as he walked back around to the front of the desk.

Hughes indicated the portrait of Washington in his Masonic garb hanging behind the desk.

"Notice the lighter area that runs almost all the way around the outside of the picture frame. That means that for along time a larger picture hung there. I suspect you figured that I'd gotten Bremer to talk. Since the only clue he had to your identity was that picture that Martha and I gave you, you had to get rid of it. But with your obsession with Washington, I knew that you'd never part with it, really." he said.

Renaldi smiled slowly.

"You're definitely smarter than I thought you were." smiled the industrialist, as he pulled a small black object from his pocket and pushed a button set into the top.

"Carter, what're you saying?" demanded Addie, coming over to grab his arm.

Carter Hughes looked down at her and then back at his father in law.

"Addie, Howard Renaldi is RAVEN. The great terrorist leader in this area."

She looked at the two with total bewilderment. It was impossible that someone like Howard Renaldi would support terrorism. It flew in the face of everything a man like him would hold dear.

"Are you serious?" she gasped, looking over a Renaldi with wide eyes.

Renaldi just stood there and smiled as he looked behind them.

"Too bad that the knowledge won't do you any good, my boy." he said with a wave at the open passage behind them.

Calmly, Hughes looked over his shoulder at the open door to the passage and was not surprised to see three members of Renaldi Security watching them, guns drawn. At a signal from Renaldi, they crossed the room and patted down both Hughes and Addie, carefully relieving Hughes of his pistol. Addie braced herself, expecting Hughes to put up a stiff fight. She was determined to help him, but Hughes made no resistance as Renaldi herded them back into his office. Leaving them standing in the middle of the floor, Renaldi returned to his desk and sat down in his chair.

"Well it is really too bad that you had to find out. We could have used you for the Washington operation." said Renaldi with regret in his voice.

"Why Howard? Why did you have her killed?" he asked.

Renaldi shrugged and relit his cigar.

"It really was an accident, just like her and you getting together, as a matter of fact. I never expected her to be at Rockefeller Center that day. You two never usually meet for lunch, that day you did. Shit happens. It did have the effect of making sure that no one would ever suspect me of being involved." he grinned. "And after all, there was no great loss. It's not like she was really related to me."

"What do you mean?" demanded Hughes, as his temper started to rise.

"You poor fool, this project has been in the planning stages for years. My real flesh and blood daughter didn't want to participate in the project. She refused to have the implant and even tried to go to the authorities. Rather than have her cause problems, I had her terminated with extreme prejudice. After all, the operation is much more valuable than any one member of my family. This Martha was her replacement and I must say that she was rather good at her part. My boy I really envied you her company in bed, as I know from experience she was a hot one. The real problem was that she actually began to believe that she was my daughter," he said with no change of expression.

"But why? What did you hope to gain?" demanded Hughes, his features flint hard as he gritted his teeth in anger.

"Why power, my boy. The only thing worth taking a risk for, more power than any one man has ever held in his hands at one time. By this time next year, I will be a virtual dictator in this country." Renaldi laughed as he sat rubbing his hands together briskly.

"So long as her death wasn't a total waste," responded Hughes dryly.

"No, actually, it has worked out rather well. She was a potential problem and now she is an asset. Dead, she is the symbol of what I have lost in this war against my country. She easily worth several million votes from the great unwashed masses."

"You're a sick man, Howard," said Carter very calmly.

Howard Renaldi shrugged and took a deep drag form his cigar.

They looked at each other in silence until Addie finally had to say something.

"So now what?" she asked, though she really didn't want to know the answer.

Renaldi looked at her and grinned around his cigar.

"Well now I am going to fly to Washington D.C. tonight and start phase two of our little operation. In spite of what you may think, I am not the man in charge of this new American Revolution, though I am a very senior member of the Brotherhood. My son-in-law will be killed by my security as you are in the process of killing poor Baxter Medford. It's a pity, you have to die, as well my dear, but you know that poor Carter has been under such a strain since the murder of his wife. You are just in the wrong place at the wrong time. It's such a pity." he shook his head slowly.

"I have one question, Howard," said Hughes, as he stood with his arms folded.

"What's that?" he asked.

"Why?" he asked simply.

"Well, it's a long story, and I'm sure that you would find it incredibly boring." he began.

"We certainly have the time." interrupted Addie.

"I like a girl with a sense of humor." Renaldi laughed, as he openly looked her up and down appreciatively.

"But to answer your question," said Renaldi, turning his attention back to Hughes, "I originally didn't have any choice. You see, there were twelve major players in the group that furnished the money for President Regean's Iran Contra operation. The fool who was overseeing the project for the National Security Council really didn't handle things the way they should have been handled and the entire operation got leaked to the press. Everyone the press could tie to that foul-up was prosecuted. Those of us who hadn't been discovered tried to keep a low profile."

He pulled a metal briefcase from beneath the desk and began to shove papers into it as he talked.

"About ten years ago, I was contacted by someone whose name I won't mention, except to say that he was from Iran. He told me that if I didn't cooperate with them, my part in the Iran Contra would be revealed to the press. Now, with all of the continuing fuss in the media about that little indiscretion, it was likely that I would go to prison. I couldn't risk that.

If I did cooperate with the terrorists, he promised that once the country was subjugated, I would come to power as the new leader. All I had to promise was that I would never lay a hand on Iran or its allies. Hey, I am a good businessman. He offered me a good deal and I took it."

"So you arranged for the murders at the Federal Building and the Rockefeller Center?" Addie probed.

"Of course. I wanted targets that would call for a great deal of attention and keep people from looking at other things. We wanted to attract all the attention that we could to New York City and we succeeded."

"Why destroy the F.B.I. office?" asked Addie, her reporter's instincts kicking in.

"Well the Sheik was one of Iran's most important agents in the United States. He was also a prime suspect in the murder of that reporter Cosack. Personally, I was all for letting him swing in the wind, but Bani-Sadr called me and ordered me to have him smuggled out of the country. The problem was that the F.B.I. was hot on his trail, so I decided that something had to be done to derail their investigation. Unfortunately, we couldn't find anyone to buy off.

Then too, we discovered that one of our people had panicked and talked to that Kahane, feller. So it was decided to take them all out at one time. These Moslems are fanatics. When a call was put out for volunteers to die for the Sheik, we had over a hundred volunteers. Deciding to use the assets that we had available, we sent some to the F.B.I. office and the rest to raid One Police Plaza. We succeeded beyond our wildest dreams. At the same time, I used it to dispose to some folks that were beginning to become royal pains in the ass." he finished as he snapped his briefcase shut.

Putting on his coat, Henry Renaldi grabbed his briefcase and walked into an alcove to the left side of the room. He touched a spot on one of the floor-to-ceiling bookcases and then pulled the case away from the wall, revealing another secret passage. As he entered, he looked back at the group standing in his office.

"Fred, come with me. George, as soon as we are gone, take them into Baxter's office and kill them. Make it look good," he ordered as he vanished into the recess, one of the security guards close behind him.

As soon as the bookcase swung shut, George stepped in front of them and swung his rifle toward the passageway.

"Come along now and make it snappy. If you cooperate then I'll make it painless." he promised, with a leer at Addie.

Without argument, Hughes obediently turned, walked across the room and entered the dimly lit passage to Medford's office. He could hear the two guards urging Addie along behind him. As he walked, he brought his hand to his belt and removed the small pager he wore at his right hip, cupping it in his hand. He had decided that he would make his move as the guards came from the dimly lit passage into the brightly lit office. For just a second their eyes would have to adjust to the change of light. That would be his best time he decided.

Swiftly, he moved along the passage and stepped into the office, placing himself out of sight beside the open panel. As he saw Addie begin to step into the room, he grabbed her arm and swung her out of the line of fire. The guards thought she was trying to escape and both tried to come through the door at the same time. They stopped in confusion when Hughes he stepped in front of them.

Addie decided that Hughes had flipped out when she saw that he had pointed his beeper at them. The guards thought it was funny also and began to laugh. Their laughter stopped rather suddenly when Hughes pressed the top button twice. There were two bursts of hissing and both guards toppled over backward.

Hughes glanced down at Addie sitting on the floor with her skirt around her waist and a baffled look on her face.

"What did you do to them?" she asked with a perplexed look on her face.

He held up the beeper for her to see.

"Nine millimeter beeper, never leave home without it."

He leaned over and grabbed one of the dropped rifles. After insuring it was loaded, he darted back along the passage toward Renaldi's office. Addie, crawled to her feet, grabbed the other rifle and ran after him.

She entered the Chairman's office in time to see Hughes vanish behind the other bookcase. Darting across the office, she reached the bookcase as it slowly swung shut. A quick dive across the remaining few feet allowed her to wedge her own body behind it. As her eyes adjusted to the darkness of the passage, she began to make out a slight light emanating from along the baseboard. Some type of indirect lighting, she quickly determined, gave at least some light to hallway. Ahead, she saw a flight of stairs that led upward. Not seeing Hughes, she realized that she was lagging far behind so she hit the stairs at a run.

At the top of the stairs, Addie saw another door. Throwing caution to the wind, she threw open the door and ran out onto a helicopter pad. She saw Hughes kneeling on the edge of the pad with his rifle pointed at the Bell helicopter that was rising from the far end. From the flashes of light coming from the end of his weapon, she could tell that Hughes was pumping round after round at the aircraft.

Glancing up, she thought that she saw Renaldi peering out of the window on the near side of the aircraft. Running to Hughes' side, she brought her own rifle up and began to fire.

She never knew which one of them had been the most successful, but she noticed that the helicopter began to smoke and waver from its course. At one point, the chopper came in low over the pad, so close, in fact, that Addie could make out the struggling pilot, his figure silhouetted against the afternoon sun. With what must have been her last shot, Addie fired directly at the pilot.

She lowered her rifle and watched the pilot clutch at his throat, one hand still clamped around the control stick. As the wind from the blades tore at her clothes, Hughes rose to stand beside her, his left arm around her shoulders. Silently, they watched the wounded pilot struggle to keep his aircraft in the air, but to no avail. Finally, he lost his valiant struggle and the helicopter dropped like a stone toward the empty streets below. The sound of the explosion reached even to their lofty position.

With her arm around Hughes' waist, the two walked to the edge of the helipad and stood watching the burning wreckage below. Addie was amazed at the amount of wreckage that littered the street, the flames from the burning aircraft reflected off the surrounding buildings made a rather pretty picture. As she watched, Hughes murmured something to her and moved away from the edge of the pad. Ignoring him for the moment, Addie felt a great feeling of relief wash over her. It was over, she thought. Letting her rifle slip from her hands to fall to the rough surface, Addie turned to speak to Hughes, but saw he was gone.

Wildly, she looked around for Hughes and started to run for the door, she was sure he had left her. As she jerked open the door, she heard some grunts coming from the other side of the large air conditioning housing to her right. Slowly working her way through the closely packed air housings, she found herself in a small partially enclosed helipad. Hughes was struggling to pull a large tarp off of a small machine. Wordlessly, she came to help him pull the cover off of his prize. The small item uncovered was a two man helicopter.

Hughes smiled and looked at Addie.

"This is the X-43, an experimental helicopter being developed by Renaldi Enterprises. I remembered that Howard mentioned that he liked to keep the experimental stuff close to home. I thought it would be close."

Addie looked at him quizzically.

"What do you plan on doing with this?"

His face was cold as he spoke.

"Someone or some group of people have taken my life from me. I plan on getting it back. Howard was going to Washington so that's where I'm going."

"Correction, buster. Washington is where we are going." said Addie firmly.

Hughes looked down at her for a moment and shook his head.

"No. I don't want to expose you to any more danger. What I have to do can best be done alone."

Addie grabbed his arm and pulled him partially around.

"Now you listen to me, Carter. I have stood by you from the time I first met you in that restaurant. I plan to stay with you until the end. Where you go, I go. Now get this through your hard head. If you go to Washington, I go to Washington."

A slow smile crossed his face. In spite of the coldness that enveloped him and had since the death of his wife, he found he liked this brash young woman. He held out one hand in an invitation.

"In that case, shall we go?"

Addie paused for a minute, brushed her hair from her face and looked up at him.

"Washington is a big place, how will we find where he was going?"

Hughes pursed his lips for a moment and then smiled his deadly smile once more.

"He wouldn't go to Washington without seeing his old friend, Senator Holling. I will pay him a visit."

In a few minutes the roof top was empty, all that could be seen was a small light moving to the west. The Spector was on the hunt.

EPILOGUE

The meeting was a somber one. The five men in the dimly lit room had debated long and hard before coming to a decision. They were elated at the success of their initial attacks on New York City, but were puzzled by their New York command structure failing to make the scheduled contact. In spite of this, it was decided to move while the iron was hot.

The muffled voice of the leader spoke softly.

"This it is decided. We began the second phase of our operation. The President must die."

About the Author

Ken Hudnall is a former radio talk show host, who has published several books ranign from a ground breaking new theory regarding Unidentified Flying Objects to a series of Southwestern Horror that incorborate Native American Legends. This book begins his second series. He lives in El Paso, Texas with this wife.